Raw Dawgin'

A NOVEL

* * *

DAVID J MATHER

Also By David J Mather

A young Peace Corps volunteer finds adventure and heartbreaking romance in the lawless foothills of the Andes.

Set in beautiful southern Chile in the late 1960's, this coming-of-age novel paints a vivid picture of a forgotten way of life.

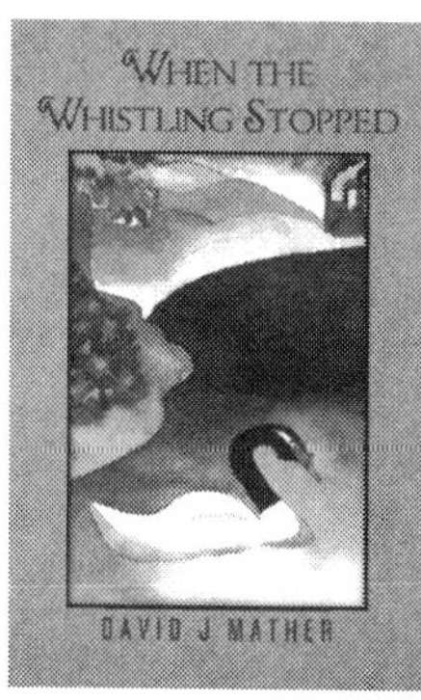

In this sequel to *One For The Road,* murder and intrigue follow a young couple's quest to expose an amoral mill owner responsible for the death of thousands of black-necked swans. The twists and turns of this eco-thriller make it hard to put down.

State Trooper Rusty McMillan goes undercover to bust marijuana smugglers on Florida's Gulf Coast. He gets the evidence he needs, but before any arrests can be made, the area is slammed by a lethal storm and Rusty is forced to join the community in a life-and-death struggle.

Raw Dawgin'

A Peace Corps Writers Book - An imprint of Peace Corps Worldwide

Printed in the United States of America
by Peace Corps Writers of Oakland, California.

For more information, contact peacecorpsworldwide@gmail.com.
Peace Corps Writers and the Peace Corps Writers colophon are trademarks of PeaceCorpsWorldwide.org.

ISBN: 1935925911
ISBN-13: 9781935925910

Library of Congress Control Number: 201893390
First Peace Corps Writers Edition, February 2018

TO
FLORIDA'S LAST FRONTIER,
HORSESHOE BEACH

ACKNOWLEDGMENTS

Raw Dawgin' is a sequel to *Crescent Beach.* Both novels take place in the fictitious town of Crescent Beach; I picked the name because it is ubiquitous in Florida. All the characters are products of my imagination: any resemblance to actual persons, living or dead, is purely coincidental.

Once again, the internet proved invaluable for my research. Among the many sites for Raiford Prison, otherwise known as the Union Correctional Institution, three in particular were helpful: "A Day in the Life of a Prisoner" by Michael Romero, "That's the Way It Is in Prison" by Charles P. Norman, and"Without the 'Rock,' Florida Inmates Get the Hard Place" by William Booth. I used the site aquaticcommons.org for info on the Florida ban-the-net law of Nov. 8, 1994. For Alzheimer's Disease, the novel "Still Alice" by Lisa Genova was particularly informative as were the internet sites familydoctor.org and webmd.com. For Florida hog hunting there was Gene Fletcher's excellent "A Hog Claim" at storyhouse.org. Gary Monroe's book "The Highwaymen" provided both background and illustrations of the colorful works of Florida's African-American landscape artists. Many internet sites were also helpful with scalloping, especially the Leenoga.com article of "Scalloping in Florida—What You Need to Know."

Enjoyed and very much appreciated were my conversations with, in alphabetical order, Marine Donny French, Captain Timmy Futch, Danny Hicks, and Carol Porter. I'd also like to thank my corps of proofreaders: Judy Barker, Wendy Beck, Allie Farrar, and Joyce Killebrew. A very special thank you to Jill Andrews who went way above and beyond in carefully reading and editing the manuscript as well as educating me in the process. And, for the fourth time and for the fourth book cover, I'd like to thank friend and artist Jennifer Brown. Finally, the proverbial 'last, but not least' thank you goes again to my wife Lindy without whose help and infinite patience, this book would not have seen the light of day.

Raw Dawgin'

Prologue

Jimmy Talbot turned off the highway into a recently turned-over peanut field. His pickup's headlights played off the extensive mobile spray irrigation system as he followed the tractor road to a thick copse of hardwoods at the far end. The road dead-ended in a circle with derelict agricultural machinery scattered between the trees. He switched off the motor and looked at his watch. Eleven-twenty. Peanuts and farming were the furthest things from his mind. Sliding off his white rubber boots, he awkwardly laced up a size-twelve pair of brogans with newspaper stuffed in the toes. He threaded several long, thick plastic cable ties making loops he kept open with small pieces of duct tape. After putting a good handful of these as well as the roll of duct tape in his jacket pockets, he pulled a .357 Magnum out of the glove compartment, took a deep breath and got out of the truck.

Tucking the pistol under his belt, Jimmy followed a faint trail through the woods. It was in the low forties, far from snake weather; still, he was cautious. He shone the flashlight all around, the last thing he needed was to get snake bit. He stumbled a couple times because of the clodhoppers, but if anyone ever checked his tracks, the man they'd be looking for would have size 12's. For the same reason, he had bought four new tires for the truck. As soon as this was over, he'd change over and pitch the old ones in the dump. He passed good-sized sweet gum, cherry, and oak draped in vines and Spanish moss before he began to hear road noise and see light through the trees. At woods' edge was a small dark parking lot, barely lit from what light came from the small church next to the highway. Jimmy had sabotaged the parking lot's two floodlights a few days earlier, correctly betting that no one would fix them before the midnight Mass. He scanned the lot, looking for the new Lincoln Town Car, but there were only older-model pickups and cars. Another pick-up turned in from the highway, its headlights dancing off the trees as it pulled up to park. A Mexican couple got out. The man tucked in his white shirt as the woman waited. Jimmy hunkered down at the base of a tree and watched them walk towards the church.

Three vehicles turned in from the highway. Jimmy looked at his watch. Quarter of. Two more followed. Rush hour, he thought. Among the cars was the Lincoln that went to the far end of the lot and backed into a space bordering the woods. The nearest other vehicle was a pick-up several spaces away. A short, very stocky man got out of the car leaving the door open and interior lit. He was wearing dark slacks and a yellow Guayabera shirt. When he leaned over to pull out a black leather jacket from the passenger side, the shirt rode up, exposing a pistol in the small of his back that lightly reflected gold and silver. Jimmy shuddered. He remembered that pistol well. Custom made Beretta 92. The man zipped up the jacket, looked around, and headed towards the church. Jimmy caught himself rubbing the palm of his right hand as he watched the Colombian walk away.

It was quarter past and organ music was coming from the church when Jimmy left the woods. Although probably not necessary, he put on gloves before he bent down and let the air out of the Lincoln's rear passenger tire. He returned to the woods where he hid behind a bushy red cedar tree only twenty feet away. El Espantoso, The Ghost, that's what the Colombian was called, but Jimmy knew his real name was Arias, the name engraved on that fancy ass gun. He was also the cold-blooded son-of-a-bitch who had shot him in the hand and threatened his twin grandsons.

Jimmy walked around. Gotta be real careful. This guy ain't no humpty; not a cartel kingpin in Miami for nothing. Jimmy sat down on a log by the cedar tree. He was up and down several times. Wonder how long the mass will go? He started massaging his right hand again. Hell of a way to spend Christmas Eve, but if everything goes right, he should be back before daylight. A few minutes later, Jimmy's head snapped up when he heard people leaving the church. He quickly stood and hid behind the cedar again, pulling the pistol from his belt. His stomach began fluttering. Stay cool now, stay cool!

Espantoso didn't go ten feet before he realized he had a flat. He immediately reversed back to his parking place. He got out and looked at the tire, then viciously kicked it before returning for his keys and opening the trunk. His neighbor in the pickup, just about to leave, took in the situation. He got out of his idling truck and walked over. Jimmy thought, get out of here! The pair began speaking Spanish while Espantoso got what he needed to change the tire. The neighbor kicked the tire and said something that they both laughed at. After the lug nuts were off, the man helped Espantoso put the spare on, then reached for the lug wrench. Espantoso wouldn't let him have it and instead took out his wallet. The man shook his head and said something, probably Merry Christmas, Jimmy thought. The two shook hands and the man drove away. The parking lot was empty. Espantoso finished tightening the lug nuts and rolled the flat back to the trunk. He flopped the tire in and was about to close the trunk when Jimmy slammed him hard from behind. Espantoso fell forward into the trunk with Jimmy putting the Magnum to his head while yanking out the Beretta and tossing it towards the woods.

"This is a 357 Magnum, Espantoso, and'll make a big hole. If you behave, we'll just have a little talk, you and me. If you don't, you're dead. Your choice."

Jimmy kept the gun tight to Espantoso's head, his other hand pushing hard on Espantoso's back. The Colombian's face was smooshed against the tire.

"No problema, no problema!"

"Hands behind your back, close together. Slowly, carefully!"

Espantoso did as he was told. Jimmy continued to keep the gun against his head as he looped one of the plastic cable ties around Espantosa's wrists and pulled it tight. Espantoso grunted when it cut into the skin. Jimmy looped three more just as tight.

"Coño!" Espantoso spat. Jimmy breathed a small sigh of relief. Step one completed. Now step two.

"Lift a leg." Espantoso did what he was told. "Now the other." "Jimmy looped both ankles and connected the two with a third,

longer loop. Espantoso was hobbled like a horse. "Now stand up and turn around."

"Jeemy! Cabrón! What thee fuck…" Jimmy slapped a piece of duct tape over his mouth, then another. A thick vein was pulsing in Espantoso's forehead, his eyes coal black, his jet black hair slicked back, and scars from early-age acne pockmarked his face. Jimmy shut the trunk and took Espantoso by the elbow, shuffling him quickly into the woods before retrieving the fancy pistol.

"Wouldn't want you to lose your cop killer, now would we?" Jimmy said, tucking the gun under his belt. "Or is it a kid killer, you sleazebag?"

When they arrived at the truck, Jimmy lowered the tailgate, saying, "Now don't get nervous. We're just going for a ride to where we can talk without being bothered." Espantoso looked from Jimmy to the bed of the truck and bolted. He didn't get far before Jimmy tripped him and slammed the barrel of the Magnum across his face a couple times, opening up a pretty good gash on the Colombian's forehead. Jimmy dragged him back to the truck and stood him up. "Now don't make me do something I don't want to, Espantoso. Just want a little chit-chat, man to man." The Colombian tried to head-butt Jimmy who stepped aside and knocked him down. Jimmy kicked him in the face and ribs until he was still. Grunting, Jimmy pulled and pushed Espantoso into the back of the pickup where he rolled him up in a tarp like a mummy, not caring whether he could breathe or not. Moving quickly, he secured the tarp with some rope and tied down another, covering the Colombian. He jumped down and entered the cab where he hung onto the wheel for a few moments with head bowed, eyes closed. Plumb wore out already, he thought. He looked at his watch. Better get moving. It wasn't until he had pulled out of the field and headed north that it clicked that it was Christmas morning. He was so zoned he wasn't sure how many vehicles he passed in the next hour. Maybe two. Once through Perry, he turned left on 98. When he crossed the Econfina River, it wasn't long before he turned onto a limestone road. The woods soon began to thicken. Jimmy loved this area. It was the Florida of the past.

Probably ain't much different from when the Spaniards arrived, he thought. Twenty minutes later he stopped the truck.

Jimmy unwrapped Espantoso and set him up leaning against the tailgate. He was conscious, but woozy. Jimmy grabbed on to one of his arms. "We're going to have our little conversation about a hundred feet from here. You gonna walk or am I gonna have to drag you?" Espantoso took a wobbly step. Jimmy escorted him through the woods until his flashlight revealed a stack of cinderblocks with a pile of chains on top. The light reflected off the chains and Espantoso's eyes widened. Eyes suddenly pleading, he turned towards Jimmy who pushed the chains off to the ground and forced Espantoso to sit on the blocks. Jimmy ripped the duct tape off Espantoso's mouth. It came away with skin and Espantoso began to bleed. "Now, ain't this pretty around here? Look at those trees and vines and all." Jimmy shined the light all around. "No one comes here much, so still lots of critters. Even fish." Jimmy picked up a chunk of limestone. He flipped it a few feet off to the side. A couple seconds later they heard a splash. "I know you can't see it, but that's a sinkhole, mostly covered up in vines. And I got no idea how deep it is, but plenty. Probably ties in with the aquifer and all that. Did you know this whole state is like a Swiss cheese underneath? No, probably didn't cuz you and your goons been too busy snorting cocaine and killing people."

Espantoso began to shake his head violently back and forth, saying, "Jeemy, don't be stupid! Don't do thees! My men weel find you and reep your heart out if you do thees!"

Jimmy ignored him and shined the light on the palm of his right hand. "Don't know if you ever saw your handiwork once it healed." Jimmy put the hand up close to Espantoso's face and flexed it. "Still bothers some, especially stormy weather. Took a good while to heal because it got all infected. That was pretty bad." Jimmy pulled out Espantoso's fancy pistol. "Yup, this cocksucker did a job on it alright. But you know what hurt the most? The burns from the muzzle flash. 'Course you used that silencer which maybe caused it to be extra bad, but even without it, I imagine it'd still hurt like hell."

Jimmy walked behind Espantoso, suddenly pulled him backwards, kneeled on his left hand, and shot the right. Espantoso, groaning, jumped to his feet. Jimmy threw him to the ground and held him with a size 12 on his head.

Espantoso's voice was muffled, but Jimmy still heard him.

"You weel die for thees, coño! They weel find you! The family weel get you!"

"Hurts like a son-of-a-bitch, don't it? But you know what? The hole in my hand…that's not what pissed me off. That's not what this is about. The threats to my family. You crossed the line there. Now, maybe you were just bluffing; trying to scare me. I ain't got no idea." Espantoso tried to shake his head, not easy to do with his face pressed into the ground. "But, considering your reputation, I figure I can't be taking no chances. So, long story short, Espantoso," Jimmy said, leaning over and putting the gun to his head, "Adíos."

Chapter One

A Big Mac first. Yeah, and then maybe go look for a woman. Wonder if anyone's had sex and a Big Mac at the same time, Bobby mused as he stared up at the bottom of his cellie's bunk. He reached up and ran a finger along the cool steel. Seventeen years he'd been looking at this hunk of metal. No, make that fourteen; there were the three at the Rock. He put his arms behind his head. Just a few more days and he'd be outta this hellhole. Thanks to Whacko, he had a place to stay in Crescent Beach where the ex lives. She's probably forgotten all about me, he thought; but, maybe not. Going to be surprised as hell when I show up, that's for sure. Bobby smiled. Can't wait to see the look on her face.

Yes siree, Raiford's going to be minus one inmate come Monday, bring it down to twenty-five hundred and ninety-nine bastards in this godforsaken concrete and steel jungle. Better than it was, though. The Rock! Now that was a tough joint: fights, rapes, stabbings all the time—when serving hard time was really hard time. Where the real baddies were. Put me right in there with them even though it was my first screw-up, my only screw-up. Judge didn't give a damn if I was drunk and crazy jealous of Tammy when I got into that bar fight. Didn't care that I'd never been in serious trouble before. What he cared about was my sending the statey who tried to 'cuff me to the hospital. Twenty years for aggravated assault and thrown in with the rapists and killers where you had to watch your step around the clock. Had to prove yourself right away or you were up the creek. The newcocks coming in from jail had no idea what was in store for them: intimidated and beat up the minute they arrived. The poor bastards not big enough to fight back ended up as lackeys and sex partners. Took plenty of lumps, but at least I never got screwed in the butt in the Rock, or in here either. Made it through. People learn quick who to mess with and who not. Rock's been closed since eighty-five, but the screws left it standing as a reminder. Like anyone who was in there could ever forget. Good riddance is what I say. Bobby suddenly heard two shrill whistle blasts from the tall towers of the steam plant. They could be heard over the entire eighteen thousand acres of the Union Correctional Center which was what Raiford was formally called now. Bobby looked at his watch. Plenty of time for a catnap before he went out to the yard to work out. He closed his eyes.

Bobby had thought a lot about his ex-wife during the seventeen years he had been in. Because he hadn't seen her since consenting to their divorce after he was sentenced, he still pictured her as the pretty nineteen-year-old, ponytailed brunette with a saucy butt. Their marriage was embellished in his mind. Two years of perfect bliss. Any memories of him knocking her around, breaking her jaw on one occasion, were pushed off to the side. They had rented a cracker shack in town under a big live oak tree. It was their honey lodge and she was his honey pot. He had a good job. Weekdays he ran the edger in the local sawmill while she worked as cashier at the local BP station. On weekends they drove around in his loud, mud-splattered truck, mud bogging with friends and drinking beers, sometimes sipping Dr. Peppers laced with Southern Comfort. She would ride up close, almost in his lap, hand on his thigh. She was his road queen.

But then he had started drinking more of the hard stuff. Made him nasty and nasty jealous. He got Tammy a fake ID and they would go to bar dances which was like rubbing salt in a wound because he would get jealous at the drop of a hat if anyone paid too much attention to Tammy. Everyone paid attention to Tammy: she was an eye-catcher and a live wire. By his second or third drink, Bobby was seriously into his cups and didn't want to dance anymore. He just wanted to drink and watch Tammy dance. So he permitted her to cut a rug. She was real good. Provocative wasn't in his vocabulary, but that's what Tammy was when she danced—didn't matter if it was slow or fast. She had more moves than a stripper. Problem was that some of the guys who didn't know her or Bobby thought she was coming on to them. They couldn't leave off at the dance floor and hit on her when she returned to Bobby at the bar. One night, a guy all decked out in cowboy duds wouldn't leave her alone. Tammy, ignoring Bobby who was drunk, flirted back. Bobby went berserk. He was fit and fast and mean as a moccasin, and took care of the cowboy quickly. In the process, though, he damaged the bar and a statey was called in. Bobby was still in a fighting mood when Officer D'Angelo tried to take him out to the cruiser. Bobby told him to fuck off and mind his own business. You don't say that to a trooper. D'Angelo brought out the cuffs and grabbed one of Bobby's arms which Bobby shook free and slammed him with an elbow to the nose. A roundhouse followed, knocking the trooper down hard. Bobby furiously kicked him in the ribs and face and crotch before Bobby's friends could react and pull him off. The officer lay in a heap on the floor. He didn't move. When Bobby calmed down, he knew he was in deep shit.

But that was seventeen years ago. Since then he had been a model prisoner, sucking up to the guards whenever possible. Other than defend himself and a friend or two on occasion, his record at Raiford was clean. And it had paid off. Aggravated battery of a police officer was a felony of the first degree which meant that it was mandatory that eighty-five percent of any sentence be served. Eighty-five percent of twenty years was seventeen. Bobby's case had been looked into and he was to be freed next Monday, two days from now. Consequently, aside from his addiction of going out to the hut yard to work out with the free weights, he was spending most of the time in his bunk. He had stopped scoring hits of crystal meth and had avoided as much of the usual interaction as possible. He was careful bordering on paranoia. He didn't want to blow it. Anything could happen at any time in Raiford and he was taking no chances.

Lying in the lower bunk with freedom just around the corner, he thought all the time now about Tammy. Whacko, his friend and former cellie, was on the outside and had located her for him. He wondered how much she had changed. Let's see, she'd be thirty-six. Probably married with half-way grown kids and fat like most other middle-age bitches. Most likely let herself go. But, maybe not. Man, they had made sweet music together! Hands behind his head, he surveyed his world. The cell was a whopping seven feet wide, just wide enough for the double bunk with the skinny mattresses, and ten feet, eight inches long. Two footlockers, sink, open toilet, concrete block walls with a single pinup calendar on the wall. Xs blocked out most of the days. The solid metal door with a three-inch by eighteen-inch Plexiglas window was wide open. This was home for fourteen of the seventeen years in Raiford.

Bobby opened his eyes and looked at his watch again. Time to go to the yard. He heaved himself up and threw some water on his face before pulling sweatpants and a sleeveless undershirt from his footlocker. He took his weightlifting seriously, read up on it, did it right. It showed.

His chiseled upper body was straight out of a magazine with the proverbial six-pack abs and dinner plate pecs. Just walking around, his muscles winked and flexed. It was Saturday afternoon and some of the black inmates were playing basketball. Bobby watched them as well as several other inmates who were shuffling counterclockwise around the yard. The count was down. Many, Bobby knew, were at the movie. Every Saturday a movie was shown three times, but that was the last place Bobby wanted to be so close to getting out. There were no guards in the theater and things happened there, scores were settled. You never went in without your group: self-preservation was a matter of numbers. But even the numbers didn't help if the Goon Squad came after you, and that was the biggest reason Bobby sucked up to the guards. The Goon Squad was made up of big tough blacks who did the guards' bidding in return for favors such as looking the other way when it came to smuggling in drugs or making buck, a potent wine, to sell to the other inmates.

Bobby walked up to the free weights corner of the yard. His buddy Virgil, a monstrous black who weighed over three hundred pounds, was just finishing his bench press routine. Bobby counted the weights. Four hundred pounds. Considering Virgil's bulk, Bobby knew this was intermediate level, but Virgil was gaining—he was pressing ten more pounds than he did two months ago. Only thirty more pounds and he'd be considered advanced. Although Bobby benched just under three hundred pounds, he weighed only one-eighty which put him almost at the elite level. Bobby was considered by everyone in the yard as the most accomplished and knowledgeable when it came to weightlifting workouts and technique.

Virgil's spotter helped Virgil settle the barbell back in the stand. Sweat coated Virgil's face.

"Virgil, my man. How's it going?" Bobby asked, as he clasped the black man's monstrous paw.

Virgil had a smile like an all ivory keyboard.

"Bobby-boy. How long you got now? Couple more days at the club here?"

Virgil's sissy, who called himself Toni, was seated on a plastic chair off to the side inspecting his fingernails. Toni was white and had a small slender frame and shaved eyebrows. Virgil was his husband.

"Monday morning I'm blowing this popcorn stand." Bobby began his warm-up stretches, targeting the groin, back, neck and shoulders.

"Who gonna show me how's it done wit' you gone?"

Bobby laughed. "Yourself, Virgil. I can't teach you anymore. You just got to stick with it, is all. You're the man, now. People going to come to you for the 'how to.'"

Virgil toweled off as Bobby rubbed talcum powder on his hands. He began his workout alternating dumbbells and barbells. Today he was concentrating on the upper body. Consequently, with more parts to train, the program was more varied than usual. His repertoire was four sets of a dozen reps for each discipline, resting a minute and a half between sets. He was all business. Lately the general public outside the walls were demanding that, like TVs, there shouldn't be bodybuilding equipment in prison. Prisoners had it too soft, they said. If prison were tougher, maybe there wouldn't be so many repeat offenders. For the most part, the TVs in Raiford had been done away with. Only those on Death Row could have small 13" black and white TVs while they waited for the electric chair they called 'Old Sparky.' The other buildings had a single color TV that up to seventy inmates at a time could watch certain times of day. The prison psychologists disagreed with the public about the weights. They argued that there was a lack of rehabilitation opportunities at Raiford. The weights, they said, at least taught some discipline and put structure in the inmates' lives. The guards lobbied for the weights because threats to take them away could keep troublemakers in line. As for Bobby, he owed his sanity to the weights. If the psychologists were correct that a weightlifting program put discipline in a prisoner's life, then he was the poster child.

A small group of inmates had come over to watch Bobby work out. He finished up with three hundred crunches holding a dumbbell behind his head and fifty pull-ups. Coated in sweat, he looked at his watch. The little group disbanded. Little longer than usual, Bobby noted: just under an hour and a half. Time to go clean up for supper. As he toweled off, he was thinking that, other than the workouts, no way would he miss the prison routine. Up at five-thirty, breakfast at six, lunch at noon, and dinner at five. Meals were tons of carbohydrates. No steak, no pork chops. Lots of beans and potatoes. Fanciest meal was fried chicken once every two weeks. But only two more days to go before that Big Mac and Coke. Fries, too, with plenty of ketchup.

On the way over to chow, he caught up on the daily gossip of the black prison community from his black cellie who was in for raping his best friend's sister and then stabbing the friend when he came after him. Bobby reciprocated with the white men's news. At dinner, Bobby poked at his food and didn't say much. His friends didn't say much to him either. Everyone knew he was getting out. Bobby was the first to leave the table, rapping on it with his knuckles before standing up, the prison way of saying 'excuse me' that was a carryover from the late 1800's. He went through the customary pat down before leaving the dining hall. The guard who body-searched him said, "Understand you're getting out Monday, Bobby."

Bobby smiled. "Yes, sir, Mr. Tom. Time's kind of standing still for me right now."

"Stay clean. Hope I don't see you back here."

"Don't worry. Made one mistake; don't plan on making another." What a job, Bobby thought, frisking prisoners coming out of chow three times a day, every day! Didn't he get tired of patting our balls? Who knows, maybe he likes it. Maybe he's queer.

Monday morning finally came. Bobby was issued khaki pants and shirt to replace prison garb. A duffel bag with all his belongings over his shoulder, Bobby walked out the front gate, smiling and saluting the guards in the towers. A white 1980 Ford Torino squatting low in the back was parked a short distance away. Whacko, Bobby's former cellmate, was behind the wheel. Whacko had greasy shoulder-length hair now and was even skinnier than before. He got out and walked back to the trunk. With a goofy, toothless smile, he opened the trunk.

"Got a surprise fer ya, Bobby."

Bobby looked in at the complete set of weights. "Damn, that's fine!" Bobby threw his duffel bag in with the weights and shut the trunk. "Where'd you get them?"

"Found 'em at a yard sale, cheap. Little bit rusty, but figured they'd make a good gettin' out present."

"The best, Whacko, the best!"

Whacko had been in the wrong place at the wrong time. A very knowledgeable but illegal drug manufacturer by trade, he had been working in his meth kitchen when two dealers arrived at the same time to buy product. They got into an argument and gunfire broke out with one of the dealers killed, the other wounded. Whacko's wife was killed by a stray bullet and the lab caught fire. The end result was that Whacko's left hand was severely burned and he ended up in Raiford where he became Bobbie's cellie. Back then he wasn't pretty to look at either. Whacko had serious meth mouth with only a few remaining good teeth. The prison dentist yanked out all the brown and rotten ones. Being razor thin, few teeth, talking cracker English, and looking crazier than hell, it wasn't long before the nickname Whacko surfaced. Most everyone picked on him until Bobby pummeled a couple of the bullies. Inmates soon learned that picking on Whacko was a direct challenge to Bobby. They became fast friends, a regular Mutt and Jeff duo.

Whacko also introduced Bobby to meth. Lots of drugs were smuggled into the prison in any number of ways. The Goon Squad had the meth trade thanks to the guards, but there was always blotter acid coming in letters. Even a passionate kiss between husband and visiting wife might include passing a condom unit of drugs, swallowed and recovered later. Bobby's job of protecting Whacko was made easier when Whacko became the resident expert on all drug imports. Whacko would tell the Goon Squad what was good and what was bad, whether or not they were being screwed. The result was that the Goon Squad paid Whacko in drugs and he shared them with Bobby. But then a Levin College of Law professor from the University of Florida reopened Whacko's case *pro bono.* The lawyer got the sentence drastically reduced because Whacko hadn't done any of the shooting. Whacko was freed, but stayed in close touch with Bobby over the years.

"So, you found her..."

"Yep."

"How's she look?"

"Sexy. Still got that cute little butt ya always talked about. Done good fer herself, too. Owns and runs a nice little restaurant right on the water." Whacko put the Ford in gear and pulled out to the highway. Bobby turned to look back at the prison. He gave it the finger. He turned back to Whacko.

"Single?" Bobby asked.

"She ain't married, but's shacked up with the local Doctor."

"What's he like?"

"Dunno. Maybe ten years older 'n her. Kinda soft looking. Looks like he ain't never done a lick o' hard work." Whacko headed west. Even though it was very warm,

Bobby wanted all the windows down. He unbuttoned the khaki shirt, put his seat back, closed his eyes. His hair was blowing all over the place. He smiled. Heaven. Whacko continued, "Rented a trailer in town there and found me a little huntin' cabin in the woods in the middle of nowhere about ten miles out to set up a kitchen. Way out in the pucker brush, tucked away in a swampy cypress area. Old guy who owns it lives in Bradenton. Never uses it now; too feeble to hunt. Rented it to me for a song and bingo, I was in business! Fact is, got a little proof of the puddin' if'n ya want to try some later. Awful good, if'n I do say so myself."

Bobby opened an eye in Whacko's direction. "Does a cat have an asshole?"

Whacko smiled. "Figgered as much." He drove for a couple more minutes. "There's a new marina in town goin' gangbusters. Told the owner about ya. Said he could use some help big time. So, ya got a job if'n ya want."

Bobby sat up. "Found my gal, got some good meth, a place to live, and a job. Goddamn, you're alright, Whacko."

Whacko smiled, proud as a peacock. "So what ya wanna do first?"

"McDonald's. I want to go to a McDonald's."

"Alachua, then. Nearest one I know of. Jest a tad off 121 here."

Twenty minutes later they pulled into McDonald's. They went inside where Bobby ordered two Big Macs, a large fry, and the largest Coke possible. Whacko didn't order anything. They sat down. Bobby began to gorge himself.

"Whoa, Bobby! Ya better be careful with that stuff. Kin go right through ya if ya ain't used to it."

"God almighty," Bobby said, mouth full, a Big Mac in one hand, and dipping a fry into ketchup with the other, "I've been craving one of these since forever!"

After lunch they jumped back into the Torino and continued west. At about Fort White, Bobby's stomach began to gurgle. By the time they hit Branford, Bobby was desperate. "Whacko, pull into that gas station quick!"

Bobby walked-ran in the classic way people do when they're about to soil their britches. When he came out of the station, Whacko asked, "Did ya make it?"

"Barely."

Whacko shook his head. "Told ya to be careful. That shit's bad fer ya."

Chapter Two

Beau came out of the bathroom showered and shaved and found Virginia in the kitchen dressed for library duty. Instead of her usual polo shirt, shorts, and flip flops, she was wearing a white blouse, navy blue cotton skirt, and black flats. Her purse was upside down on the counter with a pile of woman stuff next to it.

"Looking for something, Sugah?" Beau asked, his southern accent softening the r of Sugar.

"What does it look like! Of course I'm looking for something! My damn glasses!"

"Rather short-tempered this morning, aren't we?"

Virginia's shoulders slumped. Pushing a lock of gray hair away from her face, she looked over. "I'm sorry, dear. I'm just frustrated. I can't find them anywhere and I want to open on time. Other than the festival, this is the biggest day of the year in Crescent Beach. Someone might even take out a book." Her Charleston accent was even thicker than Beau's.

"No, Ma'am," Beau said, looking out the window. "Too fine a day to read. If anybody comes in, it'll be to use the computer. Everybody else will be out on the water trying to win prize money."

Beau reached into his shirt pocket. "Here, take mine. We'll find yours later." He was handing her the glasses when the phone rang. Beau picked up as Virginia stuffed everything back in her purse, pecked him on the cheek, and made a beeline for the door.

"Hello?...What!...Oh, for Pete's sake. Yeah, I'll come down. Don't know what I can do about it, but I'll be over in five...Yeah, bye."

Virginia had the front door open.

"Who was that?"

"Tammy. Seems someone spread roofing nails all over the public boat ramp."

"What!"

"Yeah. Trailers are queued up the length of Main Street, and Tammy's and the marina's lifts are both swamped. People are angry."

"Why don't they use the commercial fishermen's ramp?"

"Sammy's got his boat blocking it."

"It just keeps getting worse, doesn't it, dear?"

"Sure seems that way."

"I'm off. Good luck."

Beau filled up his to-go coffee mug and walked to the front door. Skillet, his fourteen-year-old black lab, watched from his beanbag.

"Co-pilot going to sleep in today?" Skillet heaved himself up and took a couple of stiff steps before wagging his tail. "Well let's go then, old man." He held the door open. Beau's house was eighteen feet up and both man and dog took their time going down the stairs. When they got to the golf cart, Beau pulled down the hinged mini-stairway that Charley had built so Skillet could climb up onto the backseat. Beau flipped the stairs back up and climbed into the front. Like always, he turned to give Skillet a pat before starting off and, like always, Skillet rode looking straight ahead with his grizzled chin resting on Beau's shoulder. When they hit Main Street, Beau saw that Tammy had not been exaggerating: trucks and trailers were parked along the edge almost to the cattle gap. People, mostly men, were standing by their rigs, smoking, talking with their neighbors, fiddling with rigging. Beau and Skillet scooted up to the boat ramp in City Park where several sports fishermen, including some up to their knees in the water, were picking up nails. A Perry police cruiser was parked close by with the officer watching from the edge of the ramp.

"Anybody know who's responsible?" Beau asked in a loud voice.

"Net fishermen!" came the answer, almost in unison. Everybody paused to look up at Beau in the cart.

"See anybody?" Beau asked.

"Nope, done before sunrise most likely."

"Then how do you know it was net fishermen?"

"Who else?" came the answer.

Good question, Beau thought. He looked down at the ramp again.

"Looks like you about got them all."

One of the fishermen said, "Yeah, and we lost a good hour or more doin' it. Boats goin' in with the slings got a head start." He spat in the water. "Sons-a-bitches netters."

Beau wondered how long it would be before the boats at the end of the line could launch. Many would probably get fed up and leave. Local businesses stood to lose a lot of money. The Cancer Foundation, too. This little prank's not good for anybody. Beau turned the cart around and headed to the commercial fishermen's ramp. He pulled up to a crowd of pissed-off men facing off. Insults were flying back and forth. Beau drove right into the crowd and forced it apart. Skillet took his chin off Beau's shoulder and looked from side to side. A burly sports fisherman said, "Hey, Pop, who the hell do you think you are?" Beau stepped out of the cart.

"I'm the mayor, son." The crowd quieted. Beau looked at the locals; saw Sammy.

"Sammy, what's going on? Is this your boat?"

Beau liked Sammy, a straight-forward mullet fisherman forced by the ban-the-net law to punch nails and do odd jobs for a living. He was a little scary-looking, though, with both unruly dark beard and hair and a big frame with a huge, hard gut. Probably weighed in over two-fifty easy. Several of the other men with him were just as burly.

"Yep, shor is, Mr. Beau."

"Why do you have it blocking the ramp?"

"Don't. Loaned it to my neighbor. It's on his trailer; so guess *he's* got it blockin' the ramp."

"Where's he at?"

"Gettin' hisself a cup of coffee."

"Well let's go get him."

"Take awhile."

"How's that?"

"Went with a friend to Perry."

"For a cup of coffee? That's twenty miles away!"

"Yep, shor is."

Beau sighed. "Then it'll have to be towed."

Sammy shook his head. "Nope. Truck's locked up tight and took the keys with 'im. Lock on the trailer hitch, too. Besides Mr. Beau, this ramp ain't for them."

The crowd started to grumble again. Beau was monkey in the middle.

"Sammy, I'm not going to ask who spread the nails or whose idea it was to block this ramp, but don't you realize this hurts the whole town? The fishing tournament is for a good cause and a lot of people aren't going to enter because of these shenanigans. Others will want a refund. Tammy and the marina will lose business. So will T selling her shrimp, the store selling beer, and every other business in town."

"I'm truly sorry about that, the local businesses and all, Mr. Beau, but they're just gettin' a taste o' what we been goin' through for these last three years. Because o' them," he added, pointing, "we can't use our nets and our livin' done got taken away. These sons-o'-bitches don't care none about us losin' our jobs. And there's some of us lost our homes, marriages broke up, and our kids is losin' respect and gittin' into drugs. Well sir, we don't like what they done and we don't like them. Our ramp is our ramp. At least they ain't got that yet. Until that happens, I say tough shit!"

The burly sports fisherman said, "Who you calling a son-of a bitch, you ignorant netter? Just because you ain't got brains enough to figure out another way to make a living ain't our fault."

Sammy launched himself at the man. They wrapped up so close that no good punches could be thrown. Sammy used his extra thirty pounds to wrestle the man down: five hundred pounds of muscle and gut hit the pavement hard. Sammy was soon working his way on top. Tangled up like they were, the other man didn't have a chance against the heavier and stronger Sammy. Beau's stentorian command to stop was ineffective. Skillet started barking. A circle formed around the two men. Sammy soon had the man pinned and was about to pummel him when the Perry cruiser screeched to a stop, its siren suddenly blasting. Sammy stopped with raised fist; with his financial situation, he didn't need problems with the law.

The officer jumped from the cruiser and pulled his nightstick out in one motion. He broke through the circle with stick upraised. Sammy got off the fisherman and, breathing hard, said, "No problem here, Officer; just a slight misunderstanding."

"Bullshit!" the burly fisherman screamed, examining a skinned elbow. "Officer, this man called me a son-of-a-bitch and attacked me."

Sammy turned back to the man and yelled, "You insulted me! Called me an ignorant netter! "

"And you are! An ignorant son-of-a-bitch redneck asshole netter!" The man was spitting mad. Sammy was ready to launch into him again, fine or no fine. The policeman quickly walked between them.

"Alright, break it up you two! Get outta here, both of you, unless you want to explain everything to the judge in Perry after you cool your heels for a week!" He looked at the crowd. "Public ramp's all clear. Y'all go on over there. Party's over. Go on now!"

A bearded fisherman in a Guy Harvey tee-shirt with a Mako shark on it wasn't happy. He spit on the ground. "Yeah and start all over at the back of the line. We won't get in the water 'til noon if we're lucky!"

"Can't help that," said the officer. "Is what it is. You just got to move along."

The man spit on the ground again. "Screw that! And screw this town! I'm outta here!" He walked quickly over to his truck and started it up. He revved the engine so that the glass-pack muffler snarled in good shape before putting it into gear and driving away.

Beau watched the trucks and trailers pull out, thinking this is bad, real bad for the town. He turned to the policeman. "Thank you, Officer. Tried to stop it, but they didn't pay any attention."

The officer put his nightstick away.

"Ugly scene. And it's not just here, Mayor. Stuff like this has been happening up and down the coast. Down Fort Myers way it's been real bad. So far it ain't been too serious around here, mostly vandalism like slashed boat trailer tires, running a screwdriver along a boat's paint job, and things like those nails. But I swear it's a time bomb for sure. Just hope no one gets serious hurt."

The policeman drove off. Beau reached for his coffee and took a swig. Sammy about said it all, Beau thought. The ban-the-net law had been pushed through three years ago by the state's well-organized recreational fishing industry, totally disrupting the lives of the commercial fishermen and their families. With more and more sports fishermen moving in, the town had become a dichotomy: two mostly warring factions. In the winter it was about fifty-fifty natives and long time residents to newcomers; but in the summer with all the vacationers and scalloping, there were about three times the tourists and sports fisherman. Beau looked beyond the ramp out into the Gulf. Mostly calm and the day was warming up in good shape. He'd bet it was going to be in the high eighties. Good day to be out on the water and feel that Gulf breeze. Beau sadly shook his head. A perfect day for the tournament if it weren't for the shenanigans. Beau saw a shrimper coming in. Has to be Tiny, he thought: hard to miss that bright new paint job. Beau took another sip of coffee.

"Seeing's as we're out and about, what do you say we go visiting, Skillet? Want to see your pal, Charley?" Judging from his tail, Skillet was all for it. They retraced their previous route, passing the line of trucks and trailers. Beau and Skillet were on the working side of town with its mix of trailers, doublewides, and cracker houses with rusty tin roofs. Because of the storm, most dwellings were up off the ground now, even the doublewides and trailers. Before, everything had been on the ground. Looking to the left wasn't the most scenic, Beau thought, especially with the yards full of marine paraphernalia. There was no landscaping and only a few trees, mostly cabbage palms. Some of the lawns were mowed, some were a foot overgrown.

To Beau's right was the creek that used to be lined with fish houses before the storm. Now there were only rebuilt docks and Tiny's and T's local shrimp emporium where, besides shrimp, people in the know could buy stone and blue crabs, white fish, and for a couple days a week, fresh vegetables. Beau slowed the golf cart down as he approached the whitewashed concrete-block icehouse with TNT SHRIMP CO. painted in large blue letters. A crude pergola topped off with palm fronds shaded a couple of waiting customers sitting on white plastic chairs. Other plastic chairs of varying color circled a fire pit. T, Tiny's girlfriend, was standing at a tank, ladling shrimp into a fisherman's bucket. Behind her was a small building that served as office with freezer space. T was barely five feet tall, cute as a button, and five months pregnant, although being so small made her look closer to eight.

"Morning, T," Beau said, stopping the cart. "Tiny's on his way in. Should be entering the channel about now."

"About time, Mr. Beau! I could use some help, tell you that. Been bonkers since before dawn." Skillet wuffed. "And a good morning to you, too, Skillet," she said, before bending back to her work.

Beau pulled away and soon passed by the humpback bridge over the creek that bisected the town. Most of the fancier houses like Beau's and the new marina were on the other side. A couple streets past the bridge, Beau turned off and soon arrived at an interior lot with several tall pines. Beau and Skillet heard a couple of loud screeches and looked up. An osprey flew out of a pine, clutching a partially eaten fish in its talons. Underneath the tree set on a large pressure-treated-pine cradle was a forty-two foot cabin cruiser, a 1957 mahogany-hulled Mathews that most people mistook for a Chris-Craft. The cradle was permanent as evidenced by the PVC pipes coming out of the ground and entering through the hull of the boat. On its transom was painted *Stingray*. The boat's captain had run aground years ago on an oyster bar just outside the main channel leading to town. For some reason he abandoned it and disappeared, leaving it to rot. Eventually it became a lover's nest for beer-drinking fishermen and their girlfriends. Charley was one of those fishermen. Unlike the others, he fell in love with the boat and eventually got the idea of salvaging it and bringing it ashore to live in. During an extremely low winter tide, he inspected the hull and discovered the damage wasn't all that serious, nothing he couldn't temporarily patch. He sump-pumped her dry and hooked a cable to Tiny's shrimp boat to tow her ashore. While attaching the cable to the bow, Charley stepped on a stingray that gigged him in the calf. He took this as a sign and named the boat *Stingray.*

Off to the side of the boat, a shiny fire-engine-red 1964 Mustang was parked in a cheap pre-fab, open-sided carport. Charley, a wiry middle-aged man, was painting the hull of the Matthews a bright blue. Dressed in flip-flops, paint-splattered blue jean cut-offs and tee-shirt, and with a red bandana tied off tightly on his head, he looked like a weather-beaten pirate. Charley put the can of paint and brush down while Beau lowered the stairs for Skillet whose tail was going a mile a minute.

"Hey ol' buddy, how's the joints this mornin'?'" Charley asked, as he kneeled down to hug and pet the lab. Skillet was beside himself. "Now think ya kin hold still a minute while maybe I looks for a little somethin' fer ya? But ya gotta sit first!" Skillet sat immediately. Charley looked at Beau. "Mornin'. Back in a jiffy." Charley climbed the aluminum ladder leaning against the boat and disappeared over the side. Stone-still, Skillet stared at where Charley had disappeared. When Charley re-appeared, Skillet almost smiled.

"Looks like you're trying to keep up with Tiny. Some color," Beau said, looking at the hull as Charley climbed down.

"Nah. Tiny painted his 'cuz o' being nagged by T. But me bein' an artist and all these days, thought it only fittin' to make the 'Ray purty. Now watch this, Beau." Charley turned his back to Skillet and pulled a doggy treat from his pocket and shifted it from hand to hand. He turned back to Skillet with two closed fists. "Which one?" Skillet took a whiff of each hand, then sat in front of Charley's right. Charley laughed and gave him the treat. Looking over to Beau, he said, "Maybelline, God rest her soul, showed me that. Said Skillet never missed and, by God, she was right!" Charley turned to look at his work. "So, what'cha think?"

"Not your typical boat color."

"Ain't your typical boat."

"True." Beau patted a scraped area. "Love this old boat," he said, thinking back five years to the storm that about wiped out the town. It was a surprise storm with no evacuation notices and a twelve-foot tidal surge at three o'clock in the morning. Beau had been swept off his feet by the surge while trying to make his way back to the house after passing out in the hot tub. He ended up freezing his butt off in the top of a cabbage palm until the *Stingray*, which had been torn loose from the pipes and old trailer it had been resting on, floated up against it. Charley had pulled him out of the tree and thawed him out in the boat's cabin. "There's been a bit of excitement downtown. Thought we were going to have a war at the commercial ramp."

"Coulda called it the Roofin' Nail War."

"So, you heard, huh? Know about Sammy's boat, too?"

"Yep. Sammy wanted me to join the fun, but I said no thanks. I told him, ain't nuthin' positive gonna come of it."

"Got that right. What can we do about all this, Charley?"

Charley shrugged.

"Don't know. This town's changin' so fast. What with all the damage from the storm and them new FEMA rules, put a lot o' pressure on folks. Then ya got Tallahassee bannin' the nets the next year causin' the fishermen to leave and the sports fishermen takin' their place. With them comin' in, real estate prices been goin' up. Townsfolk been cashin' in on that and movin' to the country. Us natives in town is becomin' a reglar indangered specie."

"Endangered."

"Whatever. But look at them boat trailers parked by the commercial ramp every mornin'—crabbers and clam farmers can't afford to live here now and got to bring in their boats from outside. That new fancy marina may be goin' blockbusters, but it's the new people who got the money goes there and it's hurtin' Tammy's business. Town meetin's ain't much more than a bunch of hens squabbling over every little tidbit and so mean-spirited that the town's gotta have its own lawyer. And now they've begun to build a condo. I mean, a damn condo! In Crescent Beach! I don't like the way this town's agoin' none. The new marina and Ralph's real estate business is 'bout the only ones to be makin' out. Ralph's gonna get rich selling all them houses and lots, but I know fer a fact he don't like the way things be goin' neither."

Beau nodded as he sat down on Skillet's seat. Charley kneeled to pet Skillet.

"Remember how the town worked together after the storm, Charley? Didn't matter who had money and who didn't. Everybody pitched in. If someone had a tractor or backhoe or some other piece of equipment and saw his neighbor in need, he'd go help that neighbor before taking care of his own problems. And Tammy, Virginia, and all the other ladies feeding the whole town day in and day out. It was beautiful thing. I'm not saying we need another storm like that; God forbid! But something. We need something to pull this town back together."

Charley looked up from petting Skillet. "Do got a bit o' good news, though."

"Glory be! What?"

"Rusty's finally retired from the State Police. Won't be long before he moves into that little cypress house on 8th Avenue."

"That *is* good news!"

"Yep. Be a mighty handy fella to have around if things git outta hand. Ain't nobody gonna mess with that boy, not if'n they got any brains."

Beau looked at his watch and stood up.

"Come on Skillet, about lunchtime. Let's see if we can give Sugah a ride home."

Beau made way for Skillet who climbed up into his rear seat.

"See you at Tammy's tonight?" Beau asked.

"Yep. Saturday night."

Beau raised Skillet's mini-stairway and they scooted off. Minutes later they pulled up to the library, one of five storefronts in a long, low concrete building. Each storefront was painted a different color. A combination groceries and fishing supplies was at one end, with Ralph's real estate office at the other. A small hardware store, an ice cream shop, and the library were in the middle. Beau pulled up to the library with its lit-up, oval red and blue neon OPEN sign, thinking that probably less people walked through this door than any other in Crescent Beach. Although underutilized and mocked by a few of the townspeople, Virginia and the others busted their butts to keep it open. Besides books, movies, and the two computers, the library sponsored and organized worthy events like the Christmas party for the town children and a monthly brunch for the town seniors. It was the driving force for the Scallop Festival which brought in a ton of money for the local businesses. People had no idea how much effort went into organizing and making the festival successful. All this passed through Beau's head as he entered the library.

Inside to the left were two simple desks with the computers, to the right a town historical display counter. Straight ahead were the stacks, and to the right of the stacks was a large reading table with several books on it. Between the reading table and the display counter was the librarian's desk. Virginia was just hanging up the phone.

"Lunchtime, Sugah. Thought maybe you'd like a ride home." Beau walked over to the large table. "Got some new ones, I see." He picked up a book and squinted at the title.

"Some are pretty good, too. You might want to take one out," she said, smiling and standing up, getting ready to go.

"Got my glasses handy?" he asked, holding the book at arm's length.

"Yes, dear." She started rummaging around in her purse. No luck. She put the purse down and searched her pockets. Then the desk top. She looked over at the computers. She glanced around the room, fervently hoping she hadn't put them down on the stacks somewhere: she'd never find them. Beau put the book down and walked over.

"Maybe you put them in a drawer."

She snapped, "Now why would I do that?" Beau thought, she's snapped at me more times in the last six weeks than in over forty years of marriage. Beau started going through the drawers. He found them in the bottom drawer. Virginia couldn't believe it. She was embarrassed. Beau didn't say anything, just read the book's title and jacket before putting the glasses in his shirt pocket. She reached out to touch him. "Beau, I'm sorry. What's wrong with me these days?"

"Nothing, Sugah. Just getting a little absentminded in your old age. Me, too. C'mon, Skillet's waiting."

Chapter Three

Norm's house was just down the street from Beau and Virginia's. Like theirs, it was on stilts and had survived the storm mostly in good shape. And like them, he was a relative newcomer to Crescent Beach. He had been a top-notch surgeon down the coast in Sarasota until his gut-wrenching divorce. He fled north to Gainesville where he worked at Shands Hospital, but soon discovered he had lost his drive. He decided to take a time out. That was nine years ago. An avid fisherman, he began fishing both coasts of northern Florida. On one of his outings, he came upon Crescent Beach in the Gulf Coast's Big Bend area. The tranquility of the simple backwater fishing village with its outstanding red drum, trout, and grouper fishing was just what he was looking for. He bought a house.

Crescent Beach was over twenty miles away from the nearest medical facility. Consequently, when Norm jumped in to help with the town's inevitable medical emergencies, one thing led to another and he soon evolved into the town's GP, veterinarian, and all around medical troubleshooter. This included stitching up plenty of argumentative patrons of the Crescent Club in the wee hours of the morning, a good deed that hadn't hurt his chances when he finally decided to woo Tammy, the club's owner. The townspeople were poor and what money he received in payment for his services barely covered the drugs he inventoried. Mostly he was paid in food: crab, fish, oysters and clams, wild and farm pig, venison, vegetables, pies, and cookies. He and Tammy ate like royalty. Problem was, Tammy was always working at the Club, so he did most of the eating.

After a long period of waiting to see who would make the first move, he and Tammy had finally gotten together five years ago. They would alternate spending the night at each other's home until the '93 Storm wiped out her house and most of her possessions. She and her two surviving pet birds moved in to Norm's and had been there ever since. It was a very comfortable house with 2 ½ baths, mostly open with kitchen, bar, dining, and living all in one large room looking out over Snowy Key and the Gulf. Besides Tammy's two large birdcages, there were a couple of leather couches, easy chairs, a large TV and stereo in the living room. Charley's north Florida land and seascape oils decorated the walls and four handmade Windsor chairs were set around a classy-looking cherry dining table. A guest bedroom and the master bedroom were in the rear.

Norm had just finished dinner and was in the master bedroom sucking in his belly to cinch up a pair of lightweight slacks. The slacks were followed by an Oxford style, short sleeve Thai shirt that didn't need to be tucked in, and leather sandals. He went out to the bar and splashed a little Jack Daniels on the rocks before sitting down in one of the easy chairs and looking out towards the Gulf. Huey, a baby blue parakeet, landed on his shoulder and began chattering in his ear. Norm put out a finger and brought the bird up to his face.

"Saturday night, Huey. You got five minutes, pardner, before you go back to your cell." Huey continued to chatter enthusiastically, bobbing his little head up and down. Norm put him back on his shoulder. Henrietta, the green cockatiel with rouge cheek circles, complained from her cage. Because Henrietta would bully Huey if they were both out and because Huey was Norm's favorite, Huey enjoyed more airtime. Tammy knew this, of course, and made it up to Henrietta when she could, but she was working all the time now, often waitressing and bartending because she couldn't afford to pay anyone, other than the cook, full time. By the time she came home she was usually exhausted and ready for bed.

Norm took a sip of Jack Daniels and decided to check on Tammy's competition before going to the Club. He went down the deck stairs, making sure the clinic underneath the house was locked—he didn't need anybody getting into the drugs he kept in the refrigerator. The clinic had been destroyed during the '93 storm, but he had rebuilt it a couple feet higher and, as mandated, with breakaway walls. The limestone avenue in front of the house ran along the crescent-shaped, white sand beach and was lined with cabbage palms rustling in the soft June breeze. The Gulf here was more like a bay and the water gently lapped the shore. The water gained a foot of depth for every mile it went out; consequently, it was extremely shallow which accounted for the only two drawbacks, at least in Norm's mind, for living here: the area was tailor-made for storm surges to roll in unobstructed and it attracted airboats like flies to sugar. Norm could put up with the surges, they were the whims of nature after all, but he had a real problem with the air boaters whose raising hell out in the marsh and around the Gulf violated the serenity and sanctity of this beautiful area and its wildlife. A minor nuisance were the golf carts on a busy weekend. One swerved around him now, four merrymakers heading to the marina on the easternmost part of town. There were no police; consequently anyone tall enough to reach the pedals could drive one of the carts, and cup-holders not holding beer bottles were a rarity.

Norm strolled by the large second homes of doctors, lawyers, and successful businesspeople from north Florida and south Georgia. All the new houses were eighteen feet up with stairways and multiple landings. Next to the stairways were cargo elevators; boats on trailers and golf carts were parked underneath. Lawns were neatly mowed, and flowering bushes and trees were artfully scattered around the lots. The avenue soon dead-ended at the new marina which consisted of a very tall metal building for boat storage and the main marina building that housed restrooms and showers, mini-market, bait shop, and bar that looked out on the Gulf. There used to be a fish processing plant here, by far the largest structure in town that sold mullet roe to the Asian market. The '93 storm, however, did a number on the buildings and although the owner had planned on rebuilding, when the new state law banned gill nets about a year later, there was no way the plant could continue. The land and what was left of the buildings were bought by Frank and his wife BeeBee, a couple from Ft. Lauderdale. Frank's timing was fortuitous. He had sold both their house and a thriving marina on the east coast at top dollar, then bought the fish house and its grandfathered footprint for pennies on the dollar because of the storm. He had immediately torn down what was left and began to build the marina. It was very possible that the loss of the fish house was the single biggest change in town: many of the natives and long time locals were out of a job and departed, creating a void that soon began to fill with sports fishermen and other boaters lured by the great fishing and new marina.

Norm heard live bluegrass music. The parking lot was overflowing. Although the marina charged basically the same prices as the Club, the newcomers to town along with the tourists flocked to the marina; and they were the ones with the money. Most nights during the summer, the marina bar was bonkers and Frank could afford to offer a whole lot of incentive like free entertainment. Part of that entertainment included his wife BeeBee. She was a looker. She also had a pair of monstrous store-bought boobs that she loved to show off. Plenty of men came in for the sweet combo of beers and boobs. Frank didn't mind as long as the cash register rang and no one got out of line. He was proud, too: he could see the envy in the men's eyes.

Norm pulled open the glass door with a large redfish etched in it and was met by a cloud of cigarette smoke. It was elbow to elbow at the bar and people were pressed together on the dance floor. A six-piece bluegrass band was in the far corner. The only more or less open area was where two couples were trying to play ring toss, a game consisting of flipping a steel ring suspended by a string from the ceiling so that it arced and caught on a hook in the wall. Despite the cigarette smoke, Norm decided to squeeze in and order a Jack Daniels: he wanted to give Tammy a full report. Sure enough, at the far end of the bar was the blond BeeBee in a turquoise halter-top. Many of the men were surreptitiously glancing in her direction while their women were looking anywhere else. Rumor had it that Frank was loaded, but even though he had all the bucks, he was a hard worker. During the day he operated the hoist and drove the gargantuan forklift to load and unload boats from storage. He tended to most of the upkeep in his free moments and, like tonight, he tended bar until closing. About the only thing Norm had ever seen BeeBee do was sit at the end of the bar drinking her Tequila Sunrises and Margaritas and reveling in the male adoration. She waved at Norm and he waved back. She was definitely a looker.

Frank was trying to keep up with drink orders behind the bar. A pretty waitress with a fistful of bills in one hand and a tray of drinks in the other threaded her way through the crowd. When Frank saw Norm he pointed to the Jack Daniels and Norm nodded. Minutes later, he brought Norm his drink. Frank was medium height, thin, with shirt-collar-length and well coiffed black hair. His white shirt was open at the chest to showcase a heavy gold chain and he wore tight black chinos secured by a belt with a big brass buckle. As hard a worker as he was and as cool as he tried to be, Norm wondered how he had scored a babe like BeeBee. What Norm didn't know was that they had impetuously married after snorting a gram of very high-grade cocaine they had scored at a casino bar in Las Vegas. What he did know was that when Frank was around BeeBee, she acted like she had stepped in something bad and couldn't shake it off her shoe.

"Evening, Doctor," Frank said, sticking out his hand. Norm took it. "Tammy know you're here?" he asked, smiling.

"She will. Looks like you're doing a heck of a business. Pretty good music, too."

Frank looked around and nodded.

"Not my first rodeo, Norm. I know what people want. And yeah, the group's good. Heard them last April at Perry's bluegrass festival. Not cheap, but it takes money to make money, I always say. How's the Club doing?"

You know damn well how the Club's doing, Norm thought.

"Fair to middling. No secret that this is the place to be these days."

"Can't help that. Like I said, it's not my first rodeo." Frank noticed he was needed down near his wife. "Got to go. Drink's on the house."

Norm lifted his glass to him as Frank hustled down the bar. Norm turned and leaned against the bar. He tried to count the people, but it was like counting hummingbirds at a feeder. He figured sixty was close enough. Tammy wasn't going to be happy. He finished his drink, threw a couple bucks down on the bar, and headed. The fresh air was a relief. Ten minutes later he arrived at the

Crescent Beach Club. Here it was, second or third busiest weekend of the year and the parking lot was maybe half full. Not good. Norm sighed and climbed up to the bar and restaurant. About the only change to the Club over the years was that the pool table underneath the bar hadn't been replaced after the storm surge took it away. Picnic tables stained with seagull droppings were out on the deck overlooking the Gulf. Inside, plastic red pepper lights hung over the row of bottles behind the long pecky-cypress bar. A Braves game was on the large TV above the pepper lights. At least, Norm thought, every seat at the bar was taken and half the Formica-topped tables had parties of two or more. He waved to Sammy and Clem at the far end of the bar before sitting down with five out of the seven members of his poker group. All were good friends. Skillet and a small ugly white dog were beneath the two tables pulled together. Beau pulled out a chair.

"Where ya been, Doc?" Charley asked.

"Scouting the competition. Quite a crowd over there."

Norm sat between Charley and Beau. Across from him in his usual spot facing the main entry door was Jimmy Talbot, a middle-aged, tan and very much weathered sports fishing guide. Jimmy was flanked on one side by Tiny, a man-mountain shrimper in his early thirties, pushing six-four and three hundred pounds. On his other side was Louie who had thinning gray hair, especially on top, and was maybe five-four in boots and tipping the scales at a buck forty-five.

"B.B. holdin' court?" Charley asked.

"Did the sun come up this morning?" Norm answered.

"Know what B.B. stands for, doncha?"

Beau rolled his eyes. "Big Boobs. Wish I had a dollar for every time you've made that observation, Charley."

Tammy stopped at their table, hands full of beers. Norm put an arm around her waist and drew her close.

"I swear you boys are like a bunch of teenagers," she said. "Can't you talk about anything besides her?" She turned to Norm. "Pretty busy over there?"

"Counted maybe sixty. Pretty good bluegrass band, too."

Tammy nodded.

"Maybe help business some if you bought a pair of what B.B.s got," Charley said.

"Watch it, Charley," Norm said.

"Jest a suggestion."

Tammy was a small, attractive brunette with a very tidy figure. At work, like tonight, she usually wore her hair in a ponytail that she pulled through the bright orange baseball cap with *Crescent Beach Club* on the front. Among other things, Norm loved the hell out of her perfect butt.

"Charley's right. Need a draw of some kind," Beau said.

"Not as if nobody doesn't know about this place, Beau," Tammy countered. Norm winced at the triple negative.

"It's all the turist fisher people that's over there," Tiny said. "Need an event to haul 'em in here. Another fishin' tournament, maybe. This one kinda fizzled what with all the goin's on with them nails on the ramp and all."

"I don't have the time and money for that, Tiny. Takes money for prizes, advertising, and everything. And after what happened I doubt if anyone's ready to donate any prizes again right off." She smiled at Norm as she pulled away. "Better deliver these beers before they get warm. Back in a few with your JD."

"Must be something we can do," Jimmy said. "Too bad the CB 250 is done with. Could of raffled off paddock passes, or maybe run a pool with big cash prizes. Maybe talk the race committee in having the trophy presentation here in the bar and a dance afterwards—call it the CB 250 Ball."

Jimmy had worn a lot of hats: fisherman, husband and father, grandfather, crabber, marijuana smuggler, racecar driver. Except for the year when he had a bullet hole in his right hand, he had driven the town's entry in the annual Crescent Beach stock car race since its inception and was still euphoric about finally winning last April. Although the field of contestants was smaller than usual, nonetheless his winning the two-hundred-and-fifty lap endurance demolition derby with top speeds of over a hundred and thirty was no small feat. The six-foot trophy was at City Hall and would remain there until next year's race. Jimmy's winning-driver trophy was proudly displayed in the living room of his house.

"Pretty hard to get people over here when you have creatures like Sammy scaring the heck out of them," Louie said, in his Boston accent that made the r in 'hard' sound like an ah. Louie was the newest member of the poker group. He had shown up at Crescent Beach only weeks before the '93 storm and impulsively bought a lot for his motorhome. The motorhome had been flooded, but survived. However the little antique MGA that he towed behind it, did not. He couldn't afford to replace the sports car so he bought an old fat-tired bicycle. He never fired up the motorhome again, jacked it up, and landscaped right up to its edge. You couldn't see in through the windshield for all the hanging plants in the cab. Louie turned to Tiny. "Why don't you talk to Sammy, Tiny?"

"Won't do no good. Every time he puts a elevator up or does some wirin' at one of them new fancy houses he gets more pissed off. Says them people on the other side of the creek is from a difrent planet and uppity-like and treats him and Clem like trailer trash. Just wants to go back fishin', but can't."

Beau looked miffed. "So Virginia, Norm, and I are uppity?"

Tiny shook his head. "Ya know he don't think that."

"It's tough," Jimmy said. "Most of us are cashing in on the tourists and newcomers. Me with my guiding, Tiny and T with bait and eating shrimp, Tammy's got this, even Charley here can sell his paintings."

Charley had been Jimmy's right hand man with crabbing and smuggling. When Jimmy turned guide fulltime, Charley morphed his God-given talent from doodling to serious art. Graduating from charcoal and pastels to oils, he began to specialize in Florida landscapes and wildlife. Norm was his best customer.

"How have sales been, Charley?" Norm asked.

" 'Bout sold out at the Cedar Key festival. People spent a fortune that weekend. Don't know where the money comes from aroun' here, what with the square grouper. business dryin' up like it has. But I weren't the only one makin' out; most everybody took in some good money. But, jest like here, the Cedar Key locals still takin' that net law pretty hard. The town put up a monument dedicated to the net fishermen outside the front door o' City Hall. It's all etched in a granite slab framed in brick and shows a man with his back to ya in a birddog boat throwin' out a net. All around him is ripples: ripples of the water and ripples of the gulls' wings above. Only colors is a pale yellow sun and skinny brown horizon. Rest is gray. Says, 'The Last Sunset.'" Charley shook his head. "Saddest thing you ever saw. Looks more like a tombstone than a monument. Even had some flowers someone put in front of it." But then he smiled. "Did meet me some pretty art students from Gainesville, though. Thought I was hot stuff."

"Youth these days!" Beau said, shaking his head.

"I believe we're getting off the subject," Louie put in. "We were talking about getting Tammy some business."

"Maybe I could paint a couple signs ya could wear front side and back and pedal around town on that rusty ol' thing ya call a bicycle. I'd even pop for new batteries for them flashlights ya got taped to the ends of the handlebars fer turn signals. Git y'all lit up. People probably flock here," Charley said.

Tiny laughed. "And what 'bout you, Charley? Ya got that rusty ol' John Deere ridin' mower. Could paint a big ol' sign fer ya, too. 'Tween the two of ya, Tammy'd have to beat the customers back with a stick."

Charley rarely drove his Mustang convertible in town. For years he had ridden an old Toro riding mower around, but it had been washed into the marsh by the storm. He eventually replaced it with a well-aged John Deere.

"Have to charge Tammy fer gas. My Deere is powerful thirsty."

"And wicked slow," Louie added.

"Whacha mean, 'slow?'" Charley asked, quickly turning to Louie. "Nuthin' runs like my Deere. She'd run circles around that ol' bike o' yurs."

"In a pig's ass," Louie countered.

Jimmy leaned back in his chair, folding his hands over his stomach. Beau caught Tammy's attention and signaled for more drinks. Norm and Tiny settled in. Seemed like not a night went by without Charley and Louie having one of their discussions.

"How fast can that Deere go, you figure?" Louie asked.

Charley thought about that.

"Dunno. Maybe six or seven."

Louie laughed.

"I doubt that. Still, I bet I can pedal fifteen if I had to."

"Yeah, fer how long? Ya couldn't beat me if'n we had to go around town three or four times. Tell ya that! And who won that race 'tween the turtle and the ol' rabbit, anyways?"

"The tortoise and the hare, Charley," Norm said.

"Whatever. Fact is, Louie here would be a suckin' air after the first lap. Probably keel over from a heart attack if'n he went two!"

Tammy set the new round of drinks down. After a sip of his scotch, Beau leaned his long frame forward, putting his elbows on the table. In his best professorial tone, he said, "Gentlemen, I do believe we have the makings of an event."

Norm and Jimmy smiled. Tiny asked, "What?"

"Just like Jimmy suggested," Beau continued, "except instead of the CB 250, we have a race between the tortoise and hare, here. We could make up a pool with all sorts of categories—winner, fastest lap, slowest lap, and so on. Set it up way before so people will get word and buy in. When they come to place their bets, they just might have a beer or two and a grouper sandwich while they're discussing odds. Odds would probably change day to day. Have some tee-shirts made up for sale, and definitely got to have a trophy for the winner. Who knows, maybe an annual trophy. Trophy presentation, of course, would have to be here. Maybe even a celebratory dance or band or something afterwards…"

Charley and Louie looked at each other, minds going a mile a minute. Norm and Jimmy got caught up in Beau's enthusiasm.

"Must be at least three miles around town, easy," Norm said. "We could set up a track, put up cones, hay bales on sharp corners. Regular grand prix! Say five laps. Bet that would about let Charley catch up and make it close."

"Catch up!" Charley exclaimed.

"Fifteen miles is a long way," Louie complained. "I'll bet I don't ride that far in a month."

"Chickenin' out already, Louie?" Charley asked.

Louie gave Charley a long look. He turned back to Beau.

"If I agree to do this, I need to train. Can't be right off."

"Be a good starter event for the Scallop Festival. That's over a month away," Jimmy said.

"When did ya say Rusty was comin' to town, Jimmy?" Charley asked, innocently.

"Maybe next week. I know what you're thinking, Charley; this race is strictly stock. No getting Rusty to soup up that lawnmower of yours."

"No law 'gainst him takin' a look." Charley turned to Beau. "I agree to do this ol' race if'n Louie does."

Louie was silent for a few moments.

"Got to come up with a good set of rules, Beau, and I'd also like to check out the route. But, if all seems fair enough, I'll do it." Louie stuck his hand out to Charley. "And I'll be putting twenty bucks on my bike."

Charley quickly took his hand. "Yur on!"

The five men hashed out rules the rest of the night. Beau said that his first mayoral act Monday morning would be for him and Skillet to plot out the course. He also said it should be held mid-week before the Festival when traffic was somewhat down. They'd have to get the water department's traffic cones to block off the intersections. The more they drank, the more complicated the rules got; but after last call, they believed they were close and called it a night. Norm helped Tammy clean up after everyone left.

"So what was all that about? That tortoise and hare thing?"

Norm chuckled as he put the broom and dustpan away.

"Beau came up with an idea to bring you more business."

"That a fact? Pray tell."

Still chuckling, Norm took Tammy's arm.

"Take awhile. Let's go home and let Henrietta out of prison first."

Chapter Four

Rusty finished hitching the dual-axle utility trailer, then checked the tire pressure. Satisfied, he climbed up into the cab of his shiny new F-150 and put the tire gauge back in the console between the seats. He pulled out of the side street and, never looking back at the apartment complex he had called home for the last twenty-two years, turned west onto Highway 40 heading towards Ocala. He was excited. Daytona Beach and the Florida State Patrol were history: he was, right this minute, opening a new chapter in his life.

He had no doubts that he had made the right decision. He was ready. No, that's not true, he thought. He had been ready for years. The interstate duty of being first on the scene for all the grizzly accidents had been a heavy cross to bear. A year and a half ago, the scale was finally tipped when a young mother flying high on meth and her three daughters had been splayed on the highway after their car ricocheted off a guardrail at eighty-five and careened across the median, flipping over in the process and banging into a semi. No one had worn a seatbelt and the little girls aged two, three, and five, lay on the highway like broken dolls, their heads busted open like melons. A scene like that stayed with you for the rest of your life.

His head was full of memories filed under *tragic, unnecessary, lives lost, lives ruined.* When he thought of his job, the word loathsome came to mind. Occasionally getting the bad guys was fine, but how he hated running the tape measure at the scene of an accident, figuring out who did what on the blood-soaked highway. But, overall, he had been lucky: he hadn't crashed on some high-speed chase, or been shot by some lunatic. Sure, he had had his share of close calls and these days, with all the drugs, you never knew what someone might do. But his name was not on a sign somewhere commemorating a highway or a bridge; he had gotten out whole.

His pension would be more than adequate for his no frills life style. No worries there. He was also covered for medical by the VA for life. He had twenty-two years in as a trooper and another eight as an MP, including three tours of duty in Vietnam. Thirty year pension, seventy-five percent of his salary—nothing to sneeze at. He was also a highly skilled mechanic and knew that unless things had changed in Crescent Beach, he'd have no problem finding part time work if need be. He had outfitted the trailer as a custom, mobile shop with about every tool imaginable including a compressor, generator, and welder. Engines and heavy machinery were his passion—he could tinker on them all day. He was lucky, too, that his body had held out. He didn't work out much, but he was active enough, moonlighting operating heavy machinery for a road construction outfit and helping out in the garage. He had lost little of his natural strength which was prodigious, and his mobility hadn't suffered too much from sitting around the barracks or in a cruiser for hours on end.

A little over an hour and a half down the road, Rusty turned onto Alternate 27, heading west towards Chiefland out of Ocala. Horse country. Well-maintained, dark wooden fences with large, elaborate wrought-iron gates lined both sides of the highway for miles. Sleek, shiny horses meandered in heat-hazy green pastures dotted with picture-perfect live oaks, and he could just see the stately roofs of mansions and luxury stables set way back. He wondered what it cost to build and maintain the fences, let alone those palatial digs of the very rich.

Quite a change entering Levy County. In Chiefland, Rusty turned onto Highway 19 and headed north towards Perry. There was more litter along the highway, and businesses and houses were anything but glitzy with lots of concrete block and rusty tin roofs. There were billboards for Jesus and Bail Bonds along with used tire emporiums in every town. Pick-ups, many with a dog cage in the rear and sporting throaty glass-packs, soon outnumbered the cars. Even though he had spent only a little over a month in this area five years ago, it was still very familiar.

Back then the area had been a hotbed of drug smuggling. On the coast, shrimp boatloads of forty-pound bales of marijuana the locals called 'square grouper' were being routinely off-loaded and then distributed all around the country. It was out of control. There was so much smuggling that a huge surveillance blimp had been tethered outside Crescent Beach, but variable weather reduced its airtime and efficacy. Consequently, Rusty had been called in to go undercover, selected because his superiors felt that his background of growing up in the mountains of north Georgia where moonshining was a way of life might enable him to better infiltrate the community. Problem turned out that he began to bond with some of the locals, among them Jimmy Talbot, the main man he was supposed to bust. When Rusty got the evidence he needed, it became his moral dilemma whether or not to use it, and the situation was complicated further when a surprise, lethal hurricane devastated the town. After working side by side with Jimmy in the life and death situation, there was no way Rusty could turn him in. Rusty never regretted that decision.

Rusty drove past the turnoff to Crescent Beach, continuing to Perry for supplies. Crescent Beach was like a remote island: he knew that chances of finding a good selection of groceries there, other than fresh seafood, were slim to none. Perry, on the other hand, was a bustling lumber town of pulp and sawmills. The stench of the Buckeye Pulp Mill greeted him miles out, reminding him of his first trip into Perry. It was in Tiny's rusty old pickup. Tiny had told him that toxins from the pulp mill were being dumped into the Fenholloway River that flowed down to the Gulf. Miles of sea grass, Tiny said, were being wiped out. Rusty came to the first traffic light on the edge of town where the road to the pulp mill went off to the right. He continued straight for another mile before pulling into the new Winn-Dixie. Several blacks were entering and exiting the store. He wondered if there were any in Crescent Beach. Five years ago, it had been all white with an abundance of Confederate flags.

Forty-five minutes later, his truck loaded with groceries and a couple cases of beer, he turned off 19 onto the Crescent Beach highway. Soon both sides of the road were filled with slash pine plantations as far as the eye could see. Tiny had told him that it all used to be oak and that a squirrel could go branch to branch from Crescent Beach to Perry without ever setting foot on the ground. Rusty smiled. This was the home stretch. That's right, *home*, he thought. This was where he wanted to live, maybe, hopefully, for the rest of his life. Crescent Beach had played a very big part in the decision to retire. He had felt, for the first time in his life, part of a community there. When he had arrived, he assumed he would be dealing with lowlifes, trailer trash, druggies. He couldn't have been more wrong. People were hardworking, church and family oriented. Unlike the glitz of south Florida, life there was real and hands on.

It hadn't hurt when one night early on he had arm-wrestled Tiny to a draw at the Crescent Beach Club. Tiny was a man-mountain, a legend, and had never been beaten or tied before. Tiny took arm-wrestling very seriously: *Never Been Beat* was painted on the transom of his shrimp boat. Word of Tiny's and his arm-wrestling spread like wildfire and the next day everybody in town knew Rusty. He quickly made friends. Weeks later he was recruited by Jimmy to drive the town's entry in the CB-250, a local stock car race that was more like a high speed demolition derby. He had placed second, the best the town had ever done. Jimmy was ecstatic and hung the five-foot trophy from the rafters of the Crescent Beach Club.

Jimmy, the man he was supposed to bust: full-time crabber and fishing guide, part time marijuana smuggler. Family man, husband, young grandfather. A real good guy, a kindred spirit. The longer the sham went on, the more lies Rusty told undercover, the worse he felt: he was the low-life, not Jimmy who was only trying to provide his family with opportunities he had never had. And Crystal, Jimmy's wife. Rusty was a life-long bachelor. One reason, for sure, was his job: so many things could happen, although other troopers married and had families. Maybe he was just using that as an excuse. Still, he had never found the woman of his dreams; but if he had, she would have been like Crystal. She was tall, attractive, a shapely farmer's daughter type—a no-nonsense, hard-working gal with liquid-blue eyes. He had asked her about her name. She told him her daddy had called her Sparkles because of her eyes, but her mother said that wouldn't do and looked up similar words in the dictionary and hit upon *crystalline* which became Crystal. Back then Rusty had found himself daydreaming about her, what-if kind of thoughts, and he had felt guilty about that, too. When he had left Crescent Beach, he never said goodbye. He wondered what she thought when she learned that he had come into town to bust her husband.

Oddly, in his limited contact with the town since, he had never heard anything mentioned about his undercover role. During the negotiations on the little cypress house overlooking the marsh, the local realtor Ralph only said that the town was appreciative of all his efforts when he and Jimmy went house to house by boat looking for survivors after the big storm. Ralph, suffering from severe hypothermia, was one of the people he and Jimmy had rescued. They also had found the bodies of the elderly lady mayor and Maybelline, the Crescent Beach Club's cook. And it was Rusty who first called into Perry for aid, got everything rolling. Even though Jimmy had learned in the storm's aftermath that Rusty was a state trooper and there to bust him, they had worked together for hours in the gravest of circumstances. In the end, there was no way Rusty could bring himself to make the arrest and, right before leaving town, he handed Jimmy the evidence consisting of a bug with a tape recording. Jimmy had smashed it with a hammer.

The Crescent Beach highway was quite a change from Daytona. No traffic. Rusty had passed one pick-up in seventeen miles. He loved it. Only a few more miles to go now. He felt like popping a beer to celebrate, but that would be stupid even though chances of being pulled over were slim to none. No trooper in his right mind would be patrolling this highway. Still, you never knew—a blow-out, a deer, a wild pig, or maybe a hunting dog, and there he'd be, stranded with a busted radiator and beer slopped all over the cab. He didn't need to start retirement with a DUI. He passed the town's dump to his right. It was just the same with the caretaker's shed, about a dozen dumpsters scattered around, and a smoldering fire burning everything from cabbage palms to tires. And there, suddenly up ahead, was the cattle gap, flanked by a cabbage palm on either side. His truck made a high-pitched *brrrpp* as he passed over. Main Street. Quite a difference from when he saw it last. Then it was covered in a thick blanket of marsh grass, seaweed, and literally tons of mud. Flotsam was everywhere, even up in the branches of the pines and in the palm fronds. Crab traps, buoys, every type of plastic container imaginable, flooded boats, cars, trucks were scattered around town. Mobile homes looked like someone had taken a huge can opener and ripped them apart. Most everything had been on the ground back in '93 when the twelve-foot tidal surge hit unexpectedly between three and four in the morning. Four lives were lost in Crescent Beach alone. It was a miracle there hadn't been more.

He saw that most of the non-concrete buildings were up on stilts now. He also noticed that the small store had been replaced by a long, low concrete building with several storefronts. He pulled up to Ralph's real estate office at the far end and picked up the keys to his new house. Ralph had known that Rusty was hoping to retire here and had contacted him when the little cypress house came on the market. It was Rusty's favorite in town and he jumped on it. With very little haggling, the deal was done quickly. The house came fully furnished which was a real bonus. It was built to stay put, constructed on rugged pressure treated posts tied together both above and below grade. It was as rugged a structure as there was in Crescent Beach. The house was also built with the highest quality old-growth cypress lumber inside and out. The builder had had a cypress sawmill in Trenton about sixty miles inland, and had sawn out only the best logs for his own use. But, two years ago, the cypress mill burned down. The mill owner had no insurance and was forced to sell the house.

Rusty crossed the humpback bridge before turning left on 8th Avenue and dead-ending at his house on a canal with one of the best views in Crescent Beach. Facing due east, the house overlooked miles of marshland that was like looking out over a golden wheat field in winter and a verdant plain in summer. With his dock only a couple stone throws from the Gulf, he hoped to buy a boat in the not so distant future. Rusty backed the trailer underneath the house, a perfect fit with more than enough room for his truck along side. He carried some of the groceries up the thick cypress stairs and, balancing bags, fumbled with the keys. The house was spiffy-clean, the AC was on, and the refrigerator humming. He made a mental note to thank Ralph when he returned from his camping trip. Rusty pulled out a beer and put it in the freezer before putting the other groceries away. Up and down he went. Many of the houses in town he knew now had elevators and Ralph had asked him if he wanted one installed. He had declined and was glad he did: good exercise. Once everything was up and organized, he made a beeline for the freezer. Grabbing the icy beer and pulling a chair out to the deck, he kicked off his shoes and sat down. That special late afternoon sunlight bathed the marsh. He took a long pull of beer as a brown pelican glided by at eye-level, following the course of the canal. He put his feet up on the railing and leaned back in his chair. Not bad, he thought smiling, not bad at all.

Chapter Five

Bobby's eyes jerked open. He knew what time it was, but still looked over at the alarm clock. Five-thirty a.m. He closed his eyes and tried to go back to sleep. Even partying late the last two nights hadn't prevented him from waking up at the usual hour. Hard to break a seventeen-year habit, he thought. He could hear Whacko snoring, even though his bedroom door was closed. Hell, he thought, walls are so thin I can hear him when he's on the throne. So, what's new? Just like Raiford. Go to sleep! But, the more he tried to tune it out, the more it bothered. It was no use. He sat up and ran his fingers through his thick curly hair. Wearing only undershorts, he went into the cramped vinyl and Formica kitchen and heated up some coffee. He sat at the little kitchen table and thumbed through a weight lifting magazine. Remorse was setting in. What was he doing? he asked himself. All sorts of phrases and aphorisms danced around his head: 'Your body is your temple'—'what goes around comes around'—'you are what you eat.' Pretty much non-stop meth the last few days. He was still stoned, he knew, but rather than feeling good, post-party depression was beginning to creep in.

Absolute worst thing I can do to my body, he thought. Shouldn't do meth more than maybe once every two weeks. Once a month be better. Don't know how Whacko does it. Controlled amounts, that's how. Plus a high tolerance. But look at him! No teeth, skinny as a rail, mealy looking skin and scraggly hair. A poster child for a meth addict if there ever was one. Do you want to look like that? Bad for the ticker, too. Your body is your temple! Shape up! ...But what's wrong with celebrating a little? Seventeen years! Getting out's worth a goddamn celebration! Just got to be careful and not get strung out.

Today was going to be big: starting his new job and later, after work, he'd go over to the Crescent Beach Club to get reacquainted with Tammy. He wanted to be totally straight by then. He had seen her at a distance a couple of times around town. She looked real good; still had that tight little bubble butt and her hair in a ponytail. Wonder if she'll be happy to see me? Been a long time. Whacko had pointed out the doctor boyfriend. Good-looking enough, but has to be quite a bit older. How old is she anyways? Couple years younger than me. Make her thirty-six. He looked at the clock. Job starts at nine. Got plenty of time to kill. He refilled his cup and walked over to the living room couch.

At a quarter to nine, Bobby left the rusty and dented trailer that was on a half-lot near the concrete block post office. The only redeeming feature of the place, other than the rent, was that the half-lot was on high ground with a beautiful live oak that had to be four hundred years old. Houses and trailers in this section of town mostly had foundations at least a few feet off the ground, but Bobby and Whacko's trailer had fallen from the concrete blocks during the '93 storm and the only reason it wasn't washed away was because it was tied to eight steel augurs in the ground. No one, though, had ever bothered to jack it back up after the storm. He started walking to work. Beautiful day, sun was out and already heating up. Bet there'll be a thundershower this afternoon, he thought. He counted six mockingbirds on his way to the marina. How many had he seen at Raiford? He didn't remember one. He stopped a couple times to listen to their medley. People probably think I'm crazy listening to birds; but the few who passed in cars or pick-ups only waved. Friendly little town, he thought, as he approached the marina.

Frank was out front, dressed in a paint-spattered tee-shirt, slacks, and topsiders. A thick gold chain hung outside the tee-shirt that softly bulged with his tumescent tummy. He had a bucket of paint in one hand and a brush in the other. Bobby noticed a couple white splatters in the well-coiffed, unnaturally jet black hair. Grecian Formula, Bobby wondered? Frank looked at his watch.

"Right on time, Bobby. Here, take over for me. It's all been primed. Doing all the window and door trim."

"Yes, sir."

"This afternoon I'll give you a lesson on the boat hoist and forklift. You ever run a forklift?"

"Yes, sir. Worked in a sawmill just before..." Bobby hesitated.

"Prison?"

Bobby nodded.

"We don't tote piles of lumber here; we handle very expensive boats very carefully. Can't make mistakes."

"Yes, sir."

"Here." He handed over the paint and brush. "At noon come on in the bar and my wife BeeBee will make you a sandwich."

Frank looked at his paint-spattered hands and headed towards the men's room on the side of the building. Bobby began to paint. He was careful, wanted to make a good impression, but it was boring. All by the hour, he thought. Compared to prison, this was big money: $6.15 an hour, a buck over minimum wage. Let's see. When I was running the edger at the mill, minimum wage was $3.35. I got paid $5.35, a couple bucks over minimum wage. So, I'm making 80¢ more an hour after seventeen years. Come a long ways, Bobby, especially when a Snickers cost 30¢ back then and 70¢ now! Man, Tammy and I had some good times back then. Some bad ones, too. Hope she still doesn't hold them against me. Hard liquor. Never again. Root of all my troubles.

Bobby had worked his way around to the grocery and marine supplies section. He could see the wall clock through the window. Five past noon. Time flies when you're having fun, he thought, as he pushed the lid down on the can. After washing the latex paint off his hands and forearms, he entered the bar. BeeBee was sitting in her usual spot at the far end wearing a sleeveless blouse and nursing a Bloody Mary. No one else was around. It was the first time he had seen her and she wasn't wearing a bra. Bobby swallowed. Seventeen years without a woman and my boss's wife looks like this! BeeBee looked Bobby up and down. For his part, it took all his willpower to keep his eyes focused on hers. She took a bite of celery. Bobby remained standing at the door as she slowly chewed; he didn't know what else to do.

"So you're the new man my husband hired."

"Yes, Ma'am."

"You have a name?"

"Bobby."

"Hi, Bobby. I'm BeeBee."

Bobby nodded.

"Frank tells me I'm to make you a sandwich."

"Yes, Ma'am. Please, Ma'am."

BeeBee didn't move.

"Call me BeeBee. I don't like Ma'am. Makes me feel old."

"Yes, Ma'…BeeBee. Sorry."

BeeBee pushed herself up from the bar.

"Grab yourself a Coke or something from the cooler. Bag of chips, too, from over there," she said, pointing to a metal stand in the corner. “Turkey, lettuce, and mayo okay?”

“Sounds perfect.”

She brought the sandwich over. Bobby was sitting in front of a window looking out over the Gulf. She leaned way over when she put the plate in front of him.

“Nice view, isn’t it, Bobby?”

“Sure is, ”Bobby said, struggling to avert his eyes from her breasts. He quickly turned back to the Gulf. BeeBee smiled at his discomfort. She returned to her barstool and drink, and watched Bobby wolf down the sandwich.

“Frank tells me you just got out of prison.” Bobby nodded. “What’d you do?”

Bobby looked her in the eye.

“Punched out a state trooper.”

“Why?”

“Was drunk.”

He turned back to the Gulf and his chips. BeeBee continued to watch him.

“You look like you kept in shape. Weights?”

Bobby nodded. “In my spare time.” He turned towards her. “Had plenty of spare time.”

“It shows,” she said, looking at his biceps. “Got a girlfriend?”

“Nope. Only been out a few days.”

“How long were you in?”

“Seventeen years.”

“Jesus, you must be horny as hell!”

Bobby didn’t say anything. Frank stuck his head in the door. Bobby noticed the paint splatters were gone.

“Looking good, Bobby,” Frank said. “Guess you met the little woman.” BeeBee frowned into her drink. “Once you finish the trim, come find me in boat storage for a forklift lesson.”

“Yes, Sir.”

When the door shut, BeeBee went over to pick up Bobby's plate, again leaning way over.

"Thank you, BeeBee," Bobby said, not giving in, eyes locked on hers.

"Bobby and BeeBee. Got a good ring to it, doesn't it, Bobby?" she said, smiling. Bobby didn't say anything. He watched BeeBee walk slowly over to the bar sink. Her velvety shorts just covered her buns. He stood up when she began to wash the plate.

"Thank you, BeeBee."

"Anytime, Bobby."

Bobby went back to painting. A couple hours later he had his forklift lesson and Frank watched him practice with a few of the smaller boats. Bobby was careful and Frank was pleased. At five-thirty, Bobby punched out and walked back to the trailer. Whacko was nowhere around and there was no note. The car was gone. Probably cooking up meth at his 'kitchen' in the woods, Bobby thought. After forty-five minutes with the barbells, he peeled off his clothes and showered and shaved in the rusty tin cubicle off Whacko's room. He put on his Goodwill best and heated some spaghetti from a can. After dinner and inspecting himself carefully in the mirror, he headed out to the Crescent Beach Club.

When he entered the bar, a bunch of men were on the far side of the room acting like it was 'old home day.' There were even a couple of dogs, a big black one and a little white one furiously wagging their tails. One of the men was the doctor. Everybody was shaking hands and patting the back of a rugged-looking man with reddish hair. Tammy was there, too, and gave the man a big hug. It was a Thursday night and there were only a few other patrons seated at the bar. Bobby followed Tammy with his eyes as she left the group and went into the kitchen. The men all sat down. The eldest, tall and distinguished-looking with flowing white hair, pulled a deck of cards from his shirt pocket and set it down in front of the man with the reddish hair.

"Rusty, the timing of your return for poker night is above and beyond. But just because we're happy to have you back doesn't mean we won't try to fleece you out of every penny you saved for retirement. Be that as it may, I magnanimously and in your honor bestow upon you the first deal," Beau said.

Smiling, Rusty picked up the cards and began to shuffle. "Five card draw, nothing wild. Ante up." Dealing, he looked around the table. "So, what's everybody been up to the last five years?"

"Tiny here got hisself engaged," Charley said.

"About time. Sally from Apalach?" Rusty asked.

"Nope," Tiny answered. "Little gal from Trenton."

" 'Little' is accurate," Beau said.

"Cute as a button," Norm added.

"An' half Spanish."

Louie corrected Charley.

"Make that half Cuban,"

"Whatever. Speaks Spanish," Charley said, picking up his cards. The others did the same.

"Met her sellin' her daddy's vegetables at a farmers' market. She's a reglar ball o' fire and a business whiz to boot. Got me makin' a little money fer 'bout the first time in my life."

"Yeah, and she also tells him when to piss and when not. Only reason he ain't got a ring in his nose is she ain't tall enough to reach it…I'ma bettin' a quarter," Charley said.

"Your quarter and another," Jimmy said. Quarters plinked in all the way around. Jimmy took one card, all the others two or three.

"Look forward to meeting her, Tiny. When's the big day?"

"Ain't decided yet."

Charley snorted.

"Ya mean *she* ain't."

"Seems to me you might want to do it pretty quickly," Beau said. Turning to Rusty, he added, "Seeing as Tiny has gotten her in a, ahem, family way."

"That true, Tiny?"

"Yup," he answered proudly. "Shor did. And I agree, Beau, sooner the better; but she says we're too busy with the shrimpin' an' all...Probably in the fall when it slows down some."

"I'm betting," plink, plink, "fifty," Jimmy said.

"I'm in," said Louie.

"Me, too," said Charley, "and I'll raise you fifty." Rusty, Tiny, and Beau threw down their cards; Louie and Jimmy threw in quarters.

"Call, " Jimmy said.

"Two pair, queens and tens."

"Beats me," Jimmy said.

Charley was about to rake in the quarters when Louie said, "Not so fast." He laid down three deuces. "Count them and weep, Charley."

Rusty gathered the cards and handed them to Tiny.

"So Ralph and Craig are on a camping trip in the northwest," Rusty said.

"Going all the way to Alaska and won't be back until the end of October at the earliest. Lucky them to beat the heat," Louie said, stacking his quarters.

"Hope they're back in time for the weddin'," Tiny said.

"Doesn't look like Craig's rebuilt on Snowy Key," Rusty said.

"Don't need ta. Shacked up with Ralph," Charley said.

"That's a rather crude way to put it."

"And jest how might you say it, Beau?"

"Cohabitating comes to mind."

So they're an item, Rusty thought. "Remember when we came back from Apalach right before the storm, Tiny?"

"Shor do. Unnatural slick calm, it was."

"When we approached town I was looking around with the binoculars and I saw them swimming naked off the Gulf side of Craig's camp. Thought it a bit peculiar."

"I think it's about the best thing that ever happened to Craig, his coming outta the closet and all. Ralph's civilized him," Jimmy said.

"And Ralph got him to get rid of that goddamn airboat," Norm put in.

Tammy came out of the kitchen.

"Rusty, you still drinking Budweiser?" Rusty nodded. "And the usual for you gents?"

"Yes, Ma'am," came the chorus. Tammy headed to the bar. Bobby was sitting at the far end.

"Be right with you," she said, barely glancing at Bobby. "Got a drink order to get out." She started to pull Rusty's draft.

"Not a problem, my Road Queen; got plenty of time."

Tammy had the beer half-poured when she pressed back on the lever. She slowly looked over. It took her a second to recognize him.

"Bobby?"

"None other."

Neither said anything as they looked at each other. "Looks like prison agreed with you," Tammy finally said, before turning back to the mug. She got the drinks together—beers for Tiny, Louie, and Charley, a scotch for Beau, and a Jack Daniels for Norm. "Be right back," she said, and hurried away. She was in a daze. Where did he come from? What's he want? What's Norm going to think? Norm and the others didn't even look up when the drinks arrived. Big kitty in the middle. She checked on the others at the bar. They were milking their beers, intent on the Braves game. She sat on the barstool next to Bobby.

"You about made me pee in my pants, Bobby. So what's up?"

"You miss me, lover?"

"Hell no, and don't call me that! What are you doing here?"

"Three guesses and the first two don't count. See you been taking good care of yourself. Still got your hair in that cute ponytail," he added, reaching out.

Tammy backed out of range.

"Bobby, don't. I got a man and he's in this room, too."

"I know that. Doctor fella."

Tammy stared at him.

"You know that?"

"Sure, but you're not hitched."

"What do you want, Bobby?"

"The old times, Babe."

"Not going to happen, not in your dreams. Norm's my man and going to stay that way."

"You never know."

"When did you get out?"

"About a week ago."

"How'd you find me?"

"Got my ways."

"Bobby, there's nothing for you here. It's good to see you and all, but you should leave."

"Can't."

"Why not?"

"Me and a buddy got a place rented here and got me a job, too. Today was my first day."

"You're kidding. Where?"

"Marina."

Tammy looked up to the ceiling. "I don't believe this!" she muttered.

"How 'bout introducing me to your doctor friend?"

"You're crazy, know that?"

"Okay. Guess I'll go introduce myself." He started to stand up. Tammy put a hand on his forearm.

"Sit down. I'll go get him."

Tammy went over to the table. Norm looked up, all smiles and put a hand on the back of her leg. "Looks like my luck has finally changed....so far," he quickly added, tapping wood three times with his other hand. Louie was shuffling the cards. Norm looked at his glass, then around the table. "Another round, gents?"

Tammy interrupted him before the others could answer.

"I'd like you to come over and meet someone first, Norm."

Norm noticed right off the tightness in her voice.

"Everything okay, Honey?"

"Yeah, fine. C'mon."

Very un-Tammy-like. The others watched Tammy and Norm walk over to Bobby who was standing with legs apart and his massive arms folded across his chest. Tammy looked from Norm to Bobby, then took a deep breath. "Norm, this is Bobby, my former husband."

Norm masked his surprise by quickly extending his hand. "Nice to meet you, Bobby." Bobby made no move to shake. After an awkward moment, Norm withdrew his hand, thinking, jerk! He also thought that he'd hate to meet this guy in a dark alley: he looked tough and fit. Norm glanced at Tammy who shrugged imperceptibly. He turned back to Bobby who continued to stare coolly at him.

"Just passing through?" Norm asked.

"Nope. Plan on sticking around long enough to get something I lost seventeen years ago."

"That a fact? And what would that be?"

Bobby smiled his best smile at Tammy. "My girl."

"Forget it, Bobby! Not a chance!" Tammy said, as she moved closer to Norm.

Still smiling, Bobby said, "We'll see, Babe." He turned back to Norm. "I asked Tammy to introduce us so I could see what my competition is." He looked Norm up and down. "And I don't see much."

Norm locked eyes with Bobby. No one said anything for several seconds. Finally, Norm reached over and gently squeezed Tammy's arm. "Think I'll go back to the game. I imagine you two have some catching up to do." He looked Bobby in the eye again. "Guess I'll be seeing you around. At least for a little while."

"Count on it, Doctor," Bobby said.

Norm returned to the table. Tammy went behind the bar to make drinks. Five sets of eyes asked Norm what was up when he pulled out his chair and sat down.

"Now don't look over," Norm said, "but I was just introduced to Tammy's ex."

It was like a bunch of balloons yanked on a string. All five heads turned towards Bobby who, watching Tammy draw beers, had his back to them. Tammy, however, saw them and couldn't help laughing.

"What's so funny," Bobby asked.

"Oh, I just reckon that everyone in Crescent Beach will know who you are by tomorrow." Her smile vanished. "Guess you didn't learn any manners in prison."

"Nope, weren't no need." he said, standing up. "Think I'll be heading back now. Frank wants me at work early. Says people come early on Fridays to get a head start on the weekend, so I want to get a good night's sleep. I'll be seeing you tomorrow night."

As Tammy watched him walk out, she wondered how well she'd sleep tonight. Norm seemed to take it pretty good, but he was a gentleman. Who knows what he was thinking. She took the drinks over and set them down. No banter from the table, all business, all eyes on the cards. She returned to the bar. As soon as she was gone, Beau was the first.

"Wasn't he in prison?"

"Raiford. Twenty years, I thought; but must have gotten out early," Norm answered.

"What was he in for?" Louie asked.

"Beat up a state trooper," Norm said, looking at Rusty.

"That's not all he beat up. Worked Tammy over a couple times if'n I'm not mistaken. Tammy said he'd get awful mean when he drank hard liquor," Charley added.

"Looks fit enough. What went down?" Rusty asked.

"When the trooper tried to put the cuffs on, Tammy's ex knocked 'im down and kicked the tar outta 'im the way I heard it," Charley said.

"Have something to do with Tammy?" Rusty asked.

"Yep."

"In a bar?"

"Yep."

"Bad combo. Still, the trooper must have been careless or cocky, or both: also a bad combo. Guess he paid for it."

"And Bobby, too," said Norm. "Tammy's always said he's not such a bad guy; just when he's drinking the hard stuff. Sort of a Dr. Jekyll and Mr. Hyde thing."

Charley changed the subject.

"Rusty, ya bein' a trooper and all, I been wondering somethin' since the storm. How come ya said ya was a construction guy? Beau here says maybe it was because ya didn't think ya could make friends with us if'n we knew ya was a law officer."

Rusty looked at Jimmy who smiled and shrugged his shoulders. Rusty hesitated. He looked around the table; everyone was waiting for his answer.

"I was undercover, Charley, and sent in to bust the guys bringing in the bales of marijuana. I thought you all knew that," he said, looking again at Jimmy.

Charley, never known for his subtlety, looked guilty as hell and yanked his head towards Jimmy. Rusty almost laughed. Jimmy did.

Tiny said, "I'll be a boiled shrimp. Don' that beat all!"

"Did you get any?" Louie asked.

"Had something to do with that bust down at Snake Creek, but mostly they were too smart for me. That and the storm kinda interrupted my investigation." Rusty looked around the table. Very seriously, he said, "And I got to tell you I felt lousy the whole time pretending to be someone I wasn't, making friends under false pretenses. But I also want you to know that I felt I was making real friends here for maybe the first time in my life. That's one of the biggest reasons why I came back. I hope this doesn't change anything."

Beau was the first to raise his glass.

"Not a chance! Welcome back, friend."

Norm was the second.

"To your retirement!"

Glasses and bottles were raised and clinked all around.

Chapter Six

In cutoffs and flip-flops and bare-chested, Rusty was enjoying a mug of black coffee when there was a knock on the front door. He didn't get up, just yelled, "Out back on the deck, Charley." When Crystal came around the corner, Rusty almost choked on his coffee. He jumped up. "Crystal," he stammered. He wished he was wearing a shirt; didn't know whether to hug her. Crystal smiled with those translucent-blue eyes fixed on his. She was wearing a faded pair of jeans and a simple white blouse with a black bra strap just visible. Her brown hair was long and straight, and there was no hiding her figure's generous curves.

"Gave up waiting for you to come around and say hi."

"Been meaning to. Things keep popping up—like Charley coming in a few minutes to see if I can soup up his lawnmower. Coffee?" he asked, pulling up an Adirondack-style chair. Crystal sat down.

"Love some. Black."

Rusty hurried off for a shirt before bringing out the coffee. She looked great.

"Where's Jimmy?"

"Headed to the keys with a client." She took a sip of coffee. "Now that's real good."

Rusty watched her take another sip. They locked eyes for a moment before he asked, "And the twins?"

"Grandyoung'uns are fine. You get their thank-you notes?"

"Sure did. Your daughter's raising them right."

"And you spoiled them rotten with that train set! But, they love it and got the whole thing set up in their basement in Tallahassee. Pretty popular with all their little buddies."

"Must be about nine now. Probably won't recognize them."

"Find out come festival time—daughter's bringing them down."

"Jimmy said things are going well. Glad for you, Crystal."

Frowning, Crystal put her coffee down.

"Not everything. Something's goin' on with Jimmy."

"What do you mean?"

"Don't know exactly. Won't let on, but he's doing things he's never done before....like having me screen the clients. If someone calls with a Mexican name—Rodriguez, Gonzales, Perez, names like that—he has me tell 'em he's all booked, whether he is or not. Now Jimmy don't care if a man's yellow, black, or green, but for some reason he won't hire out to them. And he's got a pistol in the boat now. Always checks to see it's there before a client comes. And he bought another pistol he carries around with him most the time when he's not out fishin'. Tammy told me he's always asking if she's seen any Mexican-type strangers, and poker night he's always gotta have the seat facin' the door."

"Have you asked him outright?"

She nodded.

"Says there's nothing wrong…period."

"How long has this been going on?"

"Long time now. Years."

"Is Jimmy out of the square grouper business? I mean, totally?"

"Far as I know. Other than when he's fishin', we're always together. I think I'd know."

"So you don't think it's got anything to do with that?"

She shrugged her shoulders.

"Crystal, did you know I was undercover back in '93? That I was sent in to bust guys like Jimmy?"

Crystal nodded.

"Jimmy tell you?"

She shook her head and smiled.

"Didn't take a rocket scientist to figure that out after you left."

"That's why I didn't say goodbye. Couldn't; thought you'd think me as low a life as there was."

She looked him in the eye. He always swam in those eyes.

"You were doin' your job, plain and simple…and you didn't arrest him neither."

They heard a lawnmower.

"Guess who," Rusty said, standing up. "Better get him a cup of coffee."

"Don't tell him I'm worried about Jimmy."

A few minutes later, Charley found them on the deck.

"Parked the Deere next to your work trailer, Rusty. Mornin', Crystal." Charley looked out over the marsh. "Shor is purty. Like to set up my easel here someday."

"Anytime." Rusty handed Charley a mug of coffee. Charley nodded his thanks and took a sip.

"You seen any of his pictures?" Crystal asked. Rusty shook his head. "He's as good as any of the Highwaymen, if you ask me."

Charley tipped his Gators baseball hat to Crystal.

Rusty said, "Highwaymen?"

"Group o' negro painters, couple dozen from aroun' Fort Pierce in the sixties and seventies," Charley said. "Painted landscapes an' sold 'em along Route One outta the back of their cars fer twenty bucks a pop. Heck of a lot easier and better pay than pickin' oranges and vegetables. Some of them paintings are worth thousands now. My favorite's Harold Newton who liked to paint stormy weather with big angry clouds. With his paintin's it's like ya kin feel the wind blowin' through them palms and oaks. Another one was Alfred Hair. Could paint four or five in a day and they was good, too. Jest amazin'!"

"Norm's got a few of Charley's on his living room wall," Crystal said.

"Like to see them…So Charley, what do you want done on that lawnmower?"

"Make it go faster."

"You cheatin' on Louie already?" Crystal asked, smiling.

"Ain't cheatin'! Jest gonna git Rusty to tune her up a mite. Strictly legal and accordin' to the rules."

"Beau got the course figured out?" Rusty asked.

"Yep. Three and three-quarter mile course, four laps." Charley started chuckling. "Can't wait to see ol' Louie a suckin' air. An' part of the course is the woods road connector from Third Avenue East over to the ball field road. I figger if'n I run over it a few times and churn 'er up good and rain don't pack it down, he ain't gonna have it none too easy in that sugar sand."

Crystal stood up. "I'd say that comes pretty close to cheatin'. "

"How's that? Public road ain't it?"

Crystal thanked Rusty for the coffee, and he and Charley escorted her down to her truck. When she left, Rusty walked over to the lawnmower. "Looks better than your old Toro, but not much." He lifted up the engine cover and pulled out the dipstick. "You ever change the oil in this rust bucket?" Charley didn't answer. Rusty examined the throttle cable. "This should be replaced soon: about rusted through."

"She runs purty good, though; jest needs more speed. What kin be done that don't break them rules?"

Rusty stood looking down at the engine. He took out the carburetor filter. It was filthy.

"Getting a new one of these will help, and you should run some high octane gas. We can also take the governor off by the flywheel there and direct throttle to the carburetor. And I don't think changing out the drive pulley for a smaller one would break any rules. Gotta take the axle out to do that, but that'd only take a few minutes. I can tinker with the carb and timing and make sure everything's smooth. I think in an hour or so we can maybe double your speed."

After they lifted the axle out, Rusty rummaged around in his trailer. He returned with a pulley about half the size of the original and substituted it for the old one. As he tightened the bolts, he asked Charley if anything was bothering Jimmy.

"Ya noticed, huh?" Charley said. Rusty shrugged and began to pick up the axle. "Purty dang obvious when he's eyeballin' his cards, he's also eyeballin' the front door at Tammy's. I know fer a fact Jimmy ain't scared of nuthin', but gotta admit he's been actin' mighty peculiar. He's got a gun on board his boat now, an' I seen him carry on occasion." Charley looked Rusty in the eye as he helped him put the axle in place. "You all done fer good with your law enforcin'?" Rusty nodded. "Then I got a little confession. Jimmy and I was messin' some with them square grouper. Just missed gettin' caught at that Snake Creek bust ya talked about the other night." Rusty looked noncommittal. Charley shook his head. "Only Jimmy coulda saved us that night and he did. Anyway, made us some good money over the years and was how I got my Mustang. But, some of them fellas in that business was purty rough, scary; might make a man nervous-like. But that's all behind us now. After the storm I never did no more and neither did Jimmy. Ain't no one aroun' here doin' square grouper that I know o' these days. Never see the blimp up and word is the blimp station's gonna be sold to a gas company. So, that's what's so curious. Who's Jimmy watchin' fer?"

A little over an hour later, Charley climbed onto the mower with the cleaned air filter and some high-test marine fuel in the tank. He gave her full throttle and popped the clutch. The front wheels came off the ground and he did a wheelie for about fifteen feet before the front end slammed down and he could steer again. As he motored off, Rusty could hear Charley's "Yahoo!" above the revved-up engine. Charley was all smiles when he returned. He gave Rusty a high five. "Rusty, you be the man! Louie don't stand a chance!"

While Charley was taking his test drive, Louie was pedaling back to his camper from the library. He was frustrated. Although Virginia was president of the library and had built it up, such as it was, from scratch, he was more and more involved with paying the bills, balancing the screwed up checkbook, offering computer instruction and assistance, and generally picking up the slack for Virginia who was getting downright spacey. Yes, he had been the one to send the checks out last week for the water, electricity, gas, and rent, but he never would have thought that the checks she had given him at the last minute would have been dated July instead of June. They had been returned with late fees. He should be able to talk his way out of the fees, but it was Friday afternoon after closing hours. It would be on his mind all weekend. What a pain in the butt.

Bad Dog was in the camper window jumping for joy as Louie swung off the bicycle. When he opened the door, the little white dog with a pit bull head leaped out and alternated between running tight circles around him and jumping up. Louie couldn't help but smile. Bad Dog was an ugly mutt, no getting around it, but Louie loved him. His little buddy. He had found him as an abandoned puppy out at the dump with a bad case of mange. Pink skin showed through what little hair remained on his back. That was years ago and he still had the pink back. Charley said dog and owner looked alike and that the only difference between Louie's thinning hair and Bad Dog's was that the visible skin on Louie's head was deeply tanned.

Louie's parents had come over from Greece and settled in a small Greek community in Boston where Louie grew up, went to school, and eventually got his MBA at Tufts University. Because of the degree and the fact that he was an excellent numbers cruncher, he soon found employment with a large Boston firm dealing in containers shipped all over the world. He worked his way up to become the company's top CPA, an extremely well paid and trusted position. But after thirty years of punching the clock, fighting traffic, and stressing out during tax time, Louie had had enough. Though the company paid well, the pension plan was lousy; so it was going to be a bit of a stretch when he decided to drop out. He bought the motorhome with a good portion of his savings and traded in his generic Honda towards an antique MGA. Wandering the south, he stumbled onto Crescent Beach, a backwater fishing village out of another era: tranquil and totally off the radar. He hoped it would stay that way. At poker, Louie and Charley were the usual winners. Charley called him Lucky Louie, but Louie won because he counted cards. Numbers were his friends and every move at the poker table was calculated. Luck had little to do with it. But the friendly poker competition had carried over to just about everything else which explained why both were taking the race seriously.

Louie replenished Bad Dog's food bowl and water dish before entering the camper and sitting down at the built-in dinette. On the table was a scale drawing he had made of the proposed racecourse. Beau had measured it with the odometer of his caddy: three and three-quarters miles exactly. Next to the scale drawing was a computer printout of his lap times. He had started training a week ago and had yet to do the entire fifteen miles in one shot, but he was working up to it and averaging a tad better than nine miles an hour. If he could keep that up for the full race, he shouldn't have a problem: Charley had said the lawnmower might do seven. Louie changed into a tee-shirt and pair of shorts, putting on an extra two pairs of underwear to help cushion his butt because ever since he had started training, his hemorrhoids were giving him fits. The first thing he had done in preparation for the race was to remove the duct-taped flashlights from his handlebars. The second was to oil the chain. Bad Dog accompanied him on his daily workouts and folks were beginning to call him Bad Dog Butkus in reference to the Bullmastiff that Rocky Balboa had trained with. Now, as Louie pulled his bike out from under the camper's awning, Bad Dog sprang to his feet and they went over to the Club where the race would start. Louie neatly jotted down the time and they took off. Louie's legs felt strong and he was pleased at how his stamina was improving. Pedaling down Main Street with Bad Dog proudly trotting alongside, Louie was in a good mood again; but it didn't last long. Charley pulled out of a side street hauling ass on the Deere and, with a big smile and a dismissive wave, quickly passed Louie before turning off and heading home.

Chapter Seven

"So how's things goin' at work?" Whacko asked, as he stirred a little chopped up crystal in his coffee.

"Better than with the ex," Bobby said, pulling a carton of eggs out of the refrigerator. "Scramble you some?"

"Nah, all set."

"Whacko, I swear you got to eat something. You can't just do that stuff all the time without replenishing your body."

Whacko shrugged.

"So what about the ex?"

"Nothing. Go for a beer every afternoon after work to talk her up. Been getting along fine, but ain't no spark on her end. Don't know how much her doctor friend likes it, but tough. Work's going good, though; helping bartend tonight." Bobby smiled as he sat down to eat the eggs. "Boss's wife's been coming on to me heavy. Should take a gander; pretty hot stuff."

"Careful, boy. Playin' around with married women's dangerous. Ya don't need no trouble bein' just outta prison and all. Better leave it alone." Whacko stood. "Gotta go punch the clock. Orders to fill. Probly won't be back tonight."

Whacko took a long pull of coffee in the Ford Torino before taking off. Bobby's right, he thought, been doing the chemicals too much—wore out all the time now. But if it wasn't for the crank, don't know if I could do anything anymore. He took another pull, put the car in gear, and headed out the highway towards Perry. Several miles out of town he turned onto the backwoods Steinhatchee road. The limestone was a glaring white line in the sun. A couple miles later he turned onto another limestone road, then another and another. Everywhere was slash pine plantations, hardwood hammocks, or swamp. After more than a half hour negotiating the maze, the road began to narrow even more and occasionally there were shallow channels cut into the limestone from where swamp water headed towards the Gulf. He finally arrived at the simple camp that wasn't much more than a twelve-foot square plywood box with a rickety porch, a rusty tin roof, and a window on each side of a padlocked door. The owner from Bradenton had used it for hunting deer, hogs, and turkey. But he was over seventy now and overjoyed to rent it to Whacko. Whacko always made sure to pay on time.

Whacko unlocked the door, wondering why he bothered with a lock. Someone could bust in easy enough; way out here it would only keep honest men out. He pulled the drapes back from the windows. The room was surprisingly neat and well-organized. There was a cot in a corner, and against the center of the far wall was a small gas cooking range. Flanking either side of the stove, Whacko had built solid-wood counters with storage shelves above and below. On the counters were glass beakers, carboys, medicine bottles, a large cutting board, Bunsen burners, a box of Ohio Blue Tip Matches, a Coleman stove, funnels, and coils of tubing. Below were plastic gas cans, coolers, and different size containers. On the shelves above were all the ingredients necessary to make crystal methamphetamine.

For most of his younger life, Whacko had been a loser. Unlike Louie, his family history went way back in America. Originally a family of sharecroppers from south Georgia, they had moved down to the swamps and ranchland of north central Florida just before the turn of the century, becoming some of the earliest Florida crackers who drove free-ranging cattle with long bullwhips. Education was never a priority in his family. Consequently, although plenty bright, Whacko never studied and his grades stunk. He didn't care. He was skinny and had horrible hand-eye coordination so that he didn't make either the prestigious football or baseball team in high school. He did make the cross-country team, but it was composed primarily of nerds which didn't help his social status in the least. The one class in school he enjoyed was chemistry lab. Making gunpowder opened up a whole range of possibilities. He loved experiments with violent reactions like adding water to liquid nitrogen or dropping a gummy bear into a test tube with molten potassium chlorate. When he discovered that making drugs could help him escape his world of pimply isolation and masturbation, he applied himself fulltime. Eventually it helped his social life immensely and he began to dispense his high quality homemade dope for money and sexual favors.

Whacko started pulling down the ingredients from the shelves. At Walgreens and Winn-Dixie in Perry he purchased cold medicines with the decongestant pseudophedrine. Napa provided a host of ingredients including starting fluid for the ether, brake fluid for the tolvene, road flares for the red phosphorous, and some antifreeze. From the hardware, feed, and pool supplies stores came lye, acetone and countertop cleaners, hydrochloric acid, iodine crystals, lantern fuel, lighter fluid, and a host of other scary products. As he worked heating this, filtering that, he was extremely careful. Open flame and flammable liquids was not a real great combo: he had burned down more than one meth kitchen and he definitely did not want to go through that again. He soon opened the windows to let out some of the foul stench his cookers were producing. Trying to contain the smell was a significant problem in urban areas which was one very big reason why he had jumped at renting the shed. Getting rid of waste in a town was another problem. He produced five times more stinky waste than product. There was a good pile of it behind the shack, the contaminants of which might not be as bad as spent nuclear rods, but the toxicity was still off the charts.

Throughout the day he drank several more cups of trucker's coffee that kept him hopping until a little after sunset when he finally took a break and lay down. He was jittery as hell and it was hard for him to lay still. His heartbeats were all over the map. He put his hands behind his head and began to think about Bobby never wanting to hear about the stuff that went into the meth, didn't want to know how bad he was polluting his 'temple.' It made Whacko chuckle. So proud of that bod, Whacko thought; but he should be, he worked hard at it. And proud of his smile, too—no meth mouth for him! He thought of Bobby protecting him in prison. Good guy, Bobby. His best friend. Only friend. Whacko couldn't lay still. He got up off the cot and lit a couple kerosene lamps and started arranging things on the counter for about the thirtieth time. Bobby must be bartending by now, he thought; must be bonkers at the marina what with it Saturday night and the wind layin' down.

It *was* bonkers, Bobby was flat out. He and Frank could hardly keep up with pouring pitchers of beer, making drinks, washing glasses, and topping off the little dishes of free peanuts at the bar. But, he wasn't complaining. Being busy made the time go quickly and so did the women who joked around with him. Just as the men were turned on by BeeBee, the women were titillated by his narrow waist, huge biceps and the outline of those dinner plate pecs pressing against his shirt. So was BeeBee, Bobby knew, but he was playing it cool. Even though he knew she was watching him, he ignored her. He also maneuvered so that Frank fetched her margaritas, not him.

Bobby was a natural behind the bar. He got along with everyone. He commiserated with the women that there was nothing to do in town, shook his head understandingly at the heavy-gutted men's complaints of the ignorant redneck locals, raptly listened to a dozen boring fish stories as well as paid attention to all the fishing advice dispensed by drunk, know-it-all fishermen. When the bar began to thin out, Bobby looked at the clock for the first time. Quarter to midnight. There were still several patrons at the bar, but most of the tables were empty. The waitress was giving them a final wipe before she left at midnight. Bobby'd be off at one. He glanced at BeeBee while handing a bottled Bud to a customer. At the moment, she looked like a heat-wilted blond flower, her face lax. He saw her catch Frank's eye and nod towards the sundries section of the marina. Seconds later Frank turned to him.

"Handle it okay, Bobby, if I take five?"

"Sure thing."

Frank wiped his hands on a bar towel and followed BeeBee out of the bar. At midnight the waitress smiled and said goodnight to Bobby from the door. A couple more patrons left and Bobby was almost caught up with washing the glasses when Frank and BeeBee returned. They were rejuvenated. BeeBee bounced over to her usual stool and sat down while Frank, pinching his nose and sniffing, went out to the deck to put chairs on the tables. Bobby looked over at BeeBee. The wilt was gone. She smiled and ordered a margarita. Pretty obvious, Bobby thought, as he made her drink, but it was confirmed when he brought it over. There was white powder residue coating the edge of a nostril. Bobby reached for one of the red paper cocktail napkins.

"Here. You might want to give yourself a wipe."

BeeBee's smile vanished.

"What do you mean?"

"Looks like you went to the powder room, BeeBee. Might want to wipe away the evidence," he said, quietly.

Bobby returned to the bar sink as BeeBee quickly wiped her nose. She looked at the napkin; sure enough, traces of white powder. She looked around the bar. Everyone was pretty much in their cups and no one had noticed. She licked the end of her finger, wiped up the powder and ran the finger against her gums. She watched Bobby as he washed and put away the glasses. What a hunk! Full head of curly hair, big muscles, and such a cute butt! She noticed she was damp between her legs. She started rubbing them together.

Across town Norm sat at the bar watching Tammy clean up. Sammy and Clem were the only customers left and, per usual, Clem was weaving drunk. Sammy, Clem's brother-in-law, had given up years ago trying to wean him off the hooch. When the ban-the-net law went into effect, Sammy began drinking almost as much as Clem. Sammy didn't get sloppy drunk like Clem, but he was at least a half a foot taller and weighed probably twice as much. It was understandable that if they drank the same amount, Clem would be plastered while Sammy was only buzzed.

Norm was talking in a low tone although Sammy and Clem weren't paying any attention.

"It's getting old, Tammy, and I don't like it."

"He's not doing anything wrong and he's a paying customer like everyone else."

"Yeah, well the other customers aren't your ex-husbands."

"So?"

"So what does he want?"

Tammy didn't answer.

"You, that's what! You can't deny he's been coming on to you."

"No, I can't and I won't." She stopped wiping the counter and looked at him. "But it doesn't get him anywhere, Norm."

"But when does it stop? Is this like forever or what? Maybe you like that hunk of muscle eyeballing you all the time."

"Eyeballing's better than balling, isn't it?" she said, smiling at her joke.

"Not funny."

"Seriously, it'll stop. He'll get tired of getting nowhere and, FYI, I am damn happy with the man I got," she said, giving his arm a squeeze. "Besides, I don't have the time for any messing around; things are getting too busy. We got the scallop shucking contest here to determine the Festival Queen coming up end of next week. There's the putting up the scallop lights along Main Street. And got Charley's and Louie's idiotic race along with the parade, festival, and fireworks. End of June, first week of July's goin' to be nuts."

Mollified by the squeeze of the arm, Norm asked, "When's Tiny bringing in the shucking scallops?"

"Next Thursday morning so he won't miss poker. Friday's the shucking, and following Wednesday's the race."

"Charley finish the posters and odds charts?"

"Putting them up tomorrow."

Norm looked over towards Sammy and Clem who were deep in conversation. Norm called out to them. They looked over dully.

"You two betting on the race?"

"Shor am," Sammy said.

Swaying with one hand holding on to the bar, it took Clem a couple seconds to figure out what they were talking about.

"Who are you betting on, Sammy?" Tammy asked.

"Charley. Heard he got Rusty to tinker on that ol' lawn-mower. Goes like a bat outta hell now."

"I'ma bettin' on Louie. He's too smart to git beat."

Sammy rolled his eyes.

"Bein' smart ain't got nuthin' to do with it, Clem. It's a bye-see-cul for Pete's sake. Bein' smart ain't gonna make it no faster!"

"Louie'll figger out a way." Clem took a swig of beer. He stuck out his hand. "I'ma puttin' five on Louie."

"Aw, yur drunk. Ya work too hard for yer money, Clem. Don't go throwin' it away."

"Yur chicken," Clem countered.

"No, I ain't. Yur crazy, that's all. I seen…"

Sammy and Clem began to go back and forth. Tammy went back to cleaning up the bar and Norm went over to pull a broom out of the closet.

Chapter Eight

"Two spades."

Virginia looked at her partner, Harriet, across the table and said, "Three hearts." Harriet smiled.

The well-coiffed, silver-haired lady to Virginia's left, responded, "Three spades."

Harriet, a heavy-set lady in her fifties, took a sip of her Bloody Mary. "Four hearts."

"Four spades."

Virginia countered. "Five lovers."

Everyone looked up from their cards. Harriet asked, "What?"

"Five lovers."

Why is everyone looking at me so funny, Virginia wondered.

Harriet laughed. "Oh, you mean five hearts!"

The silver-haired lady looked indignant. "Was that some sort of hint, Virginia?" she asked.

Virginia was flummoxed. "Yes, I mean no. No message to Harriet, but yes, five hearts is what I meant to say." She picked up her glass. "Who mixed the drinks today, anyway?" she joked.

The others chuckled before the silver-haired lady said, "Virginia, hearts or lovers, makes no difference: you don't have a chance. I double."

Virginia was barely paying attention. 'Lovers!' Where had that come from! It was the silver-haired lady's opening lead. When she played the king of spades, Harriet neatly laid down her hand in front of Virginia.

Virginia had learned contract bridge from her mother in Charleston and, aside from Beau and gardening, it had become the biggest passion in her life. She was a very good player and, from her thirties on, she and various partners had competed in duplicate bridge tournaments all over the southeast. As a testament to her skill, the top shelf of the large bookcase in her living room was loaded with trophies. When Beau had retired from teaching American History at Clemson, they had sold her ante-bellum family home on the outskirts of Charleston to her younger sister. Virginia had given her a heck of a deal because she wanted it to remain in the family and also hoped that her sister would keep up the prized gardens. Unfortunately, the '93 storm had affected Charleston as well as Crescent Beach. The snow and freezing cold temperatures decimated the gardens, and their replacements were a pittance in comparison.

Virginia's green thumb, though, was plenty busy in Crescent Beach. She and Beau had their greenhouse rebuilt after the storm, doubling it in size. It was divided down the middle into his and hers: one side for Beau's vegetables, the other for her prize flowers, among which were several rare strains of orchids. On their lot she interspersed flower gardens among Beau's well-cultivated dwarf citrus trees. However, no one in town played bridge, nor seemed interested in learning. She missed it. She still sometimes made the trip up to play with old friends, but South Carolina was a long way to drive. And if Beau had any free time from the ever-increasing demands of mayor, he preferred to fish any day rather than drive all the way up to Charleston. Consequently Virginia returned less and less frequently until bridge was out of her life completely.

But, that was before she had gone to Steinhatchee two years ago to meet with some fellow lady librarians. In the course of conversation, Virginia bemoaned her loss. One thing led to another and they started up a group with Virginia as teacher. It was fun. They met on Thursdays, just like Beau's poker group, and they called themselves the Stewed Tomatoes because they would always have at least one Bloody Mary per session. Because three out of the four were from Steinhatchee, they played there. Virginia took pride in how quickly the three ladies had learned the game and, although certainly not at the previous skill level, Virginia enjoyed the outings immensely.

Virginia tuned back in when the cards were laid before her. Something was terribly wrong. She looked from her hand to the dummy. All those cards and numbers. They got mixed up in her head. She saw them alright, but there just wasn't any context. Over forty years of playing bridge and suddenly she didn't have any idea what to do. Nothing made sense. She put her hand across her eyes for a couple seconds, then refocused. Nope, same thing: not a clue. The others were waiting for her.

"Virginia," Harriet asked. "Is something wrong?" Everyone looked at her.

"I don't know." Virginia hesitated. She looked around the table. "Would it be okay if Harriet plays my hand?"

"Alright, but no coaching!" came the answer.

"I think I need some fresh air and I should walk Skillet, anyway."

Virginia stood up and Harriet took her place. With all eyes on her, Virginia went out the front door. She felt disoriented. She unhooked Skillet's leash from a rocker in the corner of the shaded porch. Together they crossed the street and walked down to the public boat launch near Roy's Restaurant. She unleashed Skillet who peed a couple times while she, her mind full, looked out over the

Steinhatchee River. Several crabbers were coming in from the Gulf. When Skillet was done, she had to wait for a couple of cars before re-crossing the street. Steinhatchee was quite a bit bigger than Crescent Beach with a lot more of everything including tourists. There were several restaurants and motels along the river as well as marinas that harbored larger, deeper draft boats than those in Crescent Beach. The river offered a 24/7 deep-water channel to the Gulf whereas only airboats could go out or come in during low tides at Crescent Beach. She returned to the porch where she sat on the porch swing for a few more minutes and looked out again over the river. Her mind was racing. What is going on! What was that bid all about? Why didn't the cards make sense! Skillet put his head in her lap and she absently stroked it. Little by little she calmed down and everything seemed to realign; she felt better, refocused somehow, or was that just in her head? She had no idea how long she had sat on the porch. She returned inside.

"How'd we do?"

Harriet smiled. "Made game. That makes it two to zero, so a rubber, too. But you have to help me score all the bonuses." She pointedly looked at the silver-haired lady. "Going to be a pile with that double."

Virginia didn't have any problems tallying, and Harriet was right: it *was* a pile of points. She declined a second Bloody Mary. As the cards were reshuffled and dealt, Virginia prayed that whatever had happened had passed. When she picked up her hand, the cards made total sense. She relaxed and the rest of the afternoon passed without incident. By the end of the session, she and Harriet had clobbered their opponents. Before leaving, she pooh-poohed her momentary confusion, blaming it on the Bloody Mary. "The alcohol must have rushed right to my head," Virginia said. She was the oldest of the four. "Must be an age thing," she added, smiling.

On her return over the limestone road to Crescent Beach, she wasn't so complacent. What *had* happened? Maybe it wasn't just an old age thing. Never happened before, that's for sure. Maybe I had a mini-stroke! No, no way. Certainly nothing to do with menopause: that was history, years ago. Brain tumor! Calm down! It probably *is* just a basic spacey old age thing. Misplacing glasses, forgetting names sometime, hard to balance the checkbook, that happens with age. Hear about it all the time. And it's been going on for quite awhile now, maybe getting a little worse is all...which is understandable because I'm getting older. She laughed at herself. Why do I always think something dreadful is happening? But, I should make a doctor's appointment...or, at the very least, talk to Norm...under the condition he doesn't say anything to Beau. Norm will probably kid me for being such a worrywart. But not for a bit. Too many things coming up with the festival. After the festival I'll go talk to Norm.

But what if it is something serious? What about Beau? How would he react? Would it be progressive and non-curable like a brain tumor? Or something so mentally debilitating that he'd have to take care of me? Oh, Virginia, stop worrying! But remember, girl, how you felt when you thought he had drowned in the storm? Like your guts had been torn out and you couldn't think clearly; just a big void, like you were being sucked into a vacuum. How would Beau feel if I were a vegetable? We've been together so long that we're not just a team; we're one, one and the same. Stop it! Be reasonable! If it's anything at all, it's probably just some chemical imbalance, a diet thing, easily fixed with some sort of supplement. You know that metabolism changes radically with age...so it really might have been a reaction to the vodka. Sure hate to give up the Bloody Marys at bridge, and especially the martinis in the hot tub, but things get screwy when you're seventy years old. And it may have been just a freak thing and will never happen again. But, if it does, then I go see Norm. But no way can I even think about checking it out in the next couple weeks. Too much going on with the parade, raffle, vendors, and all. And I'm definitely not going to say anything about this to Beau, at least not right now. She turned to Skillet.

"What do you think, Skillet? Am I getting whacky? What's your prognosis?" Skillet was sitting upright in the passenger seat with chin resting on the window frame, his ears flapping in the wind and taking in the smells. He briefly turned towards her, then returned to the window and his smells. Virginia laughed. "So you think I'm being a worrywart. That's good to know." She automatically turned left at the four corners in the middle of nowhere. How long had she and Beau been together? She counted them up. Fifty-five years! And she wouldn't change one thing, not a single one! Like him taking her to the prom. He was so gangly back then; but, still, he was a great dancer. And they were so hot and heavy in his dad's Lincoln at the drive-in on Saturday nights! College had separated them and it had been agony. She had been a pre-med student at Bryn Mawr in Pennsylvania, yet still managed to visit him at the University of South Carolina every chance she got. It was at his father's summer home in Beaufort when he had proposed to her during her junior year, his senior. She smiled at the memory. He had been so nervous sitting on the swing under the live oak, one of the very few times he had ever been tongue-tied. She had known what was coming and had a hard time not hugging him before he got it out. Probably the happiest day of her life. She dropped out of Bryn Mawr the next semester, sacrificing any career in medicine she might have. Didn't matter, she had Beau, and had had Beau all these years—through grad school and his teaching career at Clemson and now finally retirement. She knew that Beau felt no regrets either. She thought of the Greek myth of Philemon and Baucis, an elderly couple who lived in humility and happiness. One day the disguised gods, Zeus and his son Hermes, came to their simple home. Earlier, the gods had been turned away from every house in the village when they had asked for sustenance. Philemon and Baucis invited them into their humble abode and shared all the food and wine they had. When the gods revealed themselves, they asked the old couple what they might want in reward for being such generous hosts. The old couple replied that they wanted to die at the same moment because they loved each other so much that they couldn't stand living without the other. Years later when the old couple died at the same time, the gods also changed them into two intertwining trees.

When Virginia and Skillet arrived at the house, Beau's golf cart wasn't there. Still at City Hall, Virginia thought. No surprise there because Thursdays were when he usually caught up on all the paperwork in his office, then quickly returned to shower before hurrying off to poker. Skillet slowly galumped up the stairs behind her. She opened the door and Skillet trotted over to his beanbag. As she closed the door, she glanced over to the living room where the display of bridge trophies caught her eye. She slowly walked over and took them down from the shelf, one by one. She hadn't looked at them close up for years. There was the *Golden Isle Sectional* trophy from St. Simons Island in Georgia, the *Mother Day's Sectional* from Highlands, North Carolina, two from the *Azalea Sectional* of Savannah, three from Charleston's *Swamp Fox Invitational,* and several more from Florida. They were all sectional tournaments because she didn't want to be away from Beau a week at a time which was necessary for the regionals, and even longer for the nationals. A long weekend away from Beau was about all she could bear.

The trophy inscriptions took her right back. Looking at the Highlands trophy, she instantly replayed every card of those two grand slams as if it were yesterday. At Savannah she remembered that ninety-year old black woman from Jacksonville who was about as good a duplicate bridge player as she had ever met. How she wished that she could have paired up with that lady! Virginia sat there, surrounded by the trophies and their memories. Then she thought of her 'four lovers' bid in Steinhatchee. She asked herself how it was possible to remember all the minute details of bridge games over thirty years ago, then make an absurd bid like that? Must have been the Bloody Mary! Speaking of…She looked at her watch. Quarter to six already. Almost time for a drink and a hot-tub. She went down to the jasmine-surrounded hot tub area to turn on the heater and circulators, then heading back up she thought, at least I'm not too old to climb these stairs a half dozen times a day. Beau arrived in the golf cart and she waited for him at the landing. She gave him a kiss and they went up the rest of the way hand in hand.

"Beau, while I'm putting on my bathing suit, could you make me one of your special mermaids?"

Beau looked at her with a 'say what' expression, but Virginia didn't see it because she rushed in to change. Beau shrugged and began to make her the vodka martini. When he went to get ice out of the freezer compartment he found a pair of frosted reading glasses. Smiling and shaking his head, he put the reading glasses on the kitchen counter. When he finished making the drink, he was careful to skewer two olives with a little pink plastic sword-like toothpick and place them in the oversize martini glass. When Virginia came out of the bedroom in her bathing suit and terry cloth robe, she saw the reading glasses in a little pool of water. She looked questioningly from the reading glasses to Beau as he held out her martini.

"Found them in the freezer, Sugah. Here's your 'mermaid.'"

"In the freezer!" She reached for the martini. "Thank you, dear….my what?"

" 'Mermaid.' That's what you asked for."

Chapter Nine

Rusty stuck his hand in the shower for the third time. Still tepid. Something's wrong with the hot water heater, he thought. He marched naked to the kitchen and opened the pantry door. He felt the hot water pipe exiting the unit. Cool. Checked the breaker. Not tripped. He sighed. Guess that comes with ownership. In Daytona he would have called the landlord who would have had a plumber at his apartment lickety-split. Consequently, he had never tinkered on a hot water heater and had no idea what to do. Should ask the guys at poker. But, first things first. He took a lukewarm shower.

Dressed, ice cold beer in one hand and bird book in the other, he went out on the deck. His favorite time of day. The weather was clear and the sun low, bathing the marsh in special early evening light. Had to be still in the mid-to-low eighties. There was a small hardwood hammock in the marsh across the canal with a spreading tree where different birds would roost. Could be blue herons, egrets, night herons, ibises, most anything. During the day a kingfisher, osprey, or even a bald eagle might be perched there, taking a break from the hunt. What would the troopers think if they knew he was turning into a birdwatcher! But, he loved it. He especially loved it when the white ibises came in one great flock. They would fly right on by the tree before suddenly veering like a swarm of big bees and touch down, muttering who knows what as they settled in. Just before sunset the cormorants passed by low, heading to their roost on the power lines out in the bay. Pelicans were always skimming the water. During low tide, blankets of fiddler crabs would move as one on the water's edge. Sometimes snowy egrets fished in tandem with red-breasted mergansers along the canal.

What a special place, and what a special place to grow up in, he thought. Kids can grab a net, a gig, or a fishing pole and be one with nature for hours. They can go out fishing in a skiff or go hunting inland; they know the maze of channels and oyster bars around here like the back of their hand. Of course, there aren't many distractions and, at the same time, they probably take it all for granted. Maybe that's why this town stays so small: when the kids grow up, they want to go where the action is. Same thing in farm country, like back home in Georgia: kids can't wait to leave. And then you get all the folk that grew up in the city or suburbia. They can't wait to get out to the country or out on the water for a weekend, swarming in just like the ibises. Guess the grass is always greener. Seems likes it's only the lucky few who are satisfied with what they have.

Georgia. Seems so far away and long ago. What a chain of events had led him here to Crescent Beach! A lifetime of events. He smiled into his beer. Shook his head. To think that he owed all this to getting busted running moonshine across state lines when he was a kid. He had grown up poor in a north Georgia rural community where moonshining was a way of life and he had become involved at an early age, initially helping with chores like cutting and splitting wood for the stills. He worked his way up to become a runner, delivering liquor mostly across county lines to the dry counties where it was sold for the biggest profit. Alcohol content could be as strong as 180 proof, but was usually between 130 and 140; whatever it was, what he hauled could definitely wind your clock. It was made from most anything: apples, peaches, barley, rye, but mostly it was corn liquor made from sacks of chicken scratch. Every still had their recipes, but what made the best liquor was the best water, and Gilmer County had the best water around.

And driving paid well. Back then several hundred dollars for a simple run down to Marietta was big, easy money. For the most part it was safe, too, when running local. Everybody knew everybody, and most everybody knew what was going on. The owner of the still Rusty ran liquor for also happened to be the local sheriff. When Rusty had gotten pinched a couple times in the neighboring dry county, it was only a matter of his sheriff paying a fine and buying back the car from the other county's sheriff. If the confiscated hooch was low quality, the cheap stuff, it would be destroyed with fanfare and lots of publicity to make the other sheriff look good. But if it was good stuff, it was taken home. Usually within a week of being busted, Rusty would be back in his '46 Ford running liquor again.

He loved that old Ford. Had a souped-up Buick engine and could top out at over a hundred-and-thirty easy. But the one time the Ford failed him was on a run into North Carolina. Even though he was only eighteen, he had been running for two years. From the local arrests and fines, both he and his car had been noticed by the Feds. They were waiting for him to cross a state line which would bring him under their jurisdiction. He was watched and when he crossed into North Carolina, they came after him. The chase was on hilly back roads through a mix of forests and fields. The trees were a blur as the Feds chased him for miles. Rusty was a hell of a driver and he also had a hell of a fast car. Consequently, he gained a little on each curve and a lot on the straightaways. He was pulling away from the Feds as he began descending a long hill when suddenly an oil line gave way, spraying a sheet of oil up through the gap between the cab and hood, coating the windshield. He couldn't see a thing. Rusty frantically rolled down his window and stuck his head out only to get a face full, totally blinding him. There was a slight curve he couldn't see and the car left the road at close to ninety miles an hour. It busted through a barbed wire fence, dragging a quarter mile of wire and rotten fence posts in its wake. The car went down into a gulley, rolled once, and the passenger side slammed into a tree. Other than his eyes full of oil and bruised here and there, somehow he was unharmed. The '46 Ford, on the other hand, was destined for the junkyard.

Having crossed state lines made it a federal offense and there was nothing Rusty's sheriff could do for him. Nor did he try. He kept his image low which Rusty totally understood. Six weeks later when Rusty stood before the judge, he was given three options. First, he could avoid prison by ratting on the sheriff. Rusty declined. The second option was that he could join the army and go to Vietnam which at that time was raging. If he successfully served a tour of duty, his record would be wiped clean. The third was he could go to prison. Rusty chose Vietnam, becoming an MP and serving three tours of duty. Returning to the States he continued with the army, training future MPs. This eventually led to his becoming a Florida State Trooper which led to his undercover mission in Crescent Beach which led to his return to Crescent Beach in retirement. Funny the way things turn out, Rusty thought.

Rusty finished his beer and headed out to poker. Unlike most of the people in town, he walked everywhere unless he needed his work-trailer. Word was spreading like wildfire about his new little business. Some already knew he was an experienced mechanic from the CB 250 stock car race five years ago, but others had heard only recently. Frank from the marina told him he desperately needed someone dependable and good. Rusty was both. Problem might be turning away work if he became too busy: he had a hard time saying no. When he arrived at the Club, Charley's John Deere was underneath alongside Louie's bicycle and Beau's golf cart. Jimmy's and Tiny's trucks were across the street next to a few other pickups. Hanging down from the deck so you couldn't miss it was a large hand-painted sign made out of a sheet. It was a work of art. It depicted a boxing ring with the two fighters in opposite corners, except instead of boxers one was a green-checkered John Deere lawnmower with eye-like headlights that made it look like a turtle as well as a lawnmower. In the other corner was a bicycle with its handlebars extending into large, laid back pink rabbit ears, two lights on the handlebars spaced to look like eyes, white wispy strands coming out of the front wheel like whiskers, and a white bunny tail on the rear fender. In the middle of the ring it said:

TORTOISE & HARE 15
A RACE FOR THE AGES
WEDNESDAY—JULY 1—3PM
HAPPY HOUR 4:30 PM
STEAK & SCALLOP DINNER 6 PM
(*RSVP*)

Smaller posters placed here and there said:

OFFICIAL RACE HEADQUARTERS
PLACE ALL BETS HERE

Another hand-painted sheet marked the official starting/finish line of the race. Smiling, Rusty shook his head. This is turning into a big deal, he thought. He climbed the stairs and went into the Club. The poker gang was seated at the customary pulled-together tables. Tammy stood alongside. On the tables was a racing helmet that was painted like a turtle. Next to it was an old man's canvas sun hat with brim all the way around and with a cord to cinch it up tight. A pair of ten-inch rabbit ears had been sewn onto the sides. Everyone was smiling except Louie.

"No frigging way! Forget it!"

"C'mon, Louie. Be a sport," Tiny said. "Look at all the work T did on it and all." He picked up the hat. "She made them ears and hand-stitched 'em on."

"Don't forget the cause, Louie," Beau said. "We are trying to bring customers within these hallowed walls. That hat will help."

"How, wearing this ridiculous thing, will it help?" Louie asked.

"Why in the spirit of the event, of course," Beau answered. "If people know you two will be adorned in such apparel, more will come out to watch…"

"Laugh, you mean," Louie interjected.

"Whatever," Charley said. "Like Beau says, it be in the spirit of the thing. That hat ain't no more ridiculous than havin' a turtle on top of my head."

"Charley, you are you, and I am me. You make a fool out of yourself all the time. I don't!" Louie countered.

Rusty sat down. He picked up the helmet and examined it. "I do believe I've seen this helmet before, but it was a different color. Was purple with glittery flecks like a bowling ball." He put the helmet back down and looked at Charley. "I'd say this is a definite improvement."

"Yep, was yur helmet alright. Jest sittin' out with all the racecar stuff doin' nuthin'. I thought this'd be a good use fer it. No one but you or maybe Tiny got a head that big; so, I got it stuffed with rags so it'll stay put."

Tammy said, "If you wear that hat, Louie, your steak and scallops would be on the house. Besides, I think you'd look cute in it."

Louie sighed. A free meal was a free meal. He looked around the table. Slowly, he reached for the hat and sheepishly put it on. To a person, the others struggled to keep a straight face which wasn't easy because Louie did look ridiculous. But when he turned to Norm and said, "Eh, what's up, Doc?" with his heavy Boston accent, everyone broke up. Beau choked on his scotch, Jimmy and Norm laughed so hard they had tears in their eyes. The other patrons at the bar, all of whom knew about the race, looked over. When they saw Louie wearing the hat, they cheered.

When it quieted down and Beau was able to clear his throat, he said in his most serious Charleston drawl, "Tammy, would you please bring Louie here a carrot and put it on my tab." The table broke up again, even Louie laughed.

Eventually they got down to poker, but it ended early. The tide had Jimmy going out early in the morning, Tiny had to go to Perry for diesel and supplies, and Louie said he and Bad Dog were training early because of the heat. Charley smugly said he didn't need to train and told Louie not to make any noise when he rode by because he'd be asleep. Before they disbanded, Rusty said, "I think my water heater went kapooey. Who works on those?"

Charley said, "Probly the element." He pointed over to Sammy and Clem at their customary spot at the far end of the bar. "Sammy does that sort of thing these days."

Beau said, "I want to talk to Sammy, too. Come on, Rusty." Rusty and Beau headed over with Skillet right behind them. Sammy stuck out his hand.

"Welcome back, Rusty."

"Seems like you and Clem are getting along better these days," Rusty said, as he shook Sammy's huge, rough paw. Sammy and Rusty were about the same height, both broad-shouldered although Sammy's shoulders were rounded like a bear's and with his huge, hard gut, probably outweighed Rusty by a good fifty or sixty pounds. Sammy put a hand on Clem's shoulder. Clem didn't notice; he was in his cups again.

"Me and Clem's come to an agreement. If'n he comes ready to work each mornin', I ain't got no problem with his drinkin'. Now, my sister don't rightly agree with me 'bout that, but whatcha gonna do?" Sammy said, a smile emerging from his bushy black beard.

"Sammy, I would like to speak with you seriously, if I might," said Beau. Sammy turned towards him.

"Yes, Mr. Beau?"

"I will say it plainly. A lot of people in this town depend on the Scallop Festival for a good chunk of their income. I am hoping that there won't be any trouble."

"So?"

"So, I know that you and some of your friends are not too happy about the net law and you blame the sports fishermen. But, plain and simple, it's the law, the state of Florida voted for it and you can't blame each and every sports fisherman who comes here. I am asking you to impress upon your colleagues that they will be hurting the town if there are any more tricks like the tacks. You almost started a war with that one."

"If'n there be a war, let it come. I mighta put on some pounds, but I used to be a Marine and can still handle myself jest fine. And we never voted for no law like that. And only reason there was somethin' to vote on in the first place was cuz it got pushed through by the "Florida Sportsman" magazine, Tourism Department, and them tree huggers from the Florida Conservation Association." Sammy took a pull on his beer. "And it went through because tourists spend over a billion bucks each year. A lot o' money passed hands in Tallahassee and they done made that law for them, not us who live and work here.

"Because of them polly-tishuns, we didn't jest lose our jobs, we done lost our way o' life. My daddy and my father's daddy was both fishermen. Same with a lot o' folks aroun' here. None of us made a heap o' money, but we was happy—happy not to punch a clock, happy to be out on the water when the sun come up or go down. The Gulf kin beat ya up some, but it was worth it. 'Cept for Mother Nature we was our own bosses, didn't have to answer to no one. Still got us some crabbers, but they gotta live outside o' town with taxes bein' the way they is now. Rest o' us is workin' fer the rich and treated like dirt. Mr. Beau, yur talking to the wrong man." Sammy hesitated. "But, I will say this: we won't do nuthin' if'n they behave and don't carry on none. Just do their fishin' and nuthin' else. Keep this town peaceful-like and quiet. So, guess it's on them's much as us."

Beau stuck out his hand. Sammy took it.

"Fair enough," Beau said. "About time for Skillet and me to head home. I believe Rusty, here, has some business to discuss."

Beau left the bar with Skillet on his heels. Sammy looked at Rusty expectantly. Rusty got right to the point.

"You know how to fix water heaters?"

"Yep."

"Mine's on the blink. Will you take a look at it?"

"I might kin do that."

Rusty nodded.

"Buy you and Clem a beer?"

Clem looked over for the first time. Sammy said, "Be appreciated."

Rusty ordered three beers. All three touched bottles when they arrived.

"So you were in the Marines?"

"Yep."

"In 'Nam?"

"Yep, was a target. Goddamn lucky to make it, I was."

"Did three tours there myself, but I was an MP. Didn't see the stuff you did."

Silence followed as they drank their beers and thought their thoughts.

"Guess that explains it," Sammy said.

"What?" Rusty asked.

"How ya handled me so easy when I was punchin' Clem here that time."

"Had to, Sammy. You would have killed him. Then both your lives would have been over."

More beer, more silence.

"Still, ya took care o' me easy-like. Not many kin do that."

"Had a hell of a lot of training. In my job I had to go up against men who had been trained, too—Marines, Rangers, SEALs, Green Berets. I had to be good or I'd be up the creek...big time. Still, I didn't have to go through the stuff you guys did in the field, or boot camp for that matter. Parris Island, right?"

Sammy nodded.

"Was a bitch! An' don' mind sayin' I was ready to quit. 'Course I had it maybe a little tougher 'cuz I was a Fat Boy."

"What do you mean?"

"Jest what I said: Fat Boy. I was pudgy-like and accordin' to my superiors I had to lose me thirty-eight pounds. Made it extry hard for me and a couple others like me. Had to do embarrassin' stuff like sidestep-march down the chow line. At each station we'd yell, Fat Boy, here! and the cookies'd slop out mini-portions of this and that. Thought up special events for us, too. I remember one time all of us was crawlin' through a slimy, stinking muddy canal in about six inches o' water. Canal musta been two football fields long. We crawled to this little hammock that had a sorta classroom amongst the marsh grass and trees. We had to sit at attention for a survival class while the sand gnats ate us alive. I mean, you know how they kin git here. Ain't, I mean, ain't no damn comparison to what them bugs was like in that Carolina swamp! They was somethin' fierce!

"Anyways, one o' them got into my ear. I tried my best, but couldn't stand it. Like I say, we was at attention and not to move a muscle. The D.I., Drill Instructor, was somewhere behind us, watchin' us. But, I had to git that critter outa my ear! And I did: got the sucker. Snuck a glance and saw it wedged under my fingernail, and just then I was smacked hard in the head by the D.I. He went up one side of me and down the other for movin'. Then he asked me if I killed the gnat. I said, Yes, Drill Instructor, and said it was in my fingernail. He told me that gnat was a very good buddy of his and that I was to take very good care of it. He'd see me after class.

"Somehow I got that gnat back to camp without losin' it. I got a little piece of wax paper and carefully wrapped it up. After lights out and we're all in our bunks, the D.I. comes in and yells, 'Fat Boy, up and at 'em!' I sprang up and stood at attention by my bunk. 'Fat Boy, you better still have my little buddy.' Yes, Drill Instructor, I said, and showed him the wax paper. 'Grab your E-tool,' he said. 'We have a burial to attend to.'

"We went I don't know how far, but a long ways and more than double time. Those D.I.'s are in some sort of shape and I was already plumb wore out before we started. We stopped somewhere and he told me to start diggin'. I dug as fast as I could but didn't gain much 'cuz he kept kicking the dirt back in. When I finally had a hole about three feet long and maybe two feet deep, he said that should be deep enough. He had me *gently* lay his 'little buddy' in the bottom. After filling the hole in, it was double time again back to the barracks....Tell ya what, Rusty. I lost them thirty-eight pounds."

Chapter Ten

"You nervous, T?" Tiny asked.

"Nope."

"Reckon I am then fer the two of us."

"No need," she said, as she tried to button her blouse across her swollen stomach. Tiny proudly watched her.

"Guess I shoulda bought ya some new duds in Perry. Nuthin' fits ya."

T gave up on the blouse and put on a lightweight sweatshirt.

"No need to be spending any money. Mother's bringing me some of her old clothes next week."

T had grown up on her parents' farm in Trenton close to a couple hours inland from Crescent Beach. Her real name was Christina though her parents soon began calling her Tina. Because of her diminutive size, her classmates nicknamed her 'Teeny Tina' which she abhorred and had led to numerable schoolyard fights. She took on kids twice her size and never lost. This indomitable spirit as well as excellent hand-eye coordination combined to make her the best female athlete in her class which in turn led to her becoming very popular by the time she entered high school. Senior year she was voted *Most Popular.* Along the way, 'Teeny Tina' had morphed into Teeny, then to T. School was way behind her now, but she never lost that competitive spirit that had made her such a good athlete, and it was this same spirit that she was bringing to the scallop shucking competition this evening.

Tiny and T walked out to his old, beat-up Ford pickup. He held the door open and started to help her up. She shook him off.

"Tiny, I'm not an invalid. I can still get up in this ol' truck."

"I jest wanted to help ya, bein' in such a delicate way and all."

She reached up and patted his cheek.

"I know, sweetheart, and thank you; but I can manage fine."

They parked across the street from the Crescent Beach Club and got out of the truck. For Floridians who had moved down from the north or for snowbirds down for the winter, the Club appeared a little shabby; maybe picturesque at best. But to native Floridians it was quintessential old Florida. Built on stilts and looking out to the Gulf, the exterior was sheathed completely in cypress, weathered gray from years of sun and storms. The wrap-around deck was also made out of cypress as were the picnic tables on the Gulf side. The roof was tin. Down below there was a slab with already a good number of people milling around, most of whom, women included, with a beer in hand. Tammy and a few other women and girls were standing together in the center of the slab next to three picnic tables set off by fluorescent-orange traffic cones. Tiny escorted T over to the tables. Tammy looked up expectantly at Tiny.

"Forget something, Tiny?" she asked.

Tiny stood there for a second before smiling sheepishly.

"Guess I'm all nervous-like. They're in the back of my truck. Be right back!" he said, and turned on his heels. Tiny threw down the tailgate and pulled out a plastic bushel basket full of scallops. Effortlessly, he brought it over to set on one of the tables. Before returning for more baskets, he said to Tammy, "Think it's gonna be a good year: plenty of 'em out there." He nodded towards the basket. "Had 'em on ice all day so they're all numbed up. Should be easy shuckin'."

Tammy had hired a couple girls to take drink orders during the competition. A good portion of the town was present and more were on their way. Even the church people were in attendance drinking lemonade and sweet tea. Tammy was doing a brisk business right across the board. Later, all of the scallops shucked during the contest, plus some others Tiny had brought in, would be offered on the specials menu upstairs. Couldn't be any fresher; first come, first serve. The bay scallop season had only opened a few days ago and people were excited to sample the new crop. The dining area, Tammy knew, would be hopping. Her job right now, though, was to run the contest. She set empty plastic containers for the shucked scallops into coolers of ice on each table along with plastic buckets on the side for the guts and shells. While she was getting organized, the dozen contestants milled about with well-wishers. Charley was standing next to T.

"You ready to keek butt, my lee-tel wetback?" he asked.

"*Si, mi sin vergüenza,* I am ready to keek butt," T answered.

Each contestant had an assistant to hand them scallops and to empty the buckets full of guts and shells off the dock. The assistants would also be keeping an eye on the competition so they could let their partner know how she was doing. T had enlisted Charley because she knew Tiny would be too nervous to be effective. Virginia came up to T and Charley.

"*Hola, Cristina,*" she said. Virginia was the only person in Crescent Beach to call T by her full name. They had bonded instantly when they had met two years ago at the library and were good friends. "*Muy buena suerte, pero creo que tu no necesitas suerte porque con tu habilidad, vas a ganar fácilemente!*"

"*Muchas gracias*, Virginia, but if I win, it will because of my 'skill' AND because of my *asistente excelente* here.

Virginia laughed. "No, with your skill in spite of your excellent assistant. Hi, Charley."

"Now that weren't funny a'tall, Miss Virginia," Charley said.

Virginia spoke more than passable Spanish. It was a four-hour drive from Charleston to Clemson University and consequently Beau had rented a small apartment for years in Clemson. Virginia would come over and audit classes, including conversational Spanish which came in handy not only at home in Charleston with the gardeners, but also when she and Beau traveled to the Caribbean side of Costa Rica where Beau bone fished and Virginia toured botanical gardens and walked the rainforest looking for orchids.

"Alright folks, five minutes to show time," Tammy announced. "Anyone not a competitor or assistant, please step back behind the cones. All contestants take your seats, and assistants get your scallops ready."

Virginia gave T a hug and peck on the cheek while Charley filled a bucket with scallops. T sat down with the other contestants who were introduced by Tammy to the cheers of family and friends. Tammy announced the rules.

"The contest will last exactly thirty minutes beginning on the hour," she said, pointing to a large wall clock hanging from a spike driven in a 6x6. "Assistants will hand the scallops to the contestants, but will not physically help in any other way, and certainly no shop vacs are allowed." There was a titter from the crowd. "Contestants can use their own knife or spoon, or the Crescent Beach Club can provide one or the other." Tammy looked around. Everyone had their own implement, stubby shucking knives outnumbering the spoons three to one. "Once the shucking is over, our panel of three judges—myself, the mayor, and Jimmy Talbot—will count and inspect the scallops which must be free of both top and bottom shell, and completely clean of any guts or mucous debris. I repeat, the scallops must be shiny clean. Each unclean muscle will not be counted AND it will be subtracted from the total of clean ones. Whoever shucks the most will be our 1998 Scallop Festival Queen. Any questions?" Tammy looked around at the competitors, elbows on the tables, spoon or knife in hand. Everyone was right-handed and wore a glove on their left. No questions. There was a nervous twitter from the audience. Tammy watched the clock as did everyone else.

Obviously age was not a prerequisite to compete. Three of the contestants were girls who could not have been more than fifteen years old. One of them, Rebecca, was Clem's daughter, a petite and skinny twelve-year-old. She was tended by her Uncle Sammy who stood hulking at her side. Rebecca's mother, Katharine, sat at the same table and would be tended by Clem who wore a clean button-down short-sleeve shirt and whose hair had been recently slicked back. Clem was reasonably sober, but looked like he'd much rather be drinking a beer than tending his wife who outweighed him by a good forty pounds. Rebecca resembled her father in not only stature, but also with her blond hair, and she and her dark-bearded uncle made a reasonable caricature of Goldilocks and Papa Bear. The other contestants included several wives of crabbers, the town's postmistress, the school bus driver, the wife of a sports fisherman who had recently moved into town, and Jimmy and Crystal's daughter Rachel who was allowed to compete even though she lived in Tallahassee. Crystal would tend her daughter.

Tammy was closely watching the second hand of the wall clock. She suddenly announced, "Ten seconds everybody! Get ready and good luck!...Five, four, three, two, one, GO!"

A mad flurry of activity. As Tiny had predicted, the ice bath had weakened the scallop muscles and it was indeed fast shucking. Deft hands quickly inserted knife or spoon, prying open and slicing clear of the shell the white cylindrical adductor muscle which was the scallop meat. Once the muscle was free from the top shell, deft fingers pushed the guts out of the way so that the muscle could be scraped clean and severed cleanly from the bottom shell. The shuckers quickly dropped the gleaming scallop meat into their plastic container set in a cooler of ice and held out a gloved hand to their assistant for another. The pitched shells rattled into the plastic pails, the sound deadening somewhat as the buckets began to fill. The hands of the shuckers were a blur.

Ten minutes later it was difficult for the throng of spectators to assess who was winning, but not hard to see who was losing. The sports fisherman's wife was by far the slowest. She easily severed the topside of the muscles, but consistently had trouble pulling the guts cleanly away to get at the lower. She was having a good time, though, as she gamely bantered with the convivial competitor across from her who was much more accomplished. Her husband, who didn't have much to do, joked with members of the crowd; but it was obvious that his wife was falling way behind. She was painfully slow. The shells from the young girls, especially Rebecca, were flying into the buckets. Rebecca, the youngest, became the darling of the crowd. Cheering and encouragement picked up throughout the contest. T and Rebecca's mother Katharine were methodical as well as extremely quick; there wasn't a wasted move. They were all business, professional.

Tiny and Rusty stood watching, side by side. Tiny was shifting nervously from foot to foot. "Rusty," he said, looking down at his watch, "tell me exactly when T starts a scallop and when she's done with it."

Rusty looked over at T who was just finishing up a scallop. Charley handed her another. "Now!" Rusty said. Then, "Stop!" Rusty looked at Tiny who looked up from his watch.

"Six, maybe seven seconds. That's purty good." Tiny looked over to Clem's wife. They timed her. "About the same," Tiny said. "Katharine's good, too. And so's Rebecca. Got her some clever little fingers, that's fer shur. Gonna be a scallop queen some day, but I don't believe she kin keep up this pace much longer. Her mother's a different story, though," he added nervously.

"What did Tammy mean saying that no shop vacs were allowed?" Rusty asked.

"That's the redneck way of cleanin' 'em. Pop the shell open and cut the muscle and git rid of the top shell jest like here. But then they use a shop vac to suck away all the guts. Jest hold the nozzle up to the scallop and poof! In the blink of an eye," he said snapping his fingers, "cleans 'em slicker than hell, jest leavin' the little muscle stickin' straight up pretty and proud in the bottom shell. Only thing is ya don't wanna be fergettin' to clean out the shop vac afterwards. Gits downright nasty and 'bout impossible to git the stink out." Tiny turned back to the shuckers. "Notice that them scallop shells got a dark side and a light? You watch, they always begin with the dark side up." Rusty saw that he was right. "That's so the clam'll be sittin' right so you can scoop him outta there good."

Tammy was over in a corner of the coned-off area leaning against a post and scanning the crowd. She hesitated for a split second when she saw Bobby staring at her. She frowned. Seconds later when her eyes met Norm's, she had no way of knowing that Norm had been watching both her and Bobby. He had seen her hesitation and the ensuing frown. Tammy smiled at Norm. Seeing the frown had warmed his insides, but no where near like the smile she bestowed on him now. He smiled back. That's my girl, he thought.

Bobby didn't know what to do about Tammy. He was continually discouraged. And now the frown. There was just no spark, none at all. He looked at the wall clock. He'd have to leave soon for work. The only reason he wasn't at work now was that Frank said he could handle the bar alone because most everybody would be here. Bobby was already dressed for work and he looked good. Tending bar weekends had freed up his daytime so he could lift weights out in front of the trailer clad only in a bathing suit. He had lost the prison pallor and was tanning nicely which contrasted well with the white silky shirt he was wearing tonight. He was also wearing black jeans and a pair of new cowboy boots financed by his first paycheck.

Bobby had seen BeeBee in the crowd. She was, at least for her, conservatively dressed in snug Bermuda shorts, flip flops, and a Guy Harvey tee-shirt. Her blond hair had been painstakingly brushed and cascaded down to the middle of her back. She looked ridiculously voluptuous. Bobby had no idea that she wasn't here to watch the contest. She couldn't care less about who became the Scallop Festival Queen. She had come because Frank had told her that Bobby'd be here, and she had been watching him, not the contest, the entire time. Now, when their eyes met, she feigned surprise and smiled big-time. He maneuvered his way over.

"Hey there," he said.

"Hey there, yourself."

"Frank let you out."

She frowned.

"He's not my keeper." She looked down at his boots. "Thought maybe you grew a couple inches. Nice boots." She looked back up at him. "Cowboys turn me on," she added.

"That a fact?"

BeeBee smiled and slowly nodded her head.

"Got to go to work in a bit," Bobby said. "When you get back, tell me who won."

"I don't care who wins. And how about you escort me back? I might get lost."

"Pretty hard to get lost. Ain't even dark, yet."

"That's too bad, not being dark."

"Why's that?"

She cocked her head and smiled.

"Because then we might just lose our way."

Bobby began to get an erection.

Fifteen minutes had passed and some of the contestants were tiring. The three girls had slowed down as well as the postmistress, Jimmy's daughter, and the crabbers' wives. Clem's wife and T and the bus driver were still going strong. Tiny and Rusty timed T again. No change: she was a little machine. Charley was urging T on; he had been keeping an eye on Clem's wife Katharine and although he had no idea who had shucked more, he kept telling T that Katharine was ripping through them. Clem was silent. He knew that his wife didn't want any urging, especially from him. Ten minutes later, most of the shuckers began stretching fingers and flexing hands in between scallops, the bus driver among them. With the exception of T and Katharine, production across the board slowed down. Tammy went over to stand underneath the clock and announced that there were only five minutes left. Although they couldn't gauge the quantities in the bowls, the crowd had a pretty good idea who the leaders were and hoarsely cheered them on. Tammy kept an eye on the clock. One minute to go. At ten seconds she began to count down. "...five, four, three, two, one, STOP! All knives and spoons on the table!" Everyone laid down her tool. "Well done!" She turned to the crowd. "How about a hand for our contestants here?" she said, and began clapping. The crowd joined in. When it quieted, Tammy spoke up again. "These scallops will now be taken up to the kitchen to be counted and the results will be announced shortly up in the Club. I might add that these same scallops will be on the specials menu for tonight. There is also a free dinner for each of the participants and for the next twenty minutes, EVERY washroom, men's and ladies', is reserved for our contestants here to freshen up. If any of you," she said, looking out over the crowd, " have to pee, you'll just have to hold it until these ladies are done." Most laughed, but some of the church ladies frowned. "Finally, thank you everyone for supporting this event, and a big thank you to each contestant for such a fine effort. I would not be surprised if a record was set here tonight. We'll see shortly."

Tammy went off to get helpers to carry up the scallops. The contestants made a beeline to wash up, and as the crowd dispersed, very few left the premises; most went upstairs. Tammy had been right: it would be bonkers at the Club tonight. Bobby and BeeBee, however, strode off to the marina side by side.

When Beau and Virginia entered the Club and saw the crowd in the bar and dining area, Beau thought it a good decision to have left Skillet at home. It was a zoo. Within the confines of the restaurant, the number of people seemed to have tripled. Every table was taken as well as the bar stools, and it was shoulder-to-shoulder most everywhere else. Virginia peeled off towards the ladies' room while Beau worked his way to the pushed-together tables along the far wall reserved for the poker gang and their family members. When Virginia joined the waiting line for the ladies' room, she was bumped into by the scallop shucking, sports fisherman's wife heading towards the bar.

"Whoops, I'm sorry," the woman said.

Virginia smiled. "No problem—pretty tough-going in this crowd."

"You're the mayor's wife aren't you?"

Virginia nodded. The woman stuck out her hand.

"I'm Jane."

"Virginia. Pleased to meet you."

"My husband and I just moved here from Minnesota. We love it; Florida's last frontier."

"Then, welcome. Beau and I are transplants, too. Charleston," Virginia said, in her thick southern drawl.

A couple women squeezed by. The ladies' room door opened. Virginia was next in line.

"Looks like my turn, Jane. Stop by our table later if you want to meet Beau. We'll be over there," Virginia said, pointing. Jane smiled and continued on to the bar. After the ladies' room, Virginia went over to the table and had just sat down when Tammy cleared out an area in the center of the room. Tiny shouted for attention, but it still took the crowd several minutes to quiet down. Tammy began reading from a piece of paper.

"Here are the results you've all been waiting for," Tammy began. "Would Katharine Cherry, T Rodriguez, and Margaret Kite please come up."

To cheers and to the hoots of Tiny and Charley, T, Clem's wife Katharine, and the bus driver slowly made their way through the crowd. Clem's wife and the bus driver stood self-consciously off to Tammy's side while T smiled at Tiny. Tammy held up her hands and waited for complete silence.

"Third place with one hundred and forty-five scallops shucked with five deductions for a final score of one hundred and forty goes to Margaret Kite. " Cheers all around. Tammy shook her hand and presented the bus driver with a Crescent Beach Club tee-shirt and a shucking knife tucked neatly in a hand-tooled sheath. She was hugged by T and Katharine before she returned to her table. Tammy waited until there was complete silence again. Even when it had quieted, she continued to wait, obviously building the suspense.

Charley yelled, "Alright, already. Come on, Tammy!" Everyone laughed, Tammy smiled.

"Before I announce the second place winner, I would like to say that her score of one hundred and ninety-seven—two hundred shucked with only three penalties—would have set a new town record. However, Katharine," Tammy said, turning to Clem's wife, "this year it is only good enough for second place." The Club erupted as Tammy presented Katharine with another shirt, a shucking knife, plus a gift certificate for two dinners at the Club. Tiny and Charley were on their feet hugging each other and hooting again. The applause was prolonged and loud. T, with an ear-to-ear grin, was engulfed in a hug from Katharine.

When it quieted down, Sammy yelled out, "Can that certificate be traded in fer beers?"

Katharine glared at her brother as she held the gift certificate to her chest. "Ferget it, Sammy! This here certificate is fer me an' Rebecca." The crowd laughed. Tammy spoke up again.

"T, congratulations." More applause. Tammy turned to the audience. "T has set the new record with two hundred and five shucked with no penalties!" The audience went wild again. Tammy presented the same prizes that Clem's wife received while the crowd quieted. A waitress made her way up to Tammy with a golden, colored-glass encrusted tiara set on a small velvety purple cushion. Tammy reached for it and turned to T. "Without further ado," she said, placing the tiara on T's head, "I crown you Crescent Beach's 1998 Scallop Festival Queen!" Once again cheers from the crowd and hoots and whistles from Tiny and Charley. When it finally quieted, Tammy asked, "Is there anything you'd like to say, T?"

T, never bashful, spoke right up. "I just think it's terrific we had such a great turnout from both the townspeople and visitors alike. That's what makes this such a special event. I also think that Margaret, Katharine, and I better watch out for Katharine's daughter Rebecca next year. I was watching her go through those scallops like nobody's business. When her fingers get a little stronger, she's going to be a force to reckon with, I'll tell you that!" More cheers. Rebecca blushed, her parents looked proud. "I'd also like to thank Tiny. Couldn't have done it without him…because without him there'd a been no scallops to shuck." Laughter. "Finally, I'm hungry; so, let's eat!" The longest applause and cheers of the night followed T to her table where Tiny gave her a careful hug and held her chair out for her. Tiny was bursting with pride.

Beau, too, was beaming. "That was a nice touch, T, acknowledging the out-of-towners." Beau looked out over the room. "It's nice to see everyone getting along for a change. They're even sharing some of the tables!"

The same two girls who had served drinks below were helping with the food. In honor of T, her table was served first. The scallops were perfectly browned and delicious. Rusty almost inhaled them.

"Damn, these are good. Never had any better and certainly not any fresher!" After another mouthful, he said, "Sure learned a lot this evening. Never knew it was just the scallop muscle you ate. About the only thing I knew was that scallops tasted good and they came out of a shell that looked like the Shell gas station sign. How do you catch them, anyways?"

Crystal asked, "You've never been scalloping, Rusty?" He shook his head. She turned to Jimmy. "We've got to take him out, Jimmy."

"Sure thing. Soon as I get a break from guiding. Pretty booked up these days."

Beau said, "Rusty, we snorkel for them and you can come out with Virginia and me in our boat anytime. Crystal, you too, if Jimmy has to work."

"You forget, Beau, I can't swim," Rusty said.

"Yur only in three to six feet of water. Eight at the most," Charley put in. "Besides, 'bout time ya learned to swim a little. Skillet can teach ya the dog paddle."

"Which reminds me," Beau added. "I'd like to ask a favor if you come out with us."

"Shoot."

"Skillet loves to swim around when we scallop, but these days Virginia and I need a hand to get him back in the boat."

"Absolutely. But how come scalloping is so big here? Never heard of people doing it over on the east coast," Rusty said.

"That's 'cuz you only find 'em these days from Tarpon Springs to Port St. Joe," Charley said. "But they 'specially like it around here 'cuz we got rivers and creeks creatin' the right mix of salt and fresh water. But years are different—good and bad. If you git too much rain, stirs up sediment and clogs their gills and kills 'em. If water's too salty, they don't do good neithers. And there ain't nearly as many around as before. Like Tampa. Done lost eighty percent o' theirs 'cuz of buildin' causeways and development."

"They been disappearin' fer a long time," Tiny added. "State's been tryin' to build up the population since the seventies. Got real serious about it five or six years ago. Closed commercial scalloping a year before the net law." Tiny turned to Rusty. "Remember Buddy Ward's where we took them shrimp in Apalach right before the storm?"

"Sure." That wasn't all Rusty remembered about Apalachicola. There was the Oasis Bar where he met his blind date Anne. They had spent a very active night in Tiny's cabin aboard the *Never Been Beat.*

"He used to buy scallops, too. Had his own processin' plant and set a quota o' nine hundred gallons o' meat per boat. Big ol' knuckle boom loader would scoop them scallops up and haul 'em away." Tiny laughed. "Most people in Apalach was sure glad when that law come."

"Why was that, Tiny?" Virginia asked.

"Stink. Town stunk to high heaven. All them scallops was loaded in dump trucks to go to the plant. With them dying, their juice an' such was a runnin' out into the streets. Then they had to haul the processed shells an' guts and stuff to the landfill, leakin' more stuff all over town. Weren't pleasant, tell ya that."

"How do you know where to find them? Are they always in the same place, or can they move around?" Rusty asked.

Louie spoke up. "They can move alright, by jet propulsion." He forked a scallop. "Think of the proportion of this muscle to the size of the clam. You saw the shells downstairs, maybe three inches at best. So this muscle is disproportionately large. A scallop is a bi-valve which means it's got two shells hinged together. When they clap those valves, or shells, together with this big muscle, it forces water out of small openings on either side of the hinge, propelling it. Can scoot up to a couple meters at a time. Sort of like Pac-Man, but instead of chomping forwards, the scallop chomps backwards."

"Whatcha mean Pack Man?" Charley asked.

Louie rolled his eyes. "You never played Pac-Man?"

"Nope. Don't know what yur talking about."

"It's only the most famous arcade game of all time, Charley," Louie said.

"Ain't many arcades around here, Louie," Charley countered.

"That ain't the only way a scallop gits around," Tiny said. Everyone looked at Tiny. "I been out at night and seen 'em riding the incoming tide. They somehow fill themselves up with air so they float. Soon as I turn on the lights and they see me, they let out the air and sink to the bottom."

Beau said, "Captain Nemo and the Nautilus."

"What's that, Beau?" Tiny asked.

"*Twenty Thousand Leagues Under the Sea,* a science fiction book where this submarine, the first and only one in the world, was going around at night sinking ships. People thought it was a sea monster. Scallops probably thought the *Never Been Beat* was the same."

"Scallops can see?" Rusty asked.

"Yep," Charley said. "Got a line o' purty little fluorescent-blue eyes on the top edge o' both shells where they close together. Ain't no doubt they kin see you. Lots o' times they like to cling to rolling moss-like stuff on the bottom, sorta like underwater tumbleweeds. When ya come up to 'em, they sinks back into the moss and hides."

The conversation on scallops slowly petered out as plates were cleared. When plates of homemade pie were brought to the table, the conversation switched to Charley and Louie's upcoming race. Tammy said that since word had gotten round about Rusty's adjustments to Charley's lawnmower, odds were running two to one on Charley. Virginia spoke up.

"No offense, Charley, but I'm putting my money on Louie here. He's been working so hard at it! How many times a day do you and Bad Dog do your training run, Louie?"

"Twice; morning and evening," he answered.

"That's good. Maybe y'all make a race outta it yet," Charley said.

"Pretty cocksure, Charley," Beau said. "Don't forget about the tortoise and hare."

"I ain't. And don't ya ferget none that I'm the tortoise, here. Got me the helmet to prove it."

"Still not crazy about wearing that hat with the ears," Louie added.

"You doing any training?" T asked Charley.

"Nope. Don't need to. My little ol' Deere's ready to go. 'Bout all I've been doin' lately is paintin' a landscape o' the marsh from Rusty's deck."

Rusty glanced over to Jimmy who was unusually quiet: he was looking out around the room. Rusty noted that Jimmy, like Crystal and Charley said, had claimed his usual spot with his back to the wall. Crystal caught Rusty's eye and nodded slightly as if to say, see what I mean? Rusty turned to Jimmy. "So you're booked up tomorrow, Jimmy?"

"Yeah, pretty much. Why?"

"Just wanted to talk a bit."

"About what?"

"Just a couple questions is all. What time you going out?"

"About an hour before high tide. Ten o'clock."

"Okay if I stop by around 8:30?"

"Sure. All gassed up and poles are already rigged; nothing much else to do. Crystal can make us a cup of joe and we'll sit out on the deck for a spell."

Rusty looked at Crystal. She smiled appreciatively with those translucent blue eyes, reminding Rusty of the last time he had sat with her and Jimmy at this table. Tammy had organized a Valentine's Day party complete with pig roast below and a killer band upstairs. There were heart-shaped balloons in the ceiling, little heart-shaped candies on the table, and lots of beer. It had been a gas. Great night! It had also been when he slow-danced with Crystal. He still remembered how her body felt: a perfect fit. He reached for his fork and guiltily began to eat his pie.

People were starting to leave. Jane, the sports fisherman's wife who had competed earlier, brought her husband over to meet Virginia and Beau. They stopped in front of Virginia. Jane said, "Hi again. I brought him over."

Virginia looked up. Her face was blank. "I beg your pardon?" she said.

"My husband…I brought him over."

Virginia's face was still blank, but she was always unfailingly polite. "Oh, how nice to meet you," she said to Jane.

"I'm Virginia and this is my husband, Beau." Beau stood and shook the man's hand. Virginia held her hand out to the woman. "And so nice to meet you. You are…?"

The woman hesitated, then reached out. "Jane. My name is Jane. It's nice to meet you, too."

Chapter Eleven

Louie had just leaned his bike up against the camper and was toweling off when he saw Rusty walking up the street. Bad Dog was flat on his stomach with all four legs splayed, panting. He, too, saw Rusty, but didn't have the energy to get up to bark. He offered a single muted woof and went back to panting.

"Morning, Rusty. Going to be a hot one."

"You're training early today."

"Saturday. Kids are out of school and if I go any later, they'll be racing me the entire time. Seems to be the town sport these days. Makes Bad Dog crazy chasing them. On your way to Jimmy's?"

"Yup." Rusty squatted to pet Bad Dog who continued to pant, his little pink tongue lolling off to one side. "Looks like Bad Dog Butkus is all tuckered out."

"So you heard about the Butkus-Rocky thing."

" A town this size? Hard not to. How's it going?"

"Like the 'Rocky' theme song says, 'Getting stronger!' But things would be better if you hadn't souped up that lawnmower."

"I didn't soup it up; didn't mess with the motor a bit. And I didn't do anything that Charley couldn't have."

"Maybe, but point is Charley *wouldn't* have. Anyway, I plan to make a race of it. Whose your money on?"

"Other than poker, I'm not a betting man."

"But if you were, who?"

"Like I say, I'm not a betting man." Rusty looked at his watch. "Got to go. Good luck Wednesday." He took a couple of steps before turning back to look at Louie. "But, I will say this: it'll be a miracle if that lawnmower doesn't rattle itself to death with the governor gone and as rusty as it is."

"Rusty, you've made my day!"

Rusty smiled and continued on to Jimmy's, thinking that it was true: Charley's lawnmower was a rust bucket and on its last legs. Charley never washed the salt off and drove it all over town. Salt air from the Gulf had corroded most of the wiring, rust had eaten at least partially through all the cables, and there were so many holes in the fender skirts that pieces flapped in the wind. Without the governor the lawnmower vibrated like a son-of-a-bitch and cables or wires could pop at anytime. A few minutes later, Rusty found himself at Jimmy's deck stairs. Mug of coffee in hand, Jimmy was looking down at him.

"You're prompt, Rusty. Eight-thirty on the nose. Come on up." As Rusty climbed the stairs, Jimmy announced his arrival to Crystal who was in the kitchen. Not more than a few seconds later, Crystal came out with Rusty's coffee.

"Thank you kindly, Ma'am," Rusty said. Although wearing faded jeans again, Crystal mock curtsied. Rusty took a sip. "Just right." Crystal smiled and went back into the house. There were a couple plastic Adirondack chairs with a small plastic table in between. Jimmy sat down and set his coffee on the little table. He motioned for Rusty to take the other chair. Rusty sat and looked out over the Gulf, wondering how to start the conversation. He saw the two oyster bars that were Jimmy's tide barometer. "Looks like about mid-tide."

Jimmy followed his gaze.

"Yep. Sure does." Silence. How to begin, Rusty thought. More silence. It was Jimmy who started the conversation.

"So what are these questions you got for me?"

Rusty thought it better if they were out of Crystal's ear range.

"How about we take our coffee down to the dock, Jimmy?"

Jimmy shrugged. "Alright," he said, standing and grabbing his coffee in one move. He led the way down the stairs. There was a long bench next to the fish cleaning station. The two men sat there.

"Jimmy, I don't rightly know how to go about asking you stuff that I know is your business. But your wife and some of your good friends are worried about you."

Jimmy rolled his eyes.

"Crystal's been talking to you. I told her before that there's nothing wrong. Who else is worried 'bout me?"

"No names, but the likely suspects. Really, Jimmy, from what I hear it makes me worry, too."

"And just what do you hear?"

"That you've got a gun in your boat now…" Jimmy started to shake his head in disgust and stand up. "Now wait a minute, Jimmy, hear me out! I can maybe understand the gun in the boat, might need it for some emergency or something, but you never carried one five years ago even though you were in the square grouper trade. Lot of people carried, but you didn't. I also hear you're packing on shore, too. You never did that before, either. You won't take fishermen out with Latin names. You ask Tammy about any strangers in town, especially Latinos. At poker or any other night at the Club, you got to sit with your back against the wall. Last night you hardly said a word you were so busy looking around. Charley says you're not scared of anything, but to me, you're sure as hell acting like it. And Crystal! For Pete's sake, she's worried to death, although she tries not to show it. She's spooked big time!"

Jimmy pulled a pack of Camels out of his shirt pocket and, flicking a fingernail across a kitchen match, lit up.

He didn't say anything for a couple of drags. Rusty looked at the man—all tan and sinewy from a lifetime of work on the water. He knew that Jimmy had quit school in the sixth grade to help his father with crabbing and mullet fishing before striking out on his own. Jimmy looked tough and was tough—a tough cracker—but Rusty also knew that his body was beat up bad from taking all the punches the Gulf and bay could throw at a smalltime operator. He could tell by the way he moved, especially when he stood up after sitting a spell. He also knew that the reason Jimmy had begun running the square grouper—bales of marijuana—was because he wanted to provide for his family, to give them opportunities he had never had. Unlike most of the other runners, he hadn't frittered away the money; rather, he had used it for his kids' education and to get a stake for a new boat and motor and everything he needed to start the fishing guide business. With his beat-up body, Jimmy knew he couldn't continue to crab much longer. He had succeeded on all counts. One of his sons was in the merchant marine, the other a high school teacher in Gainesville. His daughter Rachel was a housewife in Tallahassee and the mother of the twin boys Jimmy loved to death. And his guiding business was flourishing.

Rusty spoke up again. "Crystal and Charley both say you quit the drug trade. Doesn't matter to me one way or the other if you did or didn't; I'm not a trooper anymore. But I've been thinking, thinking about that conversation we had out on the Club's deck that night after the race. Remember that?"

"Of course I do. You was wired and I gave you more than enough evidence to arrest me."

"You told me about that Colombian who shot you in the hand. And who threatened the twins. Me, I think it's got something to do with that."

Jimmy was quiet again, obviously weighing things in his mind. Jimmy's cigarette hissed when he flicked it into the water. A pelican splashed down nearby, assuming two men on a dock meant fish scraps. Jimmy looked at the palm of his right hand, then at Rusty.

"I'll explain some things to you on one condition."

"What's that?"

"Crystal don't need to hear them."

"She knows why I'm here. That'll be tough."

"That's the way it is. Period." Rusty hesitated, then said, "Alright."

Jimmy nodded. "You're not wired again by any chance?"

"You want me to strip, Jimmy?"

"Nah, just teasing." Suddenly serious, "If I can't trust you..." Jimmy didn't finish. He lit another cigarette. "Remember I told you how that son-of-a-bitch Espantoso threatened my family and that things have a way of taking care of themselves around here?"

Rusty nodded. "Yeah, I remember."

"After the storm when you didn't arrest me, I decided to get out of the smuggling—was all done with it. I had enough money socked away for my family and there was plenty to tend to around here what with the storm damage and all. But then, in November I think it was, I was radioed by Espantoso to meet him about a job. I figured it'd be a good time to tell him I was done. I went to see him and told him, but he didn't take it good, said I couldn't quit. Had his goons go outside and grab a chicken from a pen behind the cabin where he hung out when he came up from Miami. They brought it in and Espantoso cuts a leg off. Blood everywhere and he and his goons are laughing at how the chicken's trying to get up and run around. Keeps flopping over. He turns to me and asks how I'd like my grandyoung'uns with one leg like that. Holds up his knife and says he'd need more than the shiv in his hand; said he'd need a saw. Said that I either do what he wants or he goes to Tallahassee to do them. Even tells me my daughter's address and describes where they live.

Son-of-a-bitch!" A vein stood out on Jimmy's forehead as he relived the moment. "That man was badass evil. Like I say, around here things have a way of takin' care of themselves." Jimmy looked at Rusty defiantly. "I took care of him; he ain't gonna be botherin' me or nobody no more."

Rusty was silent. Jimmy watched him closely. Finally, Rusty nodded. "So be it. Guess this world is minus one dirtball. Can't condone it, but can understand it. But if he's gone, what's this Latino thing and why the guns?"

"The last thing Espantoso said to me was, 'They will find you! The family will get you!' At first I didn't think about that at all, like fat chance. But then I start hearing stories about his cartel. How, like I protect my family, they protect theirs...except their organization is big and powerful. And they don't give up."

"How long ago did all this happen?"

"About four and a half years."

"Ancient history!"

Jimmy shook his head.

"I got friends out there. I was in the 'import' business since the seventies and know a lot of people involved in this and that. I hear the Colombians are still lookin' hard. They know he was deep-sixed by someone and Espantoso was last seen in our area; but so far I don't think they suspect me. Probably figure it was some drug competitor. But, if the shit does hit the fan, I'm praying my family won't be in the picture, that they will just want whoever deep-sixed him. I'm packing because if they ever do figure it out and come for me, I'm gonna do my best to make sure I don't go out alone. And that's why I don't take no Latinos fishing." Jimmy looked at his watch. He flipped his cigarette into the water and stood up. "Got to go change into my fishing clothes." He hesitated. "Guess you can see why I don't want Crystal to know what I done. If someone ever gets me, then you can tell her if you want—but not before." He held out his hand. "Deal?"

Rusty shook his hand and nodded. "Deal."

The two men walked to the deck stairs. Rusty handed Jimmy his cup. "Thank Crystal for the coffee, will you, Jimmy?"

"Sure thing."

Rusty was deep in thought walking home; he didn't notice Bobby pass him in the street on his way to the marina. Bobby had traded in his nightly bar garb for flip flops, cutoff blue-jean shorts, and a sleeveless tee-shirt. Muscles bulged all over. Frank was operating the controls of the boatlift when he arrived at the marina. One boat was in the sling and two more were on trailers in line. A small group of people were off to the side drinking coffee.

"Bobby, you're just in time. Got two parties need their boats taken down. Berths twenty-six and thirty-two. Bring them out would you? Twenty-six first."

"Sure thing, Frank."

Bobby turned on his heels and headed to the boat storage building. BeeBee watched him from inside the marina. When he entered the building, she turned and inspected herself in the outdoor clothing section's mirror. She turned this way and that, tugging on her halter-top before taking a hairbrush out of her purse. Meanwhile Bobby walked by the rows of elevated fishing boats—Makos, Pathfinders, Seacraft, Boston Whalers—to the big Hyster forklift at the far end. The lift had a very tall mast and long, heavily padded forks. Bobby climbed aboard and started it up. He drove to berth twenty-six that held a twenty-foot Carolina Skiff with a hundred-fifty horsepower Yamaha. Bobby gently lifted it out of its cradle. He was getting good with the forklift; Frank said he had a nice touch. Frank was an okay guy, Bobby thought as he headed out with the boat, even if he wore that stupid gold chain and had flabby arms and a pus-gut belly. He was a hard worker and good boss. How he ever snagged BeeBee, though, he didn't have a clue. BeeBee. On their walk back to the marina from the scallop shucking contest, she had said, "So you know that Frank and I do coke."

"Pretty obvious even if you didn't have that powder all over your nose the other night. Didn't need to look at your eyes either. Both of you went out all tired and came back wired."

"Have you ever done it?"

"Does a cat have an asshole? Stupid question. Of course I've done it!"

"You were in prison for seventeen years," she said, defensively. "Might not have had the opportunity."

"You kidding me! You can get anything in prison. Just need the moolah or the connections. More meth around than coke, though. Better drug: gets you higher, lasts longer."

"Yeah, and gets you hooked."

"Not if you're smart about it. I did it a bunch. No problems and whooeee, what a ride!"

"Want to do coke sometime?"

Bobby stopped walking.

"The three of us?"

BeeBee shook her head.

"Nope," she said. "Just you and me."

They continued walking.

"Don't think Frank would appreciate that much."

"Screw him."

"BeeBee, he's been good to me. And I like my job."

This time BeeBee stopped.

"Do you like me?"

He looked her up and down.

"What's not to like?"

"Frank doesn't have to know."

Bobby stopped reminiscing and concentrated on the task at hand. He stopped at the sea wall and lowered the Carolina Skiff into the water. He went back for berth thirty-two. When he was finished, he returned the forklift to the shed and walked back to the marina to see what else Frank wanted him to do. Frank and BeeBee were talking in front of the marine supplies door.

"So what's on the docket today, Frank?"

"Not much. Tide's going out now and people will probably be fishing 'til late afternoon: they won't be able to get back in any sooner. No one else has called to have his boat put in, but you never know who'll show up when. I'm going into Perry for supplies, so man the forklift and sling, check the bait shrimp, the usual stuff. I won't be back until around Happy Hour at four, so open the bar at three. If BeeBee needs anything done, tend to that... Pretty easy day with the boss away," he said, smiling at his rhyme. Bobby smiled with him, Bee Bee rolled her eyes. Twenty minutes later Frank left in his Ford Crew Cab, passing another truck pulling in with a boat in tow. It was late morning by the time Bobby was finishing up the chores. BeeBee stuck her head out the marina door as he was ladling a few dead shrimp out of the bait tank.

"Bobby, come in for a second when you're finished."

Bobby put the bait scoop in a plastic bucket by the tank and made sure the circulators were clear and bubbling before entering the marina.

"What's up?"

"Go in the bar. I've got a surprise for you."

Although brilliantly sunny outside, it was cool and dim in the bar. The windows were the polaroid-type that cut out all glare and, from the outside, you couldn't see in. Frank had spent a lot of extra money for the windows, but he said that the afternoon trade had already more than paid for them: reason being that the heavy drinkers felt a lot better about starting early when no one could see them. Bobby immediately noticed the four neat white lines on a plate at the end of the bar. Bobby wheeled around.

"BeeBee, this is not a good idea!" BeeBee was holding the *Back in Fifteen Minutes* sign they sometimes put on the marina door. Even though no one could see in, Bobby scanned the windows.

"You don't want to do a little toot with me?"

"Sure, but...here? Now?"

"Why not? Frank won't be back for hours and it's almost dead low tide. And I'll put this up in case anybody comes."

Bobby looked at the lines on the bar. His thoughts echoed BeeBee's: why not? BeeBee saw the thought process and smiled. She left to put up the sign. When she returned, a rolled up hundred dollar bill was in her hand.

"Here," she said, "You do the honors."

Bobby took the bill and snorted one line, then another. He handed the bill back to BeeBee while sniffing and snorting, trying to ingest every last bit. BeeBee did her two lines. In a very short time, the drug hit their brains. Both smiled at each other in pleasure. BeeBee licked her finger and wiped up the residue off the plate, then rubbed her finger against her gums.

"Good blow," Bobby said.

"The best Lauderdale has to offer."

They continued to look at each other. They continued to smile.

"You're alright, BeeBee."

"And you're a stud, Bobby." Sitting on a barstool, he had his arms folded and his thighs bulged below the cutoffs. BeeBee sat kitty-corner to him in her usual spot. She looked at all the muscles, lust in her face. "Can I ask you something personal?"

"Shoot."

"What did you do for sex those seventeen years? Did you screw guys?"

BeeBee's question might have angered Bobby if he weren't feeling so euphoric.

"Don't beat about the bush none, do you, BeeBee?"

"Not my way."

"No, I never did any guy. I did get oral sex on occasion, but mostly it was five against one."

"Five against one?"

Bobby held up his right hand. He spread his fingers.

"Figure it out."

BeeBee remained puzzled, then her face lit up.

"You beat off!" Bobby made an expression like, duh! "What about a woman? When was the last time?"

"Before prison."

"You're kidding me!" BeeBee looked at him in disbelief. Bobby shrugged. "What a frigging waste!" Very slowly, BeeBee leaned across the bar, her boobs in the halter top looked like they would pop out at any second until they were held in place by the bar top. "Bobby, would you like to kiss me?"

Bobby was mesmerized by her breasts. Very slowly he raised his eyes to hers. "Does a cat have an asshole?"

BeeBee smiled and leaned a little farther forward. Bobby made up the distance. The kiss was gentle, almost caressing at first. But that lasted only a millisecond. With lips still joined, Bobby was off his stool in a heartbeat. The kiss became vital, deep. BeeBee was suddenly off her stool, both stood there tugging at each other's clothing. Tee-shirt and halter top flew off. Bobby's hands were all over BeeBee's gargantuan breasts, then his mouth. BeeBee pulled his head in as he suckled. She pushed him away, and squatted and pulled off his shorts and underwear.

"Oh my God! I knew you had muscles, but this!" She began kissing and mouthing his erection. Bobby was losing it fast. He pulled her up and yanked down her shorts. She wasn't wearing panties and he bent her over the barstool. She was so ready that even as big as he was, he slipped right in. He rocked her. Moaning, BeeBee put her hands on the edge of the bar to keep the stool from tipping over. It was primeval. It was also over in a hurry. Bobby collapsed on BeeBee. That didn't last long either because BeeBee's back was about to break. She squirmed under Bobby.

"Bobby, let me up!"

Bobby pushed himself away. He was disoriented, totally spent. BeeBee grabbed her clothes and made a beeline to the ladies' room. Bobby slowly leaned over to get his clothes. He almost fell over when he got a leg tangled in his underwear. He put on his shirt and shorts and wandered over to a table where he sat down. Now that he had caught his breath and his body was relaxed, he felt very mellow. He waited for BeeBee to come out of the bathroom. She was in it for quite awhile. When she came out she was smiling.

"Man alive, Bobby, you sure pack a load! You were pouring out of me!"

"Seventeen years worth."

She walked over and stood in front of him. She hadn't brushed her tussled hair. She was a sex kitten, a Bridgette Bardot out of an earlier era. She was a pinup. What the boys in Raiford would do for a poster of her on the wall, Bobby thought. His brain and body were sending out signals. His body knew what it felt like to be in her; his brain said she was his for the taking, anytime. Frank didn't enter the picture. He got another erection. He stood up. She noticed.

"Well, well; what have we here?"

She reached out.

"More than one bullet in my revolver."

"Cannon, you mean. But not here, Bobby. You about broke me in half!"

"Where?"

"Not the house, that's for sure!"

Bobby thought about it. His erection didn't go away.

"Got a plan. Meet me in a few minutes in boat storage."

Bobby quickly left the marina and entered the large building. He started the forklift and drove it about halfway down the length of the building. In a few minutes BeeBee entered. He waved her over.

"Step onto the fork and hold on to the mast. Going up to Berth #22." Berth #22 held a large black and white speedboat with high gunnels and a straight cushy couch-like seat that spanned the stern. Bobby raised the forks up and over the boat. BeeBee stepped down into the boat. She looked around and smiled down at him.

"Perfect!"

Bobby climbed up the mast and pulled himself up onto a fork and boarded. BeeBee already had her halter off. Bobby dropped his pants. They soon lay down together on the seat.

"Let's don't be in such a hurry this time, Big Boy."

"BeeBee, you might not be able to walk after I'm done with you."

BeeBee bit him on the neck. Her hands were on his huge biceps. "Make me sore, Bobby. Make me real sore."

Chapter Twelve

Preparations were non-stop during the week leading up to the Scallop Festival. Monday morning early a flatbed truck loaded with the Scallop Festival lights slowly made its way down Main Street accompanied by a Florida Power and Light truck outfitted with a telescoping, single-man bucket. The lights were hung from the power poles running the length of the street. Each was just under six feet tall and made up of a string of lights woven around a steel frame in the detailed shape of a scallop. Each string of lights was a solid color, but the scallops alternated from red to gold to blue to green to silver. They were hardly noticeable during the day, but lit up at night they were magnificent. They gave the town a festive air.

The festival was a big deal. It was sponsored by the Crescent Beach Library and over a hundred vendors would come from all around to sell most anything: cedar and cypress outdoor furniture, crafts that varied from unique to schlock, flowering plants and citrus trees, yard sale items, commemorative tee-shirts and hats, and all sorts of food: corn dogs, burgers, cotton candy, fried mullet, hoagies, grinders, seafood gumbo, Italian meatballs and sausage. The Library always had a bake sale of cookies and pies donated by townsfolk. Tiny and T would be setting up a fryolater for shrimp meals at TNT Shrimp Company, and the crabbers would set up chairs and tables for eating blue crabs out on their docks. Paper bibs and little wooden mallets for crushing the crabs would be available at each table, and all the bits and pieces of crab would be pitched into the canal to be eaten by other crabs, starting the cycle all over again. The day of festivities would begin with the morning parade. The Library was responsible for this, too, although Virginia delegated most everything to Norm. Norm had learned soon enough that people liked to watch a parade, but few wanted to make the effort to participate in one. He complained to Tammy that it was like pulling teeth. But, there were always those who jumped right in. There would also be different amusement rides for the kiddies, different lines of new shallow-draft fishing boats would be on display, and the latest in salt water fishing gear would be on sale. Raffle tickets had been sold for weeks by the Library and local businesses. The giant raffle would be the last official event of the day. The drawing would be in City Hall. At night there would be fireworks off Snowy Key. The fireworks were legendary and drew more people than the vendors.

To organize all this was Virginia's and Louie's job. It was an immense effort. Virginia had *Post-its* scattered around her kitchen and the library to remind her of all the last minute things to do. Beau teased her that she had a *Post-it* for each vendor. The preparations were extremely time-consuming and often frustrating. The library leased a field off Main Street for the vendors, had it mowed, then mapped off each individual spot. She and Louie had to collect the money, never fun, but it didn't end there. There were always people dissatisfied: a tree was in their way or they had no shade, their neighbor had more room, they were too far away from Main St., they wanted to have their truck in their spot with them. Every year the same complaints. Most of the items in the raffle had been donated by businesses inland or bought by the Library with money given by anonymous members of the community.

Another huge time sink. A country and western band had been hired and would set up in front of the library with benches and hay bales scattered around for the audience to sit on. Then there was a myriad of other details like insurance, parking, trash barrels, Porta-potties. But, barring bad weather, each year the festival was a huge success. Consequently, everyone—natives, longtime residents, newcomers, and tourists—was very much looking forward to it.

But that was not why the streets were lined with people on this Wednesday afternoon. They were waiting for Charley and Louie's race to begin. July was peak month of the tourist season with the Fourth of July the busiest weekend of the year. The town was already packed with most everyone on vacation. And if they weren't fishing or scalloping, they were looking for something to do, and they were always looking for an excuse to party. Both Louie and Charley were two well-known locals. And people thought that the race would be a hoot: it had captured their imagination. Consequently, golf carts were haphazardly parked along the course with coolers of beer in the back. Plastic chairs lined the street as if for a parade. Joggers and speed-walkers had changed out of their spandex and come to watch. They sipped out of plastic water bottles and stretched as they waited. Kids had just gotten home from school and immediately climbed on their bikes to pedal madly around the cone-blocked course. All of them had ridden at least part of the course with Louie during his training and they were rooting for him. Many of the scallopers and sports fishermen had returned early to see the race. Lots of people were on hand: the *Tortoise and Hare 15* had turned into a major event.

Bets could be placed at the Club until five minutes before race time. There was a lot of late betting going on and the odds were being reduced somewhat, but Charley was still the clear favorite at a little under two to one. The odds were being continually updated on a large poster board tacked to a post. The picnic tables for the scallop shucking contest the previous Friday hadn't been removed. The original idea for the race, of course, was to get Tammy more business and it was happening. There had been a much larger than normal luncheon crowd with most choosing to eat below at the picnic tables close to the action. People kept trickling in to make their bets, then hung around. Although the middle of the afternoon of a workweek, people were ordering drinks and beer. It was like a bonus town holiday. Tammy had plastic baskets of free salty chips on the tables that were replenished occasionally by a waitress. In front of the slab, a fluorescent line had been painted across Main Street. The race would start and end there. Off to the side of the line under a live oak tree were Charley's lawnmower and Louie's bicycle on its kickstand. Side by side on the seat of the lawnmower were the green turtle helmet and the hat with the ten-inch rabbit ears. Charley and Louie were not present: they were riding with Beau and Skillet in Beau's golf cart checking out the racecourse.

Beau had driven north on Main Street, passing TNT Shrimp Company before turning right and crossing the Humpback Bridge.

"Every vehicle coming into town will be informed about the when, how, and where, but we can't keep all the traffic off every street. So you two have to watch out, especially at the intersections," Beau said. They approached the straightaway that ran past Norm's and Beau's and the other more expensive houses along the Gulf: one long avenue with no intersections,

"Reckon no problems here on Rich Man's Row," Charley mused out loud.

"I don't particularly care for that nomenclature, Charley," Beau said.

"If'n that means ya don't like the name, I can't help what people calls it these days, Beau. Twelve years ago was just trees and beach. Weren't no houses a'tall. Back then most everybody built on the ground and they knew it would be plumb crazy to build so close to the water. Took people with money to build safe here."

The straightaway led to the marina where cones had been set in the parking lot so that they circled around and squirted out onto the avenue parallel to Rich Man's Row. This took them back to the bridge and Main Street. They turned right, then in a short distance turned right again. They passed the Post Office and made a series of turns that took them in between the condo buildings under construction and around the ball field back to Main Street again. A long straight shot on Main Street before turning off to the public boat ramp, then a couple side streets that brought them out to Main Street again where they continued to the cul de sac at the end. Following more cones, they circled the cul de sac and headed down the home stretch to the Club. When they pulled up to the fluorescent line, there was quite the expectant crowd. A throaty cheer went up.

"You go four times around. Got it?" Beau asked.

"I imagine," Louie said. "Been pedaling it twice a day for weeks now."

"Charley?"

"Like the back of my hand, Beau."

Beau looked at his watch. "Got a few minutes yet until we count down and Tiny shoots off his pea shooter. So, go stretch, pee, meditate, or do whatever you got to do."

Louie stepped out of the cart. He said, "I got to go put ten bucks on Charley here before they stop the betting." Charley's and Beau's heads snapped around. "Just kidding." Louie walked over to his bike and began stretching.

Charley gave Skillet a pat before getting off the cart. "Guess I'll go see if I can win me some easy money." He walked up to the crowd on the slab. "Got fifteen bucks here to put on me. Any takers?"

Most had already placed their bets, and most were picking Charley to win. No takers. Charley started to put his money back in his pocket when Norm said, "I'll take that bet, Charley."

"I'll be a skun coon. You wanna bet on Louie!"

"Have to."

"And why's that?"

"Charley, what's my pet peeve in this town?"

Charley's answer was immediate. "Airboats."

"And why's that?"

" 'Cuz you don't like their noise and the way they be raw dawgin' out in the marsh botherin' all the critters."

"Yup, that and polluting the air with noxious fumes."

"So?"

"So how do you expect me to bet on your noisy, polluting combustible-engine lawnmower instead of a silent, non-invasive bicycle? It'd be contrary to everything I believe in."

"Guess you would be sort of a hippokrat at that."

"Hypocrite, Charley."

"Whatever. All I knows is that yur gonna be out fifteen bucks."

Beau loudly announced, "Will the two contestants please man their vehicles!"

"Here, Doc, you hold the money. Gotta go win me a race." Charley got a few pats on the back as he confidently walked over to his lawnmower. Louie, standing by his bike, took off his sweatpants to reveal brand new, very tight, shiny-black and padded bike shorts. His legs were the color of a freshly plucked chicken and looked like little fat drumsticks with occasional tufts of dark hair. His buns were flat and broad. People whistled and catcalled. Louie paid no attention. He was on a mission.

"Driver and rider, don your turtle helmet and rabbit hat!" Beau commanded. The crowd broke up. Beau was trying to keep a straight face. The pair looked ridiculous. Regardless, Louie kept staring straight ahead: he was zoned. Charley, on the other hand, was smiling and flexing his muscles to half a dozen cameras pointed their way.

"I will count down from five, and then Tiny there," Beau said, pointing up to the deck, will fire that itty bitty cannon and you two take off." To the crowd, he said, "If you have sensitive ears, you might want to cover them. That thing is loud." Turning back to Louie and Charley, Beau asked, "Understood?" They nodded. "Start your engine Charley, and do whatever you're going to do, Louie." Charley started the lawnmower and revved it several times. He had both hands on the wheel, leaning forward a little. Standing to the side of his bike, Louie put his hands on the handle grips and crouched into a running position. One of his ears flopped down ninety degrees. Beau raised his hand. "Okay, then. FIVE, FOUR, THREE, TWO, ONE…" Beau's hand dropped, Tiny's cannon went KABOOM, and they were off!

* * *

Earlier in the week, Whacko had returned to the trailer telling Bobby that he had made the best crystal meth of his entire career, and they made plans to smoke some of it on Bobby's day off. Bobby got Frank's permission to borrow one of the small rental aluminum boats with a fifteen horse and the plan was to go out to Coon Island for the day. Bobby had never run an outboard before, so Tuesday afternoon Frank had given him a lesson. When Bobby and Whacko arrived the next morning at the marina with a cooler full of beer and a couple daypacks, BeeBee was out on the dock. She looked incredulously at Whacko. Bobby introduced him.

"Pleased to make your acquaintance, Ma'am," Whacko said. BeeBee looked like she wasn't so pleased to make his. Whacko noticed the cones spread around the parking lot. "What's them fer?" he asked.

"You don't know about Louie and Charley's race?" she asked, cringing at his English and making a face like he was an idiot.

Bobby said, "Dumb race between a lawnmower and a bicycle."

"But a big deal here in Deadsville," BeeBee added.

"Dang, don't that beat all. Guess I been workin' too much 'cuz I didn't hear nuthin' 'bout it."

"What kind of work is that?"

"Might say I'm in the chemical business."

BeeBee looked at this scrawny, disheveled, mostly toothless man. "Right," she said. "And I'm the Queen of France."

Whacko shrugged. Frank approached carrying a couple of life jackets.

"Should be smooth sailing, boys, but for the sake of the Marine Patrol, better have these. I put in a couple dozen shrimp and a couple of poles in case you want to try your luck."

"Thanks, Frank," Bobby said, as he took the preservers and climbed down into the boat. Whacko followed with the cooler. They untied and shoved off. Frank said, "Boating rule number one, Bobby: never leave the dock until you've got the motor running."

"Why's that?" Bobby asked.

"You could be somewhere with a good current or a strong wind. Can be hell to pay if the motor doesn't start and you have to paddle back."

Bobby nodded. He pulled the starter cord and the engine fired right up. Frank and BeeBee watched the boat slowly thread the oyster bars until home free out in the Gulf. Bobby and Whacko headed south with a warm wind in their faces.

"Beats Raiford, don't it," Whacko said, smiling in the bow.

"Got that right!"

Bobby kept it at three-quarters throttle. The combination of the water's dull metallic lapping against the aluminum hull and the drone of the motor lulled them. The Gulf was at its best—calm, blue, the shimmer of a billion diamonds sparkling in the bright sun. Unlike most of Florida, there were no high-rises along the narrow strip of white sand that lined the shore. It was the way it used to be with cabbage palms, red cedar, the occasional live oak, and plenty of bugs. With a good breeze out of the west blowing inland and keeping the bugs at bay, it was a pristine paradise. But, if there were no breeze or one out of the east, the sand gnats and mosquitoes would be fierce, forcing even longtime residents and natives to flee. From the water, though, it always looked idyllic.

Bobby followed the coast for several miles at a couple of hundred yards off shore until he saw Coon Island a ways farther out. Frank had given him directions. Frank had also told him that originally the island was a couple of acres in size, but the '93 storm had washed most of it away. Now it was nothing more than a sandy spit that was a favorite for all sorts of sea birds that congregated at one end. There were no bugs because there was always a healthy breeze, plus no vegetation except for some succulents and a few low bushes in the center. They motored up to the island. Bobby tried not to disrupt the birds by pulling into a natural cove at the other end. Still, a flock of skimmers rose up as one and banked into the sun as they circled. They soon returned to the sandy point, landing amongst the other sea birds. As Bobby pulled the boat onto the beach, he marveled at the mix of willets, sanderlings, terns, and brown pelicans, all getting along fine. In prison, he mused, there were all kinds of people mixed together, but they sure as hell didn't get along fine. Whacko didn't look at the birds; he was more interested in getting the cooler ashore.

Bobby walked up to one of four thick pilings sticking out of the sand. He put a hand on one and turned to Whacko. "Used to be a house here," Bobby said.

Whacko looked around. "On this itty bitty island? Ain't nuthin' more than a sandbar."

"Frank said it used to be a lot bigger. Poor suckers had just finished building the house when it got hit by that big storm that everyone talks about around here."

Whacko put the cooler in the shade of one of the thick pilings. He opened a beer and took a swig before sitting down and opening his dope satchel. "What happened?"

"Frank says the couple who built it was from Gainesville, a University of Florida biology professor and his wife. Guess they liked to play Robinson Crusoe 'cuz they only had kerosene lamps, a little gas refrigerator and stove, and they boated in fresh water and all their supplies. Real nature nuts. They came out every chance they got. The professor studied the marine life and birds while his wife painted them. Because they didn't want anything to do with people out here, they didn't even have a radio. So, guess they were mighty surprised when that storm hit with hurricane force winds and a twelve-foot tidal surge at three o'clock in the morning.

"Frank says they were damn lucky to survive. Said the wife wrote all about it for the *Dixie County Advocate.* Said the first thing her husband did when the storm woke them was grab a flashlight to check on their boat. It was gone which meant that their life preservers were gone, too. The windows blew out and the water began to pour in and they thought that was it—the end, they would drown for sure. When the water was knee deep, her husband shined the light out at where the island should have been. No land in sight, only big waves rolling towards shore. He saved their lives. There was a cabbage palm a dozen feet away and he was able to swim to it with a rope tied around his waist. Climbed up and pulled his wife over with the rope.

"They spent the night there and the water rose to within a few feet of the top before it stopped. In the morning the water started going out again and they could see that the island had shrunk big time. Most of the remaining trees had been uprooted by the shifting sands and lay toppled over. The house was gone and these pilings were all that remained. They climbed down out of the tree and walked around the island. The temperature had dropped and it was so cold it began to snow. Things were not looking good: freezing cold, no water, no food, no way to contact the mainland. They hoped friends from Gainesville who knew where they were, would think to check on them. But, they also thought maybe Gainesville had been slammed, too, and their friends had their own problems. The professor saw something reflecting light in a tangle of seaweed and picked it up. It was a bottle of wine from the house. A little later his wife found a can of beans. There was a plastic tarp wrapped around a tree. Pieces of wood here and there, but no matches.

"With a broken board the professor dug a depression for them to sit out of the wind and pulled the tarp around them. They hunkered down with the beans and wine which they were able to open with a scrap of wood with a nail sticking through it. They rationed the wine and beans for the next two days. It was then that a boat came out looking for them. Their friends came through. That was five years ago."

"They was lucky. I'll bet…" Suddenly a cannon went off; Whacko jumped. "What the heck was that?"

"Must be they started that stupid race," Bobby said, lying down on his back next to Whacko. Even though they were miles away from Crescent Beach, the cannon report was loud and clear. Bobby began watching the clouds slowly change shape. Whacko was sitting with arms around his knees, looking back towards town.

"If I'da known about it sooner, I would've liked to watch. Don't see a bike racin' a lawnmower every day," Whacko said.

"Dumb event."

"Wanna do some crystal?"

"Cat have an asshole?" Bobby answered, quickly sitting up.

Whacko put a small rock of the crystal meth in the crack pipe and handed it to Bobby who reached for the Bic lighter. Bobby flicked the lighter and held the flame a half-inch or so from the bulbous glass pipe, gently heating the crystal. As the rock melted, it began to vaporize and when the pipe was full of smoke Bobby inhaled it through the opening at the top. He held the smoke in for a few seconds as he began to slowly twirl the still smoldering meth until it cooled off again into a shallow hard blob. He exhaled and put the pipe back on the satchel. He lay back down.

"Wow!" was all he said. A rush of over-the-top intense pleasure permeated his being. He looked at the sky again, then out over the water, then back to the birds, at Whacko his good buddy. He was in love with it all, he was so happy, he was thrilled to be alive. He turned to Whacko who was smiling at him.

"Not bad, huh Bobby?"

"The best, man, the best. This stuff's worth its weight in goddamn gold, platinum, and diamonds! Best you've ever made." Bobby lay back down, putting his hands behind his head. Whacko prepared his hit. Soon Whacko had his arms behind his head and was looking at the sky, too. Comatose pleasure. But, not for long. Bobby, energized, said, "I'm going fishing!" and jumped up.

"Ya know how?"

"What's to know? Just put a shrimp on and throw it out there. Going to catch me a whale!"

"Might be a smidgeon more to it than that," Whacko said, still looking at the sky.

Bobby went for one of the rods Frank had rigged with a Cajun thunder and a couple lead weights and a single #4 Mustad hook. He looked at the reel, trying to figure it out.

"How do you work this thing, Whacko?"

Whacko came over and showed Bobby how to flip back the bail arm and cast. He checked the drag and handed the pole back. Bobby cast a couple times. No problem. He put a shrimp on the hook and heaved it as far as he could. Whacko's head was bobbing to a tune in his head as he watched. Bobby got it out a good ways, but they both could see that the shrimp traveled farther than the Cajun thunder and hook. "Damn," Bobby said, and reeled in and put on another shrimp. He cast again with the same result.

"Here, let me show ya how to bait a hook right." As Bobby watched impatiently, Whacko slipped the hook through the backbone of the shrimp, curved it around, and exited with the tip passing through a different section of the backbone. "There, this fella aint't goin' no place 'cept in a fish's mouth."

"How do you know this stuff?"

"Case ya ain't noticed, I'm from Florida."

"Yeah, me, too."

"Yeah, but yur a landlubber. I been around the water some; Tampa Bay area back when it was civilized."

Bobby cast. The shrimp stayed on. Whacko showed him how to jig it every now and then. Bobby was impatient. He was ready for action, now. He couldn't stand still. He paced the beach as he cast, jigged once, reeled in, cast again. Over and over. Whacko cracked a beer.

"Want one, Bobby? Or, ya too busy catchin' yur whale?" Bobby ignored him. Whacko took a long pull. "Ya gotta be more patient. Let it sit a bit. Yur probly pullin' the shrimp right outta their mouths."

Bobby reeled in and checked his shrimp. Heaved it out a long ways again near an oyster bar and stuck the rod in the sand near Whacko. He felt like walking around the island, but didn't want to disrupt the birds. So, instead, he got a beer from the cooler and paced circles around the pole.

"That stuff," Bobby said, nodding towards Whacko's little canvas satchel, "must fetch a pretty good price."

"Does."

"Don't it bother you that kids are getting into it these days."

"Don't sell to no kids. Adults only. What they does with it is their business."

"In Perry, mostly?"

"Nope, only a couple black dudes there. They sell to the workers in the mills."

"How do they afford it—the workers?"

"Don't know, don't care."

"Where else?"

"All over. Tallahassee. Gainesville. Crystal River and Homasassa. Apalachicola." He laughed. "Not Dixie County, that's fer sure."

"Why's that?"

" 'Cuz there's so many backwoods labs in the hammocks it's ridiculous. Crazy fuckers, too."

Bobby looked at the fishing pole. Rock steady.

"Watch that pole for me, would you? Going to walk around a bit."

Whacko laughed.

"Guess that crystal done got ya speeded out some."

Bobby walked around the point and headed towards the birds. As he approached, the birds nervously eased towards the water. They soon ran out of room and began to fly up. Bobby felt guilty and turned around. He started taking off his clothes. Whacko looked at him.

"Going for a swim," Bobby said.

"Shuffle yur feet."

"Say what?"

"For the sting rays. They love to bury themselves in the sand. They don't want to have nuthin' to do with ya, but if ya step on one, they'll stick ya with their tail. Hurts like a son-of-a-bitch. If ya shuffle yur feet, they knows yur comin' and skedaddle."

Bobby shuffled his feet.

"Water's warmer than hell, Whacko. Like velvet. Come on in."

"No thanks." Whacko reached for another beer instead.

Swimming around, Bobby thought about Whacko and what he'd been through. When he came out of the water, he grabbed a beer and sat down to drip dry.

"You were lucky you got out of Raiford as quick as you did; know that, Whacko?"

"I don't call puttin' in ten years is gettin' out quick."

"Yeah, but you were sentenced to thirty."

"Bum rap. Ya know that; I didn't shoot nobody. Was just makin' my hooch. Goddamn dealers done the shootin'. And them crackheads hit the wrong person."

Whacko sighed and took a long pull of beer. Stared out across the water. Bobby broke the silence over a minute later.

"Loved her a lot, didn't you?"

"Yup." Whacko took another swig and set the beer down in the sand. He turned to Bobby. "Believe it or not, Bobby, I had plans back then. Had plans of gettin' a real stick-built house somewheres. Get a decent car. Somethin' besides yard sale clothes for her. That ol' gal deserved it. Stuck by me a long time. She weren't the prettiest or the skinniest, but I loved her bad. And all she was doin' was bringin' me out a goddamn baloney and mayonnaise sandwich. Watched her bleed to death and couldn't do nuthin' 'bout it. Was a terrible feelin', worst I ever had. Since then I ain't cared about much. Still don't. It don't take much to make me happy." He reached for his beer and held it up. "Beer, a little weed, some chemicals now and then, a roof over my head. Don't need more than that. I may be goin' nowheres, but I'm sure as hell enjoyin' the ride."

Suddenly the slack fishing line zinged and the fishing pole was yanked out of the sand. Bobby and Whacko lunged for it. Colliding, Whacko was sent flying off to the side like a bowling pin. Bobby grabbed the rod, the reel inches from entering the Gulf. On his knees he yanked the rod up. It bent over like a wishbone, the tugging on the other end fierce. The line began to play out with the reel whirring.

"Got me a whale for sure!" Bobby screamed.

Whacko got up slowly, gingerly. "Keep the tip up. Don't yank on him! Let him take the line and tire hisself out!"

The fish took a lot of line. Bobby went into the water up to his knees, his bright white buns contrasting with his tanned torso. The fish went off to the right, and Bobby went to the right. The fish went left, and Bobby went left. Shuffling his feet was long forgotten. Whacko came out in the water fully dressed to give pointers.

"When he eases up, pull in a bit and reel up the slack. But keep your tip up, keep the line taut. Don't know what you got. Being near that oyster bar, maybe redfish or black drum. But who knows, maybe a small shark. Jest keep him away from them oysters. Don't want him to cut the line."

After ten minutes, the fish began to weaken. After fifteen, the fish was losing; Bobby slowly reeled him in. They caught a glimpse of him fifteen feet away.

"Whooee!" Whacko exclaimed. "Lookee there!"

"What is it?"

"Redfish. A beauty! Careful now. We ain't got no net. When ya git him closer, sorta drag him into the shallow water and work him easy onto the beach."

Five minutes later, a fat twenty-six inch redfish was suffocating on shore. Whooping and hollering, Bobby and Whacko toasted each other with beers. Once the red was in the cooler, they did some more meth. Then more beers. By the time they left the island, they were wasted. The weather held just fine and they were riding the high tide on the way in which was a good thing because Bobby wasn't paying close attention to the PVC pipes that marked the oyster bars. They scooted over some that otherwise would have sheared a pin. They approached the marina dock. BeeBee had watched them coming in and was walking down to greet them.

Flying-high-cocky, Bobby said, "Watch this landing, Whacko."

Whacko was weaving in his seat and having a hard time focusing on anything. He was surprised to find the dock only forty feet away. He fumbled around for the bow line. Bobby confidently aimed for the dock. When he went to put the motor in neutral, he was going too fast to shift out. He turned the throttle the wrong way and the boat sped up instead of slowing down. Only ten feet away, he panicked and turned hard, throwing Whacko almost into the canal. The bow and midsection missed the dock, but the corner of the transom clunked pretty hard. Luckily, that section was heavily reinforced and didn't even dent. Bobby got it into neutral, but the canal was not wide and he was still heading at a pretty good clip for the seawall on the other side. He flung the lever into reverse and turn the throttle hard. The motor revved and flew up out of the water in noisy protest. Whacko lurched like a rag-doll. Bobby throttled down and the motor fell back into place. The engine stalled. Bobby pulled on the starter rope several times. No luck. He didn't realize he had the throttle all the way to off. He looked over to the marina dock. BeeBee was watching with hands on hips.

"Better throw me the bow line, Bobby, before you do some real damage." Bobby took the line from Whacko's hands. Whacko didn't seem to notice. He tossed the line to BeeBee who pulled them over. When they had tied up, BeeBee said, "You guys are trashed!"

Bobby ignored her. Instead, he pulled the redfish out of the cooler and held it up. "Take a gander. Now ain't she a beauty!"

Bobby put the cooler, along with the daypacks, on the dock. He helped Whacko out of the boat. Frank came down. He took one look at Whacko and said, "Looks like you boys have been enjoying yourselves." Bobby opened the cooler. Even doubled over, the redfish barely fit in. Frank admired it. "Know how to clean it?" he asked.

"Nope, but Whacko does," Bobby answered.

Frank looked at Whacko again. "Maybe I better clean it for you. Wait a sec and I'll go get my fileting knife. You boys got some mighty fine eating coming up."

Frank went back up to the marina while Bobby half-carried Whacko over to the Ford Torino and poured him into the front seat. On the way back to the docks, BeeBee smiled and said, "Frank's got to go to town again tomorrow to get some parts for a motor Rusty's working on. What say we visit the love boat again, Big Boy."

Frank was heading towards them with a large electric battery filet knife in hand. Feeling no pain or guilt, Bobby said, "Sounds good to me, Doll."

They met Frank at the cleaning station. Pelicans were already landing in the canal and looking up expectantly. Bobby looked around the parking lot. The fluorescent cones were gone and there were only a couple cars and pickups parked up close to the marina.

"Kinda dead around here," he observed.

Frank expertly started in on the redfish. "Everybody's over at the Crescent Beach Club. They're having that post race steak and scallop feed. It should pick up later. Pretty busy, though, this afternoon during the race." After he flipped a large flap of skin into the water, he looked over at Bobby. "So, don't you want to know who won?"

Chapter Thirteen

Charley popped the clutch, intentionally doing a wheelie for the crowd. His front wheels were off the ground for a good ten feet before the front end crashed down. The crowd cheered. Louie took off, sprinting alongside his bike, then leaped on, smashing a shin on a pedal and wobbling momentarily before gaining control. By the time he started pedaling, he was twenty feet behind Charley; but that didn't last long. Louie pedaled like a maniac and passed Charley near the TNT Shrimp Co. He was doing fifteen miles an hour while the John Deere was topping out at ten or eleven. Louie started to put some distance between them. But Charley wasn't worried. He knew, regardless of all Louie's training, there was no way Louie could keep up that pace for fifteen miles.

Louie's bicycle was an outdated tank. Made by Schwinn in the early sixties, it was a single speed relic with fat tires. The rusty frame was thick tubular steel, solid but heavy. Besides the rust, the bike just looked old, outdated, an antique. The frame arched up from the rear wheel, connected to the vertical tube that housed the seat, and continued on to where it was joined by another arched steel tube. The two heavy tubes, eight inches apart, curved gracefully until they met the frame coming up from the front wheel that housed the handlebar post. Yet another tube down low tied the whole frame together. The handlebars were quite long and the chain guard thick and wide. The bike was like a big old Buick or Oldsmobile out of the same era. The gearing was medium range so that for Louie to hit fifteen miles an hour, his legs were like a hamster spinning a wheel. Besides oiling the chain and taking off the taped-on flashlights, the only things he had done to the bike was to add a water bottle bracket to the frame and, under the supervision of a ten year old named Tommy who accompanied him on his training runs, take the handlebars out, flip them upside down, and reinsert them so that they were low and sleek. Bent over and leaning forward he looked much more like a racer. Before, with the handlebars up high, he looked like a Mary Poppins. But the handlebars didn't make the bike go any faster or pedal easier: he was already breathing hard shortly after crossing the humpback bridge.

Louie extended his lead on Rich Man's Row. There were no spectators along the straightaway. He looked behind him; no sign of Charley, but he certainly could hear him. Louie slowed down. Got to pace myself, he thought. Burned a lot of energy with that start. Pure adrenaline rush. Hauled ass. But can't expect to keep that up. Got to get back to my pace! Just like in training. That's it—nice solid, even pace. Relax. Get in a rhythm. The lawnmower can't do more than eleven at best, which means you just got to do a little more. You can do that. Just like in training. You can do that easy. Just put your mind elsewhere. You won't even feel your legs. Think about Boston…No, that won't help. Must be other things to think about. Let's see…

Louie entered the marina's parking lot. There was a crowd on the edge of the fluorescent cones. Behind the crowd was a host of cars and pickups. People were laughing and cheering. The laughs are for the hat, he thought—he could feel the ears flapping on his bare shoulders. Tammy had printed up two styles of colored tee-shirts for the event, with and without sleeves. She had given one to him and Charley. He had chosen the sleeveless style because the forecast said it would be pushing ninety with heavy humidity. On the front of the shirt, in the pocket area, *CRESCENT BEACH CLUB* was printed in bold, midnight-blue letters. On the back in the same midnight-blue was *TORTOISE AND HARE 15* in letters so big that they covered his entire back. He followed the path of cones out of the parking lot, glancing at the crowd. None of the faces registered. What did register was the fact that everyone seemed to be holding a cold beer.

As Louie exited the marina, Charley entered the straightaway. He was wearing the more conventional tee-shirt. He was relaxed, enjoying himself. Like a Sunday afternoon drive, he thought. The high revs and rattle of the Deere didn't bother him a bit. He would have thought something was wrong if it didn't rattle and vibrate. The exhaust system wasn't much more than a straight pipe; it was very loud. That didn't bother him either, but then again he was already partially deaf from all the fishing boats he had worked on over the years. He looked out over the Gulf and noticed that the tide was coming in. Cormorants were sitting on their customary perches, mostly channel markers or on the dock railings that didn't have partially driven nails sticking up to keep them off. Beautiful afternoon, hardly a breeze, and the water was calm. It was also very warm and muggy. He chuckled. Gonna take its toll on Louie fer sure, he thought. He glanced over to Norm's house. He was proud that some of his best paintings were in his living room. After all the Fourth's celebrations, he had to get back over to Rusty's. He had started to paint the marsh there on clear, late afternoons. The marsh was so beautiful in that angled, golden-yellow evening light, though it always varied a little, was never exactly the same. Maybe I should buy me a camera. Take pictures when it's just right for reference. But don't know if it'd be the same to paint from a photo. He entered the marina parking lot. The crowd cheered.

Louie could just hear the cheers for Charley. It let him gauge his lead. Plenty. He crossed the Humpback Bridge, turned right, and turned right again and pedaled past the Post Office. He was coming up to the dirt track behind the ball field that connected to the other paved road that would return him to Main Street. Shouldn't call it dirt, he thought: it's sugar sand, pure and simple, and a pain in the butt. Fine grained, it was tough walking in let alone riding through on a heavy bike. He would lose time and it was totally taxing. He entered the path, avoiding the tracks made by four-wheelers and pickups. He tried to stay on the matted leaves on the edge because it was firmer and offered better traction. Still it was impossible to avoid all of the sand. He got bogged down and had to stand up and pedal in a couple of places. Even though giving it his all, he knew Charley would be gaining on him as he made his way across. Charley wouldn't have any problem here, not with those stubby fat tires. Finally, breathing hard, he turned onto the pavement again. He soon found his rhythm and continued on to Main Street.

After Charley passed through the marina parking lot, the majority of spectators returned to the bar for refills. Frank was bustling around trying to keep up with the orders. No help from BeeBee who sat at her usual spot filing her fingernails. Frank didn't mind her not helping: he was used to it. She was his queen Bee. When the rush was over and the bar emptied again, he asked her, "Aren't you going out to watch?"

"Like Bobby said, it's a stupid race. But what else do you expect in this stupid town?"

Frank looked at her.

"You're not happy here, are you, Bee?"

BeeBee thought of Bobby's phrase, 'Does a cat have an asshole?' while rolling her eyes and looking at him as if he were a moron. "Duh!" she said. "I was happy in Lauderdale, Frank. There was plenty of action. Plenty of fun things to do. I don't know why we had to sell out and come to this...this hick town where the biggest action in six months is a damn scallop shucking contest and a frigging race between a rusty lawnmower and a junky old bicycle. Good God!" She went back to filing her fingernails.

"It was the right time to sell, sweetheart," Frank said, defensively. "We cleaned up. Same thing'll happen here. More and more money is coming to this town and we didn't pay much more than a pile of beans for this real estate. And now that the business is going so good, everything will be worth a fortune."

"Frank, you've already got plenty of money. What good is it if you can't spend and enjoy it? There are no restaurants worth a hoot, no shows, no movies, no clothes stores, no golf, no tennis, no nothing! Crescent Beach. What a joke! There isn't even a beach where you can swim. Too damn shallow to get your knees wet!"

"Aw, you've just got cabin fever. Maybe you should take a day a week and go shopping."

"Right! Go shopping in Perry. Maybe I can get a good deal on some used tires or a pair of spandex sweatpants from the thrift store!"

"I meant Gainesville or Tallahassee. Plenty of good restaurants and stores."

BeeBee thought about it. Might be fun at that. But a lot of driving. Still, her turquoise T-bird was a pleasure to drive. Good sound system with loads of good tapes. Get out of here. She thought of Bobby. Now that would be fun if Bobby came along. All sorts of ideas began to surface and none of them included Frank.

"That's not a bad idea," she said. "Of course, I'd feel kind of guilty leaving you here working, but I really should get out of here. You're right—must be cabin fever. Might be just what the doctor ordered. Wednesdays. Middle of the week when it's not so busy. Yeah, Wednesdays."

BeeBee smiled. Frank smiled, too; pleased that he had made her happy. The spectators cheered again. Frank looked out the window. "Louie's still in the lead," he said.

Louie was sweating heavily. He wiped his brow and reached for the water bottle. It was already half gone. When he finished the first lap, Charley wasn't in sight. He hadn't seen Charley since he passed him at the beginning of the race. He checked his time. Nineteen and a half minutes. Numbers began to fly around his head like pinballs. He calculated his speed and how far Charley should be behind him. He welcomed the numbers as they took his mind off his legs that were getting heavier by the minute. He had done all his training in the early mornings and evenings when it was cooler. The heat and the humidity were taking their toll. Let's see, nineteen and a half minutes to go three and three-quarters miles. That would mean I'm averaging almost exactly eleven point six miles per hour. Now if Charley is going full out, which of course he is, he'll be averaging around ten. That means it would take him twenty-two and a half minutes to do a lap. Now if I'm going one point six miles an hour faster, that would make him a full half mile behind me. Louie smiled, comforted by the thought.

Charley kept chugging along. No calculations going on in his head. He waved to friends cheering for him. He looked up at the sky. He looked at the slash pine and live oaks near the post office. Something was wrong with a couple of the pines, their needles were browning. Lack of rain. Nah, it's been this dry before. Probably the pine beetle. Should tell Beau. He'd know how to git it checked out. If it's the beetle, that critter kin run right through 'em all, kill 'em dead! Maybe they can get sprayed with something. When he came to the sandy section, he powered right through, fishtailing a little with his wheels tearing up the sand and scattering the leaf matter. Back on Main Street, he saw some sports fishing boats entering the main channel. Probably just finished scalloping, he figured. The fluorescent cones in the City Park parking area were fun to negotiate; he zipped around the tight curve as if on rails. The same for the coned curve at the cul-de-sac at the end of Main Street. When he passed the starting line, finishing his first lap, he looked up at Tiny on the Club's deck and mimed looking at a watch. Tiny yelled that he was about three minutes behind Louie. Charley nodded and gave him the thumbs up. When he passed the TNT Shrimp Co., T was smiling and wind milling her arm in encouragement. She said something in Spanish. He caught the last three words: *mi tortugita verde*—my little green turtle.

Louie was doing pretty well on the second lap until he came to the sandy track again. Even before entering, he knew it was going to be trouble. The narrow band of leaf litter had been torn up and scattered by Charley's tires, leaving more exposed sand. In response he built up momentum on the paved area, his legs like a hamster's again. The extra speed got him through the worst of it, but not all. He tried to turn out of it, to get onto another patch of packed leaves, but his front wheel plowed the sand. It stopped him cold and he had to dismount. He pushed the heavy bike through the sand, trying to run, but it was next to impossible. He was already winded from pedaling like a mad man, and now trying to run through sugar sand with legs that felt like lead, had his heart pounding. He had to rest when he arrived at the pavement. He took a sip of water. He was rationing it now. He almost felt like quitting right there and then, but an image of a gloating Charley filled his mind. He took another sip and put the bottle in its bracket. With a deep sigh, he put one foot on a pedal and pushed on the pavement a couple times with the other. He heaved his leg over the seat. He slowly worked up his speed, but he had lost any rhythm. Soon his mouth was wide open and he was sucking air. Main Street, City Park, the cul de sac. When he pedaled out of the cul de sac into the straightaway towards the Club, he saw Charley about to emerge onto Main Street. He had made up a lot of distance. Charley, fresh as a daisy, saw him at the same time and smiled and waved. When Louie passed the Club, he checked his time. Twenty-four minutes! A full five minutes slower! That frigging sand! Numbers filled his head again, but they were harder to get a handle on. But it was better trying to toss those numbers around than thinking about his legs. He finished his calculations by the time he entered Rich Man's Row. If his calculations were correct, the bottom line was that his lead had been cut in half which meant Charley was only a quarter mile behind him. Judging from where he had seen Charley, that seemed about right. He started pedaling harder. He went through the marina parking lot and back towards the humpback bridge.

Louie figured he was pedaling fast enough to be gaining a little of what he had lost. He willed himself not to look back over his shoulder, but the cheers coming from the marina made it clear that Charley was not that far behind. He dreaded the sandy stretch. What to do? Passing through the condo construction he started standing up as he pedaled. It was agonizing. He was using different muscles and they soon screamed. He built up a good head of steam and powered into the sand. He got farther than last time, but once he became mired, he gave up pedaling immediately, saving his strength. Pushing the bike, he could hear Charley getting closer. When Louie made the pavement again, he was winded, but less winded than last time. He hopped on his bike and pedaled madly towards Main Street. It was seconds later that he heard Charley slow down and the lawnmower rattle when it hit the slight drop from the pavement's curb to the sandy section.

At the corner where he turned back onto Main Street, Louie saw his little buddy Tommy who had helped him turn the handlebars around on his bike. He was waiting for Louie and anxiously looking past him. Louie tried his best to smile at the kid as he went by. The kid got on his bike and pedaled after Louie; he caught up quickly. He was Louie's personal cheerleader. "Hurry, Mr. Louie! Mr. Charley's catching up." The kid speeded up a little faster, pulling away from Louie, then slowed down. "Come on! You can pedal as fast as me, no problem. You can do it. Come on!" and he sped up a little. Louie willed himself to keep up with the kid who incrementally ratcheted it up until Louie started to make up some of what he had lost to Charley. When they approached the turnoff to City Park, the kid said, "I'll be back at the corner when you come through again. Keep it up, Mr. Louie!" Louie raised a hand off the handlebars in acknowledgment. Without the kid pushing him, he was suddenly more aware of the burning in his legs. Imperceptibly, little by little, he slowed. The sound of the lawnmower grew. By the time he rounded the cul de sac, Charley had already turned onto Main Street and was heading towards the cul de sac. When they passed each other Charley yelled out over the noise of his engine, "Got you in my sights, Louie. Ain't gonna be long now!"

Most of the people lined up to see the race thought that the *Tortoise and Hare 15* would be a fun time, something to do, an excuse to party, an excuse to leave work early. No one, with the exception of Charley and Louie, had really taken it seriously. It was just party time in July. That changed on the third lap, and by the fourth it was serious business. People were paying attention. More side bets were being made. Charley and Louie were being seriously cheered. Charley basked in the attention. Louie was so tired, so numb, and so hurting, he didn't care. He just wanted it to end. The last forty minutes was nothing less than agonizing. How the heck did those guys keep it up at the Tour de France? he asked himself. Because they're young, incredibly fit, and don't pedal a damn bathtub! You're a flabby fifty-five year old ex-number cruncher! What do you expect! He passed the Club with Charley in hot pursuit, only a hundred yards behind. Everyone at the Club was cheering. Tammy and Norm, who had been inside preparing the steak and scallop extravaganza, came out and joined Beau, Tiny, and Rusty on the deck.

"Dang," Tiny said. "This is gettin' excitin'! Hope the weather holds," he said, looking up. "Thunderheads movin' in purty quick."

"Speaking of holding, can't believe that old rust bucket hasn't fallen apart yet," Rusty said. "Got to be vibrating like a son-of-a-gun with that governor off."

"Charley always says nuthin' runs like his Deere. Says you kin beat it with a sledgehammer and it'll just keep on tickin'," Tiny said.

"I just hope Louie doesn't keel over," Norm put in. "He looks awful…in pain. Did you see the color of his face?"

"Just doesn't seem fair," Tammy added. "Him working so hard, racing his heart out while Charley's just cruising."

"No one twisted his arm to do it," Tiny said.

"Maybe not literally, Tiny," Norm said. "But we did sort of coerce him a bit."

"Shor we did, but it was for a dang good cause. Look at all the business Tammy's got these last couple days. And you can bet your bottom dollar this place'll be bonkers tonight."

"Going to have to freeze a lot of steak and scallops if it's not," Tammy said.

Beau was looking around at the mixed crowd along the street. "This whole thing has been great for the town. Look at that," he said, pointing. "Crabbers and marina people getting along for a change. Saw Sammy before the race laughing with a scalloper when he bet on Charley.

Great to see. Like at the scallop shucking. Lots of interaction. Maybe we finally turned the corner—got all this animosity settled down once and for all. Sure hope so, anyway."

"Amen," Tammy said, before returning to the kitchen. Norm followed her.

Beau watched them leave, then excused himself. "Guess it's about time I get the checkered flag ready. Won't be long now."

Chapter Fourteen

Minutes after Louie and Charley passed the Club, dark clouds moved in. The temperature dropped and it felt like heaven to Louie. It energized him and he picked up the pace. He thought of his legs as pistons. Up-down. Up-down. Just keep them moving! Entering Rich Man's Row, a brief but heavy cloudburst, one of those Florida summer afternoon toad stranglers, let loose. Cats and dogs. Louie held his face up to the rain. It cleansed the sweat. His mouth was open to the sky. He reveled in it. The tempest hardly affected the spectators. People were braving the rain in the marina parking lot as he pedaled through. Even BeeBee, umbrella in hand, had come out to watch the last lap. Half-way to the humpback bridge, the rain stopped and the sun broke through. There were puddles everywhere and the pavement soon began to steam.

Louie didn't know what to do about the upcoming sandy stretch. Most likely it would determine the winner. Charley was so close and he knew Charley would just whip through it. But, if he could just make it through without pushing the bike, he might still have a chance. But his legs! If only he had fresh legs! He turned onto Main Street after crossing the bridge, then right at City Hall. He looked over his shoulder. Charley was already on Main Street, only seconds behind him. He heard a couple people yelling encouragement to Charley. It seemed inconceivable that Charley wouldn't catch up on the sandy stretch. Louie passed the Post Office and came to the condo construction, but he didn't stand up to pedal this time; he just didn't have the strength. His thighs were like rubber. He concentrated. Pistons! Think pistons! Up-down, up-down, just keep them moving! He entered the sandy area and was surprised to find how well the hard rain had tamped the sand. It wasn't rock hard, but a lot firmer than before. He pedaled as hard as he could, which was not nearly as hard as he had pedaled during the first three laps, but he was making it! But here came Charley, the lawnmower screaming right behind him. Charley passed him with the lawnmower's rear tires kicking sand in his face.

When Charley passed him, Louie suddenly felt utterly and totally demoralized. Besides the exhaustion and the sand in his face, there was a lead balloon in the pit of his stomach. It surprised him when he made it through the sand to the pavement without getting off the bike, but so what? What did it matter? He watched in frustration as Charley sped off towards Main Street. He continued to pedal, but his heart wasn't in it. His head was down. He watched the pavement slowly pass underneath his feet. He would finish the race, congratulate Charley, and then disappear. Go commiserate with Bad Dog before going to bed for a long nap. At least the race was for a good cause, helping Tammy out who had been the lifeblood of this town for so long. And he should be proud that he had given it his all. Still, it didn't help much. He had really, really wanted to win.

"Mr. Louie! Mr. Louie!"

Louie looked up and saw Tommy coming towards him as fast as he could. He was standing up, pedaling furiously. Louie couldn't imagine trying to stand up and pedal like that now. The kid rode by, circled, and came up by his side.

"Come on, Mr. Louie. The race isn't over. You can still do it!"

Louie looked at the kid, sadly shaking his head.

"Come on! Don't give up! Come on!" The kid raced ahead, braked, until they were even, then raced ahead, braked, continually urging him on.

Alright, alright! For the kid's sake he picked up the pace. The kid smiled. The kid even got him to ratchet it up, but not much. Louie was doing nine miles an hour at best. When they hit the straightaway on Main Street, they could see Charley getting close to the turnoff to City Park. An insurmountable lead. But for the kid's sake, Louie kept on going. When they came to the turnoff to City Park, the kid stayed with him. Louie wondered if they would be able to hear the cheers when Charley crossed the finish line.

Charley entered City Park and motored around the fluorescent-coned curve like he was on rails again. He enjoyed it because the corner was tight enough and he was close enough to the ground that he felt like he did as a kid driving his homemade go-kart. The lead change immediately registered with the spectators in City Park and they cheered Charley mightily. Charley was feeling pretty good, too. He had been right, he thought. Knew Louie couldn't last. No way. But dang, he sure tried hard! Charley chuckled. And man, don't he look beat up! But, got to remember to go easy on him—don't rub it in. He smiled. Still, feels purty dang good to whip his butt! Charley headed out of City Park, following the streets to where he turned back onto Main Street again, heading to the cul de sac. Once around that, he'd be in the home stretch. About the time that Louie and the kid were exiting City Park, Charley entered the cul de sac curve, accelerating hard again like he was in the go-kart of his youth. Suddenly he felt the accelerator pedal give out. It collapsed flat on the floorboard and stayed there. He lost all speed. The motor was running fine, but it was just idling along at, appropriately, a turtle's pace.

Charley put the lawnmower in neutral and jumped out. He had a pretty good idea what had happened. He threw back the hood in a clang and looked at the carburetor. Yep, just like Rusty warned me—throttle cable done give out. Dang! It didn't take long before he came up with a solution. Need a three-foot piece of thin wire. String. Fishing line. There wasn't anyone at the cul de sac. The nearest house was a hundred feet down the road, but it didn't look like anyone was home. He lowered the hood and jumped on the lawnmower. He put it in gear and it went forward, but very, very slowly. He put it back into neutral and began pushing. It was much faster than driving it. He pushed it to the house. No one was indeed home. The house was on stilts with a barbecue area underneath. He ran around. No string. No wire. No nothing! He ran back to the lawnmower and pushed it to the next house. No one there either. Everybody's probably down at the finish line, he thought. There was a small room under the house, raised up a couple feet off the ground for summer storm surges. The door's upper half had glass panels. Charley looked inside. Fishing poles and tackle. Probably a hundred yards of monofilament inside. He tried the door, but it was locked. He was ready to smash a window and reach in and unlock the door; but thought better of it. He continued his search under the house.

The people at the Club could hear Charley's lawnmower when it was way over at City Park. Their ears followed him to when he had pulled onto Main Street and headed for the cul de sac. But then, curiously, the sound of his motor had died. Several people walked up the road to take a look. They saw Charley was in a fix and yelled the news back. Word spread like wildfire. Suddenly, Louie and the kid surfaced onto Main Street. Louie was sure that Charley had already won because he no longer heard the lawnmower. When Louie and the kid turned the corner, they saw Charley bent over the motor. Charley looked up and saw them at the same time. Louie could see the despair and frustration in Charley's face. It was like a shot in the arm! Louie shifted out of Mary Poppins mode and put everything, plus some, into his pedaling. He even left the kid behind who began cheering in glee.

Louie passed the tractor as Charley was untangling a rat's nest of old string he had found underneath the house. Once he had it straightened out, he found that both ends were frayed and he didn't have a knife. There was a tiny hole in the carburetor arm with a fragment of the old rusty throttle cable still attached it. With fingers still tingling from the Deere's vibration, Charley twisted it out. It broke off in his hand. Trying to stay calm and not hurry was next to impossible. He did his best. He tried to slip the frayed end of the string through the tiny hole. No deal—the strands just bent. He sucked on the string, bringing it to a point as he looked back at Louie. He was just entering the cul de sac. Charley tried to thread the arm again. The point bent. He sucked it again. This time it went through. Whew! He tied a quick double granny knot, then pulled on the string to see how it worked. The string was rotten. It broke. Charley clenched his fists and screamed at the top of his lungs. He looked quickly back at Louie again. He was several hundred feet away, pedaling towards him for all he was worth. Charley looked at the engine for a second, then grabbed the hood and wiggled it free from where it pivoted on rear posts. He threw it off to the side of the road. He jumped into the driver's seat and put it in gear. Holding the steering wheel in one hand, Charley leaned way out over the tractor and pinched the carburetor lever between thumb and index finger and pulled back. The tractor jerked forward. Charley lost his balance and almost shoved his hand into the radiator fan.

He rearranged his body and tried again. This time the acceleration was a lot smoother. Problem was that it was impossible to hold the steering wheel with one hand and extend himself far enough so he could grab the throttle lever with the other. His stomach was in the way. So he decided he had to somehow steer with his body. He lay across the steering wheel, pressing hard with his stomach, supporting the front of his body by planting his left hand on the fender, and grabbing the carburetor lever with his right. His legs and feet were sticking out past the mower in the rear. Basically he was lying down on the mower. He had just gotten her up to full speed and was figuring out the logistics of steering by rotating his stomach left and right when Louie swerved around him. Charley brought the lawnmower more or less under control and zeroed in behind Louie. Charley thought it would be damn tricky to pass Louie, that is if he got the chance. But that was a big if: Louie, that son-of-a-gun, was hauling butt!

They were quickly approaching the finish line. Beau was up just ahead holding a very large checkered flag that Charley had made out of an old sheet he had cut in half and tacked to a broom handle. Tiny, Norm, and Rusty were making sure the mob of people around the Club stayed out of the road. Almost everyone who had been watching the race had gravitated to the finish line—it was as if the whole town was there. The decibel level of the yelling and cheering and whistling was beyond impressive. The amount of alcohol consumed may have had something to do with that. It was quite a finish. Louie was pedaling like a hamster again, his face bright red from equal parts of exertion and determination. The brim in the front of his sweat-stained hat was pushed up by the same wind that kept the rabbit ears flat and pointing backwards. His pumping, previously pale thighs were a bright pink. Close behind was Charley, weaving back and forth, his face straining as much as Louie's and his turtle-helmeted head and neck were extended way out beyond the carburetor. He was doing his best to keep his sweaty hand from slipping into the fan. Charley's erratic weaving had the crowd backed up. Beau raised the flag up high, then whished it back and forth as Louie passed the finish line two lengths ahead and pulling away. The noise of the crowd was deafening.

Louie coasted to a stop, breathing hard and heart thumping like there was no tomorrow. His head was down. He was gasping for air. He thought he might throw up. Charley let go of the carburetor lever and the lawnmower stopped a little ways past the finish line. Resigned, he slowly pushed himself up and off the lawnmower. He turned off the engine. Tommy showed up on his bike and dismounted near Beau before the crowd closed in. Louie managed to get off his bike without falling down, and with rubbery legs pushed it to the starting line. The excited, bubbling crowd opened up for him. Charley was the first to congratulate Louie. He patted Louie on the back as Louie put the kickstand down.

"Dang, Louie, you done good!" Charley exclaimed, holding out his hand. Louie took it. Louie looked awful. "How's the ol' bod?"

"You don't want to know. What happened to the lawnmower?"

"Throttle cable broke," Charley said. "Shoulda listened to Rusty. But no never mind. I'll git ya next year fer sure. Make this an annual event."

People who heard that cheered, then groaned when Louie shook his head and said, wearily, "Not going to be a 'next year.' Sorry, Charley. One and done."

Charley looked at Louie's exhausted face and the sweat-soaked hat, shirt, and shorts. "Guess I can't rightly blame ya none. What say I buy ya a cold beer, even though I done lost a pile of money today?"

"You're on. In a second, though," Louie said, turning to look around. "I got someone to thank first." He saw Tommy standing shyly by his bike. He walked over to him and put a hand on his shoulder, looking at him for several moments. Tommy smiled. Louie shook his hand and said, "Thank you."

Beau walked up to Louie. Standing next to him, he asked for silence from the crowd. "Louie," he began. "Norm's got something for you." Norm stepped forward with a beautiful custom trophy about twelve inches tall that had been fabricated in Gainesville. It had imitation-gold cartoon characters, a rabbit and a turtle, shaking hands. The base was walnut with a brass plate engraved with:

TORTOISE AND HARE 15
July 1, 1998
WINNER

Both Louie and Charley were surprised by the quality of the trophy. Charley looked at it, saying, "Dang, if'n I had knowed this was in the bargain, I mighta done a little more maintenance to the Deere! That little ol' thing would look mighty good on a shelf in the 'Ray."

Louie accepted the trophy, smiling. "Thanks, Norm; it's a beauty." Louie turned back to Tommy. He took him by the arm and brought him forward a couple of steps towards the circle of spectators. Without letting go of Tommy's arm, Louie said, loudly, "Turns out that this race was just like the fairy book story about not giving up. Believe me, back by the ball field I *had* given up, but Tommy here brought me back. He wouldn't let me quit. He taught me a lesson. He's the man here, not me!" The crowd cheered. Louie cleared his throat and continued. "Like I said, Tommy's the real winner and I want him to have this." Louie handed the trophy to Tommy whose eyes were like saucers. Louie saw Tiny at the edge of the crowd. "Tiny, hoist Tommy onto my shoulders."

Tiny effortlessly placed Tommy on Louie's shoulders. Louie did a little pirouette with Tommy proudly waving the trophy back and forth. The crowd cheered. A great ending to a surprisingly great race. When it quieted, Louie turned to Charley. "I'll take that beer now, Charley. And a root beer for my friend here." The crowd parted to let Charley and Louie, with Tommy still on Louie's shoulders and holding the trophy, through to the stairs leading up to the Club.

Chapter Fifteen

The day after catching the redfish, Bobby was hung over more from the amphetamines than the beer. He moped around the marina. The euphoric high was gone, replaced by a low: a real downer. Yesterday he had been energized, he could do anything. Today he couldn't get geared up—everything was a chore. He was dragging and needed a pick-me-up bad! He wondered if the low was lower than the high was high. Was it really worth it? So bad for the bod. These thoughts were going through his mind when Frank came up to him. Frank smiled as he shook his head side to side.

"Moving kind of slow today, Bobby. Looks like all those beers yesterday caught up with you. I shouldn't offer, but go grab one if you want. Hair of the dog."

Bobby shook his head. "Thanks, but no thanks, Frank."

Frank shrugged. "Suit yourself. I'm off to get Rusty some parts for that motor he's been working on. You know the drill." Bobby nodded. "See you in a few hours."

Five minutes after Frank drove away, BeeBee called Bobby over. She was holding the *Back in Fifteen Minutes* sign. Bobby perked up. He hoped that meant another line or two—just what he needed. He walked into the bar as BeeBee shut and locked the door. Sure enough, four beautiful white lines all chopped up and laid out. Whether it was the coke or the probability of upcoming sex, Bobby went hard. Probably both, he thought. BeeBee came over smiling, bussed him on the lips, and, handing him the rolled up bill, said, "Be my guest, Big Boy." Within minutes they were headed to Berth #22.

After a wild bout of sex, BeeBee and Bobby lay naked, her head comfortably on his chest. He fiddled absent-mindedly with a lock of her long blond hair as he stared at the underside of the metal roof. It was very warm.

"Why did you hookup with Frank?"

Without looking at him, BeeBee answered, "Why do you think?" Before he could answer, she held up a hand and rubbed forefinger and thumb together. Bobby nodded.

"Where'd you meet him?"

"I let him pick me up on a beach in Lauderdale. Actually, I had seen him a few times before at his marina when a couple girlfriends and I partied with some guys who had boats there." She laughed. "I thought Frank was an employee because he was always on the forklift, cleaning boats, that sort of thing. You could have knocked me over with a feather when he told me he owned the joint."

"What'd you do before you got together?"

"Cashier at a Publix. So, why all the questions, Bobby?"

"Thought I should at least know a little about you, considering. And Frank, too, seeing as I've been screwing his wife." He could feel BeeBee shrug into his chest. "So you married him for his money..."

"What else? He wined and dined me big time at first. We went out to all sorts of shows and fancy restaurants. Took me out into the ocean in his cigarette boat. For a working girl like me, it was like I had tapped into Fort Knox. He'd do anything I wanted, including taking me to Vegas for five days. I screwed his brains out in Vegas and he spent money like there was no tomorrow. We scored some primo coke and flew through that town. We were having such a blast we decided to get married and when we said our 'I do's,' we were high as kites." Bobby didn't say anything. He kept fiddling with her hair. "But things changed. Soon as we got back, the honeymoon was over. It was like pulling teeth to get him to take me out. He had his prize to look at now and screw and show off; but that was it. No more shows, no nothing. He didn't want to do anything but work. But, at least it was Lauderdale. There was stuff to do. I could hang out with friends during the day. Go to the beach and get a tan. Plenty of guys at the beach."

"This the first time you played around?"

BeeBee laughed. "Hardly."

"Does he know about the other guys?"

"Nope. He can't see beyond me. He worships me. I'm perfect in his eyes, and so, if I'm perfect, then I can't possibly be screwing around." She pushed herself up and looked at him. "So yeah, there have been other guys, Bobby; but you're the best. I mean that. I knew as soon as I saw you that we'd hit it off big time." She put her head back down on his chest. Stroked a biceps. Bobby didn't know whether or not to believe her. "Then he got the opportunity to sell the marina for a small fortune. I was all for it, and not just because it was a lot of money. I thought if he didn't have the marina, he'd start wining and dining me again. So, what does he do? Looks all around the state for another marina. Can't find one that's right, but finds Hicksville here and buys this land and an old fish house and builds a goddamn marina and house! Didn't even think of asking me about it! And he works twice as hard now. Anyway, I'm stuck here. If I leave, I'll be broke and I don't want to be a cashier again. So here I stay." Her hand moved down to between his legs. "But I got some ideas. How would you like to get wined and dined, among other things," she said, caressing him, "on your day off?"

"How?" His body was responding to her caress.

"I told Frank I was sick of this place. He suggested I get out of here one day a week. I told him it was a great idea and guess what day I chose, Big Boy."

"Wednesday," he said, cupping her breast.

"So, what do you think?"

"I think Wednesday is a long way off."

BeeBee smiled as Bobby rolled over on top of her. They were too busy to hear the truck pull into the marina, but, suddenly, heard the side door open and someone say, "Frank? Bobby?"

"Oh no! Rusty!" Bobby whispered. He rolled off and grabbed his cutoffs.

"Maybe he'll go away," she whispered back, panic-stricken.

"And tell Frank that the sign was on the door and we both weren't around? And if he comes in here, why's the forklift up? And that boat he's been working on is in a ground-level berth. He might just start tinkering on it and we'd be trapped!" He grabbed his tee-shirt. "I better go," he whispered, "and see what he wants. I'll come back for you as soon as I can."

BeeBee nodded as she pulled on her panties, her gargantuan breasts swaying back and forth. "Stay down!" Bobby hissed. She ducked down quickly. He pulled the tee-shirt over his head and jumped up onto the forks. He was climbing down the mast when Rusty saw him. Bobby looked disheveled. Rusty smiled to himself. Napping on the job.

Bobby saw Rusty at the same time. "Hey, Rusty," he said, as he climbed into the driver's seat. Rusty walked up.

"Not taking a little nap by any chance, Bobby? I take it Frank's not here."

Bobby tried to looked sheepish, instead of scared to death.

"He's getting your parts. Don't tell him, okay, Rusty?"

"While the cat's away...Don't worry, mum's the word."

Bobby asked, "What time is it anyway?"

Rusty looked at his watch.

"One-thirty."

"If you come back in a couple of hours he should be here."

"I brought the trailer with all my tools so I could disassemble and clean the lower unit before the water pump and impeller go in. Like to tackle it now. Could you bring the boat out front?"

Bobby's face fell. "Right," he said. "Sure thing," and started the lift. He drove over to pick up the boat which had a big Mercury. A week ago, the owner had taken it out for about an hour when it overheated because the water from the cooling system wasn't peeing out in a steady stream. Unfortunately he hadn't noticed the faulty stream until after the motor had started missing badly. Suddenly the engine went WHAM and the dipstick blew out and hit the housing, spraying oil on the scalding hot engine which caused it to smoke like a banshee. The owner brought the boat in at an idle.

When the guy explained what had happened, Frank said, "Got to be the impeller. Usually not a big deal." But it turned out to be a big deal because the guy had run it for so long. The thermostat, water pump, and all the gaskets had melted. It was a miracle that he made it back to the marina at all. Rusty was brought in to take a look. First thing Rusty did was to check the compression. For whatever reason it was within tolerances and the motor wasn't toast. Rusty told the owner that he had been extremely lucky. How could the impeller go on a brand new engine, the guy wanted to know. He was pissed. Rusty shrugged his shoulders. Gaskets dry out during storage. Factory defect. Ports clogged by mud wasps or a plastic bag. Unusual for a new motor, but always possible. Well, it's a goddamn inconvenience, the guy said, but at least it's still under warranty.

Rusty and Frank looked at each other, and Frank turned to the owner. "Better check the fine print. Usually there's something in there that it's the operator's responsibility to always check for a steady stream when the motor's started. If there's no stream, he's supposed to shut it off immediately and contact an authorized dealer." The guy pulled out the motor manual and warrantee from the center console. Sure enough, there it was in black and white. He used Frank's phone to call Mercury. Their answer was, sorry fellah, read your manual first next time. The guy was spitting mad. Frank thought he was going to have a heart attack right there. But he didn't. Ultimately, he bit the bullet and told Rusty to fix it if he could.

Bobby was bringing the boat over to the seawall when Rusty stopped him.

"No, Bobby, not in the water—over close to the trailer here. It'll be a heck of a lot easier to work on and if I drop something, I won't be up the creek."

Bobby brought it over and lowered the boat to a convenient height. "How long's this going to take?" he asked.

"Don't know. A while. Might be ready by the time Frank gets here. Can you raise it up a smidgeon?" Bobby did as he requested. "Right there, perfect."

Bobby got off the lift. He watched Rusty take the housing off. "If somebody needs a boat pulled, I'll need to use the lift."

"If that happens, we'll just put the boat back in storage and I can work on it there."

Bobby nodded sadly. "Yeah, guess that would work. I better get busy. Give me a holler if you need something."

Bobby circled around back to the storage building. Rusty's back was to him. He entered and shut the door. He walked up to Berth #22.

"BeeBee!" he whispered. BeeBee's head appeared over the gunnel. She was thirty feet up and the steel berths covered with carpet were cantilevered out from monstrous vertical I-beams. There was no way in hell she could climb down.

"Where's the forklift!" she whispered back.

Bobby looked sick. "Rusty wants to keep the boat on it while he's working."

"Tell him you need it!"

"I tried. He said if I needed it, I could just bring the boat in here for him to work on."

"Great!"

"Yeah, big time!"

"What are we going to do?"

"I don't know."

Bobby looked around. He was trying not to panic.

"Bobby!"

"What?"

"I got to pee bad."

"Hang it over the side."

"I can't. It's too scary."

Oh, sweet Lord! "Then in the boat somewhere."

"If I do, we're not using it again!"

"Don't worry about that! I'll probably be dead anyway. Frank's going to shoot my ass!"

"He does have a gun in the truck."

"Thanks for sharing!"

They heard a truck enter. They looked at each other, their eyes huge.

"Oh Lord!" Bobby swallowed. "Gotta go."

BeeBee ducked down again as Bobby left the building. It was a customer backing up to the sling. Bobby breathed a sigh of relief. After launching the boat, Bobby realized that the sign was still hanging on the locked door. He better go get the key from BeeBee. He was walking past Rusty when Rusty said, "Bobby, if you've got a second, I could use an extra pair of hands."

"Sure thing."

"Here, hold this so it lines up. Trying to do that and get the bolt in at the same time is a bitch."

Bobby lined it up. Rusty turned his head away from the motor and was looking at Bobby while putting the long skinny bolt in by feel. "Heard you did some time at Raiford."

"Yeah, seventeen years."

"For putting a trooper in the hospital."

Bobby nodded. "I was drunk." He paused. "I heard that you used to be a trooper." Rusty got the bolt in finger tight, then reached for a socket.

"That's right. Over twenty years."

"Then I imagine that goes against the grain—what I did to that trooper, I mean."

"Nope, not especially...There, got it. One more." Rusty reached for another long skinny bolt.

"It doesn't?"

"No, just a damn shame all the way around. Didn't have to happen. Trooper must have had poor training. Because of that, he gets seriously hurt and you lose seventeen of the best years of your life."

"You think you could have prevented it?"

"Yup. Not your resisting arrest, but you certainly wouldn't have kicked my butt and put me in the hospital."

"I was pretty quick and ornery back then, Rusty. Pretty mean when I drank the hard stuff...and I had drunk plenty that night."

Rusty looked at Bobby for a few seconds before answering. "I didn't say that to be macho or brag or anything, Bobby. It's just the plain truth. I served multiple tours in 'Nam as an MP. I was highly, highly trained because I had to take care of guys who were also very highly trained; and believe me, there was no room for error with those dudes. After 'Nam, the Army didn't want me to leave: made it worth my while to stay on for another tour stateside as an instructor.

"The trooper you nailed should never have let you get close enough to take a swing. And if you charged him, there's a whole book of maneuvers to put you down and cuff you in the blink of an eye. Instead of going to Raiford, you might have gotten a year or two at best, and that trooper would not have been confined to a desk job for the rest of his career. Like I say, just a damn shame….Here, got it. Thanks, Bobby. All ready for Frank, now."

"Do you want to put the boat back in the shed and I can call you when Frank gets here?" Bobby asked, trying not to sound eager. Rusty looked at his watch.

"That's not a bad idea. I could…"

Rusty was interrupted by Frank's arrival. Bobby's stomach sunk to his ankles. Frank parked and walked over carrying a couple plastic bags. He handed them to Rusty.

"Good timing, Frank. Just finished. All set to put these babies in," Rusty said, as he opened the bags. He quickly and professionally began to insert the parts. Frank noticed right away the sign on the marina door.

"What's with the sign, Bobby?"

"Dunno."

"Where's Bee?"

Bobby shrugged. "Dunno that either. Been doing things and helping Rusty here. Maybe she went for a walk," he said, hopefully.

"Bee, a walk! Doubt it. She must be over at the house. I'll go see."

"Frank, if you wait just a couple of minutes, we can put this baby in the water and test run her. I'd like you at the controls so I can put a heat gauge on the engine under load."

"Want me to run up to the house, Frank?"

"No thanks, Bobby. Just stick with us and watch how Rusty does it. You should learn how to put an impeller in."

In fifteen minutes, the boat was in the water with Frank at the wheel and Rusty in the stern, facing the motor. The housing was off so he could check the temp. It was almost low tide so Frank was eyeballing the oyster bars as they carefully began to thread their way out to the Gulf. Rusty was watching Bobby drive the forklift back to the boat storage shed. He was going fast and the forklift clanged loudly when he hit a pothole. Should take it slower, Rusty thought; hard on the machine. For his part, Bobby was thinking about BeeBee, not the machine, as he jerked to a stop in front of Berth #22. BeeBee's head carefully appeared over the side of the boat. Bobby jumped out, shoved the forks together, and raised the lift. BeeBee stood up and looked around as the lift quickly came up. She was a mess. Her hair was all plastered down and her black bra was clearly visible through her sweaty blouse. She did not look happy. She scrambled onto the forks and Bobby lowered her down.

"About frigging time, Bobby! Here!" She flung his balled up underwear into his face.

"Couldn't get here any faster," he said, pulling the underwear away. It was soaked. "BeeBee, you didn't piss on these, did you!"

"Of course not, you boob! It's hotter than hell up there and I about sweated to death. I used them for a towel."

"Frank's back." BeeBee looked wildly towards the door. "Don't worry, he's out in the boat with Rusty. But he wanted to know why the marina door was locked and where you were. I said maybe walking. He figured you were up at the house. Man, that was close! I've been a nervous wreck for the last couple of hours!"

"Well, I'm a mess." She was still sweating. "And I'm outta here!" She fast-walked to the door and carefully looked out. No one was around. She left the shed and, with head down, began to walk quickly to the house. Out on the water, Rusty and Frank were passing the last oyster bar. Rusty saw BeeBee exit the shed and head to the house. He also saw Bobby come out and watch her. Rusty turned to look at Frank. He was concentrating on the oyster bar and hadn't seen anything. Rusty faced shore again. He watched Bobby go back into the building. Yes indeedy, Rusty thought, while the cat's away.

Chapter Sixteen

"Now don't fidget none, Rebecca! I know you're excited, but sit still," Katharine said, to her daughter. Rebecca was sitting in the kitchen of her family's rusty trailer while her mother braided her hair. Katharine's husband Clem and her brother Sammy were leaning against the counter watching. The area was small and narrow, and Sammy and Katharine's bulk made it even smaller. Rebecca continued to squirm. She was excited because the mayor had selected her to drive him in the parade today. Kids drove golf carts around Crescent Beach all the time, but not her because her family couldn't afford one. She occasionally rode with her buddies and they would scoot all around; but that didn't cut it. She wanted to drive, too. She was envious. Consequently, she had been overjoyed when for the last five days Beau had given her instructions and let her drive his cart every afternoon for a half-hour under his supervision.

Katharine finished tying off the two braided pigtails with red ribbons and stepped back, hands on hips, to inspect her work. Rebecca looked cute as a button: a little fair-haired Indian maiden. "There," Katharine said. "That oughta do it."

"Doncha look smart?" Clem said, smiling at his daughter.

"Shor does," Sammy agreed. He walked over and picked Rebecca up to hug her. "We shor is proud of ya and yur gonna be the prettiest gal in the parade, darlin'. Ain't nobody gonna hold a candle to ya."

"Oh, Uncle Sammy, you're going to rumple my dress." But Rebecca beamed. Sammy immediately put her down. He always did what his niece wanted. He was at her beck and call; he loved her to kingdom come. Sammy had never married, Rebecca was his only niece, and there were no nephews. She was the apple of his eye. Rebecca pulled her chair over to the window to keep an eye out for the mayor. She didn't have to wait long. Within minutes Beau, with Skillet in the back with his head on Beau's shoulder, pulled up in the cart. Beau was wearing the traditional mayor's scarlet sash of office. He didn't have to get out of the cart because Rebecca was out the door in a flash. She was followed proudly by her parents and Sammy. Beau lifted up Skillet's head and scooched over, making room for Rebecca to drive. Rebecca climbed in like she had done it everyday of her life. Skillet figured out what was going on and shifted position so he could put his head back on Beau's shoulder. Rebecca looked very serious as they drove off.

They turned right, off Main Street onto the ballpark road just before the cattle gap at the town's entrance. This was where Norm organized the parade lineup each year. It was ten-thirty-five. Several decorated golf carts and homemade floats had already arrived and the Perry High School band in bright red uniforms was practicing by the Baptist church a hundred yards or so in from Main Street. The four members of the Honor Guard from the Perry VFW were standing around underneath a live oak, smoking; their three rifles and an American flag set leaning against the tree. Beau got out and walked over to Norm.

"Behind the Honor Guard?" Beau asked.

"Yup. Same as always."

Beau climbed back into the cart and directed Rebecca where to go. More golf carts, floats, a skidder, towed boats, a tractor pulling a wagon, and a couple of antique cars joined the lineup. Charley was one of the last to arrive in his fire-engine-red Mustang convertible with a *Scallop Festival Queen* banner draped across the grille. T, wearing a tightly stretched white dress and the golden tiara on her head, was sitting next to him. Charley had washed and waxed the car so that he could have shaved in its reflection. In fact, maybe he had: he was freshly shaven for a change. T climbed out of the front and got into the back. She sat up high where the convertible roof was carefully tucked in the boot. Norm walked up the ballpark road, giving instructions to go slow, don't bunch, and be careful. He returned to the head of the line where a Perry squad car with a part-time rent-a-cop had pulled in. Norm looked at his watch. He talked to the part-timer behind the wheel. Norm stepped away and looked back at all the floats. He looked at his watch again. Eleven o'clock on the nose. He tugged his arm up and down like pulling a train whistle and the lights on the squad car immediately came on and the siren began wailing. The squad car slowly pulled out onto Main Street, clearing bystanders out of the way. The Honor Guard followed. The parade was on.

Rusty was standing on the edge of Main Street, just down from the library, in front of a vendor selling different sculptures made out of discarded junk like old rake heads, shovels, horseshoes, rusty old chains, various car parts. Many of the sculptures were clever, all were interesting. The display included a straight line of life-size turkey buzzards with their bodies made out of painted black mufflers and their bright red necks and heads out of tightly coiled springs and cans with welded beaks. They were perched on a tall, horizontal metal stand and their bobbing heads seemed to be looking down on Rusty. It was Rusty's first Crescent Beach parade and he didn't know what to expect. He hoped it wouldn't be a dud. It wasn't: it was Americana at its best. Beau and Rebecca followed the Honor Guard. Beau looked like the consummate, gracious southern politician with his long frame, flowing white hair, and a ready smile. Rebecca was all business. Her back was ramrod straight and her arms outstretched at ninety degrees to the steering wheel. She was diligently maintaining the exact proper distance between them and the Honor Guard. Beau was waving to the crowd and when he saw Rusty, he yelled over to meet him in the library after the parade. Rusty gave him the thumbs up. T followed Beau and Rebecca. Rusty waved and T smiled and waved back. She was holding a bouquet of roses, but it didn't hide the fact that she was pregnant. Has to be a first, Rusty thought: a knocked-up-and-showing, out-of-wedlock parade queen. Not for the first time, he wondered how she and Tiny did it, with him weighing in at almost three hundred and her not much over a hundred. He smiled as he recalled an old grade school riddle. *Question: how do porcupines make love. Answer: very carefully.* Charley was waving to everybody and had an ear-to-ear grin. He was in his element.

They were followed by the Perry High School Band. It was mostly drumming until the band reached the library and they began a fair rendition of *Seventy-six Trombones.* Next, a Ford Model A that a mechanic had driven in from the country. T and Tiny's float followed, a dory draped in fish net with a bunch of kids holding signs for TNT Shrimp Company and advertising the fried shrimp T would be cooking up later. There were a series of decorated golf carts. Tammy had a display for the Crescent Beach Club and Frank had one for the Marina. Every business in town had something in it. A few kids rode decorated bicycles. The crowd cheered heartily for the two sets of Shriners in their tasseled hats, one from Mayo circling in tiny little cars, the other from Jacksonville on tiny motor scooters.

It was a coup for Norm who had tried for years to get them to participate. Rusty cheered lustily for Jimmy and Crystal's twin grandsons who were on rollerblades darting here and there. Both sported a charcoaled mustache and were dressed as consummate sports fishermen; each held a fishing pole with a dangling painted cardboard fish advertising Jimmy's guiding business. But the biggest cheers of the day were for Louie and little Tommy who were near the end of the parade. It had been Norm's last minute idea to ask them to take part and the paint was barely dry on a pair of six-foot pink and white rabbit ears Charley had made and duct-taped on top of the roof of the golf cart. A simple stiff-hitch had been fabricated to have Louie's bike in tow. Large *TORTOISE AND HARE 15* cardboard signs were taped on the sides of the cart. Tommy, like Rebecca, was proudly driving, although unlike Rebecca, he was in a cool-man pose, driving one-handed and the other arm draped over the top of the seat. Louie was holding up Tommy's trophy and waving it back and forth. After two more floats, the town's volunteer fire engine with lights flashing and siren screaming brought up the rear.

After the fire engine passed and folks began walking around again, Rusty perused the sculptures behind him and then headed to the library. It was gangbusters inside. There was free coffee and pastries supposedly just for the vendors, although everybody who came in helped themselves. Crystal was serving the coffee. She saw him enter and smiled. He made his way through the crowded room over to her.

"I hope you saw your grandsons," he said.

She laughed. "Of course. I was a little worried about the skate thing, but they're pretty good at it."

"Liked the mustaches, too. Good touch."

"Jimmy's idea."

Without asking him, she handed him a cup of coffee, black, no sugar. Virginia came over.

"How'd you like the parade, Rusty?"

"Great! Did you get to see any of it?"

"The whole thing. Always shoo everyone out and close up for the parade," she said, in her thick drawl.

"About got everything wrapped up?" he asked.

"Gaining; almost there. Only twenty or thirty more *Post-its* to go. Then the raffle at four and all done. Just cleanup and counting money after that."

"Count me in for the cleanup."

Virginia smiled. "Thank you. I will."

Beau entered and walked up to the trio. "Perfect," he said. "Just the people I wanted to see." He put an arm around Virginia. "Now that this thing is almost over, Sugah, about time we went scalloping. Tomorrow. Hope you'll join us Rusty."

"Absolutely!"

Beau turned to Crystal. "Imagine, this weekend especially, Jimmy's booked solid. How about you coming with us?"

"Have to be sometime after ten, that's when the grandyoung'uns are going back."

"High tide's around noon, so that'd be perfect." Beau turned back to Virginia. He sighed. "Okay, Sugah, I'm yours now for a few hours. Tell me what you want me to do." Virginia took his arm and pulled him towards her *Post-its* stuck all over her desk.

Rusty thanked Crystal for the coffee and ducked out of the packed library. He sat down on a hay bale near where the band would be playing later. He sipped the coffee, looking around at the mob scene. There were lines at many of the food vendors, people were walking around drinking sodas from gargantuan cups, kids were eating cotton candy, a steady stream of boats on trailers passed on Main Street, cars were parked everywhere. Rusty had no idea that there were almost as many people out on the water. Some were out fishing for trout or redfish, but most were to the south in the best scalloping grounds. There was an absolute flotilla of all shapes and sizes anchored around the Salt and Pepper Keys. Many had gotten an early start to get the best anchorage. Others had only gotten an early start on drinking beer. The five occupants of a large party barge fell into the second category. In their early to mid thirties, they had come down from Tallahassee for a guys-only weekend. Back home they worked hard and were good family men. One was the manager of a Publix, two were contractors, another was in real estate, and the fifth had a retail sporting goods store. It was the sporting goods guy who owned the party barge and who was familiar with Crescent Beach. He had been coming for years. He talked his buddies into the outing and they had rented Tammy's largest cabin. For them this weekend was about no kids, no wives; just beer, scallops, and tall tales. Let loose a little bit.

After changing into her favorite tee-shirt and shorts, the same outfit she had worn in the scallop shucking competition, Rebecca joined up with Tommy after the parade. Even though Tommy was two years younger, they were good buddies. They pedaled over to the vendor area and left their bikes on the kickstands while they wandered around. They soon spent what money their parents had given them on cotton candy, soft drinks, and corn dogs. Eventually they climbed back on their bikes and pedaled down Main Street to the TNT Shrimp Company. T was frying up shrimp while Tiny was taking it easy, sitting at one of the extra tables they had set up on the dock. His hands were behind his head and he was watching the people at the picnic tables in front chowing down. He smiled when he saw Tommy and Rebecca glide up on their bikes.

"Well, lookee here. Guess we just got two of the most important people in town, one a drivin' the mayor hisself, and the other a drivin' a famous champeen bike racer. You two grab a sody pop and git over here and sit down!" Tommy and Rebecca grabbed root beers and came over. They were already pumped up by the kudos they had received from their peers walking around the vendor area, but hearing this from Tiny was even better. "T, kin you fix up two plates o' shrimp for our guests here?" Tommy and Rebecca were already stuffed, but what Florida kid could refuse a pile of perfectly fried fresh shrimp with gobs of tartar sauce. T brought over the plates and they dug in. Tiny watched them gobble up the shrimp like they were starving.

"So what other important activities do ya two rapscallions have planned fer today?" Tiny asked.

"Goin' fishin'," Tommy mumbled, with his mouth full.

Rebecca was a little more delicate. She swallowed before she said, "Mr. Beau said we could fish off his dock this afternoon. Said there've been some trout hanging around the edge of the grass."

"Whatcha usin' fer bait?" They looked at each other and shrugged. Tommy said, "Probably those white and pink wiggly things."

Tiny shook his head. "No ya ain't! Ya two needs to use live bait. When ya git ready to go on over there, ya come by here first. T and I'll fix ya right up. Jest bring a little bait bucket."

Tommy and Rebecca turned happy smiles onto Tiny. "Thank you, Mr. Tiny," they said in unison. The pair finished their shrimp, politely thanked T, and continued down Main Street on their bikes. They pedaled past several stands selling blue crab meals. Almost all the tables on the docks were full. They saw the crabbers taking it easy like Tiny, sitting on white plastic chairs around the fryolaters. This was a holiday. No crabbers were out on the water today, they were all in town and most of them here. They waved to the two kids as they pedaled past.

Some of the scallopers were beginning to leave the Keys so they could make it back to the raffle at four. The five guys in the party barge were ready to call it a day, too, but not because of the raffle. They had their limit of ten gallons of unshelled scallops in the coolers. Each person was allowed two gallons, although the max for any boat, no matter how many passengers, was ten. The men were stuffed, eating raw scallops with a little lime, accompanied by lots of beer. They hadn't worn tee-shirts while snorkeling and their shoulders and backs were burned. One of the contractors and the realtor were partially bald, and the tops of their heads were bright pink. All five would most likely be hurting from the sun come nighttime, or from the beers come morning, or both. Only the driver of the boat had curtailed his beer consumption, and he was the only one who was paying attention to the tide. It was dropping and they had a big boat with a big motor. Time to head in.

They arrived at the marina where Frank hoisted the barge and lowered it onto the trailer. Frank noticed that the vertical guide pipes on the sides of the trailer had been pushed out and mentioned it to the owner. "Thanks, Frank. I'll take care of them back at the cabin. I've got some nylon straps with ratchets there," he said, from the cab of his pickup. He drove off to the side of the lot, parked, and walked towards the bar. His flying-high buddies had wanted to ogle the lady with the big boobies before returning to the cabin to clean scallops. He paused to let his eyes adjust; quite a change from the bright Florida sun to the air-conditioned, polaroid-window interior. Sure enough, the four had eschewed the vacant tables looking out over the Gulf and instead were seated at the mostly deserted bar, giggling like adolescents. BeeBee sometimes took the bar on Saturday and Sunday afternoons before Bobby arrived so Frank could tend to the boats. Bobby was willing to come in early, but Frank didn't want to have to pay overtime. BeeBee had her back to them, drawing beers. She had a knowing smile on her face. For her, being ogled by young men was the next best thing to screwing them. As the sporting goods boat owner approached his friends, one of them turned to him, shaking his head with an expression like 'unbelievable' and cupped his breasts like he was holding watermelons. When BeeBee turned around to bring the beers over, he dropped his hands and smiled lasciviously at her. Anybody who wore a halter top like that deserved it, the guy thought.

BeeBee served the beers before coming up to the sporting goods boat owner. She put her forearms on the bar, leaning over so that her head and boobs formed a perfect triangle, all three about the same size. It seemed like there was no way that she wasn't going to fall out of the halter. BeeBee's smile grew imperceptibly when she saw not one of the men could keep their eyes up. "So what can I do for you, Honey?" she asked, just as one of the sporting goods guy's friends was taking a swig. He choked and stood up, quickly putting a bar napkin to his mouth. His friends broke up.

"Nothing, Ma'am," the sporting goods guy said, eventually. "Got to drive." BeeBee made a show of looking disappointed and pouted. His friends tore their eyes away from her and urged him to have a beer. C'mon, O.C., they said, we're not going back to Tallahassee, just back to the cabin. There aren't any cops. One for the road! He acquiesced and BeeBee brought him a Bud Lite draft. BeeBee enjoyed flirting with the men while waiting for Bobby to come to work. One beer turned into two, and then they finally left. BeeBee looked at her watch. Time had passed quickly and Bobby would be here in another five or ten minutes. However, it turned out she was wrong about that.

Bobby was indeed on his way to work. After he walked by the fire station and post office, he passed City Hall. Cars, trucks, bikes, golf carts were parked everywhere, and people were jostling at the door. He looked over the shoulders of the queue and saw it was jam-packed inside. That's right, the raffle, he thought. He took a left onto Main Street and headed towards the humpback bridge. He saw a very large party barge in tow, coming from the direction of the marina. It caught his eye not only because it was big, but because its white guide posts were sticking way out. Good thing no one else is crossing that narrow bridge, he thought. Down Main Street he saw two kids heading his way on bicycles carrying fishing poles. The one in front had a little yellow and white bait bucket hanging from the handlebars. The truck and party barge were going slowly and when it crossed the bridge and pulled out onto Main Street, it blocked the two kids from view.

Tommy and Rebecca had gotten their shrimp and turned onto the humpback bridge as the truck pulled onto Main Street. The driver had seen them when he looked left, then looked right to make sure no one was coming from the other way as he pulled out. Two of his buddies were in the truck with him and the other two were in the party barge. But the two in the party barge weren't standing or sitting up; they were lying down on the cushy couch-like seats, eyes closed, enjoying the soft rays of the afternoon sun. Full of beer and being gently rocked since leaving the marina, both were already half asleep by the time the boat and trailer turned onto Main Street. The trailer hugged the centerline, but the driver's side guide pole crossed it. Tommy saw it coming and deftly ducked under. It missed him by a few inches. Rebecca wasn't so fortunate. She took a direct hit to her left shoulder. There was no guardrail, only a curb about twelve inches high on each side of the bridge. She and her bike were knocked into the creek seven feet below.

No one in the truck or trailer felt a thing, and they continued up Main Street toward Tammy's. Bobby saw the kid jump off his bike and look down into the creek. The girl had disappeared. Bobby started running. The little boy began shrieking at the top of his lungs. He was blubbering by the time Bobby arrived. Bobby looked down. It was low tide. The girl lay half in and half out of the water. Oysters were all around. Her arm was in a very awkward angle. He thought he saw a bone protruding. She was bleeding heavily. Her face was in the water. Bobby leaped off the bridge. He was wearing sneakers, a good thing because he landed in a foot of water on some oysters. The landing jarred him and brought him to his knees. He extended a hand out to keep from falling over. He sliced it up pretty good on the oysters. He rushed to the little girl and very gently, very carefully supported her neck as he brought her head out of the water. He had seen enough bad stuff in prison to know that you had to be careful about neck and spinal injuries. He turned her head to the side and she coughed and threw up some water then breathed loudly enough so at least he knew that she wasn't going to drown. But blood was all over her. Bobby looked up at the kid on the bridge. The kid looked scared to death and tears were pouring down his face.

"Go to City Hall! Tell them what happened! Get help! GO!"

Thankfully, Bobby thought, the kid wasn't in shock or something. He ran to his bike and a split second later was pedaling madly to City Hall. Tommy burst into the building, pushing people out of his way. He screamed at the top of his lungs, "Rebecca's hurt bad! Boat knocked her off the bridge! She needs help bad!"

There was a stunned silence. The first to react was Rusty who barreled out of the building. Close on his heels was Norm who yelled over his shoulder, "Beau, get my bag from the Subaru at my house." Rusty and Norm sprinted to the bridge. Mostly men were the first to pour out and run after them. Beau jumped into his golf cart and speeded towards the bridge. Rusty and Norm were looking down at Bobby cradling Rebecca's head when Beau turned onto the bridge. Norm stopped him and handed him his clinic key, saying, "Surgical dressing and bandages are on the shelf to the right of the door. Bring all of it! There are several jugs of distilled spring water on the floor. Bring those, too!" A man jumped on the cart to help Beau before he speeded off. Rusty and Norm scrambled around the bridge to the bank where they jumped down into the creek. Bobby looked up at Norm, all competition and enmity over Tammy by the wayside.

"Had to turn her head some because she was face down in the water. She coughed up a little water and seems to be breathing, so no danger there, I think. But I didn't know what else to do. I know you're not supposed to move the head in something like this, but I didn't have a choice."

"You did great, Bobby," Norm said, as he began to assess. "Keep her head just like that."

Norm thought back to emergency training. What was that acronym? UABCC—urgency, airway, breathing, circulation, cervical spine immobilization.

URGENCY. Norm looked at the splayed arm with the protruding ulna—compound fracture—and the cuts bleeding heavily, some deep in the thigh area. He whipped off his belt and fastened a tourniquet around her thigh. He looked at Rusty who nodded and knelt. Rusty took the belt from Norm in one hand while he removed his shirt with the other. With teeth and one hand, he ripped the shirt in two. He handed one piece to Norm and began cleaning the mud off Rebecca's body with the other. Norm checked the deep cuts on Rebecca's head. Like Rusty, he wiped the mud and creek water off Rebecca. Shirt's not sterile, he thought, but a hell of a lot better than the creek water and stinking mud. Can't apply too much pressure here; could be bone chips and don't need to be pressing them into the brain. Plenty of open wounds. Anybody's guess about closed wounds. Definitely urgent.

AIRWAY. “Keep supporting her, Bobby,” Norm said, as he gently tilted her head and chin a bit. He eased her to where he wanted. “That’s good. Hold her there.” She was breathing, but erratically. At least the airway was clear.

CIRCULATION. Norm took the pulse at her throat, then after a few seconds at her wrist. Rapid breathing and pulse. Where it wasn’t soaked from the canal, her skin was cool and moist. He pressed the end of one of her fingers at the fingernail. It turned white, then after four or five seconds, pink. Should have taken no more than two. Delayed capillary refill. Shock.

Beau arrived and yelled to Norm. Norm looked up. He hadn’t noticed the crowd that had formed. He saw Sammy looking down in horror. Only a couple of minutes had passed. “Someone call an ambulance!” Norm yelled back. “Tell the dispatcher absolute emergency! Unconscious, severe bleeding and loss of blood, broken arm, closed wounds, and patient is in shock!” The man who lived closest sprinted to his house. Norm reached up for the medical bag and supplies, saying, “And someone go get that stretcher from the Fire Department.” Two men peeled off in a truck. Norm went back and started dressing cuts as best he could. He applied pressure to the deep cuts on the thigh area as Rusty let off on the belt.

Within minutes the truck roared back. The stretcher was handed down to Norm. The tide was dead low. Norm picked and cleared oysters and hanging brush away from the side of the creek and created a space to lay Rebecca until the ambulance arrived. He had to get her out of the water. Rusty and Norm worked the stretcher under Rebecca as gently as they could until they had most of her body supported. Norm took over for Bobby, gently cradling her head. It was then Norm noticed that the blood all over Bobby’s hand wasn’t just Rebecca’s. Bobby hadn’t said a word. Bobby and Rusty eased the stretcher to the cleared area in slow motion. Who knew what damage had been done to her backside, but they didn't dare turn her over. Rusty went back to the belt, Norm to the cuts while Bobby cradled the neck and head again. Bobby was watching her face when her eyelids fluttered and opened.

"Doctor," Bobby said. Norm looked up. Bobby nodded towards Rebecca who was looking at Bobby, most likely wondering who the heck he was.

Norm put his head in view and very gently said, "Welcome back. How do you feel?"

"I hurt all over, Dr. Norm," she said. Her voice wasn't more than a whisper.

'Dr. Norm:' good sign. "Can you tell me your name, young lady?" She looked weakly indignant. Another good sign.

"Rebecca, of course."

"Good. And what day is it?"

"Why everybody knows it's the Fourth of July."

"Good girl. This is your lucky day. You got to drive the mayor in the parade and in a little bit you're going to get an ambulance ride, too, with sirens and everything. But that will be a little while yet, so you just close your eyes and try to rest up."

Rebecca closed her eyes. Twenty seconds later she opened them. She looked confused. "What happened, Dr. Norm?"

"Looks like you went swimming off the bridge, but there wasn't any water. Next time you better wait for high tide."

"I did?"

"Not really, but sort of."

"Where's Mama and Daddy and Uncle Sammy?"

"They're very close by. Your parents will be riding in the ambulance with you. You'll be with them in a jiffy. Now close your eyes and rest."

Rebecca did as she was told and twenty minutes later the ambulance arrived. The two EMT responders immobilized her head as they conferred with Norm. They carefully shifted her to their stretcher and strapped her in. Within fifteen minutes she and her parents were on their way to the hospital. The crowd thinned out, although there were bunches here and there discussing the accident and shaking their heads. Norm, Rusty, Bobby, and Beau stood together.

"Let me look at that hand, Bobby," Norm said. It was an ugly wound. "You need stitches. Better let me take care of it at the clinic. When was the last time you had a tetanus shot?"

"Dunno. I hate shots."

Norm laughed. "Doesn't matter, you're getting one. That creek water is about two steps up from raw sewage. Infection's going to be a big deal with Rebecca."

"Did you see it happen, Bobby?" Beau asked.

"Sort of. Saw a truck pulling a big party barge going over the bridge, and the two kids on their bikes coming the other way. After they crossed each other I saw only one kid and he freaked. Got off his bike and looked over the side and started bawling. Something was up, so I ran over."

"Quick response, Bobby," Rusty said. "You may very well have saved her life. Good going."

"Just happened to be in the right place. Anyone would have done it. Just hope she's okay. Cute little thing."

"Got that right!" Beau said. "Little Tommy told us that she was hit by one of those guide poles they use to get boats on the trailer straight. Said he just ducked under it."

"Don't know about that. But do know that both poles were sticking out."

"You didn't get a license number did you?" Rusty asked.

"No, but it's probably still in town. Shouldn't be hard to find." They all looked at him in surprise. "The boat turned left, not right. Went down Main Street as if nothing had happened."

They digested that for a moment before Beau said, "Oh man! Sammy was talking to Tommy. If he found out whoever did this is still in town, all..." He didn't finish the sentence. "C'mon Rusty, let's get you a shirt and go find Sammy!" Rusty and Beau sped off in the golf cart while Bobby, hand wrapped in gauze, walked with Norm towards his clinic on Rich Man's Row.

Chapter Seventeen

Sammy headed straight to his pickup after talking to little Tommy. If the party barge were still in town, he'd find it. He jumped into his Chevy pick-up and drove past City Hall, the humpback bridge, and the TNT Shrimp Co., continually glancing down the side streets. He would drive out to the point, then to the launch area at City Park, and then all the side streets in between. It turned out that wasn't necessary. It took him less than five minutes to find the party barge. When he came up to the Crescent Beach Club, he saw it parked on the other side of the live oak trees that separated the Club from Tammy's cabins. It was parked in front of the largest cabin. He could see a guy in the party barge winching in the guide poles. Son-of-a-bitch is making it look like he didn't do nuthin', Sammy thought. Sammy continued past the club where he took a right, then his next right that took him by the cabins. The man had left the boat and joined three men on the cabin porch. All of Tammy's cabins were booked for the weekend and the little attached porches were full of vacationers. Some were grilling, others sitting on rockers staring out towards the Gulf, but most were cleaning scallops and drinking beer. With low tide most everyone had returned from the Keys.

Sammy drove very slowly by the party barge, one of the expensive ones with enormous pontoons and a honker motor. There was no mistaking it. Just like Tommy had said, it was very big and pulled by a shiny red crew cab pickup. The guide poles had been brought in with two ratcheted nylon straps hooked to the boat's gunnels. Sammy looked over to the porch behind the boat. The four men were laughing and cleaning scallops. Cans of beer were on the railing. Sammy, seething, struggled to contain himself and not jump out of the pickup and take them on right then and there. He kept seeing Rebecca all bloody, lying in the creek. And they hadn't even stopped! Hit and run! Them sons-a-bitches gonna wish they was never born! Scenarios flew through his head. So intent on payback and kicking butt, he drove past where he wanted to go. He turned around near Tiny's and returned to the crabbers' docks. He found a spot across the street and parked. He was only a couple of stone throws away from the party barge. He visited each dock. Everyone, of course, knew that Rebecca had been seriously hurt; they were all talking about it when Sammy walked up. They listened intently to the how and why it had happened. His plan was to enlist an army to go kick some ass. He had no problem.

The sporting goods guy, the two contractors, and the Publix store manager were on the porch. The realtor was inside snoozing off the beer. The four men were good-naturedly bantering back and forth with men from the neighboring cabins, bragging on how they had gotten away from their old ladies for the whole weekend and could do exactly as they pleased. The wives of the others were all presently at the raffle. The conversation shifted to other man-topics like best bait for the reds, where they were biting, size of outboard motors, best fishing boats, when a purposeful group of seven husky locals approached with Sammy in the lead. Six of the men walked up to the porch, standing in a line in front of the stairs. Without hesitating, Sammy heaved himself aboard the party barge. The sporting goods guy looked at the men. What the fuh..? When he saw Sammy, he shouted, "Hey, fella, what do you think you're doing!"

All conversation ceased. Everybody looked over from the cabins and watched Sammy in disbelief as he ripped out the gas tank line and picked up the tank and started sloshing it all over the boat. When it was empty, he tossed it away and reached for the spare. The sporting goods guy finally reacted. He jumped up to go stop Sammy, but he was roughly pushed back by the other men. The sporting goods guy's friends jumped up to help. A scuffle began while Sammy emptied the second can. He threw the can aside and jumped down from the boat. He lit a rag and threw it into the boat. WHOOSH! The boat was an immediate inferno. Cushions, carpet, decking all went up. There was prodigious heat. The aluminum began to melt and run. Sammy strode up to the sporting goods guy who was spitting mad and being held by two of the men while the other four burly locals kept his friends away.

"What the hell did you do that for!"

"You the owner?"

"Yeah!"

Sammy coldcocked him, breaking his jaw in the process. He crumpled. The men let go of him and he fell to the ground where Sammy in white fury began kicking him. The man's friends jumped on Sammy, but Sammy flicked them off with meaty forearm shivers. Sammy's friends began to wail on the three men while Sammy turned to kick the man again. The other porches emptied. The tourists soon outnumbered the locals, but the locals outweighed them by a good margin. It was a brawl. The party barge was sending up a torrent of black smoke. Two bubbas drove by pulling an airboat. It looked like their kind of fun. They chose the side of the locals because they looked more like their kind of people. They jumped into the fray and started pummeling the tourists. Over at the Crescent Beach Club, someone on the deck shouted fire.

People flooded out to take a look. Tammy came out, but not for long. She turned right around and went inside to call 911. "All hell's breaking loose in Crescent Beach!" she exclaimed. "Send police, fire trucks, and an ambulance. We need it all!" She gave the particulars. The dispatcher told her to hold the line. When the dispatcher came back on he said that Crescent Beach's fire chief had been contacted, and he'd do his best with the police and ambulance, but it was the Fourth of July and they were spread thin. One ambulance, Tammy knew, already had Rebecca in it. She went out to the deck again. A handful of men were flying down the stairs to mix it up, most likely against the locals. It was turning into a war.

Beau and Rusty were coming from Rusty's, approaching the Humpback Bridge and Main Street when they saw the smoke.

"Oh Lord," Beau said. "I hope that's not what I think it is." Beau drove through the stop sign, turning left onto Main Street. He had the golf cart floored. There was no doubt where the smoke was coming from and they could soon see the burning party barge down the side street. Beau pulled in under a live oak, a safe distance away from the fire. The squad car that had led the parade had its lights and sirens going and arrived at the street just after Beau and Rusty. It screeched to a halt fifty feet away from the boat. The part time rent-a-cop jumped out, assessed the situation, and jumped back in to radio for backup. He stayed in the car. The local fire engine arrived with its lights and sirens adding to the cacophony. The squad car was blocking the way and the fire engine driver blasted the truck's low-pitched, ear-shattering horn. Sprinting past the squad car that was trying to get out of the fire engine's way, Rusty knew that he had to find Sammy and neutralize him if there was any hope of quelling the melee. Beau wisely remained standing by the golf cart. Sammy wasn't hard to find. He was in the center of the fighting. He had a guy in a headlock with one of his powerful arms, and was slugging him with the other. Another guy was trying to bring Sammy down from behind; he had an arm around Sammy's neck. Sammy let up on the headlock and the guy he had been pummeling dropped to the ground. Sammy pried his assailant's arm loose, turned and threw him toward the burning boat. The guy fell hard, got up, and fled both the heat and Sammy. Sammy looked wildly around to do more damage. Rusty planted himself in front of him.

"Sammy, stop! You got to stop before someone's killed here. You got to stop…now!" Sammy's eyes were wild. Doesn't even know me, Rusty thought; no recognition in those eyes, only fury. Sammy looked like a goaded bear. Rusty put both hands out as Sammy ambled straight at him, carefully backpedaling, creating distance for more reaction time. "Got to stop, Sammy!" he said, again. Rusty squared up to Sammy. He knew Sammy would swing, but not which hand. Having both hands out gave him more options to defend himself. It turned out to be Sammy's right. Rusty deftly deflected it with his left forearm while at the same time drawing back and straightening his right arm with his thumb pointed down. As he pushed Sammy's punch away, he whipped his extended and flexed right forearm at Sammy, striking his face and breaking his nose. As the blow whiplashed Sammy's head backward, Rusty stepped behind Sammy and placed both hands around the nose area and yanked his head further back so Sammy was looking skyward and bent over backwards. With Sammy totally off balance and the equilibrium in Rusty's favor, Rusty pulled down his head with all his might sending all two hundred and sixty pounds of Sammy crashing to the ground with his head leading the way. Sammy lay there in a heap.

A crabber suddenly put a chokehold on Rusty from behind. Rusty's reaction was immediate and smooth and very fast. He bent down while reaching behind him to lay a hand on the guy's thigh for balance. At the same time he shifted his left leg behind the man which in turn opened up the man's front from the waist down. Bringing his balled left fist back and up, Rusty pounded the man twice in the testicles before bringing the same elbow up sharply into the guy's face. With the same arm, he then pushed the man backwards over his leg. Like Sammy, the man fell hard. Rusty spun around and drove a short punch into the guy's chin. The guy stayed down.

The street fight spread, the mass of bodies moving away from the intense heat of the burning boat. When the volunteer firefighters began spraying the party barge and truck, steam and smoke filled the air. Everyone was getting soaked. Steam was rising from the few shirts that hadn't been torn off bodies. More and more people circled the area to watch. With all the sirens, smoke, and flashing lights, word was out all over town. The raffle had reconvened when the ambulance took Rebecca away, but it was quickly deserted again, leaving Virginia, Louie, and a few others to continue drawing the winners. Concerned wives ringed the growing circle of spectators; the fight showed no sign of abating any time soon. The party barge owner still lay where he had been kicked by Sammy. The Publix store manager had gone down quickly, too; but the two contractors were giving as good as they got. The snoozing realtor woke up and walked to the screen door. At a thin five feet seven inches tall, he wanted no part of it. He quickly closed and locked the inside door.

One of the bubbas from the airboat smashed Rusty in the shoulder with the charred handle-end of a wooden paddle. Rusty figured the guy had tried for his head. His arm went numb. He backed away from the guy, shaking his arm, trying to get feeling back. The guy came at him again. Unfortunately for the guy, the feeling in Rusty's arm did come back. Like Sammy, the guy was right-handed. With a precise and lightning quick move, Rusty stepped into the guy's swing, deflecting it with his left forearm, then with the same hand slapped the guy twice, hard enough so his head snapped back with each blow, sunk a heavy right fist into the guy's gut, spun him around by the left arm while kicking a leg out. As the man fell onto his stomach, Rusty put an arm lock on him. It was the exact same maneuver Rusty had used to quiet Sammy five years earlier. Back then he was a trooper and excessive force and police brutality lawsuits and leaves of absence were always in the back of law officers' minds. He could have snapped Sammy's arm that day like a twig, but he didn't and let Sammy back up. But he wasn't a law officer anymore. He also didn't like people swinging sticks at his head. He kneeled on the guy's back and snapped his arm like a twig. The man screamed.

Rusty stood up and looked around. Tiny had waded in. Gentle giant no longer, Tiny was roughly pulling men apart, leaving several down on the ground in his wake. The fire was under control although the boat was toast and the paint job on the truck totally blistered. The firemen shifted to hosing the closest cabins. The siding was hot and more steam filled the air. Between Rusty and Tiny, the fight had abated somewhat, but several were still trading blows, while others were muckled on to each other, rolling around on the pavement and in the grass on the side of the street. The number of tourists in the melee had swelled to the point that the fight was becoming one-sided. Now's the time someone's really going to get hurt, Rusty thought. He ran up to the two firefighters manning the hose just as two State Trooper cruisers and a Sheriff's car arrived. Rusty yanked the hose away and turned it on the fighting men. It bowled a couple over and soon had everyone's attention. The fracas stopped completely when the men saw the stateys and deputies approaching. The troopers ordered everyone to sit down on the side of the street while they sorted things out. Rusty handed the hose back to the firemen and walked up to the troopers and introduced himself, telling them that he was a recently retired trooper. After he caught his breath and the adrenalin subsided, Rusty explained what had gone down. Norm arrived in his Subaru. Carrying his doctor bag, he quickly walked up to the injured. Close behind Norm came an ambulance. It was the same one that had taken Rebecca to the hospital. The EMTs hurried over to Norm who said, "You guys are working overtime today. How's the little girl?"

"Doctors are still working on her," one of them said. "Just heard over the radio that besides the broken arm, she has a broken leg. Concussed. Bleeding's contained. She'll be okay if infection doesn't rear its ugly head. Big if, considering what she was pulled out of and that compound fracture." He looked at the long line of men sitting on the ground. Several were wincing and carefully picking at their legs and arms: they looked more concerned about imbedded sandspurs than their bloody wounds. "What the hell happened here?"

"Little quarrel between the family of the little girl and the owner of the vehicle that hit her." The EMTs nodded, then began to work alongside Norm.

Sammy and the retail sports guy were brought in front of the troopers. Rusty positioned himself between the pair. The deputies and Tiny stood over the others. Neither Sammy or the retail sports guy was in very good condition. Sammy was woozy whereas the boat owner, although bent over hugging his ribs with one hand and holding his jaw with the other, was hopping mad. It was hard for him to talk, but he still made his case to the troopers.

"For some goddamn reason, this crazy son-of-a-bitch burned my boat and two of his buddies held me while he slugged me! Knocked me down and then kicked me! Guy's a lunatic!" Sammy's head was clearing. When it clicked who was talking and what the guy was saying, he saw white again and lunged for the man. He didn't get far. Rusty was the first to react and threw an elbow deep into his gut. Sammy doubled over. Rusty moved in front of him. The retail sports guy had jumped back, then grabbed his sides in pain from the sudden movement. He hugged his ribs and groaned. When he could straighten up again. "See! That son-of-a-bitch is certifiable!" he mumbled, through clenched teeth.

Sammy caught his breath. He yelled over Rusty's shoulder. "Yur lucky I didn't kill ya like ya kilt my niece, ya son-of-a-whore! Jest left her lyin' there in the creek, ya did!" Sammy started to move towards the man. Rusty put his hands on his shoulders, and shook his head.

"What!" the retail sports guy said. He looked at the troopers. "What's he talking about? Killing his niece! I tell you, this man is nuts!"

Norm, as well as the men he and the EMTs had been attending, were listening intently to the exchange. The majority had no clue why the fight had started. Norm walked up to Sammy and put an arm on a shoulder. "Sammy, Rebecca wasn't killed. She was taken to the Perry Hospital. Broken arm, broken leg, serious cuts. But she is stable. Ambulance guys just told me."

Sammy looked at Norm. Within seconds his eyes filled and his whole body sagged like air let out of a balloon. Tears began to stream down his face. He put a beefy forearm across his eyes and began to sob. His whole massive body shook. The retail sports guy looked at Sammy, then Norm. He looked at the troopers who were watching him closely. He turned back to Norm. "What are you talking about? Who's Rebecca? What happened?"

"When you crossed the bridge before coming here, did you see a little boy and a girl on their bikes?" Norm asked.

The man thought back. "Sure, they were coming down Main Street. Saw them, then looked right to make sure it was clear and pulled out. The kids were just turning onto the bridge when I pulled out."

"When you turned, your trailer clipped the little girl. Knocked her off the bridge."

Even with his broken jaw, the guy's mouth dropped. He slowly shook his head. "No way! Couldn't have! I would have felt something." Rusty, Norm, and the two troopers looked at him. Sammy was still sobbing. The man yelled for his friends to come over. Three of them stood up. The Publix manager's eye was seriously swelling and his lip was three times its normal size. The two contractors had an array of bruises and superficial cuts. The realtor who had been watching from behind the screen door, stepped out. When he walked over, one of the contractors looked him up and down.

"So where were you?" the contractor asked.

"Sleeping," the realtor lied.

"Through all the sirens. Right!" the contractor said, looking at him in disgust.

"These two were in the boat," the sporting goods guy said, pointing to the contractor and realtor. "Did you see us hit a little girl?"

"We were laying down," said the contractor. "All I saw was sky." The realtor nodded in agreement.

"Did you feel like a bump or anything." They both shook their head. "See," the sporting goods guy said, turning to the troopers.

"You might not have felt anything," Norm said. "It was probably just the guide pole. The little boy told me he just ducked under it. Wouldn't have taken much to tip her over."

The guy was already pale from pain, but he turned white. The guide pole! He looked over to the boat. No poles now, not much of a boat either. But it was possible. No, probable! Those goddamn poles! Oh Lord! The reality totally sapped what strength he had left and, not letting go of his ribs, he slowly dropped to both knees. He stared fixedly at the ground. After a few seconds he looked up at Sammy who had stopped sobbing. Sammy looked tired and resigned. He saw Sammy in a different light. He asked him, "How old is your niece?"

"Twelve," Sammy answered.

"Twelve," the man said, to himself. Silence. "I've got two girls. The oldest is twelve. Oh, Lord!"

"We're going to have to get formal statements from you and your friends here," one of the troopers said. "And from you, too," he said, looking at Sammy. "But we're also taking you in to Perry. Do we need to cuff you?" Sammy shook his head. "Who were the two that held this man while you punched him?"

Sammy looked over at his friends, then back to the trooper. "Can't say as I recall."

The trooper sighed and looked down to the sports retailer. "Point out the two men that held you."

The sports retailer looked Sammy in the eye and said, "Can't say as I recall."

The trooper looked at both men. "Alright then, into the cruiser with this one." His partner took Sammy by the shoulder and led him away. The trooper asked the sports retailer for identification. He handed the trooper his driver's license. Once the trooper had the info he needed, Norm said to the retailer, "And time for you to get in that ambulance." The guy didn't move. "You've got to get pictures of that jaw and those ribs. Could be internal bleeding."

The guy looked up at Norm. "Perry hospital?" he mumbled. Norm nodded. "Same hospital as the little girl?" Norm nodded again. "Then help me up."

The EMTs began loading the ambulance. As the bubba with the broken arm was being ushered past the troopers, he stopped and shouted, "If you're gonna throw someone in jail, throw that redheaded son-of-a-bitch in; he broke my friggin' arm!"

When Rusty turned towards the man, the man took a step back. "You attacked me with a weapon. Someone does that, he pays," Rusty said, calmly.

"The hell I did!"

"The hell you didn't!" shouted Tiny who was standing next to the two deputies. "You swung a stick at his head, hit him in the shoulder, then came at him again."

"I second that," said Beau who had come over from the golf cart.

One of the troopers said to the bubba, "Looks like you should have kept your mouth shut. Guess now we'll be taking you in for assault with a deadly weapon. Your arm can be tended to later."

"Let him be; I won't press charges…but," Rusty said, walking up until his face was six inches from the bubba's. "I want you to know, fella, that once your arm heals, you can come around and try again anytime. But just remember this: if you do, I'll break both next time."

"Easy there, Trooper," the statey said to Rusty.

"Ex-trooper," Rusty said, still staring hard at the bubba.

Tiny walked up next to Rusty and added, "And if'n there's anything left of ya after Rusty gits done, I might jest join the fun." The bubba looked at the pair, turned, and meekly walked to the ambulance cradling his arm.

The ambulance pulled away full. Those with simpler wounds were tended to by Norm in the tiny clinic below his house. Norm cleaned, stitched, and bandaged until past seven o'clock. Exhausted, he didn't feel like walking to the Club for dinner and tending bar like he usually did on the night of the Fourth. But he also didn't feel like making dinner. Sighing, he decided to compromise: he'd drive over. He hopped into the Subaru. Tammy had a Children's Special going on featuring hot dog and cheeseburger plates that came with a pile of fries and paper cups of coleslaw. It was the only day of the year that strawberry and chocolate sodas were on the specials menu, as well as hard ice cream cones, banana splits, and chocolate sundaes. Each table setting included a long sparkler and a paper American flag placemat. Usually a festive scene, the tone was muted except for the kids running around outside on the deck with their sugar high. Norm joined Virginia and Beau, Jimmy and Crystal, Tiny and T, Rusty, Louie, and Charley at their usual spot. All had come to watch the fireworks from the deck.

Norm wolfed down a cheeseburger while the others, who had eaten earlier, nursed drinks. Tammy was tending bar. Every adult in the room was talking about the ugly street fight. Beau was beside himself worrying about the town. All were concerned about Rebecca. Virginia and Louie bemoaned that almost no one had claimed the raffle prizes and they would have to contact winners scattered all over north Florida. Crystal noted how quiet it was in the restaurant. Charley described the mood perfectly when he said, "This town is just plumb wore out." The sun was going down and the kids lit sparklers. They could be seen through the windows as they waved them in circles and figure eights.

"Getting close to show time," Beau said. He scooched out his chair, preparing to stand up. "You tending bar again, Norm?" Norm nodded as he wiped his mouth.

"You're not going to watch the display?" Rusty asked. Norm shook his head.

"Fireworks are 'bout his least favorite thing," Charley said. "Second maybe to airboats."

"Fireworks are bad, Charley, but not nearly as bad as airboats," Norm said.

"Seriously, Norm? That's like unpatriotic or something. What's wrong with fireworks?" Rusty asked.

"Here we go," Louie said, sitting back.

Norm smiled at Louie before he turned to Rusty and said, "Nothing really in the big scheme of things, I suppose. But years ago my ex-wife and I were traveling around

New England so my sons could look at colleges. I wanted them to see my alma mater which was Dartmouth College in New Hampshire, so we went there, too."

"Ivy League," Louie said.

"Is that like *major league*?" Charley asked.

"You could say that," Louie answered.

"It was right around the Fourth when we arrived at Hanover where the college is. I didn't want us to stay in the fancy inn there, so I booked a cabin at a lodge in a pretty little colonial town just to the north. The town had it all. Right on the Connecticut River that separates New Hampshire from Vermont, rich bottomland farms, hills for hiking, a tiny little ski area, and the place with the cabins was right on a beautiful pond that was deep enough for trout and large enough for two nesting loon families. I have to tell you that the call of the loon for me is like the call of the wild—eerily beautiful. When I hear it, it makes me feel like everything's all right with the world. We paddled all around that pond and a couple times we even saw one of the loons swimming with a chick on its back.

"Anyway, we were at the lodge for the town's fireworks on the Fourth. There was a ball field at one end of the pond where they set them off. After a buffet dinner down by the water and just before the fireworks, my sons hopped into one of the lodge's canoes, my wife and I in another. The pond was pretty crowded with all sorts of boats which made it kind of hairy because none of the canoes or rowboats had any lights. We paddled out into the center and waited. It was quite a fireworks display, not as good as ours here maybe, but pretty darn good. We were oohing and aahing like everyone else until we heard the loons begin to freak out. It was heart-wrenching. There was no doubt that it was the loons, but their call was totally different. It was like they were screaming in terror. Then the pieces of blown up fire works starting falling on us like rain, some of them hissing as they met the water of that pristine pond. I wondered how the fish liked that…or the frogs, turtles, or what have you. I mean a lot of crap fell into the pond that night! It really turned me off. Early the next morning I went out to take a swim. Cans, plastic bags, Styrofoam cups, Burger King and Kentucky Fried Chicken wrappers, all sorts of garbage. The shore was a mess. To me the whole thing was an example of how another beautiful piece of this planet is trashed for man's amusement. I haven't watched fireworks since."

Norm looked out the window and saw the kids playing with the sparklers. "And that's beside the fact that it's dangerous." He looked at Rusty. "Two years ago, one of our volunteer firemen was helping set off the fireworks display out on Snowy Key. He lit a fuse to a mammoth rocket and it sputtered and went out. He walked up to it, not realizing that it was burning internally, inside the fuse wrapping. It exploded just as he got to it. Blew him right off the ground. Burned, shrapnel, and an eyeball was blown out of its socket. But, I'll tell you that guy is tough. A Vietnam vet. He had the wherewithal to find his eyeball, even though he was bleeding heavily, and picked it up. Held it in his hand, not that it was any good, while the others boated him to shore. Luckily we had an ambulance on standby in case of some accident like this. The EMTs tried to stabilize him in the ambulance and drove him to the ball field where a helicopter came and evacuated him to Gainesville. He was very lucky he didn't bleed out. Yup, one tough son-of-a-gun: he was back at work a month later sporting an eye patch. Has a glass eye now."

"Is he still a fireman here?" Rusty asked.

Norm nodded. "But you won't find him helping with the fireworks anymore. His wife won't let him near them."

"Medium height, stocky fellow with thick dark hair. Got some scars on his face."

"Yeah, that's him," Norm said. Rusty nodded: one of the guys he had taken the hose from. Suddenly there was a BOOM! They looked out the windows and the sky over the Gulf was lit up: the fireworks had begun. Everyone got up from the table to go outside; that is, everyone except Norm. He went over to tend bar.

The bar emptied at the marina, too, leaving Frank alone inside. Frank had been impressed that Bobby had come to work after Norm stitched him up. He told him it was above and beyond, but still didn't send him home. He put Bobby to work on the draft beer detail: he could fill glasses and pitchers one-handed. BeeBee was very solicitous. When the fireworks began, Frank shooed Bobby and BeeBee outside so they could watch. Why not? Everyone else had gone outside because even though the picture windows looked out over the water, the polarizing muted the colors. Bobby and BeeBee stood a little apart from the others, heads tilted back. BeeBee sidled up close to Bobby.

Frank had remained inside for several reasons. One, he didn't care about the fireworks. Two, it gave him a chance to get a head start on cleaning up. And three and most importantly, he didn't want to leave the cash register alone. It had been a very good evening and it was full. In excellent spirits, he began wiping down the tables, looking occasionally out the windows. He saw an exceptionally bright display with all sorts of colors as well as sparkly comet-like tails that looked like tarantula legs cascading to earth. It covered the sky and lit up the waterfront where everybody was standing. He saw BeeBee next to Bobby, and he saw her extend a hand behind him and put it briefly on a buttock and give it a squeeze. Frank froze in mid wipe. It was dark again. Did he really just see that! He stood there waiting for the next rocket to light up the sky again. When it did, he saw that Bobby had moved a little ways away from Bee, both their heads back, intently watching. He began to wipe the table again. He must have imagined it. No way; Bee wouldn't do that. She's my wife! He moved on to the next table. No, no way. But, try as he might, he couldn't get the picture of that hand out of his mind.

Chapter Eighteen

Beau, with Virginia sitting at his side, brought the boat up to Jimmy's dock. Crystal stood there waiting. Rusty, in the bow ready to fend off, thought she looked like a million bucks. Tall and with her long hair pulled back into a ponytail, she was wearing flip flops and a snugged up white terry cloth cover-up that contrasted nicely with her deep summer tan. In one hand she held a mask, snorkel, and a pair of flippers, in the other a small wicker picnic basket. Rusty didn't have to fend off; when the boat was still a foot away from the dock, Crystal gracefully stepped aboard and Beau put it in reverse. They backed around, and headed out the main channel to the Gulf. Once they cleared the last channel marker, Beau turned south towards the Salt and Pepper Keys. When the boat was at cruising speed and Crystal was done petting Skillet, the lab hopped onto the seat in the bow. He sat straight up with his ears flying out behind him as he turned this way and that, watching different sea birds pass by. It was a gorgeous summer day with blue sky, a soft breeze, and the temperature in the mid eighties. The trip to the Keys took just under an hour with little conversation. Like Skillet, everyone was enjoying the ride.

The Keys were surrounded by boats. Because it was a bird preserve and especially because the Marine Patrol put in more of a presence this time of year, no boats were pulled up on the narrow, bright white beach. Everyone was anchored. Behind the beach were sea oats and other tall, sub-tropical grasses, a ton of sandspurs, a couple of cabbage palms, and a few stunted live oaks and red cedars providing rookery for mostly egrets and herons, although there were the occasional roosting brown pelicans and cormorants. In the middle of the island was a small brackish pond. The Keys were one of Skillet's favorite areas because the water's edge always had a mix of brown pelicans, toy-looking sanderlings as well as a mix of larger sandpipers, terns, oyster-catchers, skimmers, and other seabirds. In the winter they were joined by flocks of the much larger white pelicans and assorted sea ducks, principally redheads and mergansers. Beau had to severely discipline Skillet the first time he and Virginia had come here snorkeling years ago. Usually Skillet stayed with them when they went swimming, but not this time. He didn't stick around and swam so hard straight towards the island and birds that he made a noticeable wake. Beau and Virginia were intent on finding scallops and didn't notice until they heard Skillet barking. He was streaking up and down the beach having a great time. There was an absolute cloud of birds above the island. Beau was furious. He went and got Skillet who had a very thorough lesson that the island was off-limits.

Beau pulled back on the throttle as they approached the Keys and slowly maneuvered past the boats, snorkelers, and dive flags. Dive flags were supposed to be three hundred feet from each boat, but if everyone adhered to that, there wouldn't be enough room. Consequently, people shared flags or didn't have them, and usually boaters were careful like Beau. As they idled along, searching for a good spot, Beau began to tell Rusty all about scallops.

"Perfect timing," Beau said. "Sun's almost straight up which makes them easier to see. That and they seem to like the sun, too: they'll come right up to the top of the grass on a sunny day. They like the needle and blade grass, but most of all, like Charley told you at the Club the other night, they really like those underwater tumbleweeds. They seem to congregate there."

"Any size limit, Beau?" Rusty asked.

"Nope. Just amount; two gallons in the shell or one pint of meat each, not including what we snack on out here."

Beau found a spot in a sandy channel a hundred feet or so off the largest island. Rusty threw the anchor out. He measured the depth with a paddle and was relieved to find it wasn't much more than five feet. He'd be able to stand up no problem: an important detail when someone didn't know how to swim. Maybe he could pick up scallops with his feet.

"The scallop," Beau continued, "is what's technically called a bivalve mollusk. It lives about a year and the female lays somewhere around a million eggs which hatch in March, although only a small fraction of those eggs make it to adulthood. It takes thirty-six hours for eggs to become larvae that drift in the water for a couple of weeks. After that they become what's called spat and they cling to blades of sea grass where their shells form. During all this, larvae to spat, over ninety percent of them die. The ones that don't, eventually fall from the grass to the sea bottom where they remain for the rest of their short lives. They're filter feeders which means they filter or siphon microscopic plankton, including their own babies, and May is the big growing month. Fish and Game says they begin spawning around September tenth. How they can pinpoint a date like that is beyond me, but I know it's a drop in water temperature that triggers it. That's when they're most susceptible because they use up all their energy for reproduction. They have no energy to move anymore."

"Beau," Virginia said, putting on her flippers, her mask already on. "Would you please hand me the, the… the whatchamacallit tube-thing."

"It's called a snorkel, Sugah," Beau said, handing it over."

Virginia sighed and shook her head in minor frustration. "Yes, dear, I know; but, oh never mind." She stood up, snorkel in place and net bag in hand. When she sat on the gunnel, ready to let herself in the water, Skillet started shaking.

"Stay," Beau said, sternly and pointing at Skillet. Virginia eased into the water and swam away from the boat. Skillet stayed, but was still shaking. He was watching Virginia intently. When Virginia was a safe distance away, Beau said, "Okay." Skillet leaped from the bow seat over the gunnel into the water. He started swimming toward Virginia who knew he would and was facing the boat.

"Skillet, now you stay away!" she said. The last thing she or anyone needed was a ninety-pound lab scraping a back with those toenails. Skillet obeyed and happily swam around in ever increasing circles. Virginia began to look for scallops.

Beau and Crystal got ready to go in. When Crystal took off her cover-up, Rusty tried looking everywhere but at her. He didn't succeed. A mature, lovely woman. She was wearing a dated one-piece bathing suit, something that Esther Williams might have worn. The similarities didn't end there. She, too, had a full figure with all the right curves in all the right places. She folded the cover up neatly and put it on a seat. She reached for her mask and snorkel. Rusty had to force himself to look away. In a few moments he looked back. The mask was pulled up on her forehead with the snorkel fastened by a double plastic ring threaded by the mask's strap. She began to put on her flippers. Her movements were graceful, yet matter of fact. The popular C&W song *She Don't Know She's Beautiful* popped into Rusty's head.

Virginia returned to the boat before anyone else had gone over the side. She pulled herself up onto the wooden swimming platform next to the motor and opened her bag. There were four scallops inside. She pulled them out and handed them to Beau. Virginia said to Rusty, "The custom is to eat the first scallops of the day. Brings good luck." Beau, in turn, handed them to Crystal along with a shucking knife.

"Would you do the honors, Ma'am?" Beau asked.

Rusty looked at the three of them. "Raw?" he asked.

"Absolutely!" Beau said, as he cut up a lime. Crystal smiled as she shucked the scallops. She was as fast as any of the ladies who had competed in the shucking contest a week ago. Beau squeezed some lime on each scallop and passed them around. Rusty was the last to eat his. To his surprise, it was delicious.

"Okay, then," Beau said. "In I go!" He pushed himself off the side. Crystal was next. Rusty hadn't touched any snorkeling equipment and looked down at the three snorkelers. Crystal looked up at him questioningly.

Rusty blushed. "It seems you all have forgotten that I can't swim," he said.

Crystal swam back to the boat and draped her net bag over the gunnel. "It's not deep, see?" she said, standing on the bottom. "Jump in and I'll give you a lesson. Basically you just got to learn how to float."

Rusty nervously lowered himself into the water. Crystal laughed. Once his feet touched the bottom, Rusty said, "Come on now! It's not funny!" Virginia and Beau were swimming fifty feet away from the boat, looking down, their heads moving back and forth. Skillet circled them at a respectable distance.

"I'm just laughing at the expression on your face. Here, give me your hands," she said, backing up and extending her arms. Rusty had no problem doing that. Her hands felt small, strong, and good in his. "Now push off the bottom and try to extend your legs out behind you so you're horizontal." Rusty did as she said. Hanging on to her, he could keep his head above water. She towed him around. "See, nothing to it. Now let your feet come back down, and let me show you how to tread water." The lesson continued until he mastered floating, treading water, and an advanced doggy paddle that allowed him to move clumsily around the boat by himself.

"Now the snorkel and mask part," she said, before gracefully pulling herself up onto the gunnel, shifting her butt at the last second so she sat on the gunnel facing out. She leaned over to grab the remaining mask and snorkel. Rusty saw a very full and handsome cleavage. "This is the trickiest part," she said, letting herself back down into the water. She attached the snorkel before spitting into the mask and rubbing her spit around. She laughed again when she saw Rusty's face. Rinsing the mask, she said, "Wiping it with spit helps to keep it from fogging. Here, put it on." Rusty adjusted and put on the mask. "Practice breathing with the snorkel with your head out of the water." Rusty did as she said. "Now put your head in the water a little, not deep, and practice breathing like that."

Rusty did as she said, again. No problem. He also could clearly see the bottom. Cool! After a couple of minutes he stood up, spit out the snorkel, and smiled. "Piece of cake."

"Now try it floating around. I'll make sure you don't drop down too much." Rusty started floating with a tiny leg kick and his arms awkwardly treading water out to the side. Crystal supported him with one hand on his stomach, the other on a thigh. Rusty tried to concentrate on breathing evenly, but it wasn't easy feeling her hands on him. He turned his head and saw her body underwater. Everything seemed magnified. Oh my, he thought. Crystal wanted to see if he could do it on his own and took her hands away. Unfortunately his head was still tilted towards her with the tip of the snorkel precariously close to the water. Without her holding him up, he sank a couple inches. It was enough to fill his snorkel with water and he choked.

He also panicked and took in more water. Crystal immediately yanked him up and the snorkel out of his mouth. He spit out water, croaking. Crystal wasn't laughing.

"You okay?" she asked, concern all over her face. Rusty caught his breath and calmed down.

"Yeah." He looked around. Virginia and Beau were headed back to the boat. Skillet was already resting on the swim platform. "But I think it's time you looked for scallops. You go on. I'll be fine. I'll just practice a little around the boat here. Beau and Virginia can babysit me for awhile."

"You sure?"

"Yup. Go on…and thanks." Crystal smiled and pulled the net bag off the gunnel before pulling down her mask and swimming off. Virginia and Beau dumped their scallops in a cooler and went off for more. Rusty carefully practiced around the boat. By the time Crystal returned, he felt pretty confident. He showed her and she smiled.

"You got it. Next is to learn to dive down…"

But Rusty shook his head. "I think I've had enough for one day, Ma'am. I think I'll take a break." He grabbed hold of the boat and pulled himself up and in. Crystal couldn't help but notice the large muscles working in sync across his back and shoulders. She also saw that his entire back was bright red.

"Rusty, didn't you put any lotion on your back before coming out?"

"Not hardly. Can't reach it."

"With your complexion you should have at least worn a tee-shirt in the water." She hauled herself up. Rusty tossed her a towel. She dried off and threw the towel back to him and grabbed a tube sitting on the center console. "Dry off and turn your back to me!" He did as she said. Crystal began to smear and wipe in the creamy lotion. Rusty stared out over the water as her hands played over the muscles in his back. Sunny, refreshed by the water, the Gulf calm with mini ripples lapping the boat, her hands rubbing in the lotion—just doesn't get any better than this, he thought. He felt no guilt that this beautiful woman rubbing his back was his good friend's wife; he was simply enjoying the moment. Besides, it was all innocent enough. Crystal's next sentence jarred him.

"Why didn't you ever marry?" she asked.

He had a pat answer that he had used over the years. "With my line of work, I never wanted to risk it. Something could have happened to me at anytime."

"That's pretty weak. Lots of troopers are married and have families."

Rusty was silent a couple of beats, then answered, "There's another reason: I never met the right woman." Rusty paused before adding, "I guess I never met someone like you."

Crystal's hands stopped rubbing lotion on his back immediately. Her voice was very cool. "Rusty, I am a happily married woman."

Rusty whipped his head around. His expression was a mix of she didn't know what. He blurted out, "I know that, Crystal! Believe me I wasn't trying…I wasn't trying to…I just want you to know that I think Jimmy is one hell of a lucky guy and I'm envious. That's all, honest. I'd never try…" His voice tailed off. He looked miserable.

She looked at him evenly, before smiling. "I know that, Rusty. Turn around." She finished slathering the lotion on him and slapped him lightly on the back. "All set. Guess I'll go back in now and get your share of the scallops."

Rusty smiled. "Good idea."

Crystal acted as if nothing had happened, and so did he. But they weren't fooling each other. A threshold had been crossed.

While Rusty, Crystal, Beau, and Virginia were scalloping in the Keys, Norm was in the Perry hospital checking on Rebecca. The scene was all too familiar. The smells, the noises, the bustling around, the fluorescent lights. Like most doctors, Norm had come up through the ranks, having spent plenty of late nights and early mornings patching up emergency room wounds during residency before moving to Sarasota. There he had joined the cardiology department of Sarasota Memorial and risen to become one of its top surgeons. There were a lot of old people in Sarasota and he had performed many, many open-heart surgeries. He was widely respected and in demand for lectures and instruction all over the state. He worked long hours and made great money. People would say he had it all: a beautiful wife, two intelligent kids, a house on the bay with a Lyman at the dock, two Mercedes, and belonged to the right club. But all that was before his wife went through a mid-life crisis and began messing around with the club's tennis pro. Eventually, they divorced and, embittered, Norm had moved to north Florida.

He still had those gifted hands, but now they were mostly limited to patching up the wounds caused by fishing accidents and barroom quarrels. He also gave physicals, dispensed antibiotics, treated flus and infections. If he couldn't take care of something, he still had connections at Shands Hospital in Gainesville and could get his patients in at the drop of a hat. Norm was also considered the town's emergency veterinarian. His major animal doctoring achievement was taking care of Skillet after he had been brutally attacked by a pit bull. The wounds were extremely serious and Norm had become a hero in the eyes of Beau and Virginia when Skillet survived. During hunting season he was constantly brought in dogs that had been slashed by the tusks of razorback hogs out in the woods and swamps. In the early years at Crescent Beach, he had been paid as much in food—fish, crabs, shrimp, oysters, vegetables and meat from the countryside—as in cash; but, as the complexion of the town had changed over the last several years, so had the method of payment. He was being paid in dollars a lot more often now, and was even able to bank some of it. The one thing that hadn't changed was that he still was the town's only doctor.

The first thing Norm did when he arrived at the hospital was to confer with the specialist who had come down from Tallahassee. Rebecca wasn't okay. Infection had already set in. Norm was not surprised in the least. With all those open, deep wounds plus the bone sticking out of her arm getting a dose of that foul creek water, he would have been amazed if there hadn't been any infection. Rebecca was receiving as large a dose of antibiotics intravenously as her body could handle. She had a dangerously high temperature, her skin was red and hot to the touch. Luckily it was a closed, simple transverse fracture in her leg which meant it was an even break right across the bone and only a tiny bit of reduction had been necessary. The leg had been easy to stabilize and cast in plaster. No screws or metal plates necessary. Her arm was another matter. There are two bones in the forearm area—the radius and ulna. It was the ulna that had snapped and pierced her skin. It was also a spiral fracture, running diagonally down the bone, and separated. There was significant damage to the soft tissue—muscles and ligaments—around the bone. The specialist had spent a lot of time in the operating room trying to remove all the foreign and contaminated material—dirt, pieces of oyster shell, damaged tissue—before he could realign the bone. The doctor wasn't sure if he would have to go back in, so he fixated the arm externally by attaching a long screw to the ulna through her skin above and below the fracture. He attached an external metal bar to the two screws to hold the bone in place. Even for someone as experienced as Norm, the sight of little fair-haired Rebecca with all the tubes, screws and metal bar, leg elevated in a cast, wounds all over her feverish, skinny body about broke his heart. She was sleeping when he entered her room. Her parents, Clem and Katharine, and the man who had hit her, were not.

All three were sitting close together. Katharine stared as if in a trance at Rebecca. Clem was clutching his Yamaha baseball-style hat in both hands; tears streaked his face. The sporting goods guy looked about as dejected as anybody Norm had ever seen. He was also wired up: Norm could see the external screws holding his jaw together. The man looked up, gingerly nodded hello, then looked back at Rebecca. Clem looked up, too. Norm put a hand on his shoulder. He shouldn't have. The touch of sympathy opened a floodgate of tears. Embarrassed, Clem fled the room. The same doctor who had worked on Rebecca also wired the jaw. He told Norm that the man had come to see Rebecca as soon as he was allowed out of the operating room. He had stayed the night with her, only leaving to use the john down the hall. Over the course of the night, Clem, Katharine, and the sporting goods guy got to know each other. At first it was more than awkward: Katharine had been downright hostile. But when she heard how the accident had happened and that the guy didn't have a clue that Rebecca had been hit, she began to soften. It was obvious that he was devastated. She and Clem had returned home late that night. When they came back early the next morning and found the man asleep in a chair next to Rebecca's bed, Katharine's heart went out to him as well as to her daughter.

Norm, too, had returned to Crescent Beach to spend the night. He told Tammy and called Beau about Rebecca. This meant that the whole town would know how she was by the end of the next day, which was Norm's intent: better than an announcement in a local newspaper. When Norm returned to the hospital, he found the three still at their vigil. The specialist was there, too. Norm conferred with him. Things didn't look any better and the doctor wanted Rebecca transferred to Tallahassee Memorial Health Care, his home base that had a reciprocal agreement with the Perry hospital. The specialist wanted to personally monitor her around the clock. Katharine and Clem looked at each other when the specialist told them he wanted to move Rebecca. They instantly gave their permission, but Norm knew that they were also wondering about where they could afford to stay. Even if they only commuted to Tallahassee, more than three hours one way, it would still be tough on their miniscule budget. They asked the doctor if it would be possible to stay somewhere in the hospital. The doctor sadly shook his head.

The sports retailer looked like hell warmed over. When he saw the doctor shake his head, he mumbled through his wired jaw, “We live in Tallahassee. You can stay with us. We've got three bedrooms and the girls can move in with each other and it's not more than a ten minute drive to the hospital.” Katharine and Clem hesitated. “Please. It's the very least we can do. Please...” The man's voice cracked and he buried his face in his hands. Clem pulled up a chair next to him and put an arm around his shoulders. Katharine and Clem agreed to stay in the guy's house and Norm left the three of them to sort out the logistics. Norm drove his Subaru down to the local police station to pick up Sammy. The sporting goods guy had refused to press charges and Sammy was free to go.

Chapter Nineteen

It was dark when Juan Gonzales got up out of bed, but it was dark every morning when he got up. Today was special, though. Today, in celebration of his birthday two days ago, he was going saltwater fishing. He couldn't remember the last time he had taken a full Sunday off from picking peaches or tomatoes or whatever crop was in season to go fishing. When he was working down near Lake Okeechobee, he'd drive over to the lake in his old Dodge pickup and fish in the evenings after work. If he caught a bass or a catfish, it meant fish tacos for a couple of days. The kids loved fish tacos. But that was months ago and the only fishing he had done these days was in slow moving creeks mostly full of alligator gar. He and his family were living in a beat up trailer provided by the farmer he worked for just outside the little town of Mayo. His trailer was one of five set in a row for migrant workers. The farm was something over an hour from the coast and Juan had heard of a little village called Crescent Beach where the fishing was great and you didn't need a boat: there was a small, public point at the end of the road where anglers could try their luck. He had been thinking about it for days and had fine-tuned his two cheap rods and reels that were now standing ready, along with his tackle box, by the trailer's front door.

He could hear his *señora* patting tortillas for his breakfast. Breakfast was going to be special, too: spicy *huevos rancheros* just the way he liked them. He put on jeans, a tee-shirt, and sneakers. After relieving himself and splashing water on his face, he ran a comb through his thick, jet black hair. He checked on the kids before going to the kitchen. He quietly opened their door. Sound asleep. His little angels. The two girls, four and six, shared a bed while the two older boys were in the double bunk. They were the light of his life. He softly closed the door. His *señora* was at the stove. Stocky like her husband and about the same height, something over five feet, she was dressed in a white blouse brightly embroidered at the neck and at the end of the short sleeves. She also wore a simple dark skirt and practical flats. She would be taking the children to church later and it was her Sunday best. She handed her husband his specially prepared *yerba mate* when he sat down at the kitchen table. It was unusual for Mexicans like Juan and his *señora* to drink *yerba mate* because it was a South American drink, but years ago a Paraguayan family had introduced them to the strong, caffeinated tea sipped through a metal straw. The end of the straw was bulbous and perforated to prevent sucking up the finer particles of the tea that was placed loose in a cup or gourd. Placing a hand softly on his shoulder as if to say 'good morning,' his *señora* served him the eggs. A little plate with a stack of warm *tortillas* wrapped in a cloth was already on the table.

"*Buen provecho,*" she said. Juan smiled up at her, patted her hand, and began to eat. The *señora* prepared her own *yerba mate* and went over to her rocker at the end of the kitchen where she sipped the tea and watched her husband eat. The kitchen was long and narrow with two small windows, and lit by a single overhead light. Besides the table and rocker, there was a sink, refrigerator, and gas range. Strings of red peppers and garlands of garlic hung from the ceiling. There was the unmistakable scent of cilantro and there were baskets of potatoes, onions, and carrots crowded together on the linoleum floor. Shelves full of canning jars, plates, glasses, and cups lined the walls except for above the *señora's* rocker where there was a crucifix. The carpeted living room adjoined the kitchen. It was demarcated only by where the linoleum left off and carpet began. It had one large window. An old brown fabric couch and two stuffed easy chairs faced a large TV with a small statue of Christ on top. Three of the four walls had pictures of Christ: one of Him nailed to the cross wearing the crown of thorns, one of The Last Supper, and one of Him giving a sermon on a hill. The fourth wall had colored soccer team pictures with a banner of strung-together green and red plastic Mexican pennants.

When Juan finished eating, the *señora* refreshed his *yerba mate* and cleared the table. Juan finished the *mate* quickly and stood up. His *señora* smiled; she could see that he was eager to go. He worked so hard. She was happy to see him happy. She handed him some cheese *enchiladas* wrapped in brown paper for lunch before grabbing his Los Angeles Dodgers hat and putting it on his head. They embraced by the front door. Juan picked up his fishing gear and yanked open the door that always stuck a little in a bottom corner.

"*Si Diós quiere y con suerte, comerémos pescado esta noche,*" Juan said, hoping it was true that they'd eat fish tonight.

"*Ojalá,*" she said. "*Vaya con Diós.*"

He pulled the door shut and walked towards the Dodge. The pickup had a cap and there was an old mattress, a few carpentry tools, and a large cooler in back. Juan put his fishing gear on top of the mattress and the enchiladas in the cooler. It was just getting light. Juan hesitated at the door of the truck and looked out over the fields. He never tired of seeing the mist created by the cool early morning air meeting the warm soil: it looked so soft and harmonious. He hopped into his truck and drove out of the farm, turning onto a limestone road that brought him to the paved highway. He headed west. He smiled. Won't be long now, he thought.

There was no traffic around Perry and it was only minutes before Juan turned off Highway 19 towards Crescent Beach. Twenty minutes later he crossed the cattle gap at the edge of town. Except for people entering a church to his left, there was little activity on Main St. He soon came to a mini-shopping complex on the right with five storefronts. After passing a humpback bridge, there was a bait shop on the left with a short, pretty and pregnant woman ladling shrimp. He guessed she was a Latina. She looked up as he passed and waved. He waved back. Main Street curved around softly as it followed a creek emptying into the main channel leading out to the Gulf. He passed the Crescent Beach Club on the Gulf side and to the right was a small park with a bunch of live oaks. A few hundred yards later, the road ended at a cul de sac. No one was there and there was plenty of room for him to park without disrupting traffic. He got out of the truck, stretched, and walked around. Mud flats were visible, but the tide was coming in. Perfect time to fish, he thought.

The shore was lined with boulders and other riffraff to keep storm water and spring high tides from eating away at the road. Juan sat on the largest boulder on the point. He put his arms out to either side, palms down on the large rock. He'd pull out his fishing gear in a few minutes, but right now he just wanted to look at the Gulf. He saw a couple porpoises a ways out. Not a good sign because they were probably feeding and scaring away the fish. He turned to look back along the shoreline. He could see the restaurant he had passed plus all the waterfront houses on that side of town. A boat pulled into the main channel a ways beyond the restaurant. Juan watched it approach. He could see two men. He continued to watch the boat, wondering how it would be to own such a thing. It was set up for fishing: the seats in the right place, a half dozen rigged fishing rods in holders, a radio antenna, a big powerful motor, center console and windshield. He knew he'd never be able to afford something like that, but he could still dream. The channel out to the Gulf was only fifty feet from where he sat. The two men were talking. The older of the pair was heavy set and pale, decked out in the latest sports fishing garb. The other, who was steering the boat, was very tan and wore khakis and a short sleeve shirt. He looked sinewy and fit. He reminded Juan of some of the cowboys inland at the ranches.

The man at the helm did a double take when he saw Juan. He stared hard. Juan had been around enough to know that when an Anglo had that look, it wasn't good. He quickly turned away. The boat passed him and headed out into the Gulf. Juan waited a couple beats, then nervously turned to look back at the boat. With his hand still on the wheel, the man had pivoted around and was watching him like a hawk. It was unsettling. Eyes averted, Juan got up and walked until he was out of sight at the rear of the truck. He fiddled with this and that until the boat was way out in the Gulf. What was with that guy, he wondered while getting his fishing gear together.

Juan fished for hours. He was having a great time. He caught two flounder, a baby shark, one trout, and several dogfish. He rejected only the dogfish, everything else was on ice in the cooler. It wasn't until early afternoon that he took a break to eat the *enchiladas*. He leaned his pole against the rear of the truck and took the *enchiladas* out to the large boulder he had sat on earlier. He took a bite. *Que rica*, he thought. He was so lucky to have such a *señora* who took such good care of him and who bore him such fine children. She was such a good *madre* and hard worker. Life is good. *Gracias a Diós,* he had work, food for his family, a roof over their heads, and a truck. God was looking out for them.

After finishing lunch, Juan was about to start fishing again, but the sun was warm, his belly full, there was a soft breeze, and the water gently lapped up against the rocks. He closed his eyes and fell asleep. He woke to the sound of a motorboat slowing down. It was the same boat as earlier. It was still a ways out, but he could see the two men silhouetted by the lowering sun. He thought that the sinewy man was looking at him with a pair of binoculars, but couldn't be sure. When the boat was a lot closer, he could see that the sinewy man was definitely looking at him again. It gave Juan the creeps. He looked away. He didn't want any problems. When the boat was close by, he walked back to the rear of the truck.

"Do you know that guy, Jimmy?"

Jimmy watched the Latino duck behind the truck for the second time.

"Nope. Why?"

Jimmy's client shrugged. "You just seem kind of interested in him is all."

"Don't see many Latinos around here."

"Sure seemed nervous."

"Yeah, he sure did."

In a few minutes Jimmy expertly docked his boat. He unloaded a cooler full of fish and fileted the trout and redfish in record time as the client watched.

"Damn, you're good, Jimmy," the man said.

Jimmy smiled. "Ain't my first rodeo, not by a long shot."

He sent the man happily on his way with his cooler full of filets. Jimmy walked over to his neighbor's land which jutted out into the channel. He could see that the Dodge pickup was still at the end of the road. He returned quickly to the house and went inside. Crystal wasn't home and Jimmy made a beeline to the phone. Rusty picked up on the second ring.

"Think I'm being scouted by one of them Colombians," Jimmy said.

"How's that?"

"Guy out on the point. Watched me go out this morning, waited around all day, then watched me come back in. Acted mighty nervous when I looked at him."

"Probably just fishing, Jimmy."

"Wasn't no pole I could see."

"Why do you think he's Colombian?"

"Why not?"

"Because most of the Latinos around here are Mexican, that's why."

"I ain't taking no chances. Going to check him out. Want to come?"

Rusty sighed. "You're probably dead wrong, but, yeah, I'll go."

"I'll be there before you get down the stairs."

Rusty hung up the phone and headed towards the front door. He hesitated, wondering if he should get his service pistol from the bedside table drawer. He shook his head and continued out the door. Rusty waited less than a minute before Jimmy pulled up in his truck. Rusty got in and Jimmy quickly turned around and sped towards the point.

"You know this is crazy, don't you?" Rusty asked.

"We'll see."

They passed TNT Shrimp Company. T was still bustling around as much as she could bustle with that big belly.

"T's quite a worker," Rusty said.

"That she is."

Juan had called it a day and was just climbing into his pickup when they arrived at the point. Jimmy pulled broadside in front of the Dodge and hopped out. Rusty shook his head and slowly opened his door. Juan's eyes got real big as he looked from one to the other. It was the sinewy man from the boat and a taller, stocky man he hadn't seen before. They didn't look friendly. Jimmy walked up to the driver's side, Rusty to the other.

"Who are you?" Jimmy demanded brusquely.

Juan spoke little English, but he understood that. "Juan Gonzales," he said, nervously looking from one to the other.

"What are you doing here?"

"Feeshing…"

"Then where's all your fishing gear? Both times I seen you, you didn't have no rod."

Juan didn't understand. "*No comprendo…*"

"Right! And now you don't understand me!" Jimmy looked at Rusty. "What did I tell you?" Jimmy turned back to Juan. "You're Colombian, right?"

"Colombiano? No, no, Mexicano."

Jimmy reached in and planted a finger on Juan's chest. "Colombian."

"*No, no. Mexicano.*"

Rusty didn't see any threat, the little guy was scared to death. He walked around to the back of the truck. He saw the fishing poles and cooler. He opened the cooler and saw that it was full of fish.

"Jimmy, you might want to take a look here."

Jimmy gave Juan an icy look. "You," he said, poking his chest again, "stay put!"

Jimmy walked around. Rusty flipped open the cooler. Jimmy didn't say anything. He returned to Juan.

"Why did you come here to fish?"

Juan shrugged his shoulders. "*No comprendo.*"

"Get out of the truck!" Jimmy motioned for him to get out. Juan's eye's got even bigger. He grabbed the steering wheel and shook his head. Jimmy motioned again. Again Juan shook his head. This went on until Jimmy finally opened the door and yanked him out. Juan stood there shaking.

"*Por favor, no problemas, no problemas…*"

Jimmy frisked him. He found nothing but a small Case pocketknife.

"Jimmy, for Pete's sake, he's just a guy fishing on a nice Sunday afternoon."

"Maybe." Jimmy thought for a second. "One way to find out. T can talk his lingo." He took hold of Juan's arm and started marching him to his truck. Juan balked and pulled away. Jimmy reached for the arm again. Juan backed away until he bumped into his own truck. "Enough of this crap!" Jimmy said, pulling a pistol from the small of his back. Juan's hands shot straight up in the air.

"*Por favor! Por Favor*!"

"Easy, Jimmy! No need for that!"

Jimmy ignored Rusty and motioned Juan to get in the back of the truck. Juan quickly complied. Jimmy, still holding the gun, joined him. Without taking his eyes off Juan, he said, "Drive us over to T's, Rusty." Shaking his head, Rusty climbed in and drove over to the bait shop. T came out of the little building and saw Jimmy motion with his pistol for Juan to get out. She didn't say anything until everyone was out of the truck. She walked up to the trio. A tad of relief surfaced in Juan's eyes when he saw her.

"What's going on?"

"Want you to talk to this guy," Jimmy said. "Says he's a Mexican and he's just here fishing. Want to see if it's true."

"Why else would he be here if he wasn't fishing? What have you been doing to him? Poor guy looks scared to death."

T began talking to Juan. Hearing the Spanish was a huge relief. A torrent of Spanish followed. He began rapidly answering all her questions. Rusty heaved himself up on the tailgate. Jimmy put the gun away. It didn't take more than five minutes before T turned angrily to Jimmy.

"You should be ashamed of yourself, Jimmy! Juan here is just what he says he is, Mexican. He said for some reason you kept calling him a Colombian."

"How do you know he ain't Colombian?"

"Because Mexican Spanish is Mexican Spanish. You can't fake it. Believe me, this guy is Mexican. He works on a farm over in Mayo. Two days ago was his birthday and he came over here on a rare day off to celebrate by fishing. I know that area and he told me stuff he could only know if he worked over there. I don't know who you thought he was, but he's who he says he is."

Jimmy looked over to Rusty. Rusty had an expression like, 'I told you, you were crazy.' Sheepishly, Jimmy said, "Could you tell him to climb back in the truck and I'll take him back."

T told him, and Juan started towards the truck. He suddenly turned around and walked back to take one of T's hands in both of his. "*Muchisimas gracias, Señora!*"

Jimmy drove to the point, not saying a word, and dropped Juan off. Rusty got out of the cab to shake Juan's hand. Juan didn't know what to think. Jimmy waited for Rusty to get back in and drove away. When they came to the bait house, Jimmy suddenly turned in. Jimmy said to Rusty, "If the Mexican comes down the road, flag him down, will you Rusty?" Rusty nodded, wondering what Jimmy was up to. Jimmy got out of the truck and walked up to T who was just locking up. "Got any more of them bags of frozen eatin' shrimp, T?"

"Sure do. Lots."

"Three and five pounders?" T nodded. "Good. I'd like to buy two of the five pounders."

"That's a lot of shrimp."

"I got a lot of guilt." T smiled and unlocked the door. She returned in a jiffy with the two large Ziplock bags. Jimmy asked, "How do you say, 'I'm sorry' and 'gift?'"

"*Lo siento* and *regalo.*"

Juan was coming down the street and Rusty flagged him down. Juan pulled over, wondering now what! Jimmy walked around to the driver's side. He said, "*Lo siento.*" He handed the bags to Juan. "*Regalo.*" Juan looked from the bags to Jimmy before breaking into a grin.

"*Muchas gracias.*" Jimmy nodded and Juan pulled away. A few miles out of town and after checking the rear view mirror a couple of times, Juan stopped the truck. He carried the shrimp around to the cooler and rearranged everything, putting the shrimp on the bottom. On the trip home he pondered the ways of the Anglos. Hard to comprehend. He parked the truck close to the trailer and his kids exploded from the trailer and excitedly surrounded him as he hauled the cooler inside. They crowded around, as did his *señora*, to see how he had done. Juan proudly held up each fish before putting them into the sink. He picked up the still frozen shrimp and handed them to his *señora.*

"*Camarones?*" she asked.

Juan nodded. "*Si, fue un regalo.*"

After she made room in the freezer and put the shrimp away, Juan began to tell her about his day.

Chapter Twenty

"I'm tellin' ya, Bobby, that woman's poison. Ain't nuthin' good gonna come of it. Leave it alone. Yur jest askin' fer trouble," Whacko said, climbing into the Ford Torino. Bobby walked around and got into the passenger side.

"Whacko, I jerked off for seventeen years and now that I'm finally getting some hot pussy, you're telling me to leave it be?"

"Ya don't have to tell your old cellie ya was jerkin' off. I heard ya plenty of times."

"You did!"

Whacko laughed. "Hell, yeah. I know ya tried to be quiet, but I always knew when ya came. Yur breathin' was difrent."

Bobby pictured Whacko in the bunk above him, listening. He forced the thought out of his mind. Whacko started the car.

"Anyway, you going to give me some crystal, or not?" Bobby asked.

"In the glove."

Bobby opened the glove compartment and pulled out Whacko's little canvas satchel. He looked inside. Meth, glass pipe, and butane lighter.

"Take the whole thing, pipe and all. Got me another kit at the kitchen."

"Thanks, Whacko. BeeBee's a regular nympho, but with this she'll be off the charts! She's going to screw my brains out!" Bobby put the packet inside his shirt pocket and unconsciously began rubbing his thighs in anticipation.

"So, y'all done tryin' to win back yur ex?"

Bobby exhaled. "There's nothing there. If Tammy'd show any interest, I'd still be trying; but she's made it pretty obvious she's got no interest at all. She's happy with the doctor. And he's an okay guy, too." Bobby held up his bandaged hand. "Certainly took good care of me."

"Shoulda took good care o' ya. From what I hear, ya was a hero."

They drove along in silence. Bobby spoke up again. "So, I'm messing around with BeeBee. Whacko, I'm only human. If a babe like BeeBee comes on to me—I mean, a horny broad who looks like that—I got to take advantage!"

It was Wednesday morning, Bobby's day off. He and BeeBee had made plans to go into Gainesville, the big city where they wouldn't draw attention. Whacko would drop him off at the Steinhatchee Road where Bobby would wait in the woods for BeeBee to show up in her T-Bird. Whacko would continue on the limestone roads to his meth kitchen while Bobby and BeeBee would shack up somewhere. BeeBee said she had it already worked out and had made reservations. As they drove towards the Steinhatchee Road, Bobby looked out over the countryside. A few simple houses with weathered siding and a derelict pickup or two in the yards. The land was flat as a pancake with either pine plantations or pasture demarcated by rusty barbed wire fences. A few head of light brown cattle myopically grazed here and there. The air was still. It was going to be another scorcher until the usual mid-afternoon downpour cooled things off. Other than getting married in Georgia, Bobby had never been out of Florida. He'd never seen snowcapped mountains or felt cool mountain air.

He wondered if he ever would. Probably not, he thought. Whacko approached the Steinhatchee Rd.

"How you gettin' home?" Whacko asked.

"It'll be dark when we get back. BeeBee'll let me off at the dump and I'll walk the logging trail back to town."

"Still think yur makin' a mistake, Bobby."

Bobby got out of the car. "Guess we just pick our poisons, Whacko. You're into drugs, I'm into BeeBee. So to speak," he added, smiling.

"If yur so lily white, then what's that in yur shirt pocket, lover boy?"

"Just once a week, and today's party time! See you tonight, and thanks."

Bobby shut the door and Whacko drove off. He stepped off to the side of the road where he hid behind the thick trunk of a live oak. He didn't have to wait long. The turquoise convertible, top up, arrived ten minutes later. Bobby looked up and down the highway. No one in sight—no surprise. On this highway, if there were more than a couple of pickups on the road, it would be the height of rush hour. Bobby got in and slid down low in the seat, ready to slide all the way down if they passed anyone. BeeBee gave his thigh a squeeze. Bobby smiled nervously. "Let's go," he said.

First stop was BeeBee's bank in Perry. Bobby slumped way down in the seat while BeeBee withdrew a wad of cash from her account. It looked like a lot of money.

"Won't Frank notice?" Bobby asked.

"It's my account. I told him a long time ago in Lauderdale that I didn't want to have to come to him every time I needed money. So, he set up an automatic deposit thing. Being in Deadsville, I haven't spent much. So, plenty of money. And Frank's got no reason to check. As long as I don't use a credit card, we're free and clear." She squeezed his thigh again and pulled out on U.S. 20. It was a good couple hours to Gainesville.

Bobby had no idea that Whacko used the same bank. Whacko didn't have an account, but he did have a safety deposit box. Bobby and Whacko split expenses down the middle and after rent and groceries Bobby never had much left over. Whacko never talked about his personal finances, but he never had a problem coming up with his share. Bobby guessed that Whacko was more than getting by selling drugs, but he would have been totally blown away to know that Whacko had a safety deposit box crammed full of hundred dollar bills. Whacko was a low key, but successful drug dealer. When he resumed making meth after prison, he cut out all middlemen and only sold to people with a solid reputation in the biz. It was steady income with a huge profit margin.

Bobby also would have been surprised to know that his name and signature were on a card giving him rights to the box. Whacko had no relatives he was close to, and no friend other than Bobby. And Bobby was his cellie. He had stood up for Whacko plenty in prison. If it hadn't been for Bobby, he would have certainly been reamed by big horny inmates or possibly beaten to death if he resisted. Bobby had kept the bad guys at bay until Whacko had found his niche in the prison drug trade and had been left alone. Whacko never told Bobby about the money or box because he didn't want it to affect their relationship. They were just buddies, cellies. They were like two guys who had shared the same foxhole in a firefight, except the firefight had lasted for years. Whacko also knew that he had been burning the candle at both ends for a long time and he recognized signs that his body was failing. But, he didn't care; like he told Bobby, it was all about the ride. But he did care about Bobby and that's why he had forged his name on the bank card—to give Bobby a good chunk of change and make things easier for him if he kicked. When Bobby co-signed the lease agreement for the trailer, Whacko xeroxed copies and practiced Bobby's signature until he signed it perfectly on the deposit box card. Perfectly fine with the bank to have two customers for the same box. All they were interested in was the rental income.

Whacko negotiated the labyrinth of limestone roads to the shack. When he arrived, he turned off the car and sat staring at the shack for a good ten minutes. He just didn't have the energy to get out of the vehicle. He needed a pick-me-up. He reached for the glove compartment then stopped in mid-reach, remembering that Bobby had the satchel. He sighed. It was an effort doing the slightest thing these days. He was always exhausted. He didn't tell Bobby because he didn't want to get a lecture. When Bobby was around, Whacko watched TV or sat at the kitchen table. He tried to look normal when he got up to get a beer from the fridge, but even that was an effort. He almost never made anything to eat; Bobby did all the cooking. He looked again at the shed. It was a good thirty feet away. He heaved himself out and walked heavily to the front door. He put a key in the padlock, wondering like always why he bothered to lock it. Someone would bust in or not. A stupid padlock wouldn't make any difference. He made a beeline to a cabinet where an identical canvas satchel to Bobby's was stashed. Exhausted by the short walk, he leaned on the counter as he prepared the pipe. He took a hit of meth. There, that's more like it, he thought. He felt a fluttering in his chest and could hear his heart clattering away in his ears like an old Model A with the timing off. But he felt much, much better. More energy. He looked eagerly around the room at all the ingredients waiting to be processed. He rubbed his hands together and got to work.

Whacko had his Bunsen burner going and was mixing this and that about the time BeeBee and Bobby passed through High Springs. Many people believe in fate, that everything is somehow cosmically connected, pre-ordained. Bobby was not one of those people. However, he might have reconsidered if he had known that T was at that moment at her parents' farm in Trenton and that she would be taking her father to a late afternoon physical therapy session across the street from the Hotel where he and BeeBee would be shacking up. T's father had been freeing up a bound manure spreader three weeks earlier when his helper, through a miscommunication, engaged the tractor's PTO, resulting in his knee getting tangled up with the spreader's shaft, seriously wrenching it and tearing tendons. He was operated on and had only recently begun therapy. It was his right knee and there was no way he could drive, and T's mother hated to drive in the Gainesville traffic. So, T, her father, and the therapists had worked out a Wednesday schedule which coincided with T's weekly trips to the farm to bring back fresh vegetables to sell in Crescent Beach.

BeeBee and Bobby pulled up to a four-story hotel on Rte. 121, across from Florida University's Butterfly Museum and kitty corner to a doctors' complex. Bobby looked at BeeBee in awe. "The Hilton?"

"Just the best for my lover boy. Besides, no one from Crescent Beach would ever come here." She stretched outside the car before walking to the trunk where she pulled out a non-descript suitcase. She handed it to Bobby. "Got to look legit. Our name is Leonard. Mr. and Mrs. Jeffrey Leonard and they're expecting an early arrival. They should have our room all set. And here," she said, handing him the wad of cash. "You're going to need this when we register."

A doorman opened one of the two big glass doors with a fancy *H* etched on it. It was maybe the first time in Bobby's life, outside of prison, that someone had opened a door for him. Somehow he had the presence of mind to step back and let BeeBee pass through first. She smiled at him in approval. The lobby was high-ceilinged, bright, and with comfortable-looking leather couch and chair ensembles scattered around. The desk concierge wore a dark suit, white shirt, and a red tie. There was also a bright red rose in his lapel. He smiled ingratiatingly. Bobby felt like he had entered a different world. While the concierge made out a receipt for what amounted to a week's pay at the marina, Bobby looked out the floor-to-ceiling windows to an Olympic size pool. He had never swum in anything so luxurious. He wished he had brought a bathing suit. Then he remembered Norm had said to keep his hand dry. He also guessed, knowing BeeBee, that there might not be much time for that. The concierge handed the receipt to Bobby and pushed a buzzer behind the desk. A bellboy quickly came around the corner. The bellboy looked at Bobby in cowboy boots, slacks, and a Polo shirt stretched thin against his dinner plate pecs and bulging biceps. Bobby picked up the suitcase. It looked like a toy in his hand. Bobby smiled. "Thanks, but I think I can handle it okay." BeeBee proudly took Bobby's arm and they walked towards the elevator while the concierge and bellboy ogled them in envy.

They took the elevator up to the third floor and found their room. When Bobby opened the door, BeeBee grabbed him by the shirt. "Wait a minute, Buster! I want to be carried across the threshold." Bobby put the suitcase inside and picked her up effortlessly and kicked the door shut as BeeBee put a lip-lock on him. He walked over and laid her gently down on the king size bed. He started to take off his shirt, but BeeBee quickly rolled off the bed, saying, "I've got presents first!" She went over to the suitcase and put it on a bureau. First she pulled out a black silky negligee and laid it on the bed. Next was a bright yellow bikini for her and a new bathing suit for him. In the bottom was an expensive looking, black felt cowboy hat. She walked over and put it on Bobby's head. "I told you, cowboys turn me on." She smiled at him. "Try your suit on. I'll be right back," she said, grabbing the negligee.

Bobby heard BeeBee flush the toilet as he tried on the bathing suit. A perfect fit except for the fact that he had a tremendous erection and looked like he was wearing a mini tent. He put his boots back on as well as his hat. He also got the pipe, meth, and lighter out. He laid them out on the bureau and faced the bathroom door, impatiently waiting for BeeBee. When she came out he knew right away he was going to have trouble pacing himself. Her blond hair fell over her shoulders and was set off by the black negligee. Her full breasts swayed and peeked through strategic gaps in the garment. Her nipples thrust out against the silky material. Very brief, lacey panties rounded out the outfit. For her part, she took one look at his prominent mast and literally licked her lips. She hurried up to kiss him. Her hand was in his bathing suit in a flash. Somehow he pushed her away. "Wait, BeeBee!" Her hand was still in his bathing suit.

"What?"

"You've got to try this first. It's unbelievable stuff," he said, nodding towards the bureau. "Sex with this is beyond over the top." That sounded good to BeeBee, although it was with reluctance she removed her hand. Bobby showed her how to inhale the smoke. "Basically, just like smoking pot." He melted the crystal for her and nodded when to inhale.

A few seconds later, she looked at Bobby. "Whoa!" she said. She sat down on the bed. Shivers of pleasure ran through her. "Whoa!" she said, again. Smiling broadly, Bobby sat next to her. She looked lusciously infused with pleasure. She lay back on the bed. She closed her eyes and gently rolled her body back and forth. She opened her eyes and looked intently at Bobby. She cupped her breasts and began toying with her nipples, never taking her eyes off Bobby. Bobby lightly ran the fingers of his good hand up and down the inside of her thigh before kicking off his boots and pulling down his bathing suit. He kneeled at the foot of the bed and removed her panties. He pulled her to him and buried his face. He was still wearing his cowboy hat when he surfaced. Their eyes locked.

"Ride me cowboy, ride me!" she whispered, frantically.

Bobby rode her long and hard and deep. He didn't take his hat off. It was a trophy ride.

They made love three times, alternating between margaritas at the mahogany paneled bar off the lobby and brief swims in the pool. Bobby was careful to keep his hand dry. When they were ready to leave, BeeBee wanted Bobby to drive because she was still high as a kite. She waited at the front door for him to drive around with the turquoise T-Bird. The car was certainly an eye catcher and it caught T's eye as Bobby pulled up to the portico. T was waiting at a traffic light with her father in his pickup when she recognized the car. Then she saw Bobby, wearing a black cowboy hat, get out and take the suitcase from BeeBee and put it in the trunk. BeeBee got in and they drove off. T was flabbergasted. Well, well, was all she could think. When she got home late that night, she told Tiny first thing. Tiny had many attributes, but keeping a secret was not one of them. He told Charley the next day. And Charley was worse than Tiny keeping mum about anything.

Chapter Twenty-One

Whacko did not come home that night. Nor the night after. About the time that Bobby was having his second go-around with BeeBee in Gainesville, Whacko was totally worn out from all the mixing and cooking. He needed another pick-me-up. Damn inconvenient, he thought, as he was right in the middle of mixing two flammable ingredients. Can't make a mistake here! He carefully turned off the burner and brought his meth kit from the counter over to the cot. He needed to sit down. He wearily prepared his hit. Need an extra big one this time, he thought. He heated the rock and inhaled. Better, much better, although his ears were clattering even louder than before. He put the pipe back into the satchel and stood up. Whoa, Nellie! Mighta done too much, dizzier than hell! The timing of the Model A motor of his heart was still off, but the already out-of-character high RPMs had increased twofold. Suddenly the clatter of the motor changed as he took a step towards the counter. There was a horrific clunk when the engine of his heart threw a rod straight into his chest: a deep, terrific thud, and then there was no more clattering. There was nothing. Whacko was dead before he hit the floor.

Late the next morning in Crescent Beach, Virginia was sitting at her desk trying to balance her checkbook. She couldn't make hide nor hair of it; the numbers just didn't make sense. She slammed the cover closed and rubbed her eyes in frustration and anger. She couldn't hide it any longer. Something was seriously wrong with her—her head, her vision, her memory, her vocabulary, all of the above. She would tell Beau tonight. Had to. She sighed. And that would be after telling the Stewed Tomatoes today that she would no longer be able to play bridge with them. She felt guilty about telling the girls before her own husband. But, oh Lord, how could she tell Beau? He would be so upset and worried. But it had gone on too long.

At the beginning of the week she had called Harriet who would be hosting the bridge group to tell her that she should get a permanent replacement for her. It was a tough phone call to make and Harriet wanted to know why. Virginia said that she would come over Thursday to explain. She looked at her watch. Even those numbers didn't make sense! Was it safe for her to drive? Oh Lord! She took a deep breath and tried to relax.

She got up and walked over to Skillet who was snoozing on his beanbag. He snoozed a lot these days. We're all getting old, she thought. She sat on the floor next to him and gently stroked his head. He opened his eyes, stretched out all four legs, and went back to snoozing. Petting Skillet calmed her. It wasn't the first time she had come over to pet him when she was confused or disoriented. It seemed the more upset she got, the worse it got. Stroking Skillet seemed to soothe her anxieties. After a little while, she looked at her watch again. The numbers were what they should be. She was surprised. It was already eleven o'clock! Time to get a move on! She stood up and walked over to the kitchen counter for her purse. The keys to the Caddy were, thank God, right where they were supposed to be on their little hook by the pantry door. Maybe she wouldn't tell Beau until tomorrow. Tonight was poker night. Let him have fun one last night before unloading.

She nodded to herself. Yes, I'll tell him tomorrow. She felt a reprieve of sorts, although there were still the girls to face. She looked over at Skillet and said the magic words, "Anybody want to go for a ride?" For an old dog, Skillet was on his feet lickety-split.

Skillet and Virginia took the limestone road to Steinhatchee. She stopped briefly in the middle of the bridge that arched over the Steinhatchee River at the town's edge. She loved the view looking down into town. A single crab boat was coming in from the Gulf, otherwise not too much happening on the river. Many of the docks of the fish houses were vacant; most of the crabbers must still be out. A few delivery trucks were parked in front of the restaurants and marinas, and she could see a man loading cases of beer onto a dolly. There was very little traffic on the main river road. Steinhatchee looked very sleepy today. She crossed the river and swung left and down and around to the river road. Two blocks away heading towards the Gulf and overlooking the river was Harriet's weathered wood-shingled cape. It looked like it belonged more in a Maine coastal town or on the Cape in Massachusetts than Florida. The trim around the double hung windows was painted a deep burgundy. Full flowerboxes adorned each downstairs window. But what Virginia noticed right away was that the driveway had four cars in it: everyone was already there. Virginia exited the Caddy with dread. She entered the house without knocking. All four ladies were seated at the card table, cards in hand, chatting, Bloody Marys on the table. They all turned to look at her.

It went as well as it could. What was Virginia to say except that she had a problem, but didn't know what it was? She said she was going to get checked out, but there was no way she could be depended on to play bridge in her present condition. She described some of her difficulties. No one suggested brain tumor or Alzheimer's, but it was on everybody's mind, especially Virginia's. After the confession, Virginia urged the bridge game to continue. She watched them play, walking around, smiling, peering at everyone's hand as if she still could have participated. But she couldn't have. She'd have a brief flash where everything made sense—the bids, the leads and play of the cards—but mostly she was bluffing. They had a simple lunch of crust-less sandwiches and clam chowder. They drank more Bloody Marys than usual, everybody trying to do her best to appear gay. But, Virginia felt that it was more like a wake than anything else. When she left, she promised she would be in touch with any and all news. She re-crossed the bridge and made it half a mile before the tears began and she had to pull over. As she sat sobbing on the side of the road, Skillet moved over and put his head in her lap. She stroked his head absentmindedly.

After awhile she began to drive again. She turned off the paved highway onto the limestone road. It was by rote. Ten minutes later the customary mid-afternoon downpour began. It was an exceptionally heavy one, a real toad strangler. Virginia slowed way down, the windshield wipers going a mile a minute. The events at Harriet's played over and over in her mind. The rain was really coming down, but she was oblivious; she kept on driving. When the rain stopped and the sun came out, small clouds of steam rose from the road. Puddles were everywhere and culverts were close to overflowing. Virginia surfaced from her reverie. Although she was still on the Steinhatchee-Crescent Beach Road, she looked around in astonishment, then dread. She didn't recognize a thing. She was sure that she had never been here before. She had absolutely no idea where she was!

She looked over at Skillet who had his head out the window. His head as well as his side of the seat was soaked. Stupid, she thought. She must have left the window down during all the rain. But Skillet didn't seem to mind. Like always, he was totally preoccupied taking in all the smells. She looked back to the road. Where in Heaven's name was she? She stopped at a fork. Had no idea which way to go. She was confused. How many times had she driven between the two towns? Fifty? She looked over to Skillet as if he could help. Because of the rain, she didn't see any tracks and had no idea which road was traveled more than the other. What she didn't know was that she was still on the main limestone road to Crescent Beach. She *had* been here fifty times before. Had turned right fifty times before. This time, however, she turned left. She drove along hoping for a familiar landmark. There were none. She went around a wide curve. Surely she would have remembered this curve if she had come this way. But nothing clicked. She wondered if she should turn around, but then thought that the road was in good shape and must come out on the Crescent Beach highway at some point. She kept on driving.

The forest green Caddy had been spotless when she left. Beau washed it regularly once a week, just like he had with their old Caddy that had been destroyed by the storm in '93. But it wasn't clean now; limestone caked the lower third of the body. As much as she tried, there was no avoiding the puddles, some of them like mini-lakes extending from one side of the road to the other. Virginia could see Beau shaking his head when he saw the car. Virginia kept on, going this way and that without a clue where she was headed. Mostly she was surrounded by pine plantations. She hadn't seen a house since the rain started. She looked at the clock on the dash. It didn't make sense. Oh Lord! Where are we! The pine suddenly gave way to lower swampland. There were a few live oak on island-like knolls, but mostly very large Spanish-moss-draped Cypress trees and sweet gum were scattered about. Different sized cypress knees peppered the swamp. It looked like serious gator territory. Trees on both sides canopied the road, dimming the area and making it look dark and mysterious. Virginia knew that the swamp was full of all sorts of critters besides gators: wild pigs, panthers, bobcat, and lots of snakes. It was Pogolandia. She also noticed that the water was way high in the swamp and a couple culverts couldn't handle the flow, causing different size streams to cut across the road. She drove very carefully. She had been driving for a long time. How was her gas? She looked at the dash again, searching for the gas gauge. Nothing there made much sense. There, there's the gas gauge. She leaned closer for a better look. It's…BAM! The front tires of the Caddy dropped down into a trough made by an overflowing culvert. It was a good twelve inches deep by two feet across. The hard limestone surface had been eaten away by the stream. Underneath, it was soft. The Caddy was stopped cold. Skillet flew off the seat and banged into the dash. Virginia hit the steering wheel hard. The car stalled.

Virginia was stunned for a second or two. Skillet climbed back up on the seat from the floor and looked at her. She looked at him. He looked unfazed. Labs were tough, Beau had said more than once. Wish she could say the same about herself, she thought. She felt like crying. Her shoulder hurt like the dickens. She wondered if she had broken something. She stuck her head out the window and looked down. Serious trouble. She started the car, although she already knew it would be fruitless trying to get out. She put it in reverse and tried to ease it out. The Caddy was front wheel drive; the tires spun slowly, but the car didn't budge. She tried gunning it. No luck. Put it in forward and tried the same. Tried rocking it. Nothing worked. The car had only ground its way in deeper. There wasn't a chance in hell now: the car was resting on the frame. Virginia turned it off, put her hands in her lap, and sat back, closing her eyes. Skillet put his head in her lap and she began to pet him.

They stayed like that for some time. When Virginia opened her eyes, she continued to stroke Skillet. "What do we do now, Skillet?" Hearing his name, he opened his eyes and raised his head up to her. "Do we sit here and wait, or do we go for a little walk." Skillet looked like he was up for a 'walk,' another of his favorite words. Virginia felt better; not as panicky, more together, less confused. "Let's see if I can read numbers now." She turned the ignition on and the gauges lit up. The numbers made sense. "Almost six o'clock!" she exclaimed. They had left Harriets before three! We were driving for over three hours? No way! She looked at the gas gauge, something below half. Lots of gas, that is if they could have gone anywhere. So, what to do? Surely someone will come looking for us. But when? Beau will have gone to poker and won't miss us until ten or so at the earliest. The rain has probably washed away our tracks where we went wrong. Who knows where we are? But there's still a good couple of hours or more of light. And the highway might be just ahead. Or, we could stay here, with the windows up when the bugs come and run the AC to keep from cooking; wait it out. But what about carbon monoxide? What about those people stuck in snowstorms who run their cars too long for heat? Maybe we should walk for an hour or so to see what's what. Should move around some anyway. Maybe come across a hunter or a logger. If there are any splits or turns in the road, just mark the right way back. If we haven't found anything towards dark, we can just turn around. Virginia thought about it for awhile longer before making up her mind. "C'mon Skillet, we're going for a walk."

Virginia leaned over and used her left arm to open Skillet's door. Her right hurt too much. The road bisected the swamp for quite a ways. Virginia started thinking about bugs, mosquitoes in particular as they began to walk. No problem right now, but come sunset… She put the bugs out of her mind. She looked up. It was hard to tell where the sun was because of the canopy. They entered a right hand curve when suddenly there were high-pitched squeals almost underfoot. She jumped back as two little pigs bolted out of the tall grass. The piglets ran away down the middle of the road for all they were worth with Skillet barking in hot pursuit. There was heavy sloshing to Virginia's left and a huge black sow scrambled up out of the swamp. The sow's beady eyes pierced Virginia, but when Skillet's barking and the piglets' squealing registered, it took off. Virginia saw that Skillet had almost caught up with the piglets. The sow galloped after Skillet. Virginia shrieked, half in fear for her dog and half for being left alone. "SKILLET, NO! SKILLET, NO!" She saw Skillet follow the piglets into the swamp with the sow furiously close behind. She could hear tremendous splashing and Skillet's continued barking. The barking stopped and the sloshing slowly receded until it was silent. Virginia didn't know whether to keep on walking or turn around. She stood there, fearing the worst.

After what seemed like forever, she heard sloshing again, steadier, not as frantic as before. She wondered if it was the sow coming back for her. She held her ground and waited. Although she waited less than a minute, it seemed a lot longer before Skillet finally emerged. He clambered up to the road and shook. Looking somewhat embarrassed for having disobeyed his mistress, he slowly returned to her. Virginia sunk to her knees in relief and held her arms out to a very wet lab. She was happy and angry at the same time. She hugged him then grabbed his collar and mildly shook him. "Now you STAY with me, you got that? You STAY with me!" It was a mild rebuke. She was too relieved to do otherwise.

She checked Skillet all over. Not a scratch. He must have realized that the sow would have torn him apart and quit. Good choice, Virginia thought—that sow probably outweighed him by a hundred pounds. The pair continued walking. They went around a bend and walked another half-mile before coming to yet another fork. Virginia debated whether to turn around. She swatted at the first mosquito. She'd go just a little farther. The right side was a little wider with less puddles. Virginia chose right, but not before she bent and broke branches, marking the way they had come. A little ways up they rounded another curve. Virginia stopped in her tracks. Skillet looked back at her wondering what was up. There, off in the distance, in the absolute middle of nowhere, was a little shed with a white sedan parked out front.

Chapter Twenty-Two

"T seen 'em with her own eyes."

"And with whose eyes other than hers would she have seen them, Tiny?" Beau quipped.

"Her father's. He seen 'em, too," Tiny answered, seriously. "But, o' course, he don't know who they was like T did."

News to everyone at the table except Rusty. He looked down at his cards. Tiny was spreading dirt; but none of us is perfect, he thought, and certainly not Bobby and BeeBee. He just wondered where it would all lead. Maybe Frank knew, maybe not. But, it's a sure thing that he'll find out soon; it'll be all over town now. Question is, where does it go from here? These things mostly didn't turn out well. How many times had he been called in for domestic disputes, shootings or fights between or over spouses? He had no idea, but he knew it was a lot. He didn't want to hear anymore. He changed the subject. Laying his cards down on the table, he turned to Norm. "What's the latest with Rebecca?"

Norm laid his cards down, too. So did the others. "She's been moved to the hospital in Tallahassee. Round the clock supervision, still heavily sedated with a lot of vancomycin being pumped in through an IV for staph infection. She is septic which means her whole body's swollen, inflated. They're taking cultures of the infection trying to isolate the specific type so they can most effectively treat it. Everyone's obviously hoping for the best, but at this point it's a crap shoot. The infection is beyond serious. Sammy's got his truck running and is driving up tomorrow."

"Can't believe that feller dropped the charges," Charley said, "after all Sammy did to 'im and his boat."

"The guy's devastated," Norm said. "He's taking it like he hit his own daughter. He's probably in the Tallahassee hospital right now at her bedside. In Perry, he never left her room."

"Frank said he'd been drinking earlier," Jimmy put in.

"Who doesn't when he goes out scalloping?" Louie asked, leaning under the table to pet Bad Dog at his feet.

"Frank also said he was drinkin' that light stuff they call beer," Charley added. "That crap don't hardly count."

"Doesn't matter what beer he drank. Too much time had passed. He would have been legal by the time the troopers arrived and the fighting stopped: no way he could have blown a point-o-eight B.A.C.," Rusty said.

"B.AC.?" Charley asked.

"Blood Alcohol Concentration."

"You know, guys, I think I'll call it a night," Beau said. "I'm about worn out. Besides, I never saw my blushing bride this evening." He looked at his watch. "Maybe still got time to take a hot tub with her."

"Need ya some company, Beau?" Charley asked, gathering the cards.

Beau didn't deign to answer. Charley didn't expect him to.

Louie pushed his chair away from the table and stood up. Bad Dog sprung into action. "Disappointing night for Bad Dog here without getting to visit with Skillet. He's been itching to go for awhile now. Guess we'll mosey on."

"I'm pretty done in, too, and, by the look of things," Norm said scanning the room, "Tammy doesn't need any help tonight."

"Talk to you for a second, Norm?" Beau asked.

Norm was surprised by his tone. "Sure."

"Out on the deck?" Norm nodded, and they went outside. Charley, Tiny, and Louie got up, too, leaving Jimmy and Rusty.

"Buy you a beer, Rusty?" Jimmy asked.

"Absolutely."

Jimmy went up to the bar and brought two bottles back. He sat down and they clinked bottles and took long pulls. Jimmy leaned back and put his hands behind his head.

"Doing anything special tomorrow night?" Jimmy asked.

"Nope."

"We was wondering if you'd like to come over for some scallops. Crystal met up with a boatload of tourists who like getting 'em, but not cleaning 'em. Traded her labor for a whole pile. Be lucky if the three of us can eat 'em all."

"Imagine if they're anything like her chicken, bet you and I'll have no problem eating the whole mess."

Jimmy laughed. He looked thoughtfully at Rusty. "Have a good time scalloping the other day?"

"The best! Still learning how to pick them up with my feet, though."

They both laughed. Jimmy said, "Same words Crystal used—'the best.'" He paused before adding, "She likes you a lot, Rusty."

Rusty was suddenly on his toes. "Feeling's mutual, Jimmy. You're a lucky man."

Rusty could see something was on Jimmy's mind. Maybe Crystal had told him he had come on to her. Nah, she wouldn't…and he hadn't.

"Yep, she perks up when you're around. We been married a long time, known her years longer, and I ain't never seen her perk up like that for nobody but me."

They were both silent. Both took swigs of beer.

"Remember I told you why I carried a gun around these days?"

"Of course."

"And you promised not to tell Crystal unless something happened to me?" Rusty nodded. "I've got another promise I want you to shake on."

"What's that?"

Jimmy put his beer down and leaned across the table. He looked Rusty in the eye. "I want you to promise that if anything happens to me, you'll see that Crystal's okay."

Rusty was flabbergasted. "Jimmy, nothing's going to happen to you! You're paranoid. All that was years ago. And I won't shake on something like that because, well, because it's like putting a hex on you. I won't do that!"

Jimmy sighed and folded those hard, work-veined hands on the table. He wearily looked around the room. For a brief instant, Rusty saw all the worry packed behind his eyes. Then, as if putting on a mask, Jimmy's face changed back to its hard cracker self. Rusty heard himself say, "No, Jimmy, I won't shake on it. But if anything happens to you, I'll make sure nothing happens to Crystal... Count on it."

Jimmy picked up his bottle and held it in front of him. Rusty clinked his bottle against Jimmy's and they each took a long swig, never taking their eyes off each other. Jimmy smiled. "So, we're on for scallops tomorrow night?"

"You bet!"

Out on the deck, Beau didn't know how to begin other than jumping right in. "Something's wrong with Virginia, Norm."

They were standing at the railing looking out over the Gulf.

"Like what?" Norm asked, although he had his suspicions.

Beau went through all the peculiar things he could remember that Virginia had said and done over the past several months. He also told Norm about Louie's concern for Virginia, too. Louie had pulled Beau aside on several occasions, noting some of the screwy stuff she had been doing. Beau realized that it had been Louie, covering for Virginia, who had almost single-handedly pulled off the scallop festival. As for Norm, he was only surprised by the scope of miscues. He, too, had noticed peculiarities, but most of that was her searching for the right words or repeating herself or losing her glasses.

"Does Virginia know how bad it is?" Norm asked.

Beau shrugged. "I don't know. I do know that she's frustrated. I also think the frustration, or whatever's going on, is affecting her personality. She's never, ever, been abrupt before. She's getting more and more that way."

Norm nodded. A lot of signs, and none of them particularly good. "How old is she now, Beau?"

"Seventy."

"Does she know that you're talking to me about this."

"Not a clue."

"Maybe you should tell her. Then come over to see me." He turned to look at Beau. "Like sooner than later. I'll be around all day tomorrow if you want. There are some very basic, preliminary tests we could do."

"Tests for what?"

Norm hesitated. "Alzheimer's."

Beau nodded slowly. He stuck out his hand. "Thanks, Norm. You'll be seeing us tomorrow."

Norm watched Beau slowly descend to the street. Seconds later he saw the golf cart's lights and Beau appeared briefly turning around before scooting home. When Beau arrived at his house, it took him a second or two before he realized the Caddy wasn't there. He parked the cart and hoofed it up the stairs as fast as he could. Not like Virginia at all. She should be here. He thought back to when he had left for poker. He remembered looking at the bedroom clock. Was almost six. He had hustled to meet the guys by six so he hadn't really paid attention to the fact that she wasn't home yet. But, as he thought about it now, she usually got home around five. But there had been that heavy rain. Maybe she was stuck! In a ditch somewhere or—calm down! Stop worrying! Probably left a phone message saying she'd be home late. Partying with the girls.

He entered the house. Noticed right away the vacant beanbag. He marched to the phone. No blinking on the machine. He picked it up anyway. Dial tone. What the hell! He began to pace around, got hold of himself, and went to Virginia's Rolodex and found Harriet's number. Butterflies in his stomach, he dialed the number. Harriet picked up.

"Hello?"

"Harriet?"

"Yes?"

"Beau here…"

"Hi." She sounded surprised. "How are you?"

Beau skipped the pleasantries. "Is Virginia there?"

"Virginia? Why, no. She left hours ago. She left around three. She's not home yet?"

Why the hell do you think I'm calling! "No. Did she leave before the rain?"

"Let me think. Yes…Yes, I had to close the windows. She wasn't here then."

Silence.

Beau said, "I'm sure there's a simple explanation, but I'm worried. Please call me if you hear anything."

"Sure thing."

"Thanks." Beau dialed the Club.

Tammy answered. "Crescent Beach Club."

"Tammy, Beau here. Is Rusty still there?"

"Barely; he and Jimmy are just walking out the door."

"Grab him. It's urgent." Beau drummed his fingers.

"Yeah, Beau. What's up?"

"Virginia. She hasn't come home from Steinhatchee. She left about six hours ago; I know because I called where she was playing bridge. No message on the answering machine. What do I do?"

Jimmy had returned with Rusty and was standing at his side. Rusty could hear the tension in Beau's voice. "First thing is take a couple deep breaths. So when did she leave Steinhatchee?"

"Around three."

"Rained like a bitch about then. Maybe she slid into a ditch. Flat tire. Ran out of gas. I'm sure she's fine. Wait a second." Rusty turned to Jimmy. "Virginia never returned from Steinhatchee and left six hours ago. Want to form a search party of three? You know all the roads." Jimmy nodded. Rusty talked to Beau again. "You, Jimmy, and I will go look for her in my truck. We'll be right over. First, though, do one thing…"

"What's that."

"Call Perry dispatch and give them your license plate number and make of the Caddy. Ask them if there've been any accidents involving your car." Rusty heard an intake of breath over the phone. "And Beau…"

"Yeah?"

"Don't worry. She's fine. Have a belt of scotch and we'll be right over."

Beau did as Rusty said, including the single malt scotch which went down easy. No reported accidents. He noticed the empty beanbag again on his way to the door. Rusty and Jimmy pulled up just as he stepped out on the deck. Beau two-timed it down the stairs and hopped into the cab.

A couple hours earlier, Virginia and Skillet approached the cabin. The big white sedan was a Ford. They walked up to the cabin door. Virginia knocked. No answer. Not a sound. She knocked again. Same thing. She looked through one of the front two windows. It was dim inside and she could barely see a stove with a counter on each side against the wall. There was the outline of all sorts of containers and beakers neatly positioned on the counter in between what looked like Bunsen burners and a gas hotplate. Full shelves were attached to the walls. Other than the gas stove in the middle, it reminded her a little of the chemistry lab back in high school. Funny, she thought, how vividly she could picture that classroom. She had hated chemistry. She especially had hated all the weird chemical smells. She walked around the cabin. There was a pile of vile smelling stuff behind it. Skillet took one whiff and it was enough for him. Virginia checked the driver's door of the Ford. It was unlocked. She opened the door and ducked in to see if the keys were in the ignition. Nope. She shut the door and walked up to the front door again. It was getting dark.

"Anybody home?" she asked loudly, nervously. Maybe there was a privy she hadn't seen, and somebody would come around the corner. Who knew what sort of a person would be way the heck out here. "Hello?" No answer. She put her hand on the knob and twisted. It was unlocked. She opened the door, but it only went half way. Something was holding it. She looked down. There was a man's body on the floor. She screamed, quickly stepped back, and slammed the door shut. She put a hand on the door jam to steady herself. Oh Lord! Hugging herself, she stepped away from the door and walked quickly around the car several times, thinking. Skillet sat on his haunches and watched her. Dusk was upon them and so were the mosquitoes. The air became thick with them. She ushered Skillet into the car and ran around to the driver's side while whisking the air around her. She jumped in and closed her eyes. A couple mosquitoes had entered the car with her and whined around her head. She opened her eyes and squashed two. One was full of blood. She hadn't felt a bite; must be Skillet's blood. The whining ceased and she closed her eyes again. Wondering what to do, she fell asleep. She was exhausted.

She woke up sweating heavily. It was hot in the car and Skillet was panting. They both needed water. There must be water in the cabin. But, there was also that body! The only time in her life that she had seen a dead person up close was the open casket of Beau's father in Charleston. It was pitch black outside the car. She could just see the outline of the cabin. She debated what to do. First, they needed water. No, first was to check the body. Maybe the gentleman wasn't dead! Maybe he had a stroke or fainted or something and needed help. She wasn't good at stuff like this. Beau was, but he wasn't here. She could just see the outline of the two front windows. The car was pointed right at it. She hesitated, then pulled the knob on the dash for the headlights. They lit up the front of the cabin and shined through the windows.

She left the car and squeezed into the cabin. She hadn't noticed the mix of smells. They were bad. She closed the door behind her and bent down to feel for a pulse. The neck. Nothing. The wrist. Nothing. His skin was cold to the touch. He was dead. She stood up and looked around the cabin. There were jugs, gallons of this and that, various containers, beakers, carboys, but no sink and faucet. She spied several gallons of Poland Spring Water lined up on the floor. She hoped they were indeed water. She picked one up. It hadn't been opened. She tore away the plastic flap and took a careful sip. It was fine. She found an empty bowl and took it and the water out to put in front of the car. As she watched Skillet drink, she wondered, now what?

The keys to the car must be somewhere inside. On a hook, in a drawer, on the counter. Or in the dead fellow's pants. Imagining going through his pockets made her shudder. But they should take the car if they could. No way did she want to spend the night in that cabin. And no way sweltering in the car either. She returned inside. No hook, no keys anywhere. She took a deep breath and bent down to the body. The guy was all skin and bones. She put a hand in the right front pocket of his jeans. Bingo! She turned on her heels, gently shut the door behind her, and loaded Skillet. She started the car. Within a couple minutes, the AC was blasting wonderfully cool air. Judging from the angle the car was parked, it had come from the other direction from where she and Skillet had come. She backed out and headed that way. There was no returning the other way with the Caddy blocking the road.

She slowed way down at each fork in the road and carefully looked at each to see which seemed more heavily traveled. She had a lousy sense of direction and at this point she certainly didn't have a clue anyway. It turned out that she went left at almost each road choice. The road became wider. When she eventually turned onto the main Steinhatchee Road, she still didn't recognize it; not because something was wrong with her head, but because she had never driven it at night. If she and Beau had gone to Steinhatchee for dinner or some other activity, Beau always drove. She turned left onto the Steinhatchee Road. It was the correct choice; she soon came to the paved highway. Unbelievably relieved, she turned right for Crescent Beach. She looked at the clock. It was twenty to ten. If Beau was back from poker, he must be worried sick. She looked over at Skillet. She smiled. He was conked out. Long day for him, too. Headlights approached when she was still a few miles out of town. Unusual; usually no traffic this time of night. Must be a pickup. It was. Ships passing in the night.

Rusty slowed down as the pair of headlights approached; turned and watched it go by. "1980 Ford Torino," he said.

"Must be Bobby's trailer-mate." Rusty was a motorhead and knew his cars. The old Torino had caught his eye in Crescent Beach. "Wonder where he's coming from?"

They continued to the Steinhatchee Road. As they turned, Jimmy said, "Someone's come out real recent." Limestone tracks were evident on the paved highway. "Maybe that Ford. What's Bobby's buddy's name?"

"Whacko," Rusty said.

"Fitting name," Beau added.

They drove slowly along the main limestone road. Only the one recent set of tracks. The tracks eventually turned right. They decided to follow them. Eventually the tracks brought them to the cabin.

"They end here," Rusty said. He looked over to Jimmy. "Any idea whose place this is."

"Yeah, old guy from Bradenton who used to come up here to hunt years ago. Must be a real old man now, that is if he still owns it." Rusty backed in towards the cabin, preparing to turn around. The headlights lit up the trackless road. "Wait a minute, Rusty." Jimmy peered out. "Got a flashlight?"

"Big one under the seat." Jimmy found it and stepped out of the truck. He walked down the road a hundred feet or so shining the light around. He motioned Rusty to drive up. Rusty rolled down his window.

"Two sets of tracks," Jimmy said. "One's human, the other probably a fat dog's," he said, smiling. He shone his light over to a pile of recent dog shit on the side of the road. Jimmy looked back towards the cabin. "I'm bettin' Virginia and Skillet got stuck somewhere, found the guy at the cabin, and he gave them a ride to town."

"Then why didn't we pass them?" Beau asked.

Rusty said, "Maybe we did. Maybe it was the Ford. Maybe it wasn't Whacko."

"Then where's the Caddy?"

"Let's find out. Lead the way Jimmy."

Rusty kept the lights on the road so Jimmy could follow the tracks. They came to the fork in the road. Jimmy noticed the obvious bending and snapping of branches leading to the left as well as the tracks. They continued on until they saw the Caddy. They got out and looked at it. First thing Beau noticed was that it was coated in limestone. Jimmy noticed that the stream had cut away at the road surface enough so that the Caddy was sitting on the oil pan and chassis.

"Need a tow truck, or maybe a skidder, to yank her out," Rusty said.

"That's the least of it," Beau said. "Let's go find Virginia." The three clambered back in and returned to town. Sure enough, the Torino was parked in front of Beau's house. Beau hustled up the steps as fast as he could. Jimmy and Rusty followed. Skillet didn't even hear him come in. He was zonked on the beanbag. Virginia had just put her book down and was standing by her favorite chair. She had heard Beau coming up the stairs. "Hello, Dear," she said, when he charged into the room.

"Sugah!" He ran over to take her in his arms. "I was so worried!" Virginia clung to him hard. She closed her eyes; she didn't see Jimmy and Rusty enter. Beau felt the urgency of her hug. He held her out so he could see her face. "Are you okay?"

"Yes, Dear," she said, opening her eyes. She saw Rusty and Jimmy. She looked at Beau. "But I'm afraid there's someone who isn't."

Chapter Twenty-Three

Bobby, with bed-head hair, barefoot, and only wearing a pair of hastily thrown on jeans, stood outside on the stoop of the trailer watching Rusty and Jimmy get into the truck and drive away. He watched the taillights until they went around the corner. Slowly he turned to look at the Torino in the driveway, then down at the keys in his hand. He hadn't known what to say to Rusty and Jimmy, so he hadn't said anything. Whacko dead. Hard to believe. Hard to understand. No, not really; he hadn't taken care of himself. He had been killing himself for months, if not years. But dead! Gone! No more Whacko! He'd never see his crazy, skinny cellie again. Here today, gone tomorrow. He felt empty. Deserted.

The mosquitoes drove him inside where he sat down at the kitchen table, blown away, numb, staring at nothing. Rusty told him about Virginia finding Whacko in the shack. She had said that she had no idea how he had died, but it looked to her like he just keeled over. Rusty said it didn't matter, Whacko had to be taken care of and he had called the authorities. The cops were probably there right now tending to business. Maybe there had been foul play. Another screw up like before, bad-ass dealers. No, Whacko had been too careful this time, and nobody, not even me, knew where the cabin was. Now the cops were there. The cops! Bobby jumped up from the table. They're at Whacko's frigging meth lab! They'll be here next!

Bobby made a beeline to where he had stashed Whacko's pouch with the crystal and pipe. He put a magazine on the floor and the pipe on top of it. He crushed the pipe into a thousand pieces, picked up the magazine and curved it so the pieces of pipe went into the toilet. Then the crystal. He flushed the toilet. There was a small wood-burning stove in the corner of the living room. He ripped up the magazine, crumpling up the pages, and added kindling. He started a fire and burned the pouch. He went outside to the car. With a flashlight he went through it stem to stern. Only thing he found was the registration and an insurance certificate. The kitchen was next. He looked through every drawer, every shelf, every can, the refrigerator, and freezer, under the sink, in all the detergent boxes. The only surprise was a three-quarters full bottle of Jim Beam in the back of a cupboard. Probably didn't want to tempt me, Bobby thought. He placed it on the counter. There was nothing else, no hidden stash. He went through the living room, looking under the sofa and cushions and under the carpet where it lifted at the corners. He even looked behind the pictures on the wall. On to the bathroom. He looked through the medicine cabinet, behind the mirror, in the toilet tank. Nothing. He had saved Whacko's bedroom for last. He knew his own bedroom was clean, but who knew what Whacko had in his. He entered and turned on all the lights. The bed wasn't made. He threw back the sheets and looked under the pillow, under the bed, under the mattress. Nothing. He went through the cheap dresser drawers. It was pitiful. A few pairs of brief white jockey underwear, some threadbare socks, a few tee-shirts, a couple cheap short sleeve shirts, a sweatshirt. A denim jacket, a pair of chinos and a pair of jeans, and a few long sleeve shirts were on wire hangers in the closet. Couple pairs of beat-up shoes. He went through all the pockets of the clothes. Nothing.

On the top shelf in the closet was a shoebox. Bobby took it down and took off the top. He was surprised to find a folded piece of lined notebook paper with BOBBY in big bold letters printed on it. Underneath the lined piece of paper were some document-like papers, a couple old snapshots, and a funny looking key. Both photos were yellowed with age. One was of a much younger Whacko looking serious with his arm around an overweight woman with straight long dark hair. She had a nice face. The other was of Whacko and him in the prison yard. Both were smiling. Whacko had more meat on his bones then, but not much. Seemed like a long time ago. Bobby thought back. It *was* a long time ago: more than ten years. Bobby sat down on the bed and unfolded the piece of paper.

Bobby,

If yur readin this Im probly dead. Havent been feelin too hot fer some time now and I think my ticker is messed up. Yep I know. I can hear yur told ya so but it don't matter now anyhow. What does matter is ya read this carefuly so ya kin take care of busness.

I'm leavin everythin I got to ya. I got me a safety deposit box in the Capital City Bank in Perry. Thats what the key is fer. Yur name is on a card at the bank behind where them tellers are. All ya gotta do is show some identification and sign in and they will let ya git at it. I done forged yur signatur. Purty good job if I do say so. Yule find the title to the Torino which I signed over to ya. Also made a bill of sale sayin ya payed me a hundrid bucks fer it. I left the dates fer ya to fill in and ya shud go in and regster it right away. In this box are my insurance papers too. Yur required to have liability. So ya shud git some. Shud go to the same insurance place in Perry. Purty good guy. Money wont be a problem. I think yur goin to be plum surprised when ya open that box. Wish I was there to see yur face.

I buried some ya know what behind my kitchen. Made ya a map how to git to the cabin on the backside of this letter. Stuff is at the base of the big cedar tree thirty feet or so behind the cabin. Know ya say ya ain't goin to git into it but ya always partyed with me anyhow. So if ya want it its there. If not leave it be.

Last thing is if'n Im reely dead I want to be cremated. Im hopin that ya can find me a purty spot to sprinkle me somewheres. Maybe someplace up high with a purty view. But not in the water nowheres. I dont want to feed no fishes. Ya take care now.

Yur cellie, Whacko

Bobby looked at the key, then reread the letter. He glanced at the papers and picked up the snapshots again. He looked a long time at the one of him and Whacko. He read the letter for the third time. He looked at the clock. It was late for a weeknight, just before one in the morning. He was still numb, in a zombie state. He brought the shoebox into his bedroom and placed it on the bureau. He stripped and got into bed. Tomorrow is Friday which meant he had the whole day free before tending bar. He would go in to Perry. Banks must open at nine. He switched off his light, but couldn't sleep. Pictures of Whacko flashed through his mind.

Dressed in his best clothes, which meant pressed chinos and a clean, lightweight long sleeve shirt and his cowboy boots, Bobby entered the Capital City Bank at nine-fifteen. He was handed the sign-in card by a teller who told him to see the woman in the windowed office. As he walked over to the office, he glanced at the card. There was his signature below Whacko's scrawl. Bobby smiled. It *was* a damn good forgery. Bobby, trying his best to look confident and nonchalant, entered the office. The lady at the desk was dressed in a dark pantsuit and a silky-looking white blouse. She was about his age, pretty good looking if you liked dyed blond hair teased up and sprayed rock hard. There was no ring on her left hand. Bobby was a good-looking guy, what women would call a hunk. The lady smiled brightly up at him. He handed her the card.

"Identification, please," she said. Bobby pulled out his driver's license and social security card. She took a cursory look and handed them back. She positioned the card so he could sign it and handed him a pen. Bobby signed it, noting that Whacko had signed in plenty of times. He pushed the card over to the lady who examined the signature. "Thank you, Robert."

Bobby smiled. "It's Bobby to you." She returned his smile. She took a key out of her desk and led Bobby into the safety deposit room. Bobby decided that he didn't particularly like pantsuits on women.

The room had no windows, and the two long interior walls had keyed boxes like a post office, but there were no little windows on the boxes and there were three different sizes. There was a tall, central wooden counter-like table in the middle of the room. The lady inserted her key in a medium sized box, then looked at him expectantly. Bobby looked back at her. After an awkward moment, she said, "Your key."

"Oh, right." He fumbled in his pocket, giving her his best 'aw shucks' grin. He handed her the key. She opened the little door.

"There you are. When you're done, just put the box back and shut the door. Take your time, Bobby." She smiled at him again before leaving the room. Bobby pulled the box out. It was about four inches by ten inches by twelve inches deep. He put it on the table. He was curious as hell, but he hesitated. He had butterflies in his stomach. He opened the box. Whacko would have loved it. Bobby's jaw dropped in disbelief. He couldn't believe what he saw. That son-of-a-gun, was his first thought. Besides the title, the box was full of one hundred dollar bills. There were six stacks, each held together with a rubber band. Five of the stacks looked equal, the sixth was partial. He pulled out a full stack and counted it. It took awhile: two hundred bills. He did the math. Twenty thousand dollars for a full stack. Five stacks. A hundred grand! He counted the partial stack. A hundred bills, so another ten grand. A hundred and ten grand! Holy Shit!

Bobby shut the lid of the box quickly as if someone might see what was inside. A million thoughts began flying around his head. He had no idea Whacko had dealt anywhere near this much. Was this a huge recent score? Or had all this been accumulating since Whacko got out of prison? But what to do with it! Cops know now that Whacko'd been making meth. They'll be sniffing around, looking for any illegal cash. Was it legal for them to ask about a specific client's accounts or safety deposit box? Small town like Perry, they could probably do anything they wanted. Maybe the blond went to high school with the sheriff. 'Hey, sweetie, did this guy name Whacko have any money in your bank?' He should clean the box out. Get it out of here pronto! But put it where? No way in the trailer! Bury it somewhere? Get a safety deposit box in another bank in another town? Like Mayo? But they'll probably think Whacko and I were partners. When they find out I was in prison, they'll check on me for sure. Probably ask the banks about me, too. No, safest thing is to bury it somewhere.

Bobby opened the box and pulled out the Torino title and bill of sale. He also put a couple of the bills in his wallet before putting away the box. He stopped by the blonde's desk. "I'll probably be back in a bit," he said, smiling and holding up the official looking papers. "Have to take care of a couple things at City Hall and my insurance agent's."

"No problem," she said.

Bobby left the bank. He was a busy boy. First, he filled in dates on the title and bill of sale, postdating everything by a couple weeks. He had no idea if the cops could confiscate Whacko's car, but he wanted the car to be legally his before Whacko had died. He went to City Hall and got a new registration and plates. Next was the insurance changeover; the agent was just up the street from City Hall. Once that was done, he drove to a nearby ACE Hardware store where he had an eighteen-inch section of Schedule 40 PVC pipe, four inches in diameter, cut. He also bought some PVC glue, two end caps, a shovel, and a screwdriver and pliers to change the plates. He paid with one of the hundred dollar bills. He held his breath when they marked it with a colored pen. He was relieved when it passed muster; you just never knew with Whacko. He changed the plates at the hardware store, then went to an office supplies outlet where he bought a serious looking, accordion-style folder that could be tied shut with a string. Finally, before returning to the bank, he went to a funeral parlor to get all the specifics about having someone cremated.

He emptied out the safety deposit box; everything went into the new folder. He thanked the coiffed blond again and headed back to Crescent Beach. He couldn't believe that on the seat next to him was over a hundred grand in cash. He felt nervously rich. He kept right at the speed limit. A few miles outside of Crescent Beach he turned onto a little used limestone road that dead-ended at an old cemetery. It was overgrown with only a half dozen visible gravestones. Bobby parked and strode off into the woods bringing everything with him. He pushed palmettos out of his way with the shovel, carefully looking for snakes. Prime rattler territory; no one in their right mind would walk around here, he thought. Where the palmettos thinned out he buried the entombed money halfway between two live oaks, kicking oak leaves over the spot. He left the shovel hidden under a nearby clump of palmettos and returned to the Torino. Fifteen minutes later he pulled up to the trailer. A sheriff's car was parked at the curb in front. Two youngish deputies got out when he turned off the motor. They walked up to him. They couldn't have been more different. One was large with a substantial paunch straining at the buttons of his uniform. The other was very thin. A regular Laurel and Hardy.

"You live here?" the heavy one, Hardy, asked.

"Yup," Bobby said, shutting the Torino door. "Sure do."

"You're Bobby, then," Laurel cleverly deduced.

"That's right, officer. What's up?"

"You know that your partner is dead?" Laurel asked.

"Not my partner; my friend that I share this trailer with. Yes, I was told last night."

The two policemen looked at each other, smiling shrewdly. "Did you hear that?" Hardy asked Laurel. "Not his partner." He turned back to Bobby. "Did you know that he was making meth?"

"Officer, my friend and I go way back," Bobby said, subconsciously using the present tense. "We get along because we mind our own business. Can I believe he was making meth? Yes, I can believe that. Did I know he was making meth? No, I didn't. He did his thing. I did mine. End of story."

Laurel spoke up. "Yeah, you guys go way back, all the way to Raiford where you were cellmates. He was thrown in for making meth back then. Then you guys conveniently bunk up again when you get out. You expect us to believe you weren't involved? You're the pusher, maybe."

These guys have done some pretty quick homework, Bobby thought. He shrugged his shoulders. "Might be hard for you to believe, but it's the truth. I served my time. I don't want to serve any more. I've got a good job. I'm clean. You can ask my employer at the marina if I've been anything but a straight Joe."

"Then you being such a straight Joe, you wouldn't mind if we take a little look inside your place, would you?" Hardy asked.

Bobby shrugged his shoulders again. "Help yourself. Door's open."

Bobby followed the two lawmen in. He sat at the kitchen table while they started to not so subtly search the house. When they were done in the kitchen, they moved into the bedrooms and bathroom. As Bobby listened to them, he spied the bottle of Jim Beam on the counter. Looked inviting. That rich brown color. Three-quarters full. It was the first time in seventeen years he was tempted to take a swig. He heard the toilet tank top clunk down. A short time later the two deputies came back into the kitchen. Rather than taking the civil approach of thanking him for allowing them to search the trailer, Hardy said, "Stateys been taking fingerprints where we found your friend. Expect you know it was where he was making the crystal. Better hope they don't find your prints there. If they do, we'll be back to tear this place apart. And the stateys'll probably want to come back with us. Bet they'd like to get your ass again."

Thanks for the warning, Sherlock, Bobby thought. He asked Hardy, "How did my friend die?"

"Don't know; don't care. Good riddance to a piece of white trash." Bobby wondered how many teeth he could knock down Hardy's throat if he slammed him with a hard right.

"Need you to identify the body. Think you can remember what he looks like?" Laurel asked, sarcastically.

"In Perry?" Bobby asked. Laurel nodded. "Right now? Just returned from there."

"Too bad. Today being Friday and all, best if you come in now."

Bobby looked at his watch. Still lots of time before work. "Alright. Follow you?"

"Yeah," Hardy said.

The deputies walked over to the squad car. Bobby got in the Torino. Bobby followed them in to the town morgue and identified Whacko. It wasn't as bad as he thought it would be. As scraggly as he looked and as dead as he was, at least he looked peaceful. It was all over for him and he was wherever he was. Whacko had had his ride. He told the morgue people that he would see to the cremation. He stopped briefly again at the funeral home on his way out of town. On the highway home, the finality of it all hit him. Whacko's death became real. By the time he arrived at the trailer, he was dog-tired from all the mixed emotions playing on him over the last twelve hours. He wearily went in and sat at the kitchen table. He looked at the clock on the wall. Still had a couple hours to kill before work. His eyes dropped down to the kitchen counter below the clock. There was that bottle of Jim Beam, still three-quarters full.

Chapter Twenty-Four

"You mess with that poor man, Sammy, and I'll skin you alive! You hear me!" Sammy's sister and Sammy were standing in the corridor of Tallahassee Memorial Health Care outside Rebecca's room.

"Yes, Ma'am," Sammy said, meekly. Sammy had put on his only long sleeve, Oxford-style white shirt and he was wearing a clean pair of jeans. His thick dark hair had been slicked down and combed, but it still hung over his collar and had a bowl-like indentation all around from where he had been wearing his ball cap that was now in his hands. His bushy beard looked like it always did. He nervously shifted from foot to foot.

Katharine put one hand on the doorknob while shaking a finger at Sammy with the other. "You remember, now..."

They entered the room. It wasn't much different from the Perry hospital except that the room was larger with more machines scattered around. A nurse was checking Rebecca's IVs. She walked around the sports retailer guy like he was a fixture. He was in a chair, reading a book. He looked up when Sammy and his sister entered. His eyes widened when he saw Sammy, nodded to him, and went back to his book. Sammy stood on the other side of the bed from the man as Katharine positioned herself in between at the end of the bed. She watched Sammy closely, but Sammy hardly looked at the man; he was staring at Rebecca. Seeing her surrounded by all the tubes and hanging bags and machines, and especially seeing the painful looking brace sticking out of her arm, his heart went out to her. Sammy never won at poker: his face was like a road sign. He was close to tears.

"Any change, O.C.?" Katharine asked the man.

"Not that I've noticed," the sports retailer said, although Sammy could hardly see his lips move." O.C. looked to the nurse. "Ma'am?" The nurse shook her head as she left the room.

Rebecca was still heavily sedated to mask the intense pain from the raging infection. She was maintaining now and the doctors were optimistic, but she had a very long way to go. Sammy tore his eyes away from Rebecca and asked his sister, "Where's Clem?"

"Down in the cafeteria. I made him go down. He's hardly eaten a thing in days, although he's probably drinking coffee, is all. How long did it take you to git up here?"

Sammy shook his head disgustedly. "Better part o' four hours. Dang ol' truck ain't got no git-up-and-go these days. But, she made it."

He looked back to Rebecca. Her eyes were closed. She was out of it. His eyes shifted to the sports retail guy. Sammy could see that his jaw was wired. The fact that it looked painful gave him no satisfaction. He realized now that the whole thing had been a horrible accident. The guy never knew he had hit her. He hadn't intentionally left her in the canal. Sammy had also learned that he had come to town with the PVC guiderails in place. It was when the party barge had been taken out or lowered in with the sling at the marina that they had been pushed out. And the guy had got right on to fixing them, only it was ten minutes too late by then. He turned to his sister again.

"Has she been awake at all today?"

Katharine nodded. "Off and on. Just never know when. Clem and I and O.C. here have taken shifts so that when she wakes one of us is usually here. Although we've finally convinced O.C. to go home nights."

O.C. closed his book and stood up. "Which is what I guess I'll do now, Katharine." He looked at his watch. "See you and Clem for dinner around seven?" Katharine nodded. O.C. turned to Sammy. " You're welcome to join us, Sam." Sammy didn't say anything. At the door O.C. added, "And if you don't want to make the drive back tonight, we've got a fold-out couch in the living room."

O.C. went out and shut the door. Sammy looked back at Rebecca, his face was a mixed read. Without taking his eyes off her, he asked, "So Rebecca knows who this guy is?"

Katharine nodded. "Couldn't help not to. He's been here more than we have. And they git along jest fine." Katharine gave her brother a piercing look. "She don't blame him none. She's big enough to know it was an accident, pure and simple, Sammy. No more and no less. Only thing now is fer her to git better."

"Yes, Ma'am," was all that Sammy said.

At quarter to seven, Clem's and Sammy's pickups pulled into O.C.'s driveway. The house was one of those one-story, stucco-covered concrete block houses so typical of fifties and sixties Florida. It was tan colored with a white-pebbled roof. There was a mixture of oak and magnolia trees as well as azalea gardens spread around the property. Gardenia bushes flanked the front door where O.C.'s wife greeted Clem and Katharine. Katharine said, "Sammy, this is O.C.'s wife, Mrs. Meyer."

"Please, it's Judy." Dark-haired, thin, and at least a couple inches shorter than her husband's five-ten, Judy led the trio through the living room out to a screened-in lanai area with a small pool. O.C. was sitting near a gas grill in the far corner of the lanai, reading the paper. He stood up. Two young girls were playing in the pool, trying to climb onto an inflatable shark with large evil-looking eyes and two angry lines of bright white teeth.

"Girls," Judy said. "Come out and meet Mr. Sam, then get dressed. We'll be eating in a half hour."

The girls dutifully got out of the pool. Their mother threw towels over their shoulders as they walked up to Sammy. Each dried off their hands. One might have been nine or ten. The other looked to be about Rebecca's age. They were both dark-haired and thin like their mother.

"Nice to meet you, Mr. Sam," they said, as each shook Sammy's hand, their hands disappearing in his.

"Nice to meet ya, too, little ladies." The girls smiled before disappearing to their room.

"We thought we'd cook up some burgers tonight and eat at the picnic table under the magnolia," Judy said. "It's so beautiful out. Make yourselves at home. O.C., see what everyone would like to drink while I bring out the burgers."

O.C. came over. "Got sweet tea, beer, sodas, juice, and hard stuff, Sam. What'll it be?"

Sammy had a hard time making eye contact. Looking a smidgeon off to the side, he said, "Beer'd be mighty nice."

"You got it. Two sweet teas for you?" Clem and Katharine nodded. "Coming right up." O.C. left for the kitchen. Sammy turned to his brother-in-law.

"Sweet tea, Clem?"

Clem looked a little sheepish. "Ain't had a beer since the Fourth. I swore to the All Mighty that if my little girl makes it through all this, I'd never have another drink. Reckon it's so far, so good on both counts."

O.C. cooked up the burgers while Katharine and Judy brought potato salad, chips, and a crock of baked beans out to the table. They sliced up a big fat watermelon for dessert. They also brought out a large bowl of vegetable soup and a straw for O.C. It was when Sammy was chewing one of his two large, medium-rare burgers and O.C. was slurping his soup, that he started feeling guilty. Sammy hardly said a word during the meal, just listened as he was brought up to date on everything Rebecca. After the watermelon, Katharine looked at her watch. She prodded Clem who looked like he was ready to fall asleep at the table.

"It's almost eight. Time to go." She explained to Sammy that they usually sat with Rebecca for a few hours each night. Sammy started to stand. Katharine put an arm on his. "You stay put and get some sleep, Sammy. You can have the early morning shift. It's good you're here so O.C. can go check on his store. And it's usually then that Rebecca perks up a little."

Katharine and Clem left, and O.C.'s wife and girls cleared the table and went to do the dishes and homework, respectively. Sammy and O.C. were left alone. Neither knew what to say. They sat there, both uncomfortable. Finally, Sammy asked, "That jaw o' yours hurt much?"

O.C. subconsciously ran a hand around his chin. "Not so much now."

"Don't look like much fun."

"It's not."

"How's them ribs?"

"Gaining."

"Where's the party barge?"

"At the salvage yard."

"Damn!"

"Insurance'll take care of it. They may come after you, though."

"Can't get no blood from a stone."

Silence. Sammy took a swig of beer.

"What's O.C. stand fer?"

O.C. looked embarrassed. "Just a sort of abbreviation for my first name." Sammy waited for him to continue. He didn't.

After awhile Sammy asked, “And what’s your first name?”

“Oscar.”

Sammy nodded and chewed that over. “And Meyer’s your last name?” O.C. nodded like, I know, I know. “Oscar Meyer like the hot dog?”

“You got it.”

Sammy started laughing. “Bet you heard a lot about hot dogs as a kid.” Sammy and O.C. finally made full eye contact. O.C. smiled as much as he could. His eyes smiled more.

“That’s the God’s truth.”

“You any relation?”

“Nope.”

“That’s too bad. Guess you’d be mighty rich if you was.”

“That’s a fact. Get you another beer, Sam.”

“Be good o’ ya.”

O.C. left the picnic table and returned with two beers and one straw. Sammy watched him suck down some of the beer. Sammy looked here and there before clearing his throat. “Mighty sorry about punching ya. Regret it, I do.”

O.C. looked Sammy straight in the eye. “Not as much as I regret what happened to Rebecca. I’m the one who’s sorry, Sam!” O.C. had both elbows on the table. He suddenly buried his head in his hands and it was obvious he was very close to losing it. Sammy heard a muffled, “I am just so goddamned sorry!”

Sammy waited for O.C. to get it together. When O.C. looked up again, Sammy said, “Guess we’re both sorry. And guess there ain’t nuthin’ can be done ‘bout it except to make it as easy as we can fer Rebecca. I also shor appreciate yur feedin’ me and lettin’ me stay here tonight.”

“Least I can do, Sam.”

"One thing I'd like to ask o' ya."

"What's that, Sam?"

"That ya call me, Sammy."

O.C. smiled his thin smile. "You got it."

* * *

Beau brought the breakfast tray into the bedroom. Virginia was already sitting up expectantly, smiling.

"One boiled egg, three and one half minutes exactly, toast lightly buttered, orange marmalade, coffee black, and a glass of orange juice," Beau said. "Anything else doth my Queen desire? Your wish is my command."

"Yes, Page, go get yourself a cup of coffee and humor me as I break my fast."

Bowing low, Beau said, "Yes, my Queen."

Beau returned with his coffee and pulled up a chair. Virginia was delicately chewing a bite of toast, smiling at him. A cloud crossed her face. She put her toast down and finished chewing. Beau finished taking a sip of coffee. He, too, suddenly looked serious.

"Beau," she said, exactly the same time when he said, "Sugah…" They both laughed.

"Ladies first," he said.

But Virginia was not eager to begin. "No, Page, you first."

Beau took another sip of coffee.

"Sugah,…aah…aah…" Beau was always extremely articulate except when emotionally involved. Virginia knew right away that something serious was up.

"Yes, Dear?" She smiled encouragingly.

"Sugah, you know how you have been rather, aah, spacey these days? Forgetting where you put things, can't remember words or people's names or phone numbers, misdating checks, things like that?"

Virginia's stomach turned over. "Yes, Beau."

Beau hesitated, then blurted out, "I think you should see someone about it. You know, just get checked out. I've talked to Norm and he thinks it a good idea."

Beau inwardly grit his teeth, awaiting her reaction. To his complete surprise, Virginia broke into a smile and shook her head slowly back and forth. A tear soon coursed down her cheek. She wiped it away.

"Beau, oh my dear Beau." She moved her tray off to the side, and patted the bed next to her. "Come, sit here, my love." Beau did as she said. She took one of his hands in hers and held it up to her cheek. "Of course, I will see Norm and do whatever he suggests." She chuckled. "When we interrupted each other, that's what I was going to say to you: that there's something strange going on and that I should talk to Norm." She smiled. "You know, we do this a lot, you and I. I don't know how many times we think the exact same thing at the same moment." Her expression suddenly became serious. "But I want to tell you some of the things that have been going on that you don't know about."

Virginia told him about numbers not making sense and the impossibility of balancing the checkbook. She described getting lost on the Steinhatchee Road. She said she couldn't remember recipes that she had used for years and that sometimes she had trouble tying her sneakers. About how easily she got distracted; she'd be thinking about something, then some little thing would come up, like a bird might fly by and then she couldn't remember what she had been thinking about. But what worried Beau the most was when she told him about how bridge bidding and cards no longer made sense and she had quit the Stewed Tomatoes. When she was done, he patted her hand. "Would you like to see Norm today?" Looking resigned, she nodded. He looked at his watch and stood. "It's late enough to give him a call." He left the room.

Beau returned a few minutes later saying that Norm would come over in the afternoon; that he had some questions and a few very basic tests he wanted to give her here, in her own home, where she'd be more relaxed. Virginia nodded seriously. She passed the tray to Beau who took it away and did the dishes while she got dressed. That afternoon, at four o'clock sharp, Norm rapped on the front door. Beau let him in. Virginia looked up from the couch and saw that he was carrying a clipboard. She smiled nervously.

"Hi, Norm," she said.

"Hi, yourself," he answered, coming straight over and sitting next to her on the plush leather couch. He laid the clipboard down on the rosewood coffee table while Beau sat across from them in a matching leather Lazyboy recliner. Norm couldn't help but notice the large oil painting on the wall behind the couch. It was one of Charley's estuary landscapes. Painted in ethereal afternoon light, Norm could almost feel the approaching storm with the tumultuous storm clouds filling the sky. A faint tree line was way off in the distance and up close a few egrets hunted in the marsh grass that was bending in the wind. Norm would love to have the painting in his collection. He turned to Virginia. "So tell me about what's been going on." Virginia leaned back and told him.

"Okay, Virginia. We're going to do some tests now. They really don't mean much except they can provide some hints as to maybe why these things are happening. First, I'm going to give you a name and address which you will repeat out loud. Then we're going to talk for a few minutes before I ask you to say that same name and address again. Okay?" Norm smiled. "Pretty simple, huh?" Virginia nodded. "Ready?" Virginia nodded again. "Peter Black, thirty-six-oh-five Oxford St., Boston, Mass." Virginia repeated the name and address. Norm began to talk of other things as Beau and Virginia listened. He got Virginia to participate in the conversation. After a couple minutes, he asked Virginia the name and address.

Virginia hesitated "He was from Boston, Massachusetts. Cambridge St…no, no, it was…" She shook her head in frustration. That was all she could come up with. She didn't even remember the guy's name. Norm patiently waited a few minutes before moving on. He handed her a pencil and the clipboard with a blank piece of 8 ½ by 11 paper on it.

"Now I'd like you to draw a picture of a large clock. Put all the numbers on it and draw the hands at 1:40."

Virginia began to draw. It took her a long time for such an easy exercise. She completed a circle for the face of the clock that took up most of the paper. The numbers, however, she placed in a smaller circle up in the left hand corner of the big circle, with the twelve halfway down, in the three position, rather than at the top where it should be. She also left out the ten. She made the hands the same length but they weren't anywhere near 1:40. She handed the drawing to Norm. He looked at it and put the clipboard down on the table. Beau could see it. He was poker faced.

"Now count backwards from a hundred, please, Virginia." Virginia stumbled over the numbers until Norm said, "Okay. Now the months backwards." Virginia struggled with that, too. Norm took a penlight from his pocket. He had her follow the light with her eyes. He put the penlight away and sat back on the couch. "That's it. That's all I've got in my little bag of tricks today." He looked from Virginia to Beau who were both watching him intently. Norm sighed. "Something's obviously going on and I think that you should get checked out by a specialist. There are several things they'll do—MRI, blood work, lumbar puncture perhaps. I know a guy who's really good with this sort of thing and I'll call him to set something up if you'd like.

"What do you mean by 'this sort of thing,' Norm?" Beau asked, cutting to the chase.

Norm didn't hesitate. "I think this is possibly Alzheimer's. I say 'possibly' because there are other things it could be. It's hard to definitively diagnose. Virginia, how old are you?"

"Seventy." Norm nodded.

"Any history of dementia in your family?"

"My father, I guess. But back then it was called senility."

"Although there is still a ton to learn about Alzheimer's, we do know that genetics are important. We also know that after age sixty-five, the chance of getting it doubles every five years. And two-thirds of the people who have it are women. But, again," he added, quickly, "as I say, it's hard to definitively diagnose. After lengthy tests, we can be maybe ninety percent sure."

Virginia didn't say anything. Beau asked, "If it is Alzheimer's, can anything be done about it?"

"Not much. There are a few drugs out there that retard it, like Aricept. Physical exercise slows it down as well, and supplements like Vitamin C and E, baby aspirin, and statins once a day can be beneficial: anything good for the heart is good for the brain."

Beau and Virginia were silent. They looked at each other. The atmosphere was heavy. Picking up the clipboard, Norm stood. "So, that's it then. I'll give the doctor a call if you'd like."

In unison, they said, "Please," then followed with a "Thank you."

Beau stood up to walk Norm to the door. After Norm said goodbye to Virginia, they went out to the deck. Beau shut the door behind them. "Thanks for coming over, Norm."

Norm put a hand on Beau's shoulder. "We still don't know anything for sure. Let's see what my friend says. I know he'll see Virginia right away." Beau nodded. Norm turned to go down the steps. He stopped. "Looks like I've got company." Beau followed Norm's gaze. Parked in front of Norm's house was the Ford Torino.

"That's the car of the guy who died yesterday, Bobby's housemate," Beau said. "Must be Bobby paying you a visit."

"Probably wants his stitches out," Norm said. At least Norm hoped that was the reason. He hurried down the stairs.

Chapter Twenty-Five

It wasn't more than ten minutes after he had returned from identifying Whacko that Bobby got into the Jim Beam. He took an old pint jar from the cupboard and filled it halfway. It burned but was smooth enough and went down way too easily. He sat at the kitchen table in a mindless state, not realizing how often he was raising the jar to his lips. When he went for a refill, he brought the bottle back to the table. He began to thumb through his life in a backwards progression—Whacko's dead face and skinny body, burying the money, BeeBee in bed at the Hilton, Whacko and him catching the redfish, Whacko waiting for him outside the prison with the Torino and the rusty barbells in the trunk, Whacko and him cellmates in prison, his punching the statey at the bar. He put his mind in neutral when he came to Tammy. Sweet, sweet Tammy. How old was she when he first saw her in those tight jeans. Sixteen? Seventeen? He smiled into the pint jar. 'She was just seventeen, if you know what I mean. The way she looked was way beyond compare…' And man, could she dance! She was in high school and he was working at the mill when they first started dating. The guys at work ribbed him that he was robbing the cradle, but he knew they were all envious.

Those were the days! He and his Road Queen riding the ditches. Wasn't a ditch he couldn't ride, wasn't a louder truck in the county. He loved that old truck. Was in the bed of the truck where they first got it on, just them and the mosquitoes on a lonely limestone pull-off. He was her first. She also was hot stuff. BeeBee might have all the goodies, juicier-like, but she didn't hold a candle to Tammy. Maybe that was because he had really cared for her, loved her. With BeeBee it was about the sex, pure and simple. No, Tammy was his lively lady. He smiled at the phrase. 'Lively lady.' Hadn't he read a book in prison called that?

It was Tammy who first talked about getting married; she wanted out of her family life pronto. Her mother had run off with another man, leaving her to care for four kid brothers and sisters. Her father was in and out of jobs. They were poor, lived in not much more than a shack, and swamp cabbage was often the only thing on their plates. But it was when her father started playing Peeping Tom and touching her that she began talking to Bobby about crossing over to Georgia to get hitched. She was too young to do it in Florida. They were living in Blountstown at the time and it was a quick easy drive. They got a blood test and a minister and said their 'I do's.' Tammy quit high school and they rented a little house not far from the cypress mill.

Damn, those were sweet times! We had a blast. Got her a fake ID and Saturday nights we'd go to bars and dances. Loved to watch her dance. Made me horny. Problem was, made other guys horny, too. Had to stake out my territory more than once and there were plenty of fights. Bobby took another pull on the Jim Beam. Only thing he'd had to eat all day was a quick breakfast sandwich before going to the bank. He stared at the pint jar in his hand. Wasn't long before I began to hit the liquor hard; got me some real ass-kicking stuff from Georgia. Made me meaner than ever and then I really started to kick some butt. Bad thing was, couple times I kicked her butt, too. Stopped drinking after that one time I broke her jaw. Felt real bad about that. Brought her strawberry milkshakes from McDonalds every day for two weeks. But started up again after awhile, both the drinking and the rough stuff. But the psychologist in prison said that it wasn't just the liquor that caused me to wail on her; said that violence against women had come natural because of my dad. Dad was a bull, all bulked up from working the green chain at the mill his whole life, pulling and stacking heavy boards fresh off the saw for eight hours a day, five days a week, year in, year out. He got mean when he drank, too, and he drank a lot, even at the mill. No one ever gave him any lip. But ma didn't hold back when he came home drunk and broke on Friday nights. She'd give him an earful, and he'd punch her. Was like a ritual. Could almost set your clock by it.

Wonder how everything would have turned out if I hadn't beat up that statey. I was doing good at the mill, had been promoted from the green chain to the edger. The big wigs in the office said they wanted to send me to that school in North Carolina to learn how to saw. Said I had potential. Was the first time anyone ever said I had potential. I'd have made a good sawyer, too. But that's history. I blew it. No reason to go there. Bobby stood up to go to the bathroom. Whoa! Getting a little tipsy. Good stuff. He looked at the Jim Beam. There was maybe a third of a bottle left. He went off to relieve himself. When he returned to the table, he poured a less generous drink and sat down again. Wonder if Tammy really loves the doctor? Bobby looked at his bandaged hand. The wrapping was filthy from burying the money. Maybe she's with him because he has a nice house and some bucks. Maybe now that I've got some dough, she'll be a little more interested in me.

He looked at the clock on the wall. He blinked to bring it in focus. He was feeling no pain. Getting late. Should get ready for work. He stayed put. Maybe I should play hooky. He took another sip from the jar as he thought about it. Finally, he stood up, a little unsteady, but not bad. He walked into the bathroom and looked himself over. He should put on another shirt, and definitely a different pair of pants. He splashed water on his face and changed his clothes. He put on his cowboy boots and clicked his way over to the kitchen table for one last swig. He was about to leave when he spied the black cowboy hat BeeBee had given him. He debated whether or not to wear it. Probably give BeeBee a heart attack, but the lady barflies, he knew, would love it. Screw BeeBee! He put the hat on, low over his eyes, and left the trailer. He hadn't walked far before he said to himself, "Wait a minute! You've got a car now!" He clicked his way back to the Torino and hopped in. A couple of minutes later, he parked in the Marina parking lot. Not much going on; it was still a half hour before Happy Hour. He walked into the bar where Frank was washing some glasses and BeeBee was filing her nails. She did a double take when she saw the hat. Frank noticed it right away, too.

"Nice hat, Stud," Frank quipped, smiling.

"Thanks, good friend gave it to me," Bobby said, not realizing he was slurring.

Frank turned serious. "Whacko?"

"Nope. Lady Friend. Whacko's not giving anybody much these days."

BeeBee was suddenly concentrating hard on her nails. She didn't look happy at all.

"Yeah, sorry to hear about that," Frank said.

Out of the corner of her eyes, BeeBee watched Bobby pull up a stool. He almost missed it when he sat down, had to grab the edge of the bar.

"Are you drunk, Bobby?" she asked. Frank looked closely at Bobby.

Bobby shrugged. "Maybe a little. Might say I'm grievin' over my friend."

BeeBee tossed her head in disgust. "Over him! He was nothing but a …"

Bobby was off the stool and in BeeBee's face in a flash. She was startled and jerked away from him. He leaned in close; the only thing between his face and hers was a single finger he was wagging back and forth. There was cold fury in his face. BeeBee was smart enough to keep her mouth shut. "Don't…don't you ever talk bad about him. Never! You got that?" Even slurred, each word was pure ice.

Frank quickly put down the glass and towel, and walked over to his wife. "Bobby, I know you're upset. Maybe you should take the night off. What do you say?"

Bobby stopped wagging his finger and straightened up. BeeBee didn't move a muscle. He turned to Frank. "Not a bad idea." He looked beyond Frank to the rows of bottles behind him. "What say you give me that bottle of Wild Turkey there wholesale," he said, pointing, "and take it out of my pay." It was more of a statement than a request. Frank hated to give anybody anything wholesale, but with the look on Bobby's face, he nodded and walked over to the shelf. He grabbed the bottle and brought it over. "How about a glass? Don't want to offend the little lady here by chuggin' it straight outta the bottle." Frank handed him a glass. Bobby sat on the stool closest to BeeBee. He opened the bottle and poured in a good shot. He kept the bottle in the air. "How about you, little wife? Will you join me?" BeeBee shook her head. "No?" He put the bottle down on the bar. "Won't join me, huh? Too proper; too much of a good little wife to have a drink with someone not her husband. Wouldn't be right, now would it?" Bobby sipped from the glass. Frank was watching him closely. BeeBee look terrified. Frank slowly walked over to BeeBee and put an arm around her shoulders. BeeBee leaned into him. Bobby looked at them and laughed. He downed the rest of his drink. Frank was about to say something, but Bobby stood up. He fumbled with the screw-on cap. When he had it on, he said, "Think I'll blow this popcorn stand." He held the bottle up. "Thanks, Frank." He doffed his hat to BeeBee. "And good day to you, little wife." He looked at the hat in his hand. "It is a nice hat, isn't it?" BeeBee didn't say anything. Bobby turned and left the bar.

Bobby drove back to the trailer, but didn't get out of the Torino. He turned the car off and put the seat back as far as it would go. He laid back and tilted the cowboy hat down over his closed eyes. BeeBee. Unfaithful slut. Poor Frank. Good screwin', though, and if it wasn't me, it'd be someone else. He swigged from the bottle. Not Tammy. Faithful, sticking by her man. Problem was, wrong man. Maybe if I showed her I was going someplace, that I wasn't going to be just a marina boy, maybe then. With Whacko's money I could get a new start. Send myself to sawyer school. Get a good paying, important job somewhere. Maybe Tammy'd go for me then. Yeah, maybe that'd work. Wonder what she'd think about that. He suddenly opened his eyes and pushed his hat up, took a quick nip, and started the car. Only one way to find out.

He drove over to the Crescent Beach Club and climbed up the stairs to the restaurant. He was told that Tammy hadn't come in yet; that she was most likely at home. Bobby drove over to the house and parked in front. He purposefully strode up the stairs, not even considering what he'd say or do if Norm were around. He knocked on the screen door. Tammy appeared with a gray cockatiel on her shoulder. She didn't open the door. Her face was expressionless.

"This is a surprise, Bobby. What's up?"

"How about you inviting me in so I can tell you?"

Tammy hesitated, then said, "Alright, but wait a second while I put Henrietta away." She left the door and Bobby heard the rattle of a cage door opening and closing. Tammy returned and stepped aside as she opened the door. When Bobby strode by her, she could smell the alcohol on him. Uh oh, she thought. Bobby went into the center of the large living room where he stopped. He took it all in: the fine view out over the Gulf, beautiful oil landscapes on the walls, custom wood furniture, the two large bird cages in opposite corners, and a gleaming bar with expensive bottles of liquor off to the side. Tammy followed him in. He turned to face her.

"Pretty nice digs. Can see why you wouldn't want to leave this."

"What do you want, Bobby?"

"You."

"Forget it."

"Listen, Tammy, I know that I didn't treat you right way back. But I've changed. I just want a chance with you, that's all."

"Like I said, forget it."

"What if I got me some money and learned a good profession. I might not be able to give you all this," he said, sweeping an arm around the room, "but we could have it good again."

"Bobby, it's not about this," she said, sweeping her arm around like him. "I've got a business and enough money of my own. I'm here because I love Norm. I want to be with him. He is my man, period."

Bobby's face turned dark. Tammy had seen that look before; it was indelibly stamped in her memory. Alarms went off in her head. He took a menacing step towards her, but stopped. Still, Tammy backed away.

"I think you better leave now, Bobby. No use sayin' anything more."

They heard someone climbing the stairs. Norm had walked quickly over from Beau's. As he approached the stairs, he wondered what was going on. He also wondered the best way to announce his presence. Knock on the door of his own house? Yell out 'Hi Honey, I'm home?' Clomp up the stairs? He chose clomping up the stairs. He entered the house and found Tammy and Bobby faced off in the living room. Bobby's face certainly wasn't its usual smiling self. Tammy's looked a mixture of pissed and scared.

"Hey, Bobby. What's up?" Bobby turned to him. Norm noticed right away that his eyes and movements were sluggish. He was either drunk or stoned. Norm got a whiff of the booze. Drunk. "How's the hand? Should be about time to pull those stitches out." Bobby looked dully down to his dirty bandages, then back at Norm.

"Screw the hand! And screw you!"

Oh, man, Norm thought. "What's the problem, Bobby?"

"You. You got my woman." Bobby took a couple steps towards him. Norm retreated towards the kitchen. Tammy eased her way towards the master bedroom. "But I'm gonna show her that you ain't much of a man. I'm going to whup your ass."

Norm's back bumped into the kitchen counter. "Wait a minute, Bobby. I'm no fighter."

"Don't matter, I am." Norm's eyes scanned the kitchen for something to defend himself with. There was the rectangular wooden block holding the carving knives. No, no way! No knives! His eyes fell on to a medium size cast iron pan. More reasonable, he thought. He picked it up.

"Stay clear, Bobby."

Bobby laughed. "That little ol' thing ain't going to save your butt." He took a step forward.

"Hold it!" Tammy shrieked. Both men looked over. Tammy was pointing a huge pistol at Bobby's chest. " Back off, Bobby, or so help me God I'll blow you away!"

Bobby backed off. He turned to Norm. "Well, well, Doctor. I didn't think your type would have a gun in the house."

"It's not his gun, Bobby. It's mine, and you might recall that I know how to use it. Now I think you better leave."

Bobby ignored her and walked nonchalantly over to the bar. Norm figured he was trying to save face.

"Don't mind if I have a short one, do you, Doctor?"

"Help yourself."

Bobby looked at the bottles. Fancy looking. He didn't know most of the brands. But he recognized *Scotch Whisky*. He poured himself a heavy slug. He slowly drank it as he walked around the room. He peered in at the birdcages, then stopped to look out over the Gulf. He passed a hand over the back of the couch, then felt the smoothness of the cherry dining room table. Tammy and Norm were silent. Tammy continued to point the pistol. Bobby finished the drink. He walked over to the bar and clumsily poured another. Whether all the alcohol had finally hit, or something to do with the earlier rush of adrenalin, Bobby was suddenly sloppy drunk.

"One for the road," he slurred. He downed it in one long gulp, coughed, and without looking at either of them stumbled to the front door. They could hear him slowly make his way down the stairs. Tammy lowered the gun. She and Norm looked at each other. Norm came over, took the gun away and put it on a side table. He took her in his arms and they held each other tight. They waited to hear the car start below. Nothing. After awhile, they parted and walked over to the window. They looked down and saw the front door of the Torino was open. They also saw that Bobby was sprawled on the front seat passed out.

Tammy turned to Norm. Rolling her eyes, she asked, "Now what!"

"Now I take the stitches out."

Tammy looked at him in disbelief. "You're kidding!"

"Good a time as any and he won't feel a thing. Plus, did you see that bandage? Who knows what it looks like underneath?"

Norm turned towards the door. Tammy followed him down to the clinic where he got all the necessary items.

Norm sat on the passenger side where he had good access to Bobby's hand. He took the bandage off. He was gratified that the hand was mostly clean. He wiped the hand with disinfectant pads before taking the stitches out. Tammy watched. She wondered how many times she had watched him do stitches: mostly it had been after late night brawls at the Club. When he was finished, he pulled Bobby across the seat until there was room to drive.

"Think I'll take him home," he said.

Tammy smiled and shook her head. "You're something else, know that? I'll go with you."

Tammy sat in the back and Norm drove over and parked in front of the trailer. They got out, leaving Bobby loudly snoring in the front.

"Wait a sec while I put the keys inside. Don't think he should be driving anywhere." Norm entered the trailer and tossed the keys onto the kitchen table. Tammy was waiting for him at the edge of the street. When he walked up, she told him to hold still and gave him a long, deep kiss. With arms around each other's waist, they walked home. Four hours later, a very groggy and still drunk Bobby woke up. His neck was killing him and he had to piss like a racehorse. He stumbled out of the car. His mouth felt like it was full of cotton and his head was throbbing. He entered the trailer, flipped on the lights, and made his way straight to the bathroom. After relieving himself, he went into the kitchen for a long drink of water. As he filled the glass, he noticed the bright white bandage on his hand. Where the hell had that come from? He turned and leaned back against the sink as he drank. He saw the car keys on the middle of the table. He didn't remember putting them there when he came in. But he was all fuzzy and didn't remember much. He finished the water and stumbled into his bedroom. Without taking off his boots he flopped down on his bed. He was asleep in seconds.

Chapter Twenty-Six

After seeing the doctor in Gainesville, Beau and Virginia stopped at the Publix in Jonesville to buy groceries on their way back to Crescent Beach. Beau filled the shopping cart with this and that while Virginia waited in line at the butcher and deli departments. They didn't say more than a dozen words to each other, just checked things off the list. The rest of the way home they said even less. Virginia let Skillet out when they returned and took him for a long walk. Beau schlepped the bags of food up to the kitchen. By the time Virginia returned, he had everything put away and sunset wasn't far off. Beau tried to be cheery.

"How about you get the hot tub going, Sugah, and I'll make us a pitcher of martinis?"

Virginia smiled sweetly. "Alright, Dear."

Twenty minutes later they were in the hot tub, watching the big orange ball on the horizon. Skillet was to their side, snoring softly. He was on his special platform covered in a double layer of outdoor carpet. Charley had built a ramp, like the one for the golf cart, so Skillet could trot up to the platform and be part of their hot tub tradition.

"Going to be another scorcher tomorrow," Beau said.

Virginia, her mind a million miles away, said, "Yes, Dear."

They drank their martinis in silence. The sun was almost down when Virginia started crying. Beau took the glass out of her hand and placed it and his off to the side.

"Oh, Beau, I am so sorry," she said, sobbing and turning into his shoulder. Beau maneuvered his arm around her and drew her in as close as he could. He willed himself to be strong.

"Hush, Sugah. It's alright. Life's nothing but a series of tests and we've had plenty over the last fifty years. We haven't flunked one yet, and we're not about to now."

"But, Beau," she said, looking up.

Beau put a hand gently over her mouth and smiled. "Now hush. Look out there. Just beautiful!" He lightly turned her head. "Let's make each one count." Virginia wiped away her tears as best she could and settled into Beau's shoulder. They watched the sun as it disappeared.

Early the next morning while Beau and Virginia were asleep, Louie got up after another sleepless night. The savings from his former Boston job were running precariously low causing him to toss and turn as he tried to figure out ways to reduce his already miniscule budget. It was imperative to do something about his financial situation soon. Too bad he didn't get paid for all the time he put in at the library, he thought, but at least the computer there helped him maintain his sanity. He got dressed and walked over to Bad Dog who was impatiently waiting at the front door. Bad Dog streaked out to do his business while Louie began his daily ritual of making coffee and inspecting his plants. Wherever there was a window, there was at least one plant—spider plant, African violets, aloe, various ferns, even a thick, well-pruned mini-marijuana shrub. Several plants hung from the camper awning outside. After sticking a finger in the soil of each pot, he filled a long, skinny-necked watering can and made the rounds. Many of the plants were from cuttings donated by Virginia. She had even given him a prize orchid from her special stock. Louie was very much impressed by her extensive horticultural knowledge; he'd ask her a question and she always got it right. He knew because he'd check later on the computer. After breakfast, he hopped on his bike and with Bad Dog trotting alongside went to the library. As he pedaled, for some reason he thought of the Brando movie, *The Wild One,* where Brando was the head of a motorcycle gang that took over a town back in the fifties. A classic promotional poster, now a collector's item, had been made of Brando looking tough on his Triumph. Strapped to the handlebars was a stolen motorcycle race trophy. Louie thought that if he hadn't given that trophy to Tommy, he would have proudly strapped it onto his handlebars.

When they arrived at the library, Louie pulled out his key and unlocked the door. Bad Dog went straight to his rug scrap by the desk while Louie surveyed the room as always. Like the camper, the windows were full of plants. Louie had decided to take cuttings from his and put them in the two big south facing windows. He was gratified when they went bonkers and the few patrons who came into the library complimented him on how healthy they looked. After making a pot of coffee, another library perk, he took a cup over and settled down at the computer. From where he sat, he could peer out to Main Street. At this early hour on a weekday, absolutely nothing was happening. He loved this time of day. He turned on the computer, took a sip of coffee, and was soon immersed.

He heard the door open and looked up. It was the lady with the bleached blond hair from the trailer across from the crabbers' docks. Movies, always movies. She had a handful. He stood up. He looked at the clock. Two hours since he had sat down. Time flew when he was at the computer.

"I want to swap me some movies, Mr. Louie. Got any new ones I ain't seen yet?"

"Yes, Ma'am. We got several new ones in from the Baptist Church in Perry." He knew what kind of movies she liked. Kung Fu, James Bond, action-packed. "Pretty tame, though."

While she was going through the selection, she started talking about what was going on about town. She lived alone and Louie knew that she liked to visit when she came in.

"And can you believe that the store is out of eggs and butter, both! I mean, I don't want to drive to Perry for a half-dozen eggs; that's crazy!"

"Try the Marina. They should have some."

The woman stopped going through the movies and turned to Louie.

"Not on your life! I'm not going to buy anything from that Jezebel." She glanced to her left and right, before lowering her voice. "And did you know she's playin' around with that Bobby who works there now?" She got a dreamy look in her eyes. "Not that he ain't cute as can be…but she's a married woman!"

A lot of women in town didn't like BeeBee, Louie knew. Some because they were conservative church people who couldn't condone the way she dressed and carried on. Others didn't like how their men fawned over her. Others were downright jealous of her looks.

"Now how do you know that?"

She rolled her eyes before turning back to the shelves. "Everybody in town knows. Only person who don't is her poor husband. Imagine he'll be findin' out soon enough."

Louie glanced out between the plants. He saw Virginia walking towards the library. He was wondering if he should pour her a cup of coffee when he saw her stop in front of Clem and Katharine's trailer. Katharine was loading some things into her truck.

"How's Rebecca?" Virginia asked.

"Better, thank the Lord. Gaining a little every day. Infection's under control."

"Will she be able to come home soon?"

Katharine shrugged her shoulders. "Not for a time yet. But not too long, I hope and God willin'."

"Please give her Beau's and my love, and tell her to hurry home fast."

Katharine smiled. "Will do."

Virginia continued walking, her head full of Rebecca. She stopped a half block later. Now where was I going? She tried to concentrate. For the life of me, I can't remember. Must not have been important. She turned around and walked home. When she entered the house, Beau said, "That was quick. How did he take it?"

"Who's that, dear?"

"Louie. What did he say when you told him you had Alzheimer's?"

So that was it. She hesitated. "I chickened out. I haven't told him yet. But, that's silly. I'm going to turn around right now and do it. I'll be back in a little bit."

Beau sadly watched her leave the house. He wasn't fooled. Virginia walked to the library, saying over and over under her breath, L.A.L.—Library, Alzheimer's, Louie—L.A.L.—Library, Alzheimer's, Louie. Louie was back at the computer when she entered. He stood up.

"Hi," he said. "How did your trip to Gainesville go?"

Virginia smiled bravely. "That's why I'm here. I want to talk to you about it. Come sit with me over at the big table, would you, Louie?"

"Sure thing."

They sat down across from each other with Louie wondering what this could possibly be about. Virginia didn't beat around the bush.

"Beau and I went into Gainesville so I could see a specialist at Shands. I have been diagnosed with Alzheimer's."

Louie didn't say anything. It explained everything. He felt awful for her. Awful for Beau. Son-of-a-bitch! "There was a chance it could have been a tumor, but I had an MRI. It was clean. Blood work, lumbar puncture, the whole nine yards. Clinical diagnosis is that Alzheimer's is highly probable. The only way they can tell a hundred percent is by examining the histology of the brain by autopsy."

Louie reached across the table for one of her hands. "I am so sorry, Virginia."

Virginia smiled politely. "So, looks like I'm going to have to ask you to do even more than you've already done…And Louie, I know how much you've been doing, covering for me. I want to thank you for that, too."

Louie squeezed her hand. He forced a smile. "No worries, Virginia. Don't worry about a thing."

Virginia stood. "That's what I came here to say." She laughed sadly. "Actually, twice. I came over a bit earlier, but forgot where I was going."

Louie nodded. "I saw you and was wondering why you turned around."

"Anyway," she continued, "it's going to get worse. How fast is anyone's guess. They say that I'll get totally disoriented and then, poof, my head will clear. So, there will be good days and bad. I want to come help out when I'm able."

"Absolutely." Louie walked her to the door where she stopped and turned around.

"Thank you, Louie." Louie hugged her, and she left.

Virginia was on Louie's mind all day. By the time he locked the library, he had to unload. He headed straight to Charley's. The Mustang and lawnmower were in the open-sided carport. Louie put the kickstand down and yelled up to the boat's cabin. "Ahoy! Anybody home?" Charley's head soon appeared above the railing. "Permission to come aboard?"

"Come ahead. Watch yur step now."

Louie turned to Bad Dog and pointed at him. "Stay!" Bad Dog sat and Louie slowly and carefully climbed the aluminum ladder. When he was safely on deck, he asked, "Charley, why the hell don't you build a real stairway?"

"Tax collector. They figger the '*Ray's* like a camper an' I don't get taxed none. Build me a stairway and they'll get nosy. First thing ya know, gonna git taxed fer a house." Louie nodded. Made perfect sense to him. "Come on down into the cabin and take a load off. Just got me a new shipment of suds."

Louie followed Charley down to the galley. Over the last few years, little by little, Charley had restored the boat's entire interior. The mahogany gleamed and was set off by soft hues of carefully painted walls. He had installed a stainless sink, stove, and half-refrigerator that he had found at a salvage yard and polished to a mirror finish. He had found matching nautical brass light fixtures at the same yard. Each light had a small tan shade on which he had painted small blue anchors. He had replaced every board that showed any sign of rot, sanded all the wood with at least one-eighty grit and applied four coats of a synthetic urethane oil. It was as striking as any captain's quarters anywhere. Charley opened the refrigerator. It was crammed full of beer.

"Pick yur poison," Charley said.

Louie was impressed. "Dang, Charley. Look at that." He picked out a fancy bottle and read the label. Brewed in Belgium. He handed it to Charley who stood ready with a church key. Louie looked more carefully at the selection. A lot of it was imported. "How can you afford this stuff?" he asked, as Charley handed him the beer. Charley grabbed one for himself and shut the refrigerator.

"Might say they're freebies. You know that old Airstream by the canal on west Third Street?" Louie nodded as he sat down at the galley table. "Guy was restoring it. Ripped her right apart and rebuilt her from the ground up. Only thing he kept original was a recessed cabinet over the bed with sliding panel-like doors. Wanted me to paint a beach scene on those doors with an Airstream and flamingos and the water and clouds and such. But he wanted it kinda cartoon-like, not so much real life."

"Whimsical," Louie said.

"Whatever. Anyway, I did it and he loved it. Tried to pay me, but I told him it was a fun project and didn't want no money nor nuthin'." Charley smiled at Louie. "Yes, Sir, turns out the guy's a big time beer distributor from Tampa. Every time he comes up, he brings me a case of different stuff. Just got this in yesterday." Charley took a long, satisfying swig and sat down across from Louie. "So, what's up, Louie? Usually ya got somethin' special on yur mind to pay me a visit."

Louie nodded sadly. He told Charley about Virginia. Charley didn't say a word until he was finished. Neither had touched their beers while Louie was talking. Charley broke the silence. "Now ain't that a bitch." He took a swig of beer. "And there ain't nuthin' that can stop this All-Timers?"

"Alzheimer's. Nope. Modern medicine hasn't come up with anything yet."

Charley repeated himself. "Now ain't that a bitch."

Louie felt better for unloading on Charley. As for Charley, his day had been going well. Now, not so much. The two gossiped for awhile and reminisced about the race. Talked of Rebecca and her family. Eventually, Louie stood up. "Want another brew?" Charley asked.

"No, thanks. Don't feel like it much. Better go see if Bad Dog stuck around. About time for his dinner."

"Before ya go, lemme show ya somethin'." Charley led him to the forward-most berth. Propped up against the end of the bunk was an oil painting in a dark brown, pecky cypress frame. Louie examined it up close. It was a tranquil scene of marsh and egrets and a distant tree line.

"Nice," Louie said.

"Recognize it?"

"Nope."

"That's what Rusty looks out at every day from his deck. Was jest about to wrap it up and take it to him when ya got here. Gonna be a sorta housewarmin' present."

"Why don't you give me a camperwarming present like that sometime?"

"Ya ain't got no view."

Louie couldn't argue that. The pair went out on deck. Charley held the ladder for Louie as he descended. Bad Dog hadn't moved. Louie said, "Good dog, Bad Dog." Made sense to Bad Dog who wagged his tail. Louie got on his bike and pedaled off with Bad Dog at his side. Charley watched them go, then turned to go wrap up the landscape. Fifteen minutes later he pulled up to Rusty's in the Mustang. Rusty's truck was there. Charley grabbed the painting and climbed the stairs. Rusty was out on the deck having an evening beer, gazing out over the marsh. He heard Charley and went around to investigate.

"Hey, Charley. Join me for a beer on the deck?"

"Shur, but first I want to give ya somethin', a sorta housewarmin' present." He held out the painting. Rusty was surprised. He reached out and took the package before opening the front door for Charley.

When they were inside, Rusty hefted it. Smiling, he said, "Feels like a painting."

"Maybe, maybe not."

Rusty carefully pulled the paper away from the frame. He was speechless. He held the painting up, then looked beyond it out the window, then looked back at the painting. Finally he stammered, "Charley, it's beautiful—perfect—I can't take this, it's worth a lot of money."

Charley held up his hands. "Don't want no money, but a beer'll do me jest fine."

"In the 'fridge. Help yourself." In the living room was a mantle above a gas fireplace. Rusty rushed over and leaned the picture up and stepped back. "Oh my God, it's perfect! Light's not so great. Maybe I can get Sammy to install a couple mini-spots in the ceiling."

Charley walked over and stood by Rusty. "Does look good there if'n I do say so myself." He took a swig of beer.

Rusty stood there transfixed. Finally, he said, "Let's go out to the deck and look at the real thing." They went out and sat looking over the marsh. Rusty said, "Norm's right; you really do have talent, Charley."

"Guess then I got me two talents."

"What's the other?"

Charley held up the bottle. "Drinkin' beer. An' I been doin' it a lot longer than paintin', so am a mite better at it."

Rusty laughed. He asked, "Do you ever regret that you fished and crabbed your whole life, rather than paint? I mean, maybe you'd be world famous or something."

Charley put his beer down. "If it wasn't fer all that fishin' and boatin', I don't believe I could paint none a'tall. Ya see, I been around all this so much that I feel and breathe it." Charley looked out over the marsh. "I know what some of them birds are gonna do before they does. I can smell a storm comin'. I know how the marsh grass moves with the wind. Norm says everything's alive in my painting. If'n that's true, it comes from all that fishin' and such. So, no. I ain't got no regrets about none o' that."

They heard an airboat start up deep in the marsh. It soon made conversation impossible as it headed out towards the Gulf. Rusty put his hands over his ears until it passed and was out of sight. Shaking his head, he said, "Pretty easy to understand why Norm hates those things."

Charley nodded. "Yep; his pet peave, it is." They were quiet awhile, until Charley thought of Louie's visit. "Ya hear about Virginia?"

Rusty looked over. "No. What?"

"She's got All-Timers. She told Louie who jest told me."

Rusty sighed and slowly shook his head. "How's Beau taking it?"

"Dunno. Ain't see him."

Suddenly they were interrupted by the phone. Rusty got up and went into the house.

"Hello?"

"Is this Sergeant McMillan?"

"Er, yes…"

"This is Captain Smathers, Cross City Barracks. Long time, no see. Hear you're retired now."

"Yes, sir, that's a fact."

"Lucky you. Understand you moved to Crescent Beach. Learn to swim, yet?"

Rusty laughed. "Sort of. Went scalloping the other day and about drowned."

Smathers laughed, then switched abruptly to business. "Got something to run by you, McMillan. Thought maybe from the work you did in our area, you might have some ideas."

"Yes, sir. Shoot."

"A body was fished out of a sinkhole yesterday to the west of Perry. Not much more than a skeleton because fish did a pretty good job on it. Examiner estimates the body's been there maybe four to six years."

"I assume you suspect foul play."

The Captain laughed. "You might say so. This was no spelunker. Chances are it was a gangland execution. Guy was wrapped up in chains and concrete blocks and had a single bullet hole in his head. His stature and bone structure suggest Latino. Odd thing was that he had also been shot once dead center in the hand." Rusty's stomach flip-flopped. He sat down on a stool at the kitchen counter. Smathers continued. "Got any ideas?"

"Not off the top of my head. But let me do a little digging and get back to you. Can't promise anything."

"Just a long shot calling you anyway. But, thanks. If you come up with something, I can be reached at the barracks."

"Right, Captain. Goodbye."

Rusty hung up the phone, his mind buzzing. He sat there a second or two before picking up the phone. Jimmy answered on the third ring.

"Jimmy?"

"Yeah?"

"Rusty, here."

"Take it you saw the evening news." Jimmy's voice was strained.

"No, I didn't."

"Interesting item. Seems a body was discovered in a sinkhole."

"Yeah, just heard about it on the phone from a State Police captain. Wants to know if I've got any ideas."

Silence on Jimmy's end. Then, "Do you?"

"That's what I wanted to talk to you about."

"Better come on over."

"Right." Rusty hung up the phone. He went out to the deck. "Something's come up, Charley. I got to go over to Jimmy's. Stay here and finish your beer."

Charley stood up. Rusty looked spooked. "Thankee kindly, but all set." He handed the empty bottle to Rusty. "Got to get back anyway." As he went down the stairs to the Mustang, Charley thought, now what the heck's that all about?

Chapter Twenty-Seven

The Botfly is an unusual insect. It lays its eggs on mammals and the heat from the mammal's body soon hatches the eggs. The larva then burrows under the skin or enters through tiny apertures often made by mosquitos and takes up residence. It is a parasite and feeds on its host until it reaches pupal state and leaves. While burrowing, the larva often strikes a nerve causing sharp pain and discomfort. Such it was with Frank. Suspicion and doubt were the Botfly-like eggs laid during the Fourth of July fireworks. They hatched and soon burrowed non-stop around Frank's brain. He could think of nothing else. Sure, he knew that Bee had been a wild lady in Lauderdale. And he also knew that a guy like him could never get a babe like her if it weren't for his money. He had hoped that marrying her and moving here, out of temptation's way, would make everything perfect. But, it hadn't. Marriage vows, he believed, even those made in Vegas high on coke, were sacrosanct. Bee apparently thought otherwise. He didn't really blame Bobby. Bobby was a stud, something Frank knew he could never be. And who could blame Bobby for sniffing around when Bee flaunted her body so shamelessly. No, it wasn't jealousy that was bugging him; it was the worm of infidelity. He became obsessed. He tried hard not to believe that he had seen Bee's hand caress Bobby's rear end, but the image kept flashing across his mind. His suspicions deepened when Bobby had drunkenly confronted and mocked Bee. Even drunk, how could Bobby so confidently confront his wife like that if there wasn't something going on? There was a familiarity there that just wasn't right. Frank started paying closer attention.

Bobby had smoothed things over with BeeBee and they resumed their trysts in Berth #22 on Mondays when Frank would go into town for supplies. On Wednesdays they went to the Hilton. Usually before sex they indulged in a little of BeeBee's coke. Bobby didn't own a pair of dark glasses and BeeBee never wore hers inside. Consequently, Frank began to notice that on late Monday afternoons, Bobby's and BeeBee's pupils would be unnaturally dilated. The same thing for BeeBee's on Wednesday evenings, Bobby's day off. And now she was always too tired for sex. BeeBee had a compact where she kept a little vial of coke, a bill, and a razor blade. After each tryst, she would replenish it from the main stash hidden in the bedroom of their house. Frank checked the supply. It had been depleted by almost half. Still, Bobby and BeeBee were careful, and were formal with each other when Frank was around. So, Frank was never completely sure until the Monday afternoon he came out of the Winn-Dixie with a bag of groceries in his arms. There was a folded piece of lined paper tucked under the wiper blades. He put the groceries in the truck and walked around for the note. He opened it up.

YOUR WIFE IS SCREWING BOBBY

It was a jolt. He looked around the parking lot. He didn't recognize anybody or any car or truck. He read the note again. He looked around the parking lot again. Has to be someone from Crescent Beach, he thought. Most likely a woman shopping who saw my truck and hates Bee. He smiled ruefully; which means it could be most any adult female in town. He folded the note and put it in his shirt pocket while striding back to the store. He entered and went up and down the aisles. No one there he knew. He drove back to Crescent Beach, fuming. Had to be true! The bitch! Screwing Bobby right under my nose! And if one woman knows, they all know. Must be all over town, with me the fool. When he returned to the Marina, Bobby was cleaning a boat down by the dock. Frank forced himself to calm down. He walked up to Bobby and asked how it was going. Bobby said, fine. Frank saw the large pupils. When he carried the groceries into the house, BeeBee looked up from reading a book. Her pupils were like saucers.

The following Monday, Frank left as usual for Perry. But, he didn't go far. He drove out to the point which curved around enough out in the Gulf so that with binoculars he could see the Marina store and bar. It didn't take long. Within a half hour he saw BeeBee hold the door open for Bobby and follow him in after putting the sign on the door. Frank waited. He wanted to catch them in the act. He looked in the glove box. The .357 Magnum was right where it was supposed to be. When he figured enough time had passed, he returned to the Marina, turning off his engine and coasting into the parking lot in neutral. He pulled the gun from the dash and walked up to the Marina door. The sign was still there. The door was locked. As quietly as he could, he unlocked the door. He went inside. Total silence. He tiptoed to the bar, his stomach tight with a mix of dread and excitement, his head full of righteous anger. The bar was empty. His hand with the gun dropped to his side. What the hell? Where'd they go?

Bobby and BeeBee were laying down naked at Berth #22. Bobby was leaning on an elbow, toying with one of BeeBee's nipples.

"I think I could have been in the movies. What do you think, Bobby?"

Bobby laughed. "You mean like 'Deep Throat?'"

She slapped his hand away. "I'm serious."

Bobby brought his hand back. "I know one role in a good movie you coulda played. Saw it in prison." BeeBee perked up.

"What movie?"

" 'Cool Hand Luke.'"

"That was all men!"

"No it wasn't. Don't you remember that scene when the chain gang's out working and an absolute babe comes out of a house to wash her car? She's wearing short-shorts and a tight tee-shirt. She's got boobs like yours. She gets her shirt all wet, then rubs her boobs up and down on the window. It's like she's naked and screwing the car. Squeezes the sponge she's using and white suds go all over the place."

BeeBee smiled. "Yeah, I do remember that. She was sexy as hell."

"Wasn't the greatest movie to be showing us in prison, what with that scene and Paul Newman always escaping. But, I'll bet every inmate jerked off at least a half-dozen times that night."

BeeBee smiled at Bobby. "How would Big Boy like me to rub all over you like that."

"Only one way to find out."

BeeBee rubbed her breasts back and forth, up and down Bobby's chest. She pulled away and looked. "Seems Big Boy likes it."

"Yeah, he likes it a lot. He'll show you just how much he likes it."

When Frank entered the boat storage shed, he saw the forklift. His eyes followed the mast up to the forks. The boat in Berth #22 was rocking rhythmically. Gotcha, you sons-of-bitches! Frank walked quickly to the forklift. He laid the pistol down next to the seat and started it up. He quickly reversed, dropped the forks, drove forward, and lifted the boat up off the berth. He backed out to the center of the shed and drove full tilt towards the water. The bouncing of the forklift rattled them apart. Bobby hung on for dear life as he peeked over the gunnel.

"Frank!" he exclaimed. He struggled to grab and put on his underwear. It wasn't easy. BeeBee did the same with her panties and bra. She couldn't fasten the bra with all the bouncing. Frank started angling the forks down before he came to the water. Timing it perfectly he slammed on the brakes and the boat slid off the forks and fell fourteen feet into the canal. It pivoted halfway on the way down so it landed on its side, ejecting Bobby and BeeBee. The boat slowly rolled over until it was upside down. Both Bobby and BeeBee were stunned, but okay. Frank jumped off the forklift with the gun in hand. He pointed it at Bobby. With the combination of adrenalin rush and being totally pissed, Frank was having a hard time keeping the barrel steady. Bobby didn't like the look on Frank's face—it scared him as much as the pistol. He raised his arms immediately. He was wearing only underpants. BeeBee slogged through the muddy bottom until she stood next to Bobby. She had lost her bra. Bobby didn't say a word.

"Just like a pair of rats leaving a ship!" Frank shouted. "Vermin!" He cocked the pistol. Bobby held his breath. After what seemed like forever, Frank lowered the hammer. "Bobby, you get the hell out of here! You get into that car of yours and go away. Far away and don't come back. If you do, I'll shoot your ass. That's a promise. Now, GIT!"

Bobby was out of the canal and in the Torino within seconds. Limestone flew from the tires as he peeled out. Frank never took his eyes off BeeBee. "You're a whore, know that, Bee?" He cocked the gun again and aimed towards that big left tit of hers. BeeBee put her face in her hands and began to sob. Frank moved his arm to the left and pulled the trigger. A .357 Magnum makes a hell of a noise. It also made a pretty big splash two feet to BeeBee's right. BeeBee jumped and peed her panties. Frank aimed the pistol this time to her right and shot again. BeeBee was crying and shaking uncontrollably. She looked up at him.

"Please, Frank..."

Frank did not un-cock the gun, but said, "I'll give you ten minutes, bitch, to climb out, get dressed and packed, and then you take that fucking blue pimp-mobile of yours and leave! I never want to see you again! IS THAT CLEAR!"

"Yes, Frank." BeeBee scrambled like a crab over the seawall. It wasn't pretty. When she left the marina, she drove straight to Bobby's trailer. The Torino's trunk was open and Bobby was packing his barbells. He saw BeeBee drive up. He had heard the two shots. She ran up to him.

"You're alive," was all he said before closing the trunk.

"Bobby, what are we going to do now?"

"I don't know about you, but I'm leaving Dodge, pronto. Ain't got nothing to hold me here."

"We'll go together, won't we? In the T-Bird?"

"Uh, uh. Sorry, Babe. You're going your way and I'm going mine." He turned and went back into the trailer. She followed him inside. He quickly opened and shut drawers, stuffing clothes in his duffle bag. He pulled shirts and pants out of the closet.

"Bobby!"

Bobby paused in his packing.

"Look, BeeBee, it was all about the sex. Nothing more, nothing less. We took our chances and we got caught. Now we pay the price. I'm outta here...alone."

"But I don't have any money," BeeBee said, following him into the bathroom where he cleared out his razor, toothbrush, and other stuff.

"Can't help that, Babe. Guess you blew it."

Bobby jammed the toiletries into the duffle bag and hoisted it onto his shoulder. He went out to the Torino and tossed the duffle bag into the back seat. "Only one more thing," he said, more to himself than to BeeBee who had followed him out. "Whacko."

"What?" Beebie said, looking at him like he was crazy.

Bobby went into the trailer and walked up to the wood stove. On top was a nicely crafted walnut urn. Bobby picked it up and brought it out to the Torino. He carefully strapped it in the front passenger seat. He turned to BeeBee. "Whacko's ashes." Bobby slipped into the driver's seat. "Been fun, Babe. Sorry it turned out the way it did, but with your looks, you won't have any problem. Better find someone soon, though." He started the car. "Good luck." He put it in reverse and backed out of the driveway. BeeBee, shoulders slumped, watched him drive away.

Bobby drove straight to the cemetery. He found the shovel and dug up the PVC pipe. He stashed the pipe in the trunk under a pile of barbells. As he drove off, he turned to look at the urn. "Guess you were right, Whacko. Shouldn't have messed around with a married woman. Never again, I swear." A ways down the road he remembered Whacko's meth stash behind the hunting camp. "We don't need that stuff, now do we?" he asked. "Look what it did to you. Nah, we're better off without it. Besides, we got a lot of driving to do. We got to find you a mountain with a pretty view. We're a headin' west, partner." Seconds later, he said, "Now wait a cotton picking minute!" He pulled over and opened the trunk. He pulled the cowboy hat out from a corner and put it on. When he climbed back in, he looked over to Whacko. "There. Now we're all set." Bobby was smiling. He felt really free for the first time since getting out of prison. He drove through Perry, heading towards the interstate that would take them west. There was a hitchhiker on the outskirts of Perry. He had his thumb out and a cheap, battered suitcase lay at his feet. He looked like he was down on his luck. Bobby stopped.

"Where you headed?" Bobby asked.

"North."

"I'm heading north until the interstate, then west."

"Sounds good to me."

The guy opened the back door and set his suitcase on the seat. He began to open the front passenger door.

"Sorry, you got to sit in the back. This seat's for Whacko here," Bobby said, nodding towards the urn with the seatbelt cinched tightly around it. The guy looked at the urn, at Bobby, and back to the urn. He carefully shut the door and opened the rear. He had a funny look on his face. He pulled his suitcase out.

"Thanks just the same, but I think I'll keep hitching."

Bobby shrugged. "Suit yourself. Good luck." About a mile down the road, Bobby started laughing. He turned to the urn. "Did you see the look on his face, Whacko, when I told him that was your seat?" Bobby laughed so hard that tears coursed down his cheeks.

Chapter Twenty-Eight

That's the culprit, Jimmy thought, as he looked at the broken spring in the palm of his hand. He tossed it into the wastebasket at his feet and reached for a tiny sealed plastic bag. He opened it and took out a new spring and installed it in the spinning reel. He put the reel back onto the fiberglass rod and clicked the bail arm back and forth several times. Worked perfectly. He stood up and leaned the rod next to the shop door. He returned to his workbench and sat down. He stared out the window towards the Gulf. Another fine day. Felt good having a break from guiding. Lots of things to catch up with, though; got a list a mile long. But he remained where he was, motionless, looking out at the Gulf. Finally, he turned to the large Craftsman toolbox on his workbench. He opened one of the metal drawers and pulled out a beat-up newspaper article that Rusty had brought to him several days ago.

Jimmy and Rusty had debated a long time whether Rusty should get back to Captain Smathers with any information.

"If I explain that the guy was a real bad *hombre*, a drug lord and killer, I'll bet anything that I could trade his identity for the authorities to drop the case and leave it be as a gangland execution," Rusty said. "You'd be free and clear, Jimmy."

"Maybe from the good guys, but not the bad. Once the Colombians know Espantoso bit it around here, they're going to come knocking for sure. Besides, I don't believe the cops will find any evidence to lead them to me."

Rusty rolled his eyes. "Jimmy, shooting him in the hand. That was like leaving a calling card. With any digging at all, they could put two and two together. Maybe they could make a case against you, maybe not, but they'd sure as hell figure out that you did it."

Jimmy looked at the scar in his hand. That was a mistake, shooting Espantoso in the hand. It had given him a lot of satisfaction, though. "I screwed up there. Doing that was dumb; I'll admit that. I just figured no one would find him in a million years."

"Didn't you say that Espantoso's goons held you when he shot you?"

"Yeah. So?"

"So you don't think they'll figure it out—Espantoso disappeared from Old Town, no trace, five years ago. Then on statewide, maybe nationwide TV news it's reported that a short man with heavy bones, most likely stocky, was discovered with a bullet in his head AND a bullet in his right hand. And that he was shot around five years ago. I think either way, identified or not, the boys from Miami will have a pretty good idea."

He looked away from Rusty, not saying anything for a few minutes. When he looked back, he said, "You're right. Probably just a matter of time now." He sighed. "What would you do if you was me, Rusty?"

Rusty shrugged his shoulders and looked sadly at his friend. "Tough frigging call."

In the end, Rusty telephoned Smathers and the deal was worked out. Jimmy read the article for the umpteenth time.

TALLAHASSEE TIMES
Wednesday
August 1, 1998

As was reported in the TIMES ten days ago, two amateur archaeologists, scuba diving in a remote flooded sinkhole near the Wacissa River west of Perry, discovered a man's skeleton wrapped in chains and concrete blocks. Two bullet holes were found, one in the victim's head and the other in his right hand. Through a lead provided by retired State Trooper Rusty MacMillan of Crescent Beach, the remains have been identified as those of Jose Arias, also known as El Espantoso, a drug trafficker from Miami with ties to a Colombian cartel.

Forensic experts believe the body had been in the sinkhole for at least several years, and authorities are attributing the death to a gangland killing. State Police Captain Smathers told the TIMES, "Dental records from Miami have positively confirmed the identification of this man. This was an execution, plain and simple, within the ranks of a notorious drug ring operating out of Miami. We are not going to pursue this case. The state of Florida is better off without this criminal."

In related drug trafficking news, it has been announced that the Department of Defense has closed Blimp Station Number Thirteen. Established in 1978 outside of Crescent Beach, the blimp station was used in aerial surveillance of the Big Bend area of northern Florida. Citing continual downtime of the blimp due to weather and mechanical difficulties along with a drastic drop in smuggling activities in the area, a spokesman from the Department of Defense said that the facility would be sold to a local LP gas company.

Jimmy put the article away and stood up. Time's awasting, he thought. That impeller ain't going to check itself. He gathered some tools together and left his shop for the boat. He undid the lines and moved the stern closer into shore where he had poured a three foot by four foot cement slab to stand on in the water. It allowed him to work on the prop area of the raised up motor without the muck sucking the sandals off his feet. He retied the boat and got to work. He wanted to check the impeller and water pump housing. It didn't take him long to remove the lower unit. He had it in his arms with his back to the street when a new, black Ford crew-cab pickup pulled up. It looked recently washed and waxed and its shiny spinner hubcaps shone brightly in the sun. A fiberglass cover, the same color as the truck, was over the bed and the dark tinted windows were up all the way around. The center of the license plate was stamped **Miami-Dade.** The passenger side window lowered and a Latino aimed a camera at Jimmy.

"*Hola,* Jeemy." Jimmy whipped around with the heavy lower unit still in his hands. The Latino shot several pictures of the surprised Jimmy. "Smile, you're on Candeed Camera," the Latino said. The camera had motor-drive and he took a host of shots. The Latino put the camera away as Jimmy put the lower unit on the dock and began to slowly edge around the side of the boat. The Latino put his elbows on the door and watched Jimmy. He was smiling. "Long time no see, Jeemy." Jimmy had immediately recognized the man: one of the two goons that had held him when Espantoso shot his hand. "How ees thee hand, eh? That Espantoso, he was a bad *hombre,* no? I deed not like holding you like we deed." He shook his head sadly. "No, I think it was not fair, three against one. But me, I just follow orders." Jimmy was at the side of his boat. He shifted his butt onto the gunnel and slid in. The Latino's eyes closely followed his movements. "But Espantoso, he ees not aroun' any more. But I theenk you know that. And I theenk maybe I should thank you. Once Espantoso deesapeared, I go up the ladder, no? I am a man who is respected now in the family." Jimmy's hand rested above the center console drawer. The Latino started to roll up his window, but stopped it halfway. "Good luck, Jeemy, I think you will neeed it. *Adíos.*" He nodded towards the driver side and finished rolling up the window. The pickup slowly drove off. Crystal, looking worried, came down from the deck.

"Who was that, Jimmy? That truck came by three times in the last hour."

Jimmy climbed out of the boat onto the dock. He walked up to Crystal and put an arm around her waist. "Just some old business acquaintance who has come up in the world. Wanted to show off his fancy truck. C'mon, I'm starved. How about I take a break and you fix me something for lunch?" The pair walked up to the house. Jimmy was disgusted with himself. Both hands full, back to the street, no gun, and standing in a foot of water! Bet your ass that ain't gonna happen again!

A week later in Naples, Florida, a beautiful burgundy Porsche pulled in and parked across the street from the main post office. A tall, extremely good-looking blond haired man got out and crossed the street. He looked to be in his late thirties or early forties. He went straight to the post office box section in the building. He took out his key and opened his box. As expected, there was a brown manila envelope curled inside. It was addressed to Jonathan White, one of his several aliases. There was no return address. The postmark was Miami. The man smiled and returned to his car. He hadn't had any breakfast, nor did he feel like making any. He locked the envelope in the car and strode down a block to a little hole-in-the-wall breakfast place owned and run by a Peruvian.

"*Buenos dias, Don Pedro. Como esta hoy día?*" the blond man said, as he pulled a newspaper from the stand and put it on the counter. He spoke fluent Spanish. It was a necessity in his business, especially because of his clients in the Miami area.

"*Muy bien, Señor. En que puedo servirle?*" the Peruvian asked.

"Sopaipilla y un café Colombiano para llevar…grande y negro, por favor."

"Con mucho gusto." The Peruvian put some fried bread in a little brown bag and filled up a large to-go cup with black coffee. "*Quiere miel para la sopaipilla?*" he asked.

"*Sí, como no.*"

The Peruvian put two little packets of honey in the brown bag that was already dappled here and there where the grease had bled through. The blond man paid, saying, "*Muchas gracias y que tenga un muy buen día.*"

The Peruvian smiled. "*Igualmente, Señor.*"

The blond man walked back to the car, secured his breakfast goodies, and pulled out into traffic. It didn't take long before he arrived at the Hamilton Harbor Yacht Club where he owned a wetslip for his fifty-six foot cabin cruiser. The boat, like his car, was an eye-catcher. Sleek with her fourteen-foot beam, painted 'fighting lady yellow,' her immaculate bright-work reflecting the sun, and powered by a pair of big Detroit diesels, the *Pituca* was the classiest boat by far at the marina, possibly in all of Naples. Built in 1963, it had been collaboratively designed by two legends in the boating world: C. Ray Hunt, the granddaddy of the deep V hull, and Fenwick Williams, the granddaddy of the catboat. *Pituca,* a Spanish idiom meaning fancy or well-dressed lady, was painted on the stern in gold leaf. As an in-your-face to his parents, homeport was Greenwich, Conn.

He parked in his reserved spot and walked down to the boat. He ate the *sopaipilla* on deck as he read the newspaper at a round, weathered-gray teak table. Behind him were the fancy-ass buildings of the marina; in front of him, on the other side of the canal, was a shoreline thick with mangroves. When he finished eating, he put the newspaper aside, wiped his hands, and opened the manila envelope. There was a single sheet of paper inside and four photos. He looked at the photos. Each was of a tan, tough-looking man, dark haired, wiry, and holding the prop and lower unit of an outboard motor. Lining the photos up on the table, the expression of the man changed from surprise to anger. The blond man put the photos together and thumbed them like a deck of cards, like the old fashioned cartoons where slight changes in each picture created movement. It didn't work. He put the pictures down and looked at the concise typed message.

JIMMY TALBOT
FISHING GUIDE
DARK HAIR/ABOUT 6' TALL/ 180 LBS.
100 12TH AVENUE
CRESCENT BEACH, FLORIDA
CAPABLE/MOST LIKELY ARMED
HALF DOWN, BALANCE UPON COMPLETION

The blond man went over to his phone and called the Cayman Islands. $25,000 had been put into his account three days ago. He hung up the phone and went down to the living area below where he pulled out a Florida Gazetteer. He sat down in a plush easy-chair and located Crescent Beach. Way up north, six hours, maybe more, he thought. Would have to pass by Tampa. He thought about that. Maybe I could take in a Devil Rays game. They were doing lousy again, of course; might even lose a hundred games this year, but what do you expect with their payroll. But they had McGriff and Boggs, both great players and McGriff was a Tampa native. Boggs had his home in Tampa, too. End of their careers maybe, but still fun to watch. Probably be next year when Boggs gets number three thousand. Love to see that. He looked at the map again. Could take the Sunshine Skyway that goes right by Tropicana Field. Better do it on the way up, though; never know how long a job will take.

Baseball was his passion from little league on. As a kid he worshipped and emulated the pros, wearing wristbands and eye black, imitating their moves at the plate. He had always followed the Red Sox, and Yaz was his favorite. He played through prep school, but left it for girls and partying and drugs when he went to the University of Miami. However, he never lost his love of the game. He was also a blueblood and an only child. He had grown up in Greenwich, Connecticut, and his parents were both high-powered New York City lawyers. They divorced when he was ten years old, their Type A personalities just couldn't mesh long term, even for the sake of their son. After the divorce, he lived with his mother who got the way-too-large house in Greenwich, but his father still spent as much time with him as possible. The boy was impossibly spoiled and he soon learned to play both parents to his advantage. He was a very handsome teenager with a Robert Redford smile that he turned on at will. He was a charmer.

He was also a ne'er-do-well. He never worked at school from the first grade on. He got atrocious grades, cheated on tests, smuggled booze and drugs into his prep school, and broke training of the varsity baseball team by sneaking butts. He got caught smoking pot which meant automatic dismissal from his prestigious prep school, but his wealthy and influential parents pressured the headmaster and he was given a second chance. In his senior year his father figured out that his son had made money over the past four years by charging clothes at Brooks Brothers to him which he then sold to fellow students for half price. The money he made mostly went towards buying pot. When his father confronted him, his son boldly lied to him. The incessant lies caused both parents to lose patience. Against his father's wishes, the mother gave the boy a credit card to use at the University of Miami. Big mistake. Major debt. Major fees. Major drug use. Once they got that straightened out, the boy swore he would toe the line. When less than a month later he got kicked out of the university for cheating on final exams, they disowned him.

So, what to do? In Miami, no money. Parents said tough, don't call us anymore. The one thing he did know was where and how to get drugs. Being a charmer, he also had a ton of friends at the University. He began to deal. He was very good at it and the Colombian boys began to take notice. One thing led to another. He studied Spanish on his own so he could better communicate with his employers. He picked it up very quickly. The Colombians began to have him diversify. With his patrician good looks, he could go places they couldn't, like the fancy hotels in Key Biscayne, to make contacts and deals. He could waltz into any of the highbrow establishments. He looked like he just stepped off the tennis courts. His smile was his passport.

He was a man absolutely without feeling and scruples. The Colombians soon realized this and broached the subject of assassinations. Would he be interested? He asked the going rate. When he heard, he said sign me up. He was trained in weaponry in Colombia. Had a couple preliminary jobs down there. Like the Spanish, if he put his mind to it, he was a fast learner. When he returned to the States, he was given more and more jobs, mostly drug related. He was discreet, creative, and good. He slowly branched out and picked up a few other clients around the country. He never became seriously involved with women. With his looks and money, they were easy marks. After cocktails on the *Pituca*, a lavish dinner at the marina's five star restaurant, a couple winning smiles, women were putty in his hands. But, with his profession, he could not permit any entangling alliances.

He got up from the easy chair and walked up to a broad cabinet with two large rosewood panel doors, their round brass knobs side by side. He pulled the panel doors open, exposing a large world map with pins stuck into different cities and towns around the globe. The ends of the pins had little colored balls, each color signifying a different client. There were a few pins in Europe, several in Colombia, some clustered around Miami, Orlando, Chicago, New York and Newark, and Detroit. Nothing in north Florida. The majority of the pins were red and represented the Colombian cartel that had first employed him. They were by far and away his best customer. There was a clear glass jar in the corner of the cabinet full of pins. He selected a red one. Crescent Beach wasn't on the map, but he stuck the pin in as close as he could.

Chapter Twenty-Nine

Out on Rusty's deck, Jimmy told Rusty about the Latino with the camera. He concluded with, "And I just don't know what I can do other than be careful as a son-of-a-bitch and try to watch my back. Can't have a bodyguard babysit me 24/7. Out of the question."

"Need a dang camera at the cattle gap; see who's coming into town," Rusty said.

"Could come in by boat, too."

Rusty frowned. "True enough."

"Maybe your captain friend would guard me for being such a good guy taking care of Espantoso."

Rusty rolled his eyes. "Right."

A quandary.

"I asked Tammy to keep an extra sharp lookout for Latinos, and Charley, too. Both of them pay pretty good attention to the comin's and goin's around here," Jimmy said.

"I'll definitely keep my eyes open, too. And maybe in the wee hours I'll take the occasional walk around your place. Maybe Charley and a couple others could, too. Not like having a bodyguard, but couldn't hurt. Sort of like a community crime watch thing."

"And what do I tell them? That I want them to stick their necks out because some bad ass Latinos may come after me because I deep-sixed their boss five years ago? Can't ask them to do that. And I won't."

More silence. Two brown pelicans cruised by low, following the canal in front of the marsh. "Do you have any motion sensor lights around your place?" Rusty asked.

"Nope."

"Might be a good idea."

"Yup."

The next day Jimmy installed motion sensor lights. Crystal, walking back from the store, stopped a little ways from the house. She watched Jimmy putting up the lights for a few minutes before continuing on. She didn't say anything to Jimmy about the lights. Didn't ask him, why now, all of a sudden? She also didn't ask him about the gun he had begun carrying all the time. Or why he bolted out of bed at the slightest noise. It was like they had a tacit agreement of, don't ask, don't tell. But Crystal did ask Rusty who only shrugged and looked away. Crystal couldn't shake the feeling that the mysterious black pickup had something to do with it.

The days of August passed hot, muggy, and quickly without incident other than Frank put the marina on the market and closed the bar. People began keeping a close eye on tropical storms and hurricanes that were springing up everywhere. On the twenty-first of August, Texas was hit by Tropical Storm Charley. Hurricane Bonnie hit North Carolina at the end of the month. New storms were being formed off Africa, intensifying over the Atlantic, and moving towards the Caribbean. On September third, Hurricane Earl swung up from the Yucatán and made landfall in Panama City. Other than extremely high water, some rain and wind, Crescent Beach was unscathed. The townspeople breathed a big sigh of relief.

After Hurricane Earl weakened and disintegrated, the big news was Rebecca's homecoming from Tallahassee. The infection had cleared up, the cast was off her leg and she could walk fine, albeit with a slight limp that was being addressed with physical therapy. The screws and external brace had been removed from her arm, but it was still being protected by a combination brace and sling. Almost the whole town turned out to celebrate her arrival on a late Friday afternoon; Clem and Katharine's trailer was surrounded by people. Picnic tables had been hauled in to the front yard recently mowed by Sammy. People had emptied their freezers of red fish and trout to contribute to a fish fry in her honor. Sammy and his new, very good buddy O.C. were the chefs. O.C. and his family were staying at one of Tammy's cabins. Rebecca called them her Tallahassee family. The whole town knew how O.C. and his wife had taken Clem and Katharine in, and they were treated as if they were long time Crescent Beach residents. Tammy wouldn't hear of them paying for their cabin.

The crowd was a mix of townspeople and the sports fishing families who knew about the accident. Many were acquaintances of O.C.'s from Tallahassee. Others had been in town when the accident happened. But the townspeople and tourists celebrated Rebecca's recovery together. They gathered around and cheered as Beau presented Rebecca with a 'key to the city.' Right after the presentation, O.C.'s eldest daughter, Rebecca's new best friend, rode up on a shiny bicycle. She got off the bike and walked it up to Rebecca. "This is for you, Rebecca," she said, self-consciously. "It's from my Daddy's store." The crowd clapped. O.C. watched Rebecca's face. Her smile was ear to ear.

The next night Sammy spent his entire savings on taking O.C. and his family, his sister and brother-in-law and Rebecca out to dinner at the Club. The Club was especially packed due to the marina bar closing. Clem sat to

Sammy's left, O.C. to Sammy's right. Clem was still on the wagon, but Sammy made up for it and drank both their shares. By the time they finished dessert, he was drunk. He stood up to toast O.C. He whistled shrilly to get everyone's attention and he made damn sure that the entire restaurant was quiet before he began. Tammy shook her head behind the bar. Here we go, she thought.

"I beg everybody's pardon fer interuptin' yur dinner, but I wancha to hear this. This here world is made up o' all difrent kinds of people. Rich people, poor people, educated people, people like me who never had much schoolin', fishermen who do it for a livin', and fishermen who do it for a sport. I always kinda felt that it was me against them who was difrent cuz I didn't believe we could never see eye-to-eye. Didn't want them kind o' people around. Sorta like red ants and black ants. They don't like each other much and don't git along. I wancha to know that over the last couple o' months I learned somethin' big, and that is, it don't matter none, the differences don't matter.

"I been sittin' all night here with a man whose jaw I broke. I did it fer lots o' reasons. The big reason was I thought he did somethin' he didn't. I was wrong, but never gave 'im a chance to explain. Why didn't I give 'im that chance? I'ma thinkin' it was because he was difrent, he was one of them sports fishermen I couldn't stand even though I never talked with one, never listened to anything they had to say. I was wrong, dead wrong. This man here has about the biggest heart and is about the nicest guy I ever met." Sammy, tears in his eyes, looked down to O.C. "I jest wanna apologize to O.C. here in public. And I also wanna make a toast. Now I ain't never toasted no one in my whole life, but I seen it done." He raised his beer bottle. "Here's to ya, O.C., yur one goddamn fine man!" The place erupted. O.C. stood up and hugged Sammy. When they sat down, the noise of table conversation picked up again. Tammy was beaming over by the bar. She wished Beau could have heard Sammy's little speech, but he was back home with Virginia. Tammy looked over to Sammy's table. He was wiping his eyes. When he saw her looking at him, he signaled for another beer. She hopped right on it.

Tiny and T were home during Sammy's toast. After a late dinner, T was taking a shower while Tiny did the dishes. Tiny was scrubbing baked bean residue off the bottom of a cast iron pot, recalling the first time he had ever seen T. By chance he had stopped at the Farmers' Market in Fanning Springs where T was standing behind a crude plank table lined with jars of honey and heaped high with an assortment of vegetables. He bought some corn and fell immediately in love when she smiled at him. Even though Fanning Springs was over an hour and a half from Crescent Beach, Tiny began to make the trip religiously every Saturday. Painfully shy at first, Tiny forced himself to make conversation. Over time the small talk progressed from pleasantries and the weather. They talked about farming, fishing, diesel motors, high schools, sports, manure versus chemical fertilizer, the pollution of the local fresh water springs and the Gulf. She told him that her name was Christina, but to call her T. He said call him Tiny. T began to look forward to the visits as much as Tiny. Whenever the market was rained out, they both felt cheated. It took most of the summer before Tiny worked up the courage to ask her out. She had to help him along.

"T, I've been thinking…I was wondering…" Tiny stopped in mid sentence, suddenly interested in the vegetables on her neighbor's table.

"Yes, Tiny…you were wondering?"

Tiny looked nervously back at her. T knew exactly why he was nervous. "Yeah, I was wonderin' if maybe, ya know, maybe…T, would ya like to do somethin' together sometime?" he stammered. "Ya know, a dance or a picnic or," he brightened, "fishin' or somethin'."

T didn't hesitate for a second. "There's a church supper tomorrow in Trenton. I was going to go with my parents. Do you want to take me?"

Tiny had a big open face. His grin took up most of it. "Shor would!"

"One thing, though…"

"What's that?"

"I can't go with a hippie. You got to cut that ponytail off."

Tiny smiled into the cast iron pot. He had kept his hair short ever since. The bathroom door opened and a very large seven months pregnant T waddled out of the bathroom past Tiny dressed in only panties and a bra. She went into their bedroom and lay down. The ceiling fan was going full blast. T sighed with pleasure and closed her eyes. She was awakened sometime later when she felt something moving on her swollen belly. She opened her eyes. Tiny lay next to her, propped on an elbow, gently going round and round her belly with his big index finger.

"Only a couple more months," she said.

Tiny stopped with the finger, his expression serious. "T, we gotta git hitched."

"When do you want to?"

"Tomorrow!"

T laughed and took hold of Tiny's gigantic hand. Hers was like a child's in his. "After storm season. You got to finish with your shrimping first and take care of the *Never Been Beat* if we get weather. Looks to be a bad season."

"Can't wait 'til the end of storm season. No way! The baby'll be born by then." Tiny was as easy going as they come, but not in this case. "Ain't no way my son or daughter's gonna be a bastard. We're gonna git married before, and that's that! We're settin' a date tonight, T. Right now!"

T sighed; there was no getting around it this time. "Alright. Go get a calendar." Tiny was up in a flash. He went to the kitchen and removed the Yamaha Outboard

Motor calendar from the wall and was back in seconds. He handed it to her. She scanned October. "How about the 31st? That's a Saturday."

"Cuttin' it kinda close, ain't it?"

"It'll be fine. And it'll give my parents plenty of time to spruce up the farm."

Tiny didn't argue. He was ecstatic that she had finally agreed on a date. He knew her parents would be relieved, too. "Maybe ya should call them now, give them the news."

T looked at the bedside clock. She yawned. "Tomorrow'll be soon enough. Too late to call tonight. I'll do it before I go to the library tomorrow."

"Been goin' there a lot."

"So have a lot of people. Everyone wants to help out with Virginia. She still goes there like clockwork, but sometimes it's too much and needs help with the simplest thing. Louie helps her check out books and movies, and often just sits with her. With some of us helping, he can get some other stuff done or just get a break."

T's parents were overjoyed to hear the news the next morning. After making the call, T walked over and unlocked the library with the key Louie had made for her. Good day to be inside, she thought; looks like more weather moving in. Tiny better think twice about going out tonight. A half-hour later she saw Virginia and Skillet coming up the street. Skillet was on a leash which was a new look. Seemed like he was leading Virginia rather than the other way around. When they entered the library, T knew right away it was not one of Virginia's better days. Virginia unleashed Skillet who went over to sniff Bad Dog's scrap of carpet. Virginia sat down at the desk. There was a pile of new books donated by a church to be inventoried, but Virginia only stared at them. T would give her a little time to see if she could get it together before offering to help. The library door opened and a smiling

Rebecca came in. Virginia seemed not to notice. T gave Rebecca a hug, being careful with her arm.

"You're here bright and early. You after a book or a movie, young lady?"

"Movie. I've got a friend here from Tallahassee and I thought maybe we could watch a movie this afternoon before she goes home."

"Help yourself. They're in the same place they've always been."

Rebecca walked towards the movie shelves. She stopped in front of Virginia and said, "Morning, Miss Virginia."

Virginia looked up and smiled at the polite, pretty young girl. "Why hello there yourself. Aren't you a cute little thing. What happened to your arm?"

Chapter Thirty

"Tide'll be comin' in around one, Joe; so, should leave here about eleven. Bit of a hike, but worth it if you want reds," Jimmy said.

"Perfect. Give me plenty of time to get there."

"You going to stay over in one of Tammy's cabins?"

"That's the plan."

"Alrighty then. See you Saturday."

Jimmy hung up. Crystal looked up from her darning. "Joe Who, Jimmy?"

"Bentinini."

"The federal judge from Atlanta?" Jimmy nodded. "My, my. Getting up in the world, aren't you."

"He's a good guy…a regular Joe."

"Hah, hah."

"Seriously; he is. Funny as hell. He's always tellin' wop jokes."

"Italian, not wop!"

"He's Italian and that's what he calls 'em. He's always got a pant load of stories. Fun to be out with." Jimmy stood up. "Think I'll stretch my legs before I hit the hay." He went out the front door to the deck. Crystal knew he was checking the motion-sensor lights.

Twenty miles to the north of Crescent Beach was an isolated county campground on the Gulf with a public boat launch, a single dock, and a couple of porta-potties. It was a beautiful area with scattered live oak and cabbage palms and almost like an island with marsh on one side, the Gulf on the other. Midweek it was usually deserted, especially now after Labor Day. The lights of a Chevy pickup with a camper in the back and towing a boat pulled in and parked. The blond man from Naples was behind the wheel.

He was tired. The drive had taken longer than he thought. U.S. 19 was a real rat's nest coming out of Clearwater. He should have stopped in Crystal River for dinner because restaurants farther north were a joke, absolutely nothing decent in Chiefland, Fanning Springs, Old Town, and Cross City. He had to settle for some terrible Mexican in Perry before he went to the Winn-Dixie for supplies. The only good thing about the day was that McGriff had hit a home run that afternoon and the Devil Rays won due to a botched fly ball that got lost in the roof's trusses. Definite home field advantage, ten times worse than playing the Green Monster at Fenway. But, he thought, the Devil Rays need every bit of help they can get. He got out and went straight to the camper. He was ready for bed and didn't plan on getting up early. Plenty of time tomorrow to reconnoiter.

In the late morning he left the boat on the trailer and, thanks to his Florida Gazetteer, found his way on obscure limestone roads to Crescent Beach. He had rented the boat and camper from a friend who ran a small marina on the Manatee River outside of Tampa. There was no paper trail; no credit card involved. His friend always welcomed cash deals. First thing the blond man did when he crossed the cattle gap was to locate 100 12th Avenue. Tiny town. He located it within five minutes and drove slowly by: cracker house on stilts with the dock directly across the street. No one was around. A smart looking boat with rigged fishing poles was tied to the dock. It wasn't going anywhere soon because it was dead low tide. There couldn't be much more than a foot or so of water by the dock, and oyster bars and mud flats peppered the Gulf close in. He drove all over town. He parked on the point at the end of the road where there was a cul-de-sac. He pulled out binoculars and could just see Jimmy's dock and boat. He looked out to the Gulf, then back to Jimmy's, then out to the Gulf again. Anchored somewhere out there would afford a perfect spot to monitor Talbot's movements.

He drove back to the campground where someone had parked an old pickup with a rickety trailer. He launched his boat and tied it to the public dock before starting a charcoal fire. He hoped to have an early dinner and get in the camper by dusk because he had discovered last night that there was a healthy crop of mosquitoes. Because there was no wind, the no-seeums were out and would be until dark. Mosquitoes and no-seeums! Give me the *Pituca* and Naples any day, he thought. While the coals were catching, some yo-yo in an airboat began making a racket out in the marsh. He was gunning his boat, going around and around, scattering the egrets and herons, flattening channels of marsh grass. The airboat finally came in; a good ol' boy in dirty overalls, baseball cap, and ear-muffs was at the controls. The blond man went into the camper, no reason to be seen unless absolutely necessary. Through the camper window, he watched the guy back up the rickety trailer. He obviously had done it many times before; there was not a wasted move. For his final parting act, the good ol' boy gunned the airboat up onto the trailer. Bullets of water sprayed forty feet out behind the two-bladed prop. The roar was deafening. When the guy drove off, tranquility returned. It was as if the world could breathe again.

Early the next morning, the blond man checked and re-checked the tide chart. Judging from what he had seen yesterday, there was no hurry to go down to Crescent Beach: no way Talbot could go out first thing. There was plenty of time to have a cup of java and scramble up some eggs. The boat he had rented was intentionally non-descript. A ten-year-old Carolina Skiff with a well-used, but dependable fifty horse Mercury on the back. It was not an eye-catcher, but that was the point: there must be hundreds of similar boats in the area and it wouldn't draw attention. The motor ran smooth as silk and it only took him a half-hour to make the trip. He anchored way off Crescent Beach, as far as he could and still see Talbot's boat clearly with the binoculars. He couldn't believe how shallow it was. Way out here and still maybe five feet. It would have been thirty or forty at least, this far off shore at Naples. No wonder there were so many airboats around.

He settled in to wait. He had a couple fishing poles sticking up out of holders so he'd at least look legitimate if anyone came by. Although he hated fishing, too damn boring, he looked the part. He was wearing a broad-rimmed fishing hat, a silky lightweight, long-sleeve fishing shirt with lots of pockets, cutoff blue jeans, and sneakers. His friend had loaned him the rods as well as the large tackle box. He looked through the binoculars. Nothing happening. He couldn't see any fishing rods sticking up from Talbot's boat like yesterday, but then again, maybe he was too far away. The tide was coming in. He waited. He took off his shirt—good chance to work on his tan. He put some lotion on his face and upper torso. Eventually the tide shifted and began to go out again. Still, no action. He waited until late afternoon. Only once did he see movement: Talbot came down to the boat, climbed aboard, and fiddled around with something, then left. The blond man looked at the horizon. The sun was low. He pulled up the anchor and put on his shirt. Tomorrow was another day.

"Any problem with that Atlanta traffic?" Jimmy asked, as Joe Bentinini slowly extricated himself from the BMW.

"Nothing more than usual," Joe answered, shaking hands. "Good to see you, Jimmy."

"Likewise. Want to stretch your legs a bit before we head out?"

"I'm good. Do want to say hello to the Mrs., though."

"Shopping day. Crystal took the truck into Perry, but she'll be here when we get back."

The pair walked down to the dock and within minutes were following the coast north. "Goin' about forty miles to some creeks with lots o' reds," Jimmy said, over the hum of the gigantic four-cycle Yamaha. Joe nodded and smiled. He was happy to be out on the water. Hardly a cloud in the sky, the unmistakable smell of salt in the air. Joe watched an osprey soaring up high. On patrol. Suddenly the osprey went to hover mode, its wings fluttering. It swooped down thirty feet, but pulled up. Joe smiled. False alarm, he thought; the fish must have spooked. He continued to watch the osprey. Another flutter, but this time the osprey dove all the way. After crashing into the water, it took off with a fat fish in its talons. Most likely a mullet, Joe thought. Joe loved his job, but he also loved the outdoors. Being at his desk day in and out got to him. It was like a prison sometimes. He needed this. This was his tonic.

Jimmy stood at the controls, Joe was at his side. Both were wearing Polaroid sunglasses. They passed miles of isolated coastline, narrow white beach lined with mostly cabbage palms, Florida's state tree. Jimmy had the motor at three-quarters throttle and they were flying with the wake low, clean, and perfectly symmetrical. Way behind them was a boat heading north, too. Neither Jimmy or Joe noticed. There was no way that the boat behind them could keep up with Jimmy, but the blond man at the helm wasn't worried. They'd only get so far ahead, and he had his binoculars. He also had a Heckler & Koch MP5K submachine gun tucked in the folds of a blue plastic tarp.

Jimmy and Joe pulled up to a creek barely twenty feet wide. Jimmy raised the motor and began to pole. He was careful not to splash or create any pulsations that would startle the fish. Joe already had a rod in hand rigged with spinner bait. The water was rising which meant the reds could come in closer to the oyster bars where they fed on crabs, shrimp, and marine worms. They could see the wakes and swirls of several fish.

"They're in here alright," Joe said, in a low voice. "Look, there's a crawler! Good size!" He pointed excitedly at the exposed dorsal fin and part of a redfish back. "How far do I lead him, Jimmy?"

"Try casting towards that little clump of oysters. Looks like he's headin' for it."

Joe made an excellent cast. Seconds later he had a strike. It was quite a fight, but Joe was a good angler. Jimmy netted him at the boat's side. Joe took one look at the beauty and high-fived the smiling Jimmy.

"Where's the tape, Jimmy?"

Jimmy reached into the center console compartment. The tape was right next to his pistol. He measured the fish, and re-measured it to be sure.

"Lucked out. Twenty-six inches. One more inch and it woulda been illegal," Jimmy said. A keeper could not be longer than twenty-seven inches, nor less than eighteen. Limit was only one per fisherman. "Better ease up, Joe. Can only bring two back."

"Not on your life. We may only bring two back, but the law doesn't say anything about catching a hundred."

They fished the creek a while longer before Jimmy picked up and visited another. By mid afternoon, they had fished at least a half dozen creeks before they moved out to the grass beds for trout. They had caught plenty of reds, but only kept one more—a twenty-two incher.

They also had their limit of trout by the end of the day. As Jimmy lowered the motor to head home, Joe told another of his wop jokes. Jimmy didn't know how he could remember them all. Joe began, "You see there was this German, French guy, and Italian on the top of the Eiffel Tower. The German looks out at Paris spread all around beneath them and says…"

The man with the blond hair was anchored in the pass between a couple of islands and the coast. Talbot, he knew, would return this way and take the pass rather than go way out and around the islands. Impossible not to see my boat, he thought. He disconnected the gas line between the tank and the motor and stowed it in the center console. He replaced it with one heavily sun-cracked that leaked. Nice of Talbot to head north today, he thought; won't take but a half-hour to return to the camper. The blue plastic tarp was folded in half in a corner of the stern. He drew back the top fold and picked up the submachine gun. Originally designed by Germans in the nineteen-sixties, it was just over a foot long and could fire nine hundred rounds a minute. There was no stock, just a pistol grip behind the trigger and a vertical fore grip. He had brought three 9mm, thirty round magazines. He installed one of them. It curved down below the barrel. The gun was lethal and lethal looking.

He watched Talbot approach through the binoculars. He pulled up the anchor. When he could see Talbot with the naked eye, he held up a paddle with a red shirt tied to it and began waving it back and forth. The boat veered towards him. When it got close, it slowed down to minimal wake.

Jimmy had a pair of binoculars around his neck. "What's the problem?" he asked.

The blond man offered one of his best, most disarming smiles. He held up the gas line and bent it back to show how badly it was cracked.

"Gas line's leaking. Pump it up and it squirts all over the place. Lot of gas in the bilge. Don't dare to run it and don't have a radio. Think you could give me a tow to the shore yonder and call Sea Tow?"

"You bet. Joe, coil up that rear line and toss it over when I get close."

Joe nodded and went to the stern. Jimmy eased his boat up.

"Sure do appreciate it," the blond man said, smiling again. "Should have replaced it a long time ago."

It was over in less than a minute. While Jimmy concentrated on his approach, the blond man pulled back the tarp. He quickly picked up the gun and riddled Jimmy with a blast of twenty rounds. Joe was frozen with the line in his hand, he absolutely could not move. The blond man turned the gun on him and shrugged. "Sorry, fella. Collateral damage." He emptied the rest of the magazine into Joe. The blond man calmly changed magazines, then riddled the waterline of Jimmy's boat. It began taking on water. He put the gun down and replaced the gas line. He was right, it didn't take a half-hour to return to the camper. No one was around. He pulled out fifteen minutes later. By midnight, he pulled the Porsche into his reserved spot at the Naples marina.

* * *

There had never been so many boats hovering off Crescent Beach, especially before sunrise. Beau and Virginia were in their boat, along with Rusty and Louie. Charley was with Norm and Tammy. Tiny and T were in the big shrimp boat with a host of other people. Sammy and his family were with O.C. and his family on O.C.'s new party barge. Almost every boat from town that was seaworthy was out, full not just with locals, but with anglers from all over the southeast and even some from the northeastern states. Crystal, of course, was in a boat packed with her family: her daughter with her husband and the twins as well as her two other sons, the high school teacher from Gainesville and the merchant marine sailor who had flown in from Marseilles. At sunrise they would scatter Jimmy's ashes.

Jimmy had spent his entire life on the water. Crystal knew that his favorite time of day was when he went out early. How many times had he told her that he never, ever tired of seeing that big old orange sun come up over the marsh? She was dressed entirely in black. The men in her boat all wore black suits, even the twins. The clothes matched the mood—somber and sad. Besides fishing, Jimmy had been a family man. He had also smuggled marijuana, but it was to get the money he needed to educate his children, not to squander away. It was protecting his family that eventually led to his death, cut him down still in his prime and productive years. He was a very capable man, widely liked and universally respected for his knowledge of the Gulf. He was God-fearing and church going. He was a huge part of past and present Crescent Beach. The whole town felt as if a jagged hole had been ripped in the fabric of the community. Everyone, like Crystal, grieved.

After the ashes were spread, the boats returned to shore. Tammy had set up a breakfast buffet. Most everyone attended. The Club had never been so crowded. People spilled over to the deck. When the deck was full, it spilled over to the slab below. Rusty stood leaning against the deck railing, elbow to elbow. He couldn't begin to estimate how many people were there. He hoped there would be enough food, but thought, no way. He wasn't hungry. He felt empty. He also felt that he had failed Jimmy. But what could he have done? He went over it in his mind, again and again. And poor Crystal! He had failed her, too. But what in hell's name could he have done! He stayed at the railing a long time. After a while, the crowd began to thin out. He stayed put.

Crystal eventually came out, surrounded by family. She saw Rusty at the railing. Her expression turned hard. She told her family that she would meet up with them later. She walked up to Rusty.

“I think you owe me an explanation.” Her voice was ice cold; Rusty felt stabbed. He told her everything: of Espantoso shooting Jimmy in the hand and threatening the twins, of what Jimmy did to Espantoso, the discovery of the body in the sinkhole, the deal made with the authorities.

“So, it was you who made it possible for the police to identify the body!”

Rusty nodded. “That’s what Jimmy and I thought best. The law would never come after him that way and it was already all over the press about the hand. The Colombians would have probably figured it out.”

“Probably! Bullshit! Maybe they would have figured it out, maybe not. But this way they knew for sure. When that Colombian was identified, Jimmy didn’t have a prayer. That was dumb! That killed my Jimmy! Why didn’t you tell me about all this? We could have done something!”

“I promised Jimmy not to tell you anything. And what could we have done? Tell me that! I’ve been racking my brain for the last several days and can’t come up with a thing.”

“You’re racking your brain now! A little late isn’t it! Goddamn it to hell, Rusty, you should have told me!”

She glared at him, then turned abruptly and marched off.

Chapter Thirty-One

On a cool, mid October evening, Charley and Louie were sitting at a little table outside Louie's camper discussing their pig hunt. They were going to try to catch a couple of razorbacks to fatten up for a couple weeks, then roast on Tiny and T's wedding day.

"Louie, you may be smart as hell with numbers and computers and sech, but you don't know nuthin' about hawg huntin'," Charley said. "If'n I say we got to leave by four-thirty tomorrow morning, we got to leave by four-thirty!"

"Why so early? Pigs sleep, too, don't they?"

Charley rolled his eyes. " 'Course they do. But they feed early an' that's when we should go after 'em, and we gotta drive out first to Ol' Man Butler's and git his dogs an' truck. Don't 'spect me to be usin' the Mustang, do ya?"

The next morning, Louie was at the camper door when Charley pulled up in the Mustang. He gave Bad Dog a pat on the head before joining Charley in the front seat and they rode in silence the few miles out to the sixteen hundred acre Butler farm. When Charley had told Old Man Butler that he wanted to cook a pig or two for Tiny's wedding, the farmer quickly offered use of his truck and dogs, and said for Charley to take as many of his marked wild barrows as he needed. He also offered a pen where the hogs could be fed corn to take the gaminess out of the meat. Charley pulled into the farmyard. There was already a light on in the farmhouse.

"Jest shy of ninety years old and already up and around," Charley said, shaking his head in admiration. He parked alongside a mud-splattered pickup with four kennels in the back. Charley shined a flashlight around the bed of the pickup. In two of the kennels were Walkers, in the other two, pit bulls. There were some short lengths of rope, a stout pole, a couple of first aid kits, and other odds and ends. There was a Winchester .30-30 in the rear window rack. A box of ammo was on the seat. Old Man Butler had everything ready. Charley checked to see if the Winchester was loaded. There was only one round. He put in several more. He wasn't planning on shooting a pig, but you never knew what might happen. Better to have a little security, Charley thought. The key was in the ignition. Charley started the truck, turned on the lights, and they slowly drove down past the farmhouse until they came to a gate.

"Gonna be a number of these to open and close afore we git where we're goin'."

Louie hopped out to take care of the gate. When he was back in the front of the truck, he asked, "How come so many dogs?"

"Like to work in pairs. Them Walkers is the *bay* dogs. When they catch scent of a hawg, they bay like hell. When they got 'em cornered, they howl. That's when we let them pit bulls loose. They's the *catch* dogs. Their jaws is awful strong and they kin hold down a full-size boar if'n they want. Usually takes hold of it by its face or ear until we git there to kill or tie it off.

"Lotta different kinds o' dogs used fer hawgs. Ya got yer Catahoula Cur, Blackmouth Cur, Mountain Cur…them's all *bay* dogs. Florida Cracker Cur, American Bulldog is two other kinds o' *catch* dogs."

They drove through a series of fields and woods, passing through several gates. It was daylight when they entered an area of live oak, cabbage palm, and scrub palmettos. Charley put it into granny gear. "This is about where Old Man Butler said hawgs been hangin' out lately. Keep a close eye off to the side and let me know if ya see any signs of rootin'." Louie unrolled his window and looked out. "Ain't no season fer hawgs or limits if yur on private property. State's overrun with 'em; all sixty-seven counties got 'em. These razorbacks probly got relatives from DeSoto days, back when the Spanish was aroun'. An' pigs is still escapin' from farms every year. They go wild faster than any other farm animal. Make the wild pig race all mixed up. Sometimes ya kin git *listed* hawgs which got a streak of white hair across their back and shoulder. Even got some fancy-ass, escaped pigs from high falootin' gun clubs mixin' in. Pigs like Eurasian and German Mountain Boar."

Charley suddenly put on the brakes and put the truck in neutral. He got out and knelt at the side of the road. "Come on over, Louie, and take a gander." The ground looked like a rototiller had been through it. Cloven hoof marks were all around. Charley and Louie walked up the road a little ways. The ground was torn up everywhere between the palmettos. "Lookin' for acorns and other stuff. Eats lots o' things. Believe they ain't far. Looks awful fresh. C'mon, let's put on some snake leggin's and let them Walkers go."

The dogs immediately were on the trail. They zigzagged out of sight. The woods road went in the same general direction, so Charley and Louie followed in the truck. They stopped a couple times to listen. One time the barking stopped.

"Lost their scent," Charley said. Almost immediately, the barking began again. Charley smiled. "Found it." It wasn't much longer before the pitch of the baying changed; it was more urgent, frantic. Charley let the pit bulls out, each wearing a cut vest to protect vital organs from goring or bites. They bolted from the kennels. Charley, with ropes draped around his neck and the Winchester in hand, led the way through the scrub as fast as he could go. Louie, carrying the pole, did his best to keep up: it wasn't easy with all the palmetto and catclaw vines. Charley yelled back over his shoulder. He was already out of breath. "Gotta try to git there quick so them dogs don't chew on 'em too bad, or vice-versa. Besides tusks, them pigs got wicked teeth called *tushes* top and bottom. Don' wanna hafta ask Norm to do any stitchin'."

Louie was panting as hard as he did during the *Tortoise and Hare 15*. "Those dogs can cover some ground!" he wheezed.

"Hawgs ain't too shabby neithers; kin go twenty-five miles an hour if'n they want. Now careful 'round them palmetto. Rattlers like to hang out there, and a rattler ain't got no friends. Jest enemies."

The barking was louder and louder. They soon heard grunts and piercing squeals.

"Bulls got 'im," Charley said, beginning to jog. The noise increased until Charley and Louie burst onto the scene of the two pit bulls, tails wagging, holding down a good-sized barrow. It wasn't going anywhere. It was exhausted, on its side, and could barely turn its head. The dogs took turns going after the ears. " 'Bout perfect size," Charley said. "Probly dress out around seventy pounds." He leaned over the dogs trying to get a good look at the ears. He turned and smiled at Louie. "One of Butler's alright. Hot diggety!" Charley handed the Winchester to Louie and began to tie the legs of the hog.

"How do you know it's one of his?"

"Ears are marked. See the crop split." The top of the left ear had been snipped off, and then a straight, thin notch was cut going down from the crop.

"When?"

"People catch 'em when they're young with a cane pole and rope, then mark 'em. It's like brandin' 'em. All sorts of marks is made, like a simple split, crop under half crop, V cut, overbit, lots of 'em. Not supposed to take a hawg that's already marked unless it's yurs. Against the rules out here. The males git cut the same time. Lookee there," he said pointing. "No nuts. Man did that, not nature." Charley stepped away from the pig. "There, all hawg-tied." Charley pulled the pit bulls off. He had to wail on one with the pole before it got the message. He inserted the pole through the tied legs. When he finished, he looked around, taking in landmarks. "I'm thinking that the road ain't so far off. I'll hoof it back to the truck and bring it close as I can. Keep them pit bulls away." He took the Walkers and the Winchester back with him

Louie stood between the hog and dogs. He looked down at the razorback. No white hair on this one. Prehistoric looking with the backbone raised above the body like that, he thought. He involuntarily shuddered as he looked at the tusks. Those could do a job on somebody for sure. He heard the truck coming. It didn't sound very far away. Louie would never tell him, but he was continually impressed by Charley. Charley may be backwoods, but he was capable right across the board.

Charley pushed his way through the palmettos. He looked down at the pig, then smiled at Louie. "Now comes the fun part." Charley took hold of one end of the pole. Louie took the other. They hoisted the pig.

"Good Lord!" Louie said. The pig weighed well over a hundred pounds.

Charley laughed. "Never said it'd be easy. C'mon, we'll take breaks."

Yelling at the pit bulls to quit snipping at the hog, they slowly, made their way back to the truck. They stopped several times. Louie was having a hard time. By the time they arrived, Louie's arms were so heavy, he could barely lift his end of the pole as they loaded the pig behind the kennels.

"Got jest enough room fer one more," Charley said. Massaging a shoulder, he turned to the pit bulls. "Kennel up!" The two dogs jumped up to the tailgate and scrambled into the cages. Charley shut the kennel doors. " 'Bout time fer some coffee and biscuits, doncha think?"

Charley retrieved the thermos, a bag of biscuits, and some jerkey. They found a log and, after first checking for snakes on the back side, sat down. Charley, mouth half full of biscuit, said, "Understand ya might be gittin' yurself a full time job."

"Yup."

"So Beau and Norm are gonna do it?"

"Sure looks that way. Probably do the closing with Frank around the time of the wedding. Frank wants out and the price is right. Norm found a couple doctors from Gainesville as silent partners."

"Ya gonna run the lifts and all that?"

"Nope. Clem'll do that. I'll run the books and sell stuff out of the marina. Looking into getting a Mercury dealership. Plan is to gut the bar and put in a showroom and parts department. Rusty doesn't want a full time job, but has agreed to be the on-call mechanic."

"That should work out slick. Be good for Tammy, too."

"Hope so. And God knows I need the money."

The two men finished their breakfast and climbed back into the truck. They passed through more gates and passed gray, silty-soil fields that had been turned over. Sixteen hundred acres was a lot of property. They came to a freshwater swampy area where Charley found some more tracks. The scenario with the dogs was pretty much the same, except that everybody had to run in and out of swamp and Louie was scared to death that he'd get bit by a moccasin or a gator. He had recently read a newspaper article about some little dog that had been eaten by an alligator on a golf course. He had thought of Bad Dog. Now he thought about himself.

The pig took them on quite a jaunt, but the dogs finally cornered it in a raised hardwood hammock. Charley and Louie were close. They heard tremendous thrashing, barking, grunts, and then one of the dogs yelping in pain. Even after the long chase, this pig clearly wasn't going down easy. The two men approached cautiously with Louie a few steps behind Charley. They were under the canopy of low, gravity-defying, very thick live oak branches extending way out. They still couldn't see the pig. Charley levered the Winchester just in case. It jammed. "Damn!" he exclaimed. The thrashing continued.

"What's wrong," Louie asked, nervously.

"Gun's…"

The pig suddenly shot out of the palmettos, straight at Charley with the dogs in pursuit. Charley jumped aside, poking the rifle barrel at the pig like a spear. Part of the barrel disappeared in its mouth. A bloody face pit bull lunged for the ear area. There were no visible tusks: it was one royally pissed-off sow. The pig turned to bite the pit bull. Scored a direct hit. More blood from the dog's face. Louie snapped out of the frozen-in-terror mode the same time the pig saw him. It charged. Louie screamed and took two steps before jumping up and grabbing one of the live oak branches. He quickly drew his feet up which he wrapped around the branch just as the other pit bull got hold of the sow's face. Charley thought of clubbing the pig, but knew better. He backed away to let the dogs do their work. All four were harassing the pig—it began to move in a tight circle, trying to fend off the dogs. Charley held the gun at the ready like a baseball bat.

The pig had no chance and slowly weakened. It was sad. Charley respected that sow: she was valiant. After turning this way and that, defending herself against the frenzy of the pit bulls tearing at her ears and the Walkers lunging in to nip, the sow finally collapsed. Like the dogs, she had her share of wounds. Charley located the ropes that he had dropped. When he was sure the sow was held down for good by the pit bulls, he tied her up. Louie didn't see any of the fight even though it was going on almost beneath him.

"You kin come on down now, Louie."

Louie, still hanging on to the branch like a possum, looked over to Charley with the pig at his feet. Charley was examining the bites on the Pit Bulls. Louie lowered himself to the ground. He walked over.

"Holy Mother Teresa!" was all he could say.

"Purty excitin', huh?" Charley's heart was still thumping a mile a minute.

Louie looked down at the sow, her chest heaving. He could just see some tusks, but they were much smaller than the barrow's. He didn't see any brand on the ears, although it was hard to tell because they were pretty torn up. "Don't see any mark."

"Nope. She ain't never been caught."

Louie looked at the bleeding pit bulls. "Those little tusks do that?"

Charley shook his head. "Tooshes. Sows bite more than anything. This one shor did. Gonna have to doctor these dogs and her up. Don't need no screwworms."

"Screwworms?"

"Yeah. Flies that smell blood and lays eggs in wounds. Eggs hatch and larvae burrow in. Problem is, they never leave again. Keep feedin' off skin, then off tissue like muscles, and keep on eatin' until whatever critter they be feedin' on dies. Only way I hear to git rid of 'em is to spray some insecticide in the wound area and pick 'em out with tweezers. Nasty critters alright." Charley looked around the hammock, then down at the pig. He picked up the pole and inserted it like before. He looked at Louie. "Ready?"

Louie sighed and nodded.

"Let's have at it then."

It took some time to get back to the truck. By the time they had the pig loaded and the dogs and pig doctored from the first aid kits, it was mid afternoon. It was a long, slow drive back to the farm. With the sun pouring through the windows, Louie soon fell asleep. Charley got all the gates and didn't wake him until they arrived at the farm. Charley backed up to the pigpen.

"Up and at 'em!" Charley said, gently shaking Louie's shoulder. Louie surfaced and was climbing sleepily out of the pickup when Old Man Butler walked up.

"How'd it go?" he asked.

"Couple yur dogs got bit by the sow, but not too bad," Charley said.

Old Man Butler walked around to examine them. "Ain't but scratches. Looks like you got 'em doctored good." He looked at the pigs. He nodded. "You did fine. Any problems?"

Charley reached into the cab and pulled out the Winchester. "Only that yur rifle jammed right when it was a mite hairy."

The old man took the rifle from Charley and looked at it. "You put these bullets in it?"

"Yeah?"

"That's why. Had a bad action for years. I just keep one round in; that way she don't mess up. Just need one anyway."

I shor wish you had let me know that, Charley thought. But he didn't say a word.

Chapter Thirty-Two

Rusty was as nervous as a schoolboy. He paced around the kitchen. He walked over to look at Charley's painting over the mantel, but never saw it. He went out on the deck where he jammed his hands into his pants' pockets. He looked out over the marsh, but didn't see that either. Finally, he shook his head in disgust and marched over to the kitchen counter. He picked up the phone and dialed.

"Hello?"

"Hi. Rusty here."

There was a pause before Crystal said, in a neutral tone, "Hi. What's up?"

"You planning on going to the wedding?"

"Of course. Just about the whole town is."

"Was wondering if you might want to car pool?"

Silence; then, "Is this your way of asking me if you can take me to the wedding?"

"Guess so." Rusty's stomach was tight.

"Alright."

"Do you know how to get there?"

"Been there several times. Takes about an hour and a half."

"Ceremony's at two. Pick you up a little after noon?"

"I'll be waiting."

They said their goodbyes and Rusty sagged onto a kitchen stool. Was he less or more nervous now? It was hard to tell. More, he figured.

Rusty pulled up to her house at ten past noon on Saturday. He was only halfway out of the car when Crystal appeared at the top of the deck stairs. She was wearing a sky blue, three-quarter length dress and practical simple black flats. Her thick, well-brushed brown hair fell past her shoulders. She had a small pocketbook in her hand. Rusty thought she looked swell. If she was nervous, she didn't show it. I'm just a ride, he thought: we're saving gas. He hurried around to open her door. She gave him a half-smile as she settled in. He scurried back around. He hopped in the truck and put it in drive. "We're off," was all he could think of to say.

Crystal was silent. Rusty racked his brain for something, anything, to say. He should have said how nice she looked, but she might think that a come-on. A couple miles out of town, he said, "Tiny's a nervous wreck. He's been a basket case all week. He's worried that T's going to have the baby any second because she's so big and already past the due date. Charley said that when they scalded and scraped the hogs, he about took the poor pig's skin right off. Charley said he had to take over before it looked like a Swiss cheese."

Crystal laughed. "He's been a bachelor a long time, although not as long as you." More silence. Rusty tried to interpret something out of that. Nothing. It was the simple truth. "But, I agree," Crystal continued. "T's cutting it awful close. Looks to me like the baby's dropped down some, too."

They were halfway to Perry when Crystal asked, "Have they made any progress finding Jimmy's killers?"

Rusty was all business. "Some. When they found out that it was Jimmy who the killer or killers were after, not the judge, and that he or they were most likely connected with the Colombians in Miami, they began focusing down there. Originally they thought it was the judge who was the victim, not Jimmy."

Crystal turned in the seat to look at him. "Why the judge?"

"Seems he was a notorious liberal and handed out stiff sentences for racial and hate crimes. Had some death threats on occasion. If the judge hadn't been killed, I imagine they would have lost interest in the case pretty quick, what with Jimmy's history. But, the family of the judge as well as the legal community there are putting on a lot of pressure to get the killer. FBI's been called in. They're not letting this one go. They also have some leads. One of them is a guy they've been watching for a few years. They know he's done work like this before for the Colombians, but they never had a slam dunk case. The FBI passed out a few photos of the guy to see if anyone around here had seen him. The State Trooper captain from Cross City showed me one. If they're right and this guy is the killer, no wonder he got so close to Jimmy. He looks like the all American, fair-haired boy. Anything but a Latino."

"Hope they give him the chair if it's him!" Crystal spat.

"If they can figure out for sure that this guy did it, but can't prove it, I just might take care of it."

Her head spun around. "What do you mean?"

"I mean I might take care of it."

"No you won't, Rusty McMillan! That's how this whole thing started! You want to throw away your life, too!"

"No, it started because your family was threatened. Jimmy didn't have the slightest doubt that Espantoso would follow through with his threats if he didn't do what Espantoso wanted. He was caught between a rock and a hard place. I don't know what I would have done in his place. Probably the same."

"Wasn't Espantoso's real name Arias?" Rusty nodded. "I found a fancy gun when I was cleaning out Jimmy's workshop. Might be real gold and silver. Has Arias engraved on the handle."

"Jimmy told me about that pistol. A Beretta. That's the one that put the hole in his hand."

They came to the intersection with U.S. 19.

"Which way?" he asked.

"South."

He turned right.

"You know, I can see the Colombians' side of it. In their business, they can't lose face. When one of theirs is eliminated, they have to retaliate. And the way the business is run, it's like one big family; this was payback for one of their own. You do one of us, we do one of you. But if they hired this guy, he's a mercenary—lowest of the low. No family or honor involved. Strictly for money. There's no doubt in my mind that this world would be a better place without that scum on it....and it would be payback for Jimmy."

"Nope. No good, Rusty. Just get that idea out of your head right now!"

They drove through Cross City. They hit the only traffic light in Old Town. Waiting for it to turn green, Rusty said, "I didn't tell you everything Jimmy said to me." The light turned. Rusty drove looking straight ahead. "He knew they would come for him sooner or later, and he asked me to take care of you, to make sure you'd be okay if something happened."

Crystal began to cry softly. Rusty was pissed at himself for bringing it up. Crossing the Suwannee River and entering Fanning Springs she collected herself. Just past the inspection station she said, "Take a left on 26, Rusty." She reached in her purse for a tissue. She always made sure she had a pile of tissues when she went to weddings. She dried her eyes and looked at him. "What did you say?"

"What did I say what?"

"When he asked you to take care of me."

He looked straight into her eyes for a second, before looking back to the road.

"I said I would."

She nodded to herself.

"And going to get yourself killed or going to prison for the rest of your life is taking care of me? That makes a hell of a lot of sense!...Take a left at that curve."

They entered farmland. The road system in Trenton was laid out in a grid of rectangles. Within many of the rectangles were large farms and ranches. Crops included melons, peanuts, corn, squash, beans, most anything. Big round hay bales dotted the fields as well as cattle and dairy cows grazing in pastures under the shade of spreading oaks. Large open equipment sheds were here and there. Farmhouses were set way back in. It was beautifully pastoral, although the beauty masked the reality that many of the crops required prodigious amounts of water, millions of gallons that were seriously depleting the limestone aquifer. The copious amount of fertilizers was entering this same aquifer as well as mixing with the surface water on its way to the rivers and Gulf. The wonderfully clear springs that fed these rivers had begun to bubble up full of nitrates. Streams that had sandy bottoms were being covered in green slime.

"Seems to me you can take care of yourself just fine, Crystal. You don't need me… And I don't like to stick my head where it's not wanted."

Crystal was leaning against the passenger door, watching Rusty. She noticed his face was flushed. In a small voice she said, "Who said you weren't wanted?"

Rusty's head snapped over. They looked at each other intently until Crystal smiled. "Might want to watch the road." Rusty tore his eyes away. He jerked the wheel a little to get back on track. Luckily there was zero traffic in the area. A reduced speed sign came up. He slowed down. A little church was on the right. Behind it, backed up against some woods was a small parking lot with a couple light poles.

"That's the church of the minister who's doing the service," Crystal said. "It's going to be a bilingual service because T's father has invited a lot of Spanish-speaking friends to the wedding. There are a lot of them around here. Most of that church's congregation are Latinos... Turn right on that next road. We're close now, just a couple miles." Rusty turned right and they soon passed a large peanut field with a large mobile irrigation system. Rusty glanced at it. It was still full of peanuts. A tractor road bisected the field and disappeared into a thick copse of woods.

"Hardly need all that equipment this year," Rusty said, nodding towards the field. "With all these storms and rain they haven't even been able to harvest yet."

Crystal looked over at the field. There was no way that either of them could have known that this was the same field Jimmy drove through on Christmas Eve five years ago. Crystal looked backed to the road.

"Your next left."

They turned in. The long driveway was lined with cars and pickups.

"Guess we're not early," Rusty said. He looked around. "Wow! Pretty impressive. I had no idea T's family had an operation this size."

The long driveway led to a large, extended one-story brick house surrounded by live oaks and azaleas. It was well-manicured and the grass of the big front lawn was cut short as a putting green. Behind the house was a series of barns and sheds, all in tip-top condition. The tractors, dozer, baler, and other farm machinery had been cleared out of a long equipment shed and parked in back of the shed to form a giant horseshoe. Within the horseshoe were several rows of rectangular hay bales divided by an aisle. The bales faced the open end of the horseshoe where there was a tall stool to the side of a single table covered by a vestment embroidered with a red cross, and nothing but God's good green earth beyond.

More bales of hay had been arranged inside the open-sided equipment shed forming a large semi circular area in front of a stage. A microphone as well as musical instruments were on the stage. There was smoke coming from the far end of the shed where a small circle of men had gathered around Charley and Louie who were sitting in chairs in front of a large trailer-hitched steel pig-cooker. A pitcher of beer and two cups were sitting on the ground between the chairs. Charley was holding court. He and Louie had switched from coffee to beer some time ago.

"We try to keep 'er aroun' two hundred and twenty-five degrees," Charley said, as he stood up to check the cooker temperature. He threw a couple of pieces of firewood in and surveyed what was left in the woodpile. "Me and Louie been at it better part of seven hours. Gone through close to a third cord or more o' hickory. Gettin' close to crispin' time now." Louie stood and opened up the cooker. He picked up a large bowl and basted the pigs with a vinegar and pepper base mop. "Aside what Louie here's doin', we also injected brine an' such direct with a big syringe into them piggies. Should be juicy-loosey and fall off the bone when we git done with 'em…What's the meat thermometer say, Louie?"

Louie stuck the thermometer in the pigs.

"Both around a hundred and ninety."

"Time to fire her up," Charley said, throwing more hickory on the fire. He turned to the small circle of men. "Now if you gents kin set me up with a table yonder, be mighty 'preciated. We'll be puttin' them pigs on it purty quick now and gotta let them sit durin' the ceremony. Gotta cool at least a half hour before I kin cut 'em up. Besides," he said, proudly, "gotta go change into some other duds, bein' the best man and all."

The horseshoe quickly filled with people who sat on the hay bales. Most of the men and a few of the women had cups of beer. The first two rows of hay bales had bright ribbons tucked into the twine. They were reserved for family. A short Latin sat on the stool playing classical music on a guitar. He was Cuban and a good friend of T's father. He was very good. Beau sat next to Norm and Tammy. Virginia was in the house with T.

"How's Virginia doing, Beau?" Norm asked.

"Not so good. About as many bad days as good. You never know. Sleeps a lot, though she's getting plenty of exercise. When she's not with me at the house, or at the library, she takes long walks." Beau smiled sadly. "Used to be that she took Skillet for walks. Now it's like the other way around."

The front two rows of bales began to fill. People started looking around. It was getting close. The guitar music changed. The minister appeared before the table. Tiny and Charley soon came to the table from where they had been standing off to the side. Tiny was wearing some brand new black jeans and a white western-cut shirt with pearly buttons. He looked uncomfortable in front of the crowd. Charley, though, was looking out, big smile on his face. Occasionally he waved hello at someone. He was wearing a white shirt, too, and clean jeans. His hair had been recently slicked back. His right hand, though, he kept in his pocket. He was clutching the wedding ring.

The bridal procession was brief. Rebecca with no trace of a limp was the flower girl. She held a bouquet as she slowly walked up the aisle. Her bright smile was returned by everyone. Virginia was the maid of honor and followed Rebecca. Virginia, looking as uncomfortable as Tiny, made her way towards the front. Beau caught her eye and smiled encouragingly. Rebecca sat down in the front row. Virginia remained standing up by the table. The guitarist stopped. Silence. Then he began with a very beautiful and intricate version of the wedding processional. Every head turned. Tiny was smiling ear to ear. T was walking up the aisle on the arm of her father. He was still using a cane because of the manure spreader accident. T's eyes were locked on Tiny's. Her smile matched his. T's mother had made her a white satin wedding dress. A store bought dress was not an option with T so big. The pair took their time walking up to the minister. T couldn't move any faster. It was an effort. She was huge.

The service was sweet. The minister went back and forth from English to Spanish. Even the vows were in both languages. The Latinos got a chuckle as Tiny stumbled over the Spanish with a horrible accent. But they loved the effort. With the two cultures mixing and the beautiful view over the green fields, it was like all was well with the world.

After the ceremony, everyone hustled into the shed. A feast had been laid out and, between gulps of beer, Charley professionally carved up the pigs. They were perfectly done. Many of the Mexicans came up to shake his greasy hand. There were no tables, but people had no problem balancing their plates on their laps. The band began playing. Towards the end of the meal, the band switched from bluegrass to a slow waltz. Time for T and Tiny's first dance as a married couple. Tiny led T out to the area in front of the band. He hunched over her and was careful of her belly. They danced awkwardly, but everyone in the shed was smiling and whistling and loving it. Suddenly, T's smile disappeared. "Ohhhhh!"

Tiny snapped straight up. "What, T!"

T gasped and grabbed Tiny's arm. The satin dress became blotched and water ran down her leg. She looked down at her belly. "Oh, my God, Tiny! The baby!"

Tiny looked around in a panic. He looked for Norm. He didn't have to. Norm had been watching them dance like everyone else. He was at their side immediately. "Take her to the house, Tiny." Tiny didn't have to be told twice. He very gently lifted her into his arms, and as smoothly as he could, walk-jogged to the house. "Anybody else here a doctor?" Norm shouted. No reply. Then I guess it's up to me, he thought. He had never delivered a baby. He hurried towards the house. T's mother joined him and hurried alongside. Norm explained that he had never delivered a baby before and it might be a good idea for her to call a doctor who had. Meanwhile he'd do his best.

T's mother nodded. "After we get her in bed, I'll call. There are some others here who have experience in this sort of thing."

"Good," Norm said. "Go get them!" T's mother peeled off.

T's father limped after them, but not before he told everyone to stay and continue with the celebration.

After awhile, the music started up again. Groups discussing Tiny and T slowly dispersed and couples began to dance. There was a crowd around the kegs of beer. Charley had pulled his chair close to the band and had his own personal pitcher. Beau and Virginia, Louie and Tammy were sitting together on bales. Virginia was vacantly watching people dance while Louie, Beau, and Tammy were talking about Louie's working for the marina. They were surprised when Virginia spoke.

"What about the library, Louie? Who's going to do that if you're working full time?"

Beau looked at Virginia. Her eyes were focused. Welcome back, Sugah, he thought. He reached for her hand.

"Got that covered, Virginia," Louie said. "A woman from New Hampshire's moved into town and is looking for something to do. She's been helping out a lot and is real organized. Said she'd take it over. She's got the library today and tomorrow. Maybe if we get back in time this afternoon, you can meet her."

"I'd like that." She turned to Beau. "What time is it, Dear?"

Beau looked at his watch. "Past five."

"No way, today, Louie. Maybe tomorrow. Besides," she said, smiling and giving Beau's hand a squeeze, "Beau and I will be taking a hot tub when we get back."

Rusty and Crystal were also sitting on bales. The band began playing a Willie Nelson song that was a favorite of his. "Love that song," he said.

"Me, too."

Rusty hesitated, then said. "Guess it wouldn't be proper if we danced."

"Why not?"

"Just because of…you know."

"I don't care if you don't."

"You don't?"

"Nope. And aren't you supposed to be taking care of me?"

"That's what I told Jimmy."

She smiled. "I can't dance alone, now can I?"

Rusty led her to the dance area. He took her in his arms. They fit just like before. It felt the same—wonderful. Crystal shifted slightly and suddenly the inside of her thigh was touching the inside of his. Her blue cotton dress was thin. It dawned on him that Crystal was taking control. That was fine with him. He closed his eyes. Hers were already closed so they didn't see Tiny walk quickly up to the stage. Others did and stopped dancing. They knew it was good news because Tiny had a smile so big he could have tripped over it. The music stopped. Rusty and Crystal looked up. Tiny was at the microphone. Both hands were in the air with thumbs up. "It's a gurl!" he boomed. That was all. As the wedding crowd cheered, he turned on his heels and hurried back to the house. The music started up again. Everyone was laughing and patting each other on the back, hugging, and shaking hands. It was a good excuse to give Crystal a hug, so Rusty did. It came close to more than that. They resumed dancing.

Although several hours had passed before Tiny's announcement, no one had left. But now that everyone knew that things were fine, the party began to wind down. After a few more songs, the band left the stage. People began to leave. Charley was weaving. Soon only Tiny's closest Crescent Beach friends remained. They were hanging around, hoping for a glimpse of the baby. Norm came out of the house and joined them. No other doctor had come, but everything had gone perfectly, he said, thanks not to him, but to some very capable Mexican women. Eventually Tiny came out for a beer. He looked exhausted. The women pressured him for a look at the baby. He quaffed the beer, smiled, and asked Norm if it would be okay. No reason why not, Norm answered. They marched as one up to the outdoor patio. Tiny went into the house. He soon returned with the baby wrapped in swaddling clothes. Crystal pulled material away from the little face. The baby yawned.

Virginia said, "Oh, how precious! She looks just like Christina!"

Louie quipped, "Good thing."

"Can I hold her?" Virginia asked.

Tiny looked at Beau and Norm. They nodded. Tiny nervously handed the baby to Virginia. Charley took a close look at the baby. "Don't know how ya kin say that she looks like T." Newborns all looked like hairless baby mice to Charley. He turned to Tiny. "Whatcha named her?"

All eyes were on Tiny. "Was gonna call her Maria after T's grandmother. But T's father just come up with a better one. We're gonna call her Boda. "

Virginia started laughing. It was music to Beau's ears. "Perfect," she said, looking down at the baby. "Little Boda. That's perfect, Tiny!" Tiny smiled proudly.

"Now what in blazes kinda name is that!" Charley asked.

Virginia said, "It's Spanish, Charley."

Charley rolled his eyes. "I figgered that. What's it mean?"

Virginia smiled. "Wedding, Charley. It means wedding."

About The Author

David Mather began visiting the Big Bend area of Florida's Gulf Coast in 1999, becoming a resident in 2006. The area and its people inspired *Raw Dawgin'* and *Crescent Beach.* He has also written two earlier novels based on his experience in southern Chile while serving in the Peace Corps.

Made in the USA
Coppell, TX
13 February 2026

71982735R00210